瑞蘭國際

高效拆解！

新制多益TOEIC® TEST 990滿分攻略

附終極模擬測驗

濱崎潤之輔　著／葉紋芳　譯

※本書係根據日本旺文社《新TOEIC®テスト990点攻略》（新TOEIC®測驗990分攻略）一書，
再配合最新題型重編修訂而成。

前言

當我持續奮戰卻還跨不過900分的高牆時，在一年內日以繼夜使用數十本多益聽讀測驗的參考書來學習。然而，無論我再怎麼努力都無法讓分數提高。於是我從基礎來修正學習方法，並改為徹底專注於一本書的學習方法。半年後的正式測驗，我的分數不但成長了100分以上，更高達970分。

之後，我將990分視為目標而繼續努力，都能不斷地接近990分。但是，我知道如果單靠當時的方法，一定無法實現滿分的目標。因此，藉由練習各種教材和學習方法來驗證成果，同時重新審視「自己的努力是如何的不足」，嚴以律己並自我激勵。結果，我真的抓到要領、達到目標了。這意味著，「只要秉持著不放棄並繼續挑戰的心情，任何人都能靠努力和能力來達到990分的境界」。

本書不但集結了以990分為目標的學習者會遇到的盲點試題，而且能帶領大家有效地累積練習，完全沒有一題讓大家白費工夫。出現在選項中較難理解的詞句，不管是正確答案或錯誤答案，希望各位都能好好地掌握、確實理解。此外，為了因應日本2016年多益測驗「新制題型的變更」，我將《新TOEIC®テスト990点攻略》（新TOEIC®測驗990分攻略）一書配合新制再重新修訂完成這本書。也因為新制的轉變，我會繼續研究題型，並參加所有的正式測驗。期待各位全心衝刺這本書後，可以培養完整迎戰新制多益聽讀的實力。

考900分及990分所需要的訓練，還是有「差異」的。各位要徹底累積練習，連準備這兩種分數之間的「小差異」都要練習到。衷心希望這本書能幫助努力不懈的各位，早日拿下「猶如高不可攀之金字塔頂端」的990分！

濱崎潤之輔

目 次

前言 …… 3
如何使用本書 …… 6
關於TOEIC L&R多益聽讀測驗 …… 8
關於隨書附贈的MP3音檔 …… 10

攻略篇

Part 1 照片描述 …… 11
贏得990分的解題技巧及攻略法 …… 12
Training 基礎練習 …… 16
Practice Test 實戰試題 …… 23

Part 2 應答問題 …… 29
贏得990分的解題技巧及攻略法 …… 30
Training 基礎練習 …… 34
Practice Test 實戰試題 …… 42

Part 3 & 4 簡短對話＆簡短獨白 …… 53
贏得990分的解題技巧及攻略法 …… 54
Part 3 Training 基礎練習 …… 64
Part 3 Practice Test 實戰試題 …… 72
Part 4 Training 基礎練習 …… 84
Part 4 Practice Test 實戰試題 …… 92

專欄 如何提高聽力技巧 …… 104

Part 5 句子填空 …… 105
贏得990分的解題技巧及攻略法 …… 106
Training 基礎練習 …… 110
Review of Training 複習基礎練習 …… 123
Practice Test 實戰試題 …… 132

Part 6 段落填空 …… 145
贏得990分的解題技巧及攻略法 …… 146
Practice Test 實戰試題 …… 152
專欄 破解「插入句題型」與「句子歸置題型」 …… 160

Part 7 文章理解 …… 161
贏得990分的解題技巧及攻略法 …… 162
Training 基礎練習 …… 167
Practice Test 實戰試題 …… 196
專欄 Part 7的「最進階」解題步驟 …… 216

結語 …… 217

Final Test 終極模擬測驗
試題 …… 220
正確答案一覽表・預測成績換算表 …… 270
解答與解析 …… 272

Training 基礎練習 答案卡
Practice Test 實戰試題 答案卡
Final Test 終極模擬測驗 答案卡

如 何 使 用 本 書

本書結構說明如下。請好好把握每單元的特點，將能更有效地善用攻略篇。

▶贏得990分的解題技巧及攻略法

首先確認贏得990分的解題技巧。寫完範例後，再閱讀「HUMMER式密技」來掌握每一個重點吧！

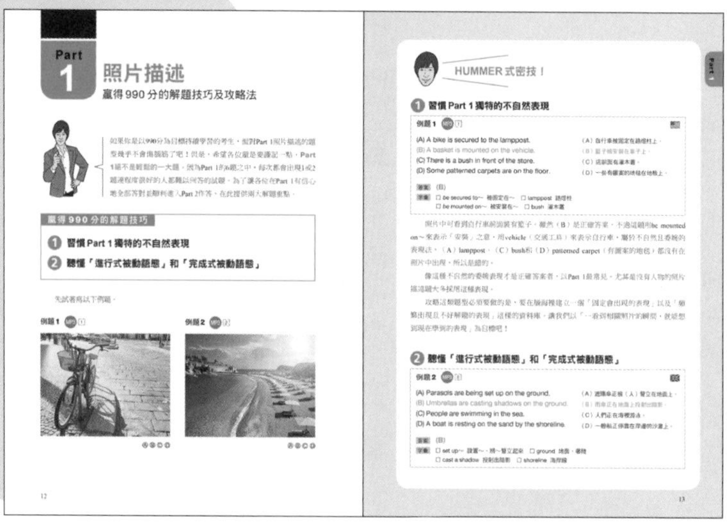
Part 1 照片描述
贏得990分的解題技巧及攻略法
贏得990分的解題技巧
1 習慣Part 1獨特的不自然表現
2 聽懂「進行式被動語態」和「完成式被動語態」
HUMMER式密技！
1 習慣Part 1獨特的不自然表現
(A) A bike is secured to the lamppost.
(B) A basket is mounted on the vehicle.
(C) There is a bush in front of the store.
(D) Some patterned carpets are on the floor.
2 聽懂「進行式被動語態」和「完成式被動語態」
(A) Parasols are being set up on the ground.
(B) Umbrellas are casting shadows on the ground.
(C) People are swimming in the sea.
(D) A boat is resting on the sand by the shoreline.
12
13

▶Training 基礎練習

每一單元（Part）都有基礎練習，是為了要贏得990分需要學到的必備能力。題型與TOEIC　L&R正式測驗不同。

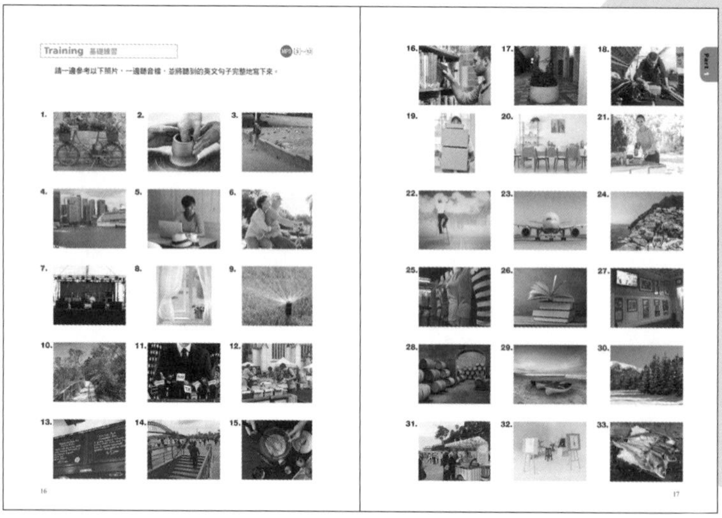

▶Practice Test 實戰試題

從「贏得990分的解題技巧及攻略法」和「Training基礎練習」兩部分學到的內容，就用寫試題來確認吧！

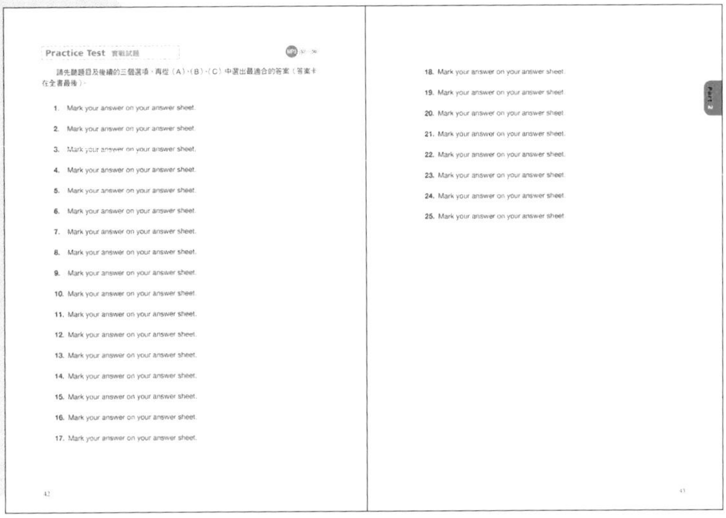

Practice Test 實戰試題

請先聽題目及後續的三個選項，再從（A）、（B）、（C）中選出最適合的答案（答案卡在全書最後）。

1. Mark your answer on your answer sheet.
2. Mark your answer on your answer sheet.
3. Mark your answer on your answer sheet.
4. Mark your answer on your answer sheet.
5. Mark your answer on your answer sheet.
6. Mark your answer on your answer sheet.
7. Mark your answer on your answer sheet.
8. Mark your answer on your answer sheet.
9. Mark your answer on your answer sheet.
10. Mark your answer on your answer sheet.
11. Mark your answer on your answer sheet.
12. Mark your answer on your answer sheet.
13. Mark your answer on your answer sheet.
14. Mark your answer on your answer sheet.
15. Mark your answer on your answer sheet.
16. Mark your answer on your answer sheet.
17. Mark your answer on your answer sheet.
18. Mark your answer on your answer sheet.
19. Mark your answer on your answer sheet.
20. Mark your answer on your answer sheet.
21. Mark your answer on your answer sheet.
22. Mark your answer on your answer sheet.
23. Mark your answer on your answer sheet.
24. Mark your answer on your answer sheet.
25. Mark your answer on your answer sheet.

▶Final Test 終極模擬測驗

在攻略篇的學習結束後，來試試終極模擬測驗吧！試題比正式測驗稍難。隨書附預測成績換算表，可以用來算出預測成績。

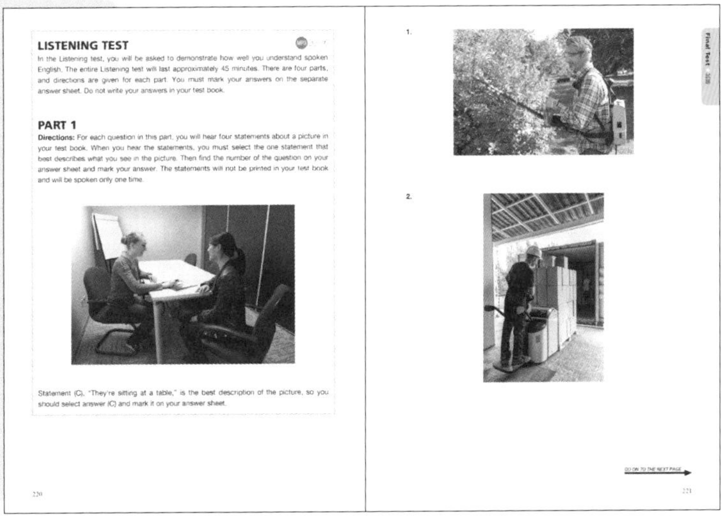

LISTENING TEST

In the Listening test, you will be asked to demonstrate how well you understand spoken English. The entire Listening test will last approximately 45 minutes. There are four parts, and directions are given for each part. You must mark your answers on the separate answer sheet. Do not write your answers in your test book.

PART 1

Directions: For each question in this part, you will hear four statements about a picture in your test book. When you hear the statements, you must select the one statement that best describes what you see in the picture. Then find the number of the question on your answer sheet and mark your answer. The statements will not be printed in your test book and will be spoken only one time.

Statement (C), "They're sitting at a table," is the best description of the picture, so you should select answer (C) and mark it on your answer sheet.

1.

2.

追加！

專題

收錄「如何提高聽力技巧」、「有效利用學習的空檔加速閱讀」等內容，彙整主要單元中的重點、加碼撇步！日後對各位將很有幫助。

關於TOEIC L&R多益聽讀測驗

什麼是TOEIC L&R（多益聽讀測驗）？

✷ 由美國研發而成的全球通用測驗

TOEIC（Test of English for International Communication 國際溝通英語測驗）是檢定英語溝通能力的全球通用測驗。該測驗是由美國非營利的測驗機構ETS（Educational Testing Service 教育測驗服務社）研發而成。TOEIC® L&R（TOEIC® Listening & Reading Test）即是測驗「聽力」和「閱讀」兩種英語能力。

✷ 得分範圍在10～990分之間

得分並非表示考生的能力合格與否，而是以5分為進分單位，得分範圍在10～990分來評定五種層級的英語能力指標。

✷ 作答採劃卡方式

作答方式是，將認為是正確答案的選項編號劃記在答案卡上。不能在試題紙上作答。

多益聽讀測驗的形式與內容

✷ 分為Listening（聽力）與Reading（閱讀）兩大部分，共有200題

多益聽讀測驗如下所示，分為聽力與閱讀兩大部分。200題要在2小時的時間內作答完畢，中途沒有休息。

Listening（聽力） 約45分鐘・100題	Part 1	照片描述	**6**題
	Part 2	應答問題	**25**題
	Part 3	簡短對話	**39**題
	Part 4	簡短獨白	**30**題
Reading（閱讀） 約75分鐘・100題	Part 5	句子填空	**30**題
	Part 6	段落填空	**16**題
	Part 7	文章理解　單篇閱讀	**29**題
		多篇閱讀書	**25**題

測驗時間

原則上實際的測驗時間及地點，以該月份場次之應考資訊上所載為準。請隨時至官方網站查閱最新訊息，所有訊息以官方網站最新公告為準。

報名費用 NT＄1,600（適用特殊優惠辦法之考生請詳閱官網說明）

受理報名方式

正式測驗採下列方式報名。依報名方式而有不同的報名期間及繳費方式。

❶網路報名

至官方網站報名。報名費用請以信用卡（美國運通、大來卡、銀聯卡除外）或在兩大超商以7-ELEVEN ibon及全家FamiPort機器支付。

❷通訊報名

官網不提供報名表下載服務，僅接受正本報名表申請。報名表請至公司臨櫃索取或來電索取，只能使用2B鉛筆填寫報名表，繳費方式為郵政匯票（請掛號郵寄），郵政匯票受款人：忠欣股份有限公司。

❸臨櫃報名

資料不全者將不予受理。因個資法相關規定，報名表上的考生個資使用同意書須考生親筆簽名，請考生本人親自來臨櫃以現金報名，非本人恕不受理報名。受理時間為週一至週五（國定假日除外），上午九點至下午五點三十分（中午不休息）。

❹APP報名

請上網至官網報名須知下載。報名費用請在兩大超商以7-ELEVEN　ibon及全家FamiPort機器支付。

?如何聯絡我們

ETS臺灣區總代理　忠欣股份有限公司

地　　址：(106) 台北市復興南路二段45號2樓

辦公時間：週一～週五（國定假日除外）每日9:00至17:30

電　　話：(02) 2701-7333

傳　　真：(02) 2708-3879

客服信箱： service@examservice.com.tw

TOEIC®測驗官網：http://www.toeic.com.tw/

※以上為2018年8月官方提供之公開資訊。請隨時至官方網站查詢當月實際開放報名之測驗考區及最新資訊，所有訊息以官方網站公告為主。

關於隨書附贈的MP3音檔

本書中的聽力測驗音檔，分成「攻略篇」及「終極聽力測驗」兩個QR Code，皆可在書封找到，請自行以智慧型手機下載喜歡的QR Code掃描器掃描聆聽。在書中，音檔以MP3圖案與數字方框標示。請參考以下收錄內容一覽表，確認MP3音軌編號後善加利用。

攻略篇 QR Code

（播放時間約61分鐘）

單元	軌數
Part 1	1～18
Part 2	19～56
Part 3&4	57～77
Part 2 正解	78～82

Final Test 終極聽力測驗 QR Code

（播放時間約49分鐘）

單元	軌數
Part 1	1～ 7
Part 2	8～33
Part 3	34～47
Part 4	48～58

如何掃描 QR Code 下載音檔

1. 以手機內建的相機或是掃描 QR Code 的 App 掃描封面的 QR Code。
2. 點選「雲端硬碟」的連結之後，進入音檔清單畫面，接著點選畫面右上角的「三個點」。
3. 點選「新增至「已加星號」專區」一欄，星星即會變成黃色或黑色，代表加入成功。
4. 開啟電腦，打開您的「雲端硬碟」網頁，點選左側欄位的「已加星號」。
5. 選擇該音檔資料夾，點滑鼠右鍵，選擇「下載」，即可將音檔存入電腦。

Part

1 照片描述

Part 1

照片描述

贏得990分的解題技巧及攻略法

如果你是以990分為目標持續學習的考生，面對Part 1照片描述的題型幾乎不會傷腦筋了吧！但是，希望各位還是要謹記一點，**Part 1絕不是輕鬆的一大題**。因為Part 1的6題之中，每次都會出現1或2題連程度很好的人都難以回答的試題。為了讓各位在Part 1有信心地全部答對並順利進入Part 2作答，在此提供兩大解題重點。

贏得990分的解題技巧

1 習慣Part 1獨特的不自然表現

2 聽懂「進行式被動語態」和「完成式被動語態」

先試著寫以下例題。

例題1 MP3 1

Ⓐ Ⓑ Ⓒ Ⓓ

例題2 MP3 2

Ⓐ Ⓑ Ⓒ Ⓓ

HUMMER式密技！

❶ 習慣Part 1獨特的不自然表現

例題 1 MP3 1

(A) A bike is secured to the lamppost.
(B) A basket is mounted on the vehicle.
(C) There is a bush in front of the store.
(D) Some patterned carpets are on the floor.

（A）自行車被固定在路燈柱上。
（B）籃子被安裝在車子上。
（C）店前面有灌木叢。
（D）一些有圖案的地毯在地板上。

答案 (B)

字彙 □ *be* secured to～ 被固定在～ □ lamppost 路燈柱
□ *be* mounted on～ 被安裝在～ □ bush 灌木叢

照片中可看到自行車前面裝有籃子。雖然（B）是正確答案，不過這題用be mounted on～來表示「安裝」之意，用vehicle（交通工具）來表示自行車，屬於不自然且委婉的表現法。（A）lamppost、（C）bush和（D）patterned carpet（有圖案的地毯）都沒有在照片中出現，所以是錯的。

像這種不自然的委婉表現才是正確答案者，以Part 1最常見。尤其是沒有人物的照片描述題大多採用這種表現。

攻略這類題型必須要做的是，要在腦海裡建立一個「固定會出現的表現」以及「頻繁出現且不好解題的表現」這樣的資料庫。讓我們以「一看到相關照片的瞬間，就能想到現在學到的表現」為目標吧！

❷ 聽懂「進行式被動語態」和「完成式被動語態」

例題 2 MP3 2

(A) Parasols are being set up on the ground.
(B) Umbrellas are casting shadows on the ground.
(C) People are swimming in the sea.
(D) A boat is resting on the sand by the shoreline.

（A）遮陽傘正被（人）豎立在地面上。
（B）雨傘正在地面上投射出陰影。
（C）人們正在海裡游泳。
（D）一艘船正停靠在岸邊的沙灘上。

答案 (B)

字彙 □ set up～ 設置～、將～豎立起來 □ ground 地面、著陸
□ cast a shadow 投射出陰影 □ shoreline 海岸線

照片中可看到很多豎立起來的傘，影子正投射在地面上。這題的關鍵在於是否理解casting shadows，正確答案是（B）。（C）的描述在照片中只有海，並沒有看到有人在游泳。（D）的shoreline描述符合，不過照片中並沒有船，所以不正確。

這題我想關注的是（A）。它是現在進行式被動語態，在表達「遮陽傘目前正被人豎立起來」的持續動作，這個選項當然不是正確答案。然而，如果換作是Parasols have been set up on the ground.（遮陽傘已被豎立在地面上了。）這句呢？這時因為「被豎立」的動作「已完成」，所以就能成為正確答案。

由於現在進行式被動語態（are being set up）和現在完成式被動語態（have been set up）乍聽之下難以區分（都有set up），因此對於想要在Part 1拿到滿分的考生來說，要完全聽懂其中差別變得非常重要。為了準確聽懂並100%理解內容，累積這方面的聽力訓練是必要的。

超越！進階技巧

我們再來看一下有關進行式被動語態和完成式被動語態的說明。請想想看，以下哪一個例句能夠正確描述照片內容呢？

(1) Pottery is being exhibited on the shelves.
（陶器正被展示在架上。）

(2) Pottery has been set up on the shelves.
（陶器已被設置在架上。）

雖然這題應該一看就可知現在完成式被動語態的（2）是正確答案，但實際上（1）也是正確的。

聽到主詞是事物且句型為進行式被動語態時，往往會認為是「人正在對事物做什麼動作」。但是，（1）並非在表達什麼「動作」在持續進行，而是在表達「被展示」的被動「狀態」目前正持續著。由此可知進行式被動語態的情形，不限於一定是人正在做什麼動作。*be* being exhibited（被展示著）、*be* being displayed（被陳列著）和*be* being reflected（被映照著）等即是符合這樣的「狀態」表現。以下再舉幾個例句：

Some merchandise is being displayed in front of the store.
（一些商品正被陳列在店前面。）

Some buildings are being reflected in the water.
（一些建築物正被映照在水中。）

贏得990分之路

例題2 選項（B）的casting shadows並不是很難的措辭。不過，一看到照片即預測「或許會來個casting shadows」而等著語音播放，這是TOEIC L&R多益測驗的進階學習者必備的能力。

本單元每次出現1～2題難度較高的題型，大多包含不太熟悉的表現方式，也不會出現在其他單元。因此，必須要盡量掌握Part 1可能會出現的表現。**為了將可能成為答案的固定表現以及稍有難度的表現建立一個資料庫**，我推薦各位用本書進行聽寫練習。因為藉由正確地認識發音，並將它寫出來的方式，可以一目瞭然是否已真正學會該表現。

下一頁開始，共有51題日後正式測驗有可能會出現的例句。以Part 1獨特的不自然表現為主，包括進行式被動語態及完成式被動語態等，都是精心挑選而成。

準備Part 1時最重要的就是，徹底重複進行簡單的訓練，如此一來就可以確實培養實力。除了聽寫練習之外，希望各位要一遍又一遍地進行交叉、重複及跟讀練習，直到完美掌握51題例句為止。

一旦精通了這些表現，相信各位對於Part 1難題的解答能力大幅提升，應該有實質的感覺。

總結

迎戰Part 1，就用聽寫練習來建立正確答案的資料庫吧！

Training 基礎練習

MP3 3～12

請一邊參考以下照片，一邊聽音檔，並將聽到的英文句子完整地寫下來。

1.

2.

3.

4.

5.

6.

7.

8.

9.

10.

11.

12.

13.

14.

15.

16.

17.

18.

19.

20.

21.

22.

23.

24.

25.

26.

27.

28.

29.

30.

31.

32.

33.

34. 

35. 

36. 

37. 

38. 

39. 

40. 

41. 

42. 

43. 

44. 

45. 

46. 

47. 

48. 

49. 

50. 

51. 

Training 基礎練習 原文與翻譯

MP3 3～12

Part 1

3

1. Some baskets are mounted on a bicycle.
（一些籃子被安裝在一輛腳踏車上。）

- □ mount *A* on *B* 在B上安裝A

2. Some people are molding some clay.
（一些人正在塑造黏土。）

- □ mold 塑造～
- □ clay 黏土

3. Some stones have been used to create a wall.
（一些石頭已被用於製作牆壁。）

4. Some high-rise buildings overlook the water.
（一些高樓層建築物俯瞰著水面。）

- □ high-rise building 高樓層建築物
- □ overlook 俯瞰

5. The woman has turned away from her computer.
（女性已將臉轉離她的電腦。）

- □ turn away from～
  將（臉、眼睛等）轉離～

4

6. A man's head is sheltered by his hat.
（一名男性的頭被他的帽子保護著。）

- □ *be* sheltered by～ 被～保護著

7. Some equipment is suspended over the stage.
（有些裝置懸被掛在舞台的上方。）

- □ *be* suspended 被懸掛著

8. Some drapes are partially covering the window panes.
（有些窗簾局部蓋住玻璃窗。）

- □ drape 窗簾
- □ window pane 玻璃窗

9. Water is being sprayed from the equipment.
（水正從裝置噴灑出來。）

- □ *be* sprayed from～
  從～噴灑出來

10. A walkway is bordered by a low fence in the park.
（人行道被公園內的矮籬笆圍住。）

- □ *be* bordered by～ 被～圍住

5

11. Some microphones are placed on the podium.
（一些麥克風被放在講台上。）

- □ podium 講台

12. Some things are being stored in boxes outside.
（一些東西被收在戶外的箱子內。）

- □ *be* stored in～ 被保存在～

13. A chalkboard is displaying menu items.
（黑板顯示著菜單項目。）

- □ chalkboard 黑板

14. The staircase has railings on both sides.
（樓梯的兩側有欄杆。）

- □ staircase 樓梯

15. Someone is stirring ingredients with a utensil.
（某人正在用道具器具攪拌食材。）

- □ stir 攪拌～
- □ utensil 器具

6

16. A man is browsing some books in the store.
（一位男性正在店內隨意翻閱書籍。）

☐ browse 隨意翻閱～

17. There are patterned floor tiles on the porch.
（門廊上鋪著有圖案裝飾的地磚。）

☐ patterned 有圖案裝飾的
☐ porch 門廊

18. A mechanic is carrying out an inspection in the workshop.
（技師正在工作坊進行檢查。）

☐ carry out～ 進行～
☐ inspection 檢查
☐ workshop 工作坊、研討會

19. A stack of boxes is being transported by the man.
（一堆箱子正由男性搬運著。）

☐ transport 搬運～

20. A tablecloth has been draped on the table.
（桌布已被鋪在桌上。）

☐ drape 垂掛～

7

21. A woman is sorting things into containers.
（一位女性正將物品分類到容器內。）

☐ sort 分類～
☐ container 容器、貨櫃

22. A man standing on a ladder is applying paint to the wall.
（一位站在梯子上的男性正將油漆塗於牆上。）

☐ apply *A* to *B*
將A塗於B、將A用於B

23. An aircraft is taxiing on the ground.
（一架飛機正在地面上慢慢滑行。）

☐ taxi
（飛機）慢慢滑行

24. Houses are crowded together on the hillside.
（房子聚集在山坡上。）

☐ *be* crowded 聚集

25. Many clothes have been displayed inside the shop.
（很多衣服已被陳列在店內。）

8

26. Several reading materials have been piled on the desk.
（數本讀物已被堆在書桌上。）

27. Some artwork has been hung on a wall.
（一些藝術作品已被掛在牆上。）

☐ artwork 藝術作品
☐ hang 掛～

28. Some barrels have been laid in the warehouse.
（一些大桶子已被放進倉庫。）

☐ barrel 大桶子
☐ warehouse 倉庫

29. Some boats have been resting on the beach.
（一些船已停在海灘。）

☐ rest 靜止、停擱

30. Some trees are casting shadows on the land.
（一些樹正在地上投射出陰影。）

9

31. Some customers are being served at the food cart.
（一些客人正在小餐車邊被服務著。）

□ *be* served 被提供服務

32. Some easels have been set up in the studio.
（一些畫架已被擺置在工作室。）

□ easel 畫架
□ *be* set up 被擺置、設立

33. Some fish are being chilled on ice.
（一些魚正被用冰冷藏著。）

□ *be* chilled 使冷藏

34. An item has been taken out of the display case.
（一項商品已被取出展示櫃。）

35. Some plates have been set next to the sink.
（一些盤子已被放在水槽旁邊。）

10

36. Some protective gear is worn by the players.
（一些防護裝備被球員們穿著。）

□ protective gear 防護裝備

37. Some sacks have been stacked in a warehouse.
（一些袋子已被堆放在倉庫內。）

38. Some foods are being displayed in a glass case.
（一些食物陳列在玻璃櫃內。）

39. Some vehicles have been left unattended on the street.
（一些車輛已被留置街上無人看管。）

□ *be* left unattended 被留置而無人看管

40. A car's trunk has been opened.
（車子的後行李箱已被打開。）

11

41. Heavy machinery is in use at a construction site.
（建築工地裡有重型機械正在運轉中。）

□ *be* in use 正在使用中、正在運轉中

42. The man is feeding a board into the machinery.
（男性正將板子推進機器內。）

□ feed 將～推進（機器）、對～餵食

43. Some people are wearing gardening gloves.
（一些人正戴著園藝手套。）

□ gardening gloves 園藝手套

44. A vehicle has been raised in the air in the workshop.
（工作坊裡有一輛車已被抬在空中。）

□ *be* raised in the air 被抬在空中

45. The woman is crouching on the ground.
（女性正蹲伏在地上。）

□ crouch 蹲伏

12

46. The women are holding different types of clothes.
（女性們正拿著不同種類的衣物。）

47. They are wearing headphones on their heads.
（他們頭上正戴著耳機。）

□ wear 戴著～

48. There are multiple levels of shelves in the library.
（圖書館內有多層書架。）

□ multiple levels 多層

49. A man is doing chores in a kitchen.
（一位男性正在廚房做家務。）

50. Some documents are being examined by the women.
（一些文件正被女性檢查著。）

□ examine 檢查～

51. Some people are working on a sewing project together.
（一些人正一起做著縫紉工作。）

□ work on～ 從事～

Practice Test 實戰試題

MP3 13～18

聽完四句英文描述後，請從（A）、（B）、（C）、（D）中選擇一個最能符合照片內容的答案（答案卡在全書最後）。

1.

2.

3.

4.

5.

6.

1.

13

(A) Some luggage is being unloaded out of an airplane.
(B) An aircraft is taxiing on the runway.
(C) The airport terminal has been closed.
(D) A ramp has been connected to the aircraft.

（A）一些行李正被從飛機卸下。
（B）一架飛機正在跑道上滑行。
（C）機場航站已經被關閉。
（D）活動梯已被連接上飛機。

答案　(D)

解析　這題關鍵在於是否知道（D）的ramp就是指「上、下飛機用的活動梯」。不過，即使不知道這個單字，還是可以聽懂其他選項的描述跟照片狀況明顯不同而選擇（D）吧！（A）因為照片沒有行李，所以描述錯誤。（B）雖然也是錯的答案，還是希望各位要記住taxi當動詞是指「（飛機）慢慢滑行」。（C）描述航站關閉，從照片中無法判斷。

字彙　□ runway 跑道　□ ramp 上下飛機用的活動梯、斜坡、（往高速公路的）入口坡道

2.

14

(A) An alley runs toward an archway.
(B) A path leads to the porch.
(C) Pedestrians are walking along the street.
(D) The ground is shaded by a lamppost.

（A）一條小巷朝向拱廊延伸出去。
（B）一條小路通向門廊。
（C）行人們正沿著街道行走。
（D）地面有被街燈遮蔽的影子。

答案　(A)

解析　（A）的alley和（B）的path兩者都是「小街道」，照片裡的小街道跟有扇形的建築物相連，因此（A）是正確答案。（B）的porch（門廊）是常常會出現的單字。（C）描述的pedestrians（行人）在照片裡沒有看到，所以不正確。（D）描述的街燈在照片裡也沒看到，所以不正確。

字彙　□ archway（上面為拱形的）拱廊　□ pedestrian 行人

3.

15

(A) The doorway has been cleaned by the brush.
(B) The porch is being cleaned with the brush.
(C) A chair has been set next to the door.
(D) A chair is being set by the brush.

（A）門口已被用刷子清理乾淨了。
（B）門廊正在被用刷子清潔。
（C）一張椅子已被擺放在門旁。
（D）一張椅子正被（人）擺放在刷子旁。

答案 (C)

解析 這是進行式被動語態和完成式被動語態的混合題，屬於錯誤選項會讓人混淆、難度較高的題目。但是只要能確實聽懂（C）的has been set就不成問題。從照片中並無法判斷打掃是否完成或是正在進行，因此（A）、（B）都不正確。至於（D）的描述，由於圖中未呈現椅子正在被人擺放的動作，所以不正確。

字彙 □ doorway 門口、出入口

4.

16

(A) Some flowers are being arranged by the doorway.
(B) Some people are using tap water by the window.
(C) Some people are decorating the windowsill with flowers.
(D) Some flowers have been arranged on the windowsill.

（A）一些花正被（人）擺放在門口。
（B）一些人正在窗邊使用自來水。
（C）一些人正在用花裝飾窗台。
（D）一些花已被擺放在窗台。

答案 (D)

解析 （D）表達了花排列在窗台的狀態，所以是正確答案。照片裡的花並沒有正在進行擺放，位置也不是在門口，所以（A）是錯誤的。照片裡沒有人物，也沒有tap（水龍頭），由此可知（B）是錯誤的。（C）描述的應該是人們在拍攝這張照片之前所進行的動作，而不是目前正在進行的動作。

字彙 □ tap water 自來水

5.

17

(A) Some writing tools have been collected in a container.
(B) Some office supplies are being scattered on the desk.
(C) Some people are putting cups on the desk.
(D) Some writing materials are in use at the desk.

（A）一些文具已經被收集在容器內。
（B）一些辦公用品正被分散在桌上。
（C）一些人正把杯子放在桌上。
（D）桌子上的文具正在（被人）使用中。

答案 (A)

解析 （A）用現在完成式被動語態have been collected（已經被收集）明確地表達照片的狀況。（B）的being scattered（被分散）和照片的狀況不相符。（C）描述的people（人）和cups（杯子）並沒有在照片裡。（D）的be in use（正在使用中）是否為真，無法從照片來判斷，所以不適合作為答案。

字彙 □ writing tools 文具 □ office supplies 辦公用品（常用複數形） □ writing materials 文具

6.

18

(A) The man is checking out some reading materials in the library.

(B) Some people are examining some library books.

(C) A librarian has been staffed at the counter.

(D) The man is returning some library books at the counter.

（A）男性正在圖書館借出一些閱讀資料。

（B）一些人正在查閱一些圖書館書籍。

（C）一名圖書管理員已被安排在櫃檯。

（D）男性正在櫃台歸還一些圖書館書籍。

答案 **(C)**

解析 請記住（C）的staff（安排人員）可當動詞。be staffed一般是指（人員）「被安排」。（A）的checking out（借出）無法從照片來判斷，因此不是正確答案。（B）的examining some library books（查閱一些圖書館書籍）的動作並沒有出現在照片裡，（D）的returning（歸還）也無法從照片來判斷，所以都不正確。不要憑想像來選答案，這點非常重要。

字彙 □ check out～ 借出～

Part

2

應答問題

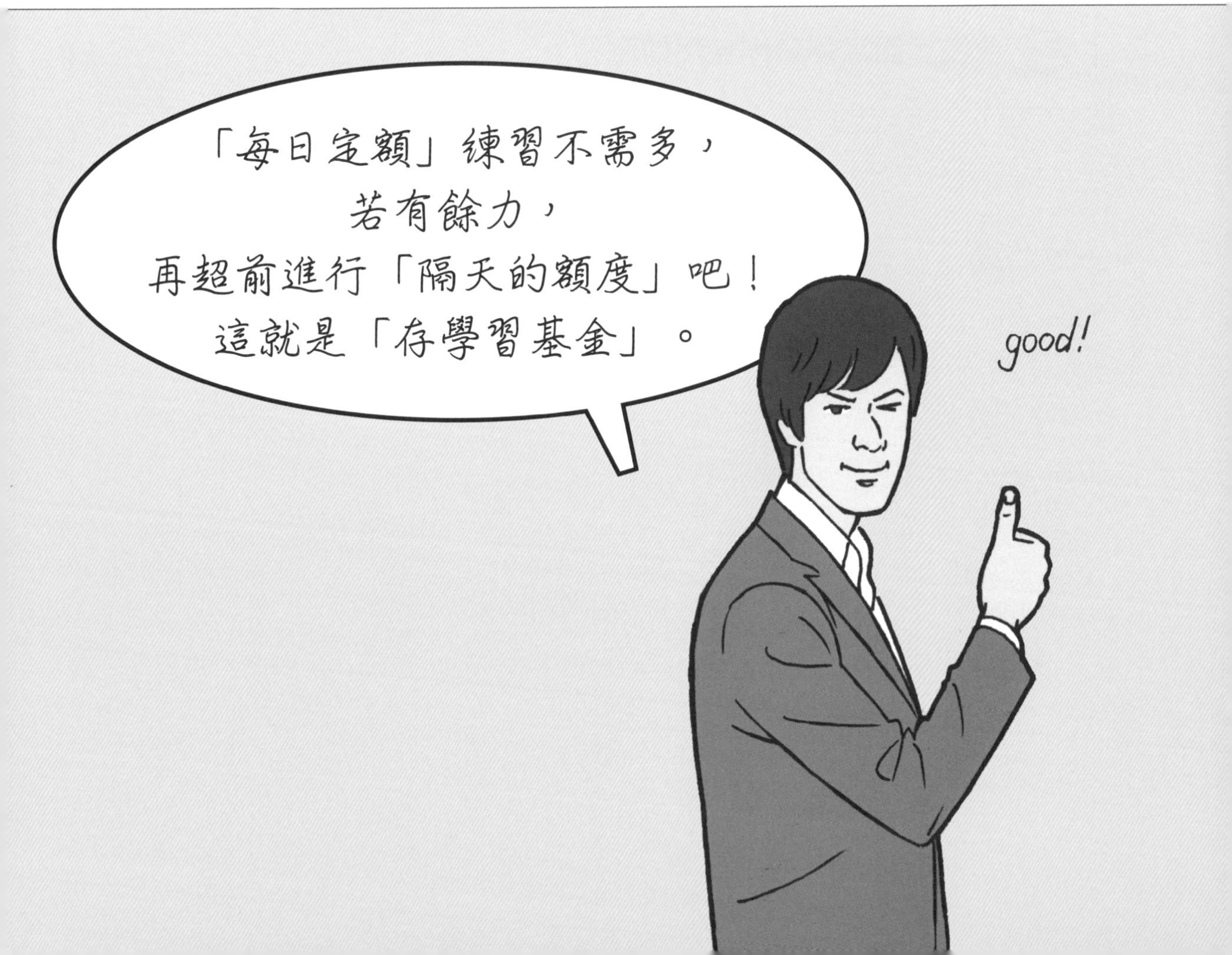

「每日定額」練習不需多，
若有餘力，
再超前進行「隔天的額度」吧！
這就是「存學習基金」。
good!

Part 2

應答問題

贏得990分的解題技巧及攻略法

即使是平時大小考經常獲得聽力滿分的考生，對Part 2有絕對自信的人應該也不多吧！與其他大題相比，Part 2更考驗考生的專注力，因為它會突然來個連程度很好的人都難以作答的「變化球」問題。為了完美通過這大題，所必備的能力，就是**面對變化球問題的瞬間爆發力**。讓我們延續Part 1的聽寫訓練，繼續來建立更完整的正確答案資料庫吧！

贏得990分的解題技巧

1 習慣「對提問作非直接的回答」

2 習慣「對陳述句作自然的應答」

先試著寫以下例題。

例題1 MP3 19

Mark your answer. Ⓐ Ⓑ Ⓒ

例題2 MP3 20

Mark your answer. Ⓐ Ⓑ Ⓒ

HUMMER式密技！

❶ 習慣「對提問作非直接的回答」

例題 1 MP3 19

How was your flight from Toronto?
(A) I will arrive there this evening.
(B) No, it's from Vancouver.
(C) Actually, I was asleep for most of it.

你從多倫多飛來的航程如何？
（A）我今天傍晚會抵達那裡。
（B）不，它是從溫哥華來的。
（C）事實上，我大部分時間都睡著了。

答案 (C)

這題是在詢問有關搭機的感想。雖然（C）對於「航程如何？」的提問沒有直接回答，但是描述了飛行過程中所做的事，建立了自然的對話，所以是正確答案。（A）說的是自己預計抵達的時間，沒有針對問題回答。（B）的No不能用來回答以How（如何）為開頭的問題，且內容也不是直接的感想，所以是錯的。

對於How was your flight?（你的航程如何？）這樣的直接提問，一般期待的回答應該是「舒適的」之類的感想。但是，因為Part 2會出現像這種**「非直接的回答」才是正確答案的變化球題目**，大家必須特別注意。為了對這類的題目游刃有餘，希望各位在平時練習時，就要加強**一聽到提問時就能瞬間100%理解考題**的訓練。

❷ 習慣「對陳述句作自然的應答」

例題 2 MP3 20

Look, these are our latest sweaters.
(A) What other colors do you have?
(B) From a dependable supplier.
(C) I bought it at the bookstore.

你看，這些是我們最新款的毛衣。
（A）你有其他顏色嗎？
（B）來自可信任的供應商。
（C）我在書店買的。

答案 (A)

字彙 □ dependable 可信任的

看了毛衣後，（A）針對陳述內容做相關回應，所以是正確答案。（B）比較像是在回答「貨源、品質控管」相關的詢問，（C）的bookstore（書店）不適合當購買毛衣的地方，且sweaters（毛衣〈複數形〉）用it（第三人稱單數）來表達也不恰當。

對於陳述句類型的題目，因為不是直接提問，往往令人難以預測將出現什麼樣的應答選項。當遇到這類的變化球問題時請特別注意，有時會以「疑問句」作為正確答案。因此除了要完全聽懂陳述句的內容及應答方說了什麼之外，也要專注於選擇「陳述句內容和應答形成自然互動」的組合。

超越！

進階技巧

為了在Part 2成功達陣，各位一定要確實檢視題目內容和每一個選項是否可以形成合理的對話。因此，希望以990分為目標的學習者一定要試著用以下的流程來作答。

①聽懂題目內容，完整記住並用英文複誦
②聽到選項（A）的內容 → 判斷這則對話是否成立
③用英文再複誦一次題目
④聽到選項（B）的內容 → 判斷這則對話是否成立
⑤用英文再複誦一次題目
⑥聽到選項（C）的內容 → 判斷這則對話是否成立

雖然難度有點高，但藉由這種方式就不會因為忘記「問題是什麼？」而感到不安，可以確實地檢視題目和選項的關係。

那麼，如果遇到像以下題目是很長的選擇疑問句時，又該怎麼辦呢？

Has your notice of resignation been acknowledged yet, or haven't you submitted it yet?
（你的辭呈是否已得到受理，或是你尚未提出？）

像這種情形，建議大家先擷取最少的必要資訊，再與選項做重複對照。以這題為例，必要資訊就是resignation acknowledged, or haven't submitted（辭呈被受理了或還未提出）。

剛開始練習時，或許會覺得要先把英文換成中文才比較容易思考。不過一旦習慣了，自然就不需要這種模式，直接用英文思維來理解反而更能夠完全記牢。如果你的目標是990分，希望一定要達到那樣的程度才行。

贏得990分之路

Part 2是需要**瞬間爆發力**的一大題。尤其是像例題中提到的「變化球」問題時，不僅要理解播放出來的句子內容，還需要有能力瞬間理解對話的場合及說話的意圖。

和Part 1一樣，就從下一頁的聽寫訓練來建立一個「正確答案的資料庫」吧！透過加強資料庫的方式來熟悉**「很多種變化球」**，將是**瞬間理解對話的最佳對策**。在了解「球的種類」之後，我們就只剩下累積更多的實戰試題，繼續進行「在瞬間將球打擊出去」的訓練而已了。就讓我們用模擬試題及練習試題來反覆進行訓練吧！「攻略篇」MP3音檔78～82更收錄了Part 2 Practice Test實戰試題的正確答案對話，希望各位能夠加以活用並建立穩固的正確答案資料庫。來反覆進行訓練吧！

另外，由於Part 2的題目和選項都只能聽聲音作答，所以比其他大題更要求**專注力**。請考生們務必**調整呼吸，冷靜地作答**。重啟心情面對每一題，知道即使遇到無法抱持自信作答的問題時，也不能拖累後面的題目。如果聽力部分（**共佔95～97題以上**）可以全部答對，大約就有**495分**到手（獲得滿分的最低量尺會依該次問題的難易度而有差別），因此做好斷、捨、離的工夫並轉換心情，全力專注在下一題吧！

總結

用聽寫練習來建立正確答案的資料庫，
提高迎戰「變化球」的「瞬間爆發力」吧！
重啟心情面對每一題，保持「專注力」也很重要！

Training 基礎練習

MP3 21～31

請聽音檔，並將聽到的英文句子完整地寫下來。共55題。

Training 基礎練習　原文與翻譯

MP3 21～31

21

1. Could you replace the ink cartridge in this copier?

（你能更換這台影印機的墨水匣嗎？）

Would you wait until this afternoon?

（你能等到今天下午嗎？）

2. The company outing is for all the staff, right?

（公司旅遊是為了所有員工，對吧？）

I heard everyone's invited.

（我聽說每個人都被邀請了。）

3. Why don't I ask for the vice president's ideas?

（我何不來問問副董事長的想法？）

Could you tell me what he says later?

（稍後你可以告訴我他說什麼嗎？）

4. Our company has lost a lot of essential employees.

（我們公司已失去很多重要的員工。）

We have to recruit immediately.

（我們必須馬上徵人。）

5. When do you expect the copier to be delivered?

（你預計影印機何時會送到？）

I heard it left the warehouse yesterday.

（我聽說它昨天離開倉庫了。）

22

6. Would you like me to move my suitcase?

（你想讓我搬走我的行李箱嗎？）

No, it's not in the way.

（不，它不會擋路。）

7. I'd like to know who has the documents from the meeting.

（我想知道誰有會議文件。）

Mr. Takeuchi may have the leftover ones.

（竹內先生可能會有剩餘的文件。）

HUMMER老師小重點 像1.這種提問，一般往往會猜它的回答是「好，我來做」或「不，我無法做」等，不過請記住它也有可能像這題用「暫緩」的回答方式喔！7.請把leftover（剩餘的）的用法背起來。當在本單元的Training基礎練習及Practice Test實戰試題，或是模擬測驗中遇到不懂的英文表達方式時，不妨將它匯整成單字簿背起來吧！

8. Excuse me, on which floor is Mr. Kei's legal office?
（打擾一下，紀（Kei）先生的律師事務所在哪一樓？）
Oh, it's above us.
（喔，在我們樓上。）

9. I'm worried renting this device may cause a problem.
（我擔心租用這個設備可能會引起問題。）
I don't think you should be worried about that.
（我認為你不該擔心那個。）

10. Is this the finalized list of attendees, or will more people come?
（這是最後確定的參加者名單，或是還會有更多人來？）
This is the list of the attendees who've responded so far.
（這是目前為止已回覆的參加者名單。）

23

11. Which means of transportation should I use to get there fastest?
（我應該使用哪一種交通方式才能最快到那裡？）
You're in a rush, right?
（你在趕時間，對吧？）

12. When will we receive the commission checks?
（我們何時會收到佣金支票？）
Mr. Taka said on the same day as our payday.
（塔卡（Taka）先生說會和我們發薪日同一天。）

13. I can't believe how crowded this restaurant is.
（我不敢相信這家餐廳居然這麼擁擠。）
That's because it received a great review in the newspaper yesterday.
（那是因為它昨天在報紙上得到很好的評價。）

14. Please tell me how long you've been an attorney.
（請告訴我你擔任律師多久了。）
It'll be two years next February.
（明年二月即將兩年。）

15. Your business cards can be picked up at the HR department.
（你的名片可以在人資部門被領取了。）
Oh, they're ready?
（哦！它們準備好了？）

HUMMER老師小重點 10.的提問有點長，把它縮短為finalized list of attendees, more people come來複誦吧！至於像11.及15.的應答方式，在多益測驗中也不時會出現，它是將原本問題的內容簡潔地換個說法，表達再次確認的口吻。也因為這類的回答內容短，因此特別需要專注力。

24

16. We are likely to see prices rise for many everyday items.

（我們可能會看到很多日常用品價格上漲。）

That's what I think too.

（我也那麼認為。）

17. Which route will you take to get to the top?

（你將採取哪條路線攻頂？）

We'll go past the small park.

（我們將經過小公園。）

18. Do you know who was absent from the meeting this morning?

（你知道今天早上是誰缺席會議嗎？）

I have no idea, but I'll go find out.

（我不知道，不過我會去查明。）

19. This copier still isn't fixed, is it?

（這台影印機還未被修理，是嗎？）

I thought it was.

（我以為（被修理）好了。）

20. There was heavy traffic last night.

（昨晚交通繁忙。）

I think it was even worse this morning.

（我認為今天早上更糟。）

25

21. Should I leave the document on your desk or hers?

（我應該把文件放在你的桌上或是她的桌上呢？）

Could you file it in the cabinet in the corner?

（你可以將它歸檔在角落的櫃子裡嗎？）

22. Aren't Mr. Iwanaga and Mr. Hisamitsu coming to the party?

（岩川（Iwanaga）先生和久光（Hisamitsu）先生不來參加派對嗎？）

I think they'll be in Gombe State then.

（我想他們人那時候會在貢貝州（Gombe State）。）

23. Do you know when your fitness club membership expires?

（你知道你的健身俱樂部會員資格什麼時候到期嗎？）

Actually, I renewed it last week.

（事實上，我上週延長效期了。）

HUMMER老師小重點 17. 的回答提到了 go past～，意思是「通過、經過～」。19. 的回答 was 後面，省略了問題描述的 fixed（被修理）。20. 的回答 it，指的是問題描述的 heavy traffic（交通繁忙）。

24. What did Mr. Yoshi talk about at the meeting?
（吉（Yoshi）先生在會議上談了什麼？）
Oh, nothing special.
（喔，沒什麼特別的。）

25. Would you like some coffee?
（你要不要來點咖啡？）
Do you know whether they serve decaf or not?
（你知道他們是否有提供無咖啡因的咖啡嗎？）

26

26. You have to use a swipe card to enter the room.
（你必須使用磁卡進入房間。）
I have to get the card from the management office, don't I?
（我必須從管理室拿到卡，對嗎？）

27. I'll call you when your consultant is ready.
（當你的諮商顧問準備好時，我會叫你。）
Thank you so much. I'll take a seat.
（非常感謝你，我會找位子坐下來。）

28. Do you want to eat lunch at your place or mine?
（你想在你家或我家吃午餐？）
Actually, I'd prefer to eat out today.
（其實，我今天比較想外食。）

29. I'd like to move this copier over to the corner.
（我想把這台影印機搬到角落那邊。）
Actually, I prefer it by the window.
（其實，我比較喜歡它靠窗邊。）

30. We should hold an annual celebration for all our employees.
（我們應該為我們的所有員工舉辦年度的慶祝活動。）
Oh, that'd be a nice gesture, I think.
（喔！我想那會是一種友好的表示。）

27

31. Can I please use this copier?
（我可以使用這台影印機嗎？）
Unfortunately, it's not working.
（很遺憾地，它無法運作了。）

HUMMER老師小重點 有些提問的正確答案會出現像24.這種意想不到的閃躲式回答，所以平日練習時，多思考這是否「可能」成為合理對話的選項是非常重要的。另外，請把25.的decaf（無咖啡因的咖啡）及26.的swipe card（磁卡）的用法記起來。27.的I'll call you雖然有可能用於表達「我會再打電話給你」的意思，但這題的情況明顯是指「我會告知你」，聽到答句時要能馬上反應過來才行。

32. Did sales increase in Canada last year?

（去年加拿大的銷售額有增加嗎？）

To tell the truth, the figures aren't in yet.

（說實話，這些數字還沒出來。）

33. If you have many things to do, you could ask Ms. Matsuda for some help.

（如果你有很多事情要做，你可以向松田（Matsuda）女士求助。）

Oh, thank you for letting me know.

（喔！謝謝你讓我知道。）

34. Tommy, would you rather work alone or as a team?

（湯米（Tommy），你寧願自己做還是團隊合作？）

It doesn't make any difference to me.

（這對我而言沒有差別。）

35. We've met at the annual conference, haven't we?

（我們在年會上見過面，不是嗎？）

Hmm, I don't believe so.

（呃，我不這麼認為。）

28

36. Did you bring the receipt with you?

（你帶收據了嗎？）

It's in my wallet.

（它在我的錢包裡。）

37. I'd like to purchase three tickets for the performance.

（我想買三張表演的門票。）

For what time?

（什麼時候的？）

38. I heard the orchestra performance will be outdoors.

（我聽說管絃樂隊的演出將在戶外舉行。）

Oh, hopefully, it won't rain tonight.

（喔！希望今晚不會下雨。）

39. There is a spill on one of the tables.

（有打翻的東西在其中一張桌上。）

Could you tell me which table it is?

（可以告訴我是哪一張桌子嗎？）

HUMMER老師小重點 針對34.的提問，可成為正確的應答選項除了「這對我而言沒有差別」之外，其他如 Either is fine.（兩者都好。）／I don't care.（我不在意。）／It doesn't matter to me.（這對我而言都無所謂。）等說法也可以，也請一併記起來喔！

40. More toner cartridges will be delivered next Monday.
（下週一會有更多的碳粉匣被送來。）
Good, we're running low.
（太好了，我們快用完了。）

29

41. Let's not tell the instructors about the issue until Friday.
（在星期五前，我們都別告訴教師這個問題。）
OK, let's wait.
（好，我們等吧。）

42. Rachel went to the event last week.
（瑞秋（Rachel）上週參加了這個活動。）
I wish I could have joined her.
（我真希望當時能和她一起。）

43. I tried the new restaurant across from our building.
（我試了我們大樓對面的新餐廳。）
Oh, what did you think?
（哦，你覺得怎麼樣？）

44. I need to have these pants dry-cleaned immediately.
（我需要立即讓這些褲子被乾洗。）
Would you like me to drop them off for you?
（你想要我幫你拿過去嗎？）

45. You should get Finn's input on this important issue.
（你應該取得芬恩（Finn）在這個重要問題上的意見。）
I'll call him after lunch.
（我午餐後會打電話給他。）

30

46. This vending machine won't take my bill at all.
（這台自動販賣機完全不接受我的紙鈔。）
Let me insert it for you if you don't mind.
（如果你不介意，讓我幫你放看看吧。）

47. I was impressed by your wonderful painting.
（我對你的精彩畫作感到驚艷。）
Actually, I think it still needs a few changes.
（事實上，我認為它還需要一些修改。）

HUMMER老師小重點 將40.的be running low（快用完）與run short of～（～不夠）一併背起來。42.的I wish I could have joined her.這種與過去事實相反的假設語氣，即使是因為以聽力方式出題而較具挑戰性，也希望各位能聽懂意思。如果對文法有任何一點疑問時，請務必每一次都查閱文法書，直到確認自己已完全了解並熟悉該文法，這點非常重要。

48. My back feels good since we started using new chairs.
（自從我們開始使用新椅子後，我的背感覺很好。）
They seem to be more comfortable than the old ones.
（他們似乎比舊的更舒服。）

49. Mr. Morrison will give us a cost estimate for the event.
（莫里森（Morrison）先生將會給我們此次活動的成本估算。）
I think it'll probably cost a lot.
（我覺得它可能會花費很多。）

50. You're getting a raise next month, right?
（你下個月將得到加薪，對吧？）
According to my boss.
（據我的老闆所言是這樣。）

31

51. Could you replace the fluorescent lights now?
（可以請你現在更換日光燈嗎？）
I'm sorry, they don't arrive until Monday.
（很抱歉，它們週一之前不會到。）

52. Isn't Mr. Kato in charge of cleaning the windows today?
（今天不是加藤（Kato）先生負責清洗窗戶嗎？）
Actually, I've been doing it since last week.
（事實上，我從上週開始就一直在做了。）

53. How was your holiday in your home town?
（你在家鄉的假期如何？）
Unfortunately, my vacation was canceled.
（很遺憾地，我的假期被取消了。）

54. When will the guests arrive here?
（客人將何時抵達這裡？）
I heard they left the station just now.
（我聽說他們才剛離開車站。）

55. Showing this handout to a third party may cause a problem.
（將這份資料展示給第三方可能會引起問題。）
It'll be fine.
（不會有事的。）

HUMMER老師小重點 像53. 這類有關感想的提問，有時也會出現意想不到的答案，請牢記這種回答方式。而對於55. 這類說話者表達的擔憂，除了回答「沒問題」和「不會」之外，其他例如「同意（是的）」或「提議（向某人確認）」等等也是常見的正確答句。

Practice Test 實戰試題

MP3 32～56

請先聽題目及後續的三個選項，再從（A）、（B）、（C）中選出最適合的答案（答案卡在全書最後）。

1. Mark your answer on your answer sheet.

2. Mark your answer on your answer sheet.

3. Mark your answer on your answer sheet.

4. Mark your answer on your answer sheet.

5. Mark your answer on your answer sheet.

6. Mark your answer on your answer sheet.

7. Mark your answer on your answer sheet.

8. Mark your answer on your answer sheet.

9. Mark your answer on your answer sheet.

10. Mark your answer on your answer sheet.

11. Mark your answer on your answer sheet.

12. Mark your answer on your answer sheet.

13. Mark your answer on your answer sheet.

14. Mark your answer on your answer sheet.

15. Mark your answer on your answer sheet.

16. Mark your answer on your answer sheet.

17. Mark your answer on your answer sheet.

18. Mark your answer on your answer sheet.

19. Mark your answer on your answer sheet.

20. Mark your answer on your answer sheet.

21. Mark your answer on your answer sheet.

22. Mark your answer on your answer sheet.

23. Mark your answer on your answer sheet.

24. Mark your answer on your answer sheet.

25. Mark your answer on your answer sheet.

1.

32

I was just wondering if you could move these books for us.
(A) Yes, I'd like to go to that movie.
(B) By when?
(C) This book was made into a film this year.

我在想你是否可以為我們移動這些書。
（A）是的，我想去看那部電影。
（B）什麼時候之前？（問期限）
（C）這本書今年被拍成電影。

答案 (B)

解析 這題是用I was just wondering if～來表達禮貌的請求。（B）的回答因為過於簡短，所以很難立即聽懂。如果聽不懂時就暫且保留，繼續聽下一個選項吧！（A）的movie（電影）跟move（移動）發音類似而容易混淆。（C）雖然也出現單字book（書籍），但無法與陳述句構成合理的應答對話。

字彙 □ I was just wondering if you could *do*～ 我在想你（們）是否可以（為我們）做～（表達請求）
□ *be* made into a film 被拍成電影

2.

33

Do you think I should follow Mr. Takatori's advice about this problem?
(A) Would you tell me what he said?
(B) No, I don't take his class.
(C) By the end of this month.

關於這個問題，你認為我應該遵從高取（Takatori）先生的建議嗎？
（A）你能告訴我他說了什麼嗎？
（B）不，我沒上他的課。
（C）到這個月底。

答案 (A)

解析 因為原本就不知道高取先生的建議是什麼，所以（A）順勢詢問其內容是合理的。若只有聽到（A）很難確定它就是正確答案，不過因為（B）和（C）都不是合理的應答，可用刪去法判斷。在TOEIC L&R多益測驗中，雖然有些選項很難立刻判斷是否正確，但是不正確的選項通常會很明顯表現出它是錯的。因此，各位要聽完其他選項後再用刪去法來判斷喔！

3.

34

Our company has lost a lot of excellent employees over the past ten months.

(A) Unfortunately, that's true.

(B) That's a consistently excellent company.

(C) Would you like me to hire you?

過去十個月，本公司失去了很多優秀的員工。

（A）很遺憾地，那是事實。

（B）那是一家始終很優秀的公司。

（C）你希望我僱用你嗎？

答案 (A)

解析 （A）針對陳述句表示「認同」，所以是正確答案。其他表達方式如「補充說明（這的確是本公司有史以來最嚴重的損失）」、「建議（刊登求職廣告如何）」、「否定（當然不是這樣）」等也可當作合適的應答。對於「非疑問句問題」的回答方式有很多種，因此難度較高。

字彙 □ consistently 始終

4.

35

They're our latest shoes.

(A) I bought it last night.

(B) This is the latest news on the issue.

(C) How are they selling?

它們是我們最新款的鞋子。

（A）我昨天晚上買了它。

（B）這是有關該議題的最新消息。

（C）它們賣得如何？

答案 (C)

解析 為了在測驗時能即時想像對話的狀況，大家不妨利用每天的訓練來鍛鍊想像力吧！尤其需要注意「題目為陳述句」的題型。如這題的描述是介紹鞋子，其中以（C）的回應最自然。（A）的it（它）如果換成them（它們），就可以代表陳述句中的shoes（鞋子），這樣的語意，在特定的情境下或許也能成為正確答案。（B）雖然也提到latest，但故意用類似shoes發音的單字issue來混淆，且無法與陳述句構成合理的對話。

字彙 □ latest 最新的 □ issue 議題、問題

5.

36

Will the company provide software training for all new employees?

(A) That's what I heard.

(B) At the company's outing.

(C) I'd like to use the training room.

公司將為所有新進員工提供軟體培訓嗎？

（A）我是這樣聽說的沒錯。

（B）在員工旅遊時。

（C）我想使用培訓教室。

答案 (A)

解析 （A）針對提問表示「認同」，所以是正確答案。（B）是針對when（何時）或是where（何地）的問題才會有的回答。（C）雖然使用與題目中一樣的單字training（培訓），但是無法構成合理的對話。

字彙 □ outing 郊遊、外出

6.

37

Do you know who has the device I'd like to use today?

(A) The device is very simple to use.

(B) I saw Mr. Sherrick using it.

(C) You can put them on the shelf.

你知道誰有我今天想要用的儀器嗎？

（A）這個儀器操作簡單。

（B）我看到謝里克（Sherrick）先生使用它。

（C）你可以把它們放在架上。

答案 (B)

解析 針對提問者想知道「誰有儀器？」，（B）用「看到使用的人」來間接回答，所以是正確答案。（A）只有描述儀器操作簡單，不是適當的回答。（C）和題目內容無關。

字彙 ☐ device 儀器 ☐ simple to use 操作簡單

7.

38

The dentist is on this floor, isn't it?

(A) Oh, it's one flight up.

(B) Sorry, this is my floor.

(C) You should consult a dentist immediately.

牙醫在這一樓層，不是嗎？

（A）喔，它是在往上一樓。

（B）對不起，我的樓層到了。

（C）你應該立刻看牙醫。

答案 (A)

解析 針對「確認牙醫在哪一樓層」的提問，可預測會聽到「回答樓層」或是「不知道」等應答選項。但正確答案（A）卻是回答「往上一樓」。one fight up是「往上一樓」的意思，請各位也一併記起來！（B）是想從電梯出來的人當下說的話。（C）雖然提到dentist（牙醫），但無法構成合理的對話。

字彙 ☐ This is my floor. 我的樓層到了。

8.

39

This is the latest catalog, isn't it?

(A) They're the latest best sellers.

(B) No, I think we have enough time.

(C) Yes, could you send it to the client?

這是最新的目錄，不是嗎？

（A）它們是最新的暢銷品。

（B）不，我認為我們有足夠的時間。

（C）是的，你能把它寄給客戶嗎？

答案 (C)

解析 （C）用it代表latest catalog（最新的目錄），希望對方能將它寄給客戶，所以是正確答案。（A）的敘述雖然包括問題句中的the latest（最新的），但講的卻是暢銷品，因此不正確。（B）如果只有回答No就是正確答案，然而 I 後面的敘述並不符提問內容，比較像是在回應「趕得上截止日期嗎？」這類問題的答案。

9. 40

Have you got the packet for the event yet?
(A) I haven't checked my post today.
(B) I had trouble getting a bucket yesterday.
(C) I waited in line at the event.

你已經收到活動用的小包裏了嗎？
（A）我今天還沒確認郵件。
（B）我昨天為了得到水桶吃不少苦頭。
（C）我在活動中排隊等待。

Part 2

答案 (A)

解析 針對提問者想知道「小包裏是否已送到？」，（A）回答「還沒確認郵件」，是最適當的答案。（B）用了與packet（小包裏）發音相似的單字bucket（水桶），但答不對題。（C）雖然也出現event（活動）這個單字，但是卻與題目的packet一事毫無關係，因此無法構成對話。

字彙 □ have trouble *doing* 為了做～吃不少苦頭

10. 41

Do you know when we get repaid for transportation and accommodation costs?
(A) I got an airline ticket yesterday.
(B) I had a great time.
(C) Maybe you should ask Ms. Motegi later.

你知道我們何時可以取得交通與住宿費的退款嗎？
（A）昨天我買了一張機票。
（B）我度過了一段美好的時光。
（C）也許你稍後應該去詢問茂木（Motegi）女士。

答案 (C)

解析 針對提問者想知道「交通和住宿費何時會退款？」，（C）說「最好問其他人（＝自己不知道）」，這是合理的對話。至於（A）和（B）都不是針對提問來回答，所以不是正確答案。

11. 42

This store is busy even on weekdays.
(A) Do you believe he is busy?
(B) I have every Thursday off.
(C) I agree.

這家商店即使在平日也很熱鬧。
（A）你相信他很忙嗎？
（B）我每週四休息。
（C）我同意。

答案 (C)

解析 從題目的陳述內容可知，這家店平日就是人氣鼎沸。（C）表示同意該句話，所以是正確答案。（A）和（B）的busy（忙碌的）及Thursday（週四）雖然是與該陳述句有關的單字，但句意都不是合理的應答。

12.

43

How long have you been in our company? (A) This company was established five years ago. (B) He's been here for two years. (C) I've only just joined.	你在我們公司上班多久了？ （A）這家公司成立於五年前。 （B）他在這裡已經兩年了。 （C）我才剛加入。

答案 **(C)**

解析 對於詢問工作的年數，（C）回答「才剛加入」，所以是正確答案。請注意這種問題的答案並不限於具體的時間。（A）和（B）雖然都有提到具體的年數，但是（A）是指公司成立的年數，（B）是回答第三人稱的工作年資，因此都不是正確答案。記得在聽選項內容時，必須要經常保持警覺去聽選項的主詞、時態及數字。

字彙 □ establish 設立～

13.

44

I have a package for you. (A) We'll pack fragile items. (B) Mr. Shimizu is going to come pick it up. (C) That'll save the trip to the bank.	我有一個包裹要給你。 （A）我們將包裝易損壞的物品。 （B）清水（Shimizu）先生會去拿。 （C）那就能省去要跑銀行一趟了。

答案 **(B)**

解析 針對「有包裹」的陳述，以（B）回答某人要過去拿最正確。其他像「我過去拿」、「請直接幫我保管」、「請幫我帶過來」等也可當作是正確的回應。（A）雖然是用package（包裹）的相關字pack，但是句意不符，（C）是與問題陳述無關的內容。

字彙 □ pack 包裝～ □ fragile 容易損壞的 □ save the trip to～ 省去跑～一趟

14.

45

I'm surprised to see many prices have increased. (A) I am, too. (B) What will be the prize? (C) Yes, between Monday and Wednesday.	我很訝異看到很多價格上漲。 （A）我也是。 （B）獎品是什麼？ （C）是的，從週一到週三。

答案 **(A)**

解析 對於「物價上漲」的陳述，（A）用I am (surprised), too.（我也很訝異。）來表示「同意」，所以是正確答案。（B）是故意使用與surprised（訝異、驚訝）和prices（價格）發音相似的單字prize（獎品）為陷阱選項。（C）是與問題陳述完全無關的內容。

15. 46

You'll choose the fastest route, right?
(A) Ms. Mori did the job fastest.
(B) I didn't choose the class, actually.
(C) I'm thinking about taking the expressway.

你會選擇最快的路線，對吧？
（A）森（Mori）女士做得最快。
（B）事實上，我沒有選這堂課。
（C）我正在考慮走高速公路。

答案 (C)

解析 這題是提問者在確認要走哪一條路線。可預料的回答如「Yes／No」，後面再接具體的路線說明，或是「還沒決定」等。選項（C）具體地說明選擇的路線，所以是正確答案。（A）是故意使用問題句中也提到的單字fastest（最快速）作為陷阱選項。（B）的choose（選擇）雖然和題目中有相同的單字，但無法構成合理的對話。

16. 47

Do you know who isn't coming to the banquet tonight?
(A) I was invited to the celebration.
(B) No, let me go check.
(C) I'll be waiting, so please get ready.

你知道今晚誰不來參加宴會嗎？
（A）我被邀請參加慶祝會。
（B）不，我來查看看。
（C）我會等著，所以請做好準備。

答案 (B)

解析 針對「是否知道有誰不來」的提問，（B）回答「不（知道），我來查看看」，所以是正確答案。（A）的celebration（慶祝會）雖然和banquet（宴會）意思相近，但不是針對問題來回答。（C）是向還沒做好（出門）準備的對方所說的話。

17. 48

That escalator hasn't been fixed yet, has it?
(A) To the next floor.
(B) Mr. Taya said it was.
(C) By taking the escalator.

電扶梯還沒被修好，是嗎？
（A）到下一樓層。
（B）田谷（Taya）先生說修了。
（C）坐電扶梯過去。

答案 (B)

解析 針對「確認電扶梯是否已修好」的提問，（B）用傳聞的句型表達it（＝escalator 電扶梯）已修了，所以是正確答案。（A）故意用電扶梯相關的用語來誤導作答。（C）雖然提到escalator，但答非所問。

18.

49

I'll teleconference with Mr. Kono this evening.	我今天傍晚將會和河野（Kono）先生進行電話會議。
(A) The conference was held in room 201.	（A）會議在201室舉行過了。
(B) Please tell me when you're done.	（B）當你結束時請告訴我。
(C) Yes, it was too long.	（C）是的，太長了。

答案 **(B)**

解析 雖然這題很難預測會出現什麼樣的應答選項，但是如果一開始即正確聽懂陳述句並牢記它，當你聽到（B）回答「當你結束時請告訴我」的時候就能斷定它是正確答案了。（A）的時態與陳述句不符，如果將was held（被舉行過）改為will be held（將被舉行）就是正確答案了。（C）是在對過去發生的某件事陳述感想，所以無法構成合理的對話。

字彙 □ teleconference with～ 與～進行電話會議

19.

50

Our client will arrive on an overnight flight from Chicago, right?	我們的客戶將從芝加哥（Chicago）搭紅眼班機抵達，對吧？
(A) Unfortunately, it was canceled.	（A）不幸的是，它被取消了。
(B) At this time, it's engaged in repairs.	（B）這時候，它正在維修中。
(C) Are we almost there?	（C）我們已經快要到那裡了嗎？

答案 **(A)**

解析 這題是提問者在確認客戶的抵達方式。（A）提供班機已取消的新資訊回應對方，所以是正確答案。（B）答非所問，因此不是正確答案。（C）是對一起到達目的地的人所說的話，用來回應這題是不適當的。

字彙 □ overnight flight 紅眼班機 □ *be* engaged in repairs 修理中

20.

51

You have to be in the hotel lobby at five o'clock.	你必須在五點到飯店大廳。
(A) At the reception desk.	（A）在接待櫃台。
(B) The banquet has been canceled.	（B）宴會已被取消。
(C) OK, I'll be there without fail.	（C）好的，我一定會在那裡。

答案 **(C)**

解析 針對「必須在五點到飯店大廳」的陳述，（C）回答「我一定會在那裡」，所以是正確答案。（A）是回應「詢問地點」的回答，因此不是正確答案。（B）是故意用banquet（宴會）讓人與陳述句中的hotel（飯店）誤作聯想。

字彙 □ reception desk 接待櫃台 □ without fail 一定、務必

21.

52

I didn't have time to check the bulletin board today.
(A) I can see you're busy.
(B) He's on the board of directors.
(C) That's nice of you to say.

我今天沒有時間查看公告欄。
（A）我知道你今天很忙。
（B）他是董事會成員。
（C）你人真好，感謝你這麼說。

答案 **(A)**

解析 這題很難預測會出現什麼樣的應答選項。（A）是對說話者表達的感受作出自然的反應，所以是正確答案。（B）雖然也有提到board這個單字，但是題目指的是「公告欄」，而（B）是指「董事會」，所以無法建立合理對話。（C）是在向對方所說的話表達感謝時的應答。

22.

53

I'd like you to stop by Shinsuk's office to pick up your new ID card.
(A) I'll do it immediately.
(B) OK, I'll pick you up at the train station.
(C) You need the credit card information.

我想請你順路到辛薩克（Shinsuk）辦公室去取你的新身分證。
（A）我馬上去做。
（B）好的，我會去火車站接你。
（C）你需要信用卡資料。

答案 **(A)**

解析 針對說話者委請對方去拿身分證，（A）回答「我馬上去做」（do it＝pick up my new ID card 領取我的新身分證），所以是正確答案。（B）是指去接人而不是身分證，所以回答不正確。（C）回答的內容也是跟題目內容完全無關，因此不是正確答案。

字彙 □ stop by～ 順路去～　□ pick up～ 取～　□ pick＋人＋up 接人

23.

54

The conference room is too hot, isn't it?
(A) I'll call for an urgent meeting with them tonight.
(B) We have a mild climate here.
(C) Could you lower the temperature?

會議室太熱了，不是嗎？
（A）我今天晚上將和他們召開緊急會議。
（B）我們這裡氣候溫和。
（C）你能降低溫度嗎？

答案 **(C)**

解析 對於「會議室太熱了（所以不做些什麼嗎？）」這樣的提問，像「我不覺得熱」、「那就開窗戶吧」、「開冷氣吧」等都可當作適當的回應。（C）用降低溫度來回應，所以是正確答案。（A）提到的meeting（會議）雖然是conference（會議室）的相關單字，但是無法構成合理的對話。（B）回答的是當地的氣候，內容完全跟題目內容無關。

24. 55

This restaurant has wireless Internet access, doesn't it?

(A) It was so good to eat.

(B) No, this location doesn't have it.

(C) I spend a few hours a day on the Internet.

這家餐廳有無線網路存取，不是嗎？

（A）太好吃了。

（B）不，這個地點沒有它。

（C）我一天花數小時上網。

答案 (B)

解析 針對「是否可使用Internet（網路）？」的提問，（B）回答這裡沒有它（it＝wireless Internet access無線網路存取），意指不能使用網路，所以是正確答案。（A）是與restaurant（餐廳）相關的內容，因此不是正確答案。（C）雖然是有關使用Internet的內容，但是答非所問。

字彙 □ spend *A* on *B* 花A在B上

25. 56

Did you go to the performance with Ms. Albright yesterday?

(A) I wanted to go, but I couldn't leave work.

(B) She brought him to the park.

(C) Her performance is always flawless.

昨天你有和奧爾布萊特（Albright）女士一起去看表演嗎？

（A）我想去，但是我無法離開公司。

（B）她帶他去公園。

（C）她的表現總是無懈可擊。

答案 (A)

解析 針對「是否有一起去看表演？」的提問，（A）表達「雖然想去但因為工作而無法去」，所以是正確答案。（B）的內容完全跟題目內容無關，（C）的her（她）不知道是指哪一位，而且也無法和問題構成合理對話。

字彙 □ flawless 無懈可擊、完美的

Part

3&4

簡短對話＆簡短獨白

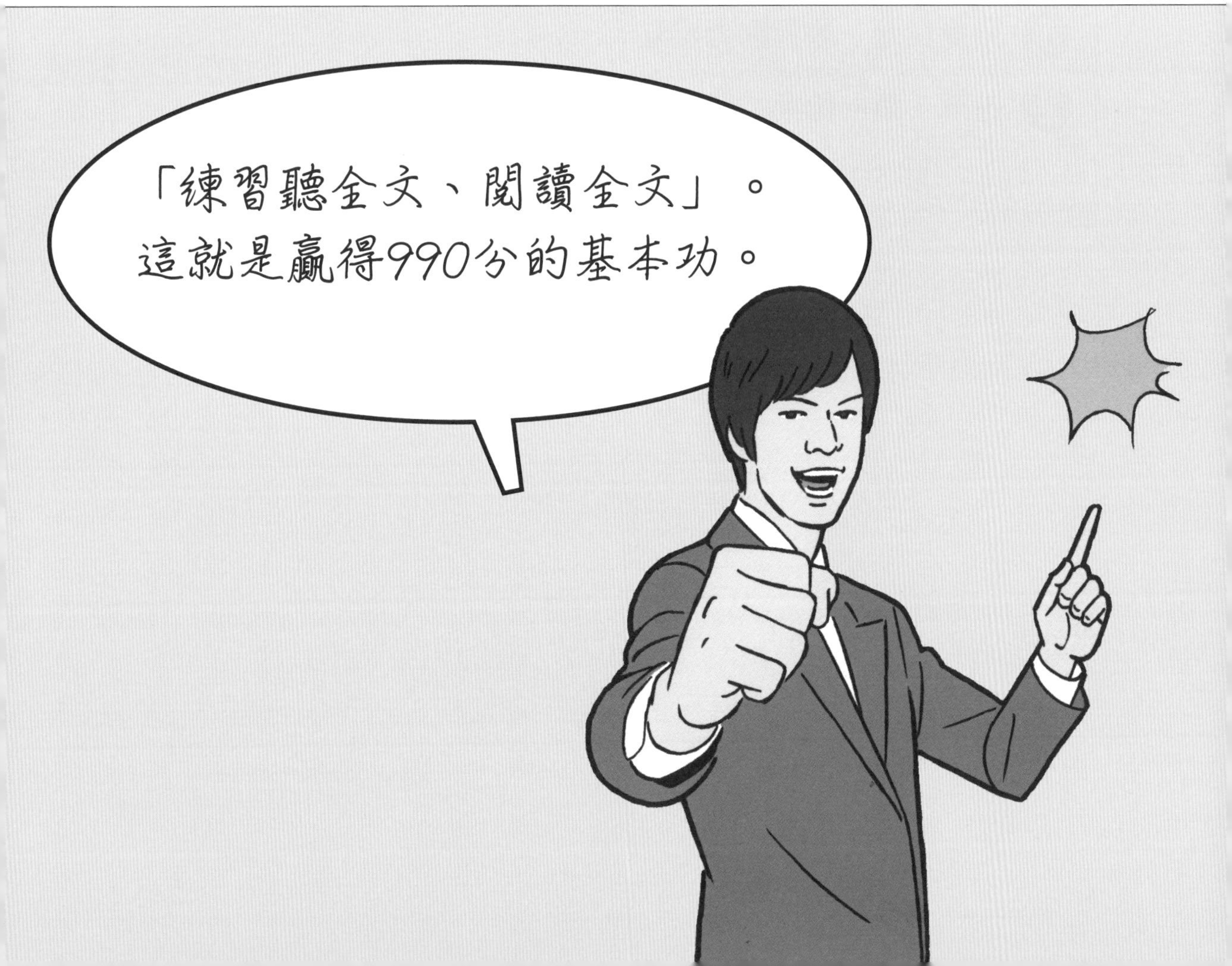
「練習聽全文、閱讀全文」。
這就是贏得990分的基本功。

Part 3&4 簡短對話＆簡短獨白

贏得990分的解題技巧及攻略法

Part 3和4的攻略法基本上是一樣的。以990分為目標的進階學習者，應該都能100%聽懂並理解Part 3的對話和Part 4的獨白內容。不過要贏得990分，單靠「聽力來理解內容」是不夠的。建議大家**要趁語音播放之前的空檔，先預覽試題本上的題目和選項（包括搭配的圖表）**，盡可能從中收集接下來要聽的重點，這樣在聽語音時，就能快、狠、準地直接作答。如果能學會**這種積極的聆聽方式**，相信要完全答對Part 3和4絕不是夢想。

贏得990分的解題技巧

① 預覽試題、收集聽力重點

② 破解「單一線索」題型*

*「單一線索」題型：意指試題的答案出處在全文中只出現一次的題型。

先試著寫以下例題。無論如何，請各位預覽試題後再來作答吧！

例題1 MP3 57

32. What does Louie want to know about?
(A) The right time to register for a convention
(B) His co-workers' thoughts about a convention
(C) An effective way to start up a new convention
(D) The official profiles of speakers at a convention

33. Why does the woman say, "I'm considering it"?
(A) She probably will not attend.
(B) She has not made up her mind yet.
(C) She has not gotten a confirmation e-mail.
(D) She has to get her boss' permission.

34. What does the woman imply about the convention?
(A) Employees should go as a team.
(B) This year's presenters are excellent.
(C) Only one day of participation is necessary.
(D) Most of the attendees are not very serious.

32. Ⓐ Ⓑ Ⓒ Ⓓ **34.** Ⓐ Ⓑ Ⓒ Ⓓ
33. Ⓐ Ⓑ Ⓒ Ⓓ

例題2 MP3 58

35. Look at the graphic. Why is the customer questioning the validity of her coupon?
(A) It is a Friday.
(B) It is only for drinks.
(C) It is just before 4 P.M.
(D) It is May 14.

36. What will Amy do for the customer?
(A) Apply a discount to all her drinks
(B) Bring her a free appetizer
(C) Give her another coupon
(D) Make the lemonade without ice

37. What does the customer need to do her work?
(A) A bigger table for spreading out her things
(B) A code for using the Internet
(C) Another writing utensil
(D) A quieter corner of the restaurant

35. Ⓐ Ⓑ Ⓒ Ⓓ **37.** Ⓐ Ⓑ Ⓒ Ⓓ
36. Ⓐ Ⓑ Ⓒ Ⓓ

例題3 MP3 59

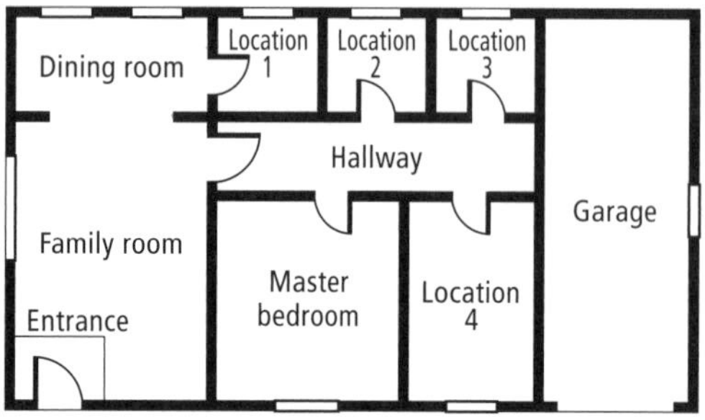

71. Why is the speaker making the call?
(A) To convey a decision
(B) To set up an appointment
(C) To request some information
(D) To officially hire the listener

72. Look at the graphic. Where does the speaker plan to put her new laundry room?
(A) Location 1
(B) Location 2
(C) Location 3
(D) Location 4

73. What will the speaker and the listener do on Monday?
(A) Draw up a blueprint of her idea
(B) Talk about a schedule
(C) Choose materials for a project
(D) Discuss an estimate for a job

71. Ⓐ Ⓑ Ⓒ Ⓓ **73.** Ⓐ Ⓑ Ⓒ Ⓓ
72. Ⓐ Ⓑ Ⓒ Ⓓ

HUMMER式密技！

① 預覽試題、收集聽力重點

聽力普遍被認為是一種「被動」的能力，不過在Part 3&4就要「主動出擊」。因為題目和選項（包括搭配的圖表）都是印在試題本上，透過預覽的方式，我們就可以在語音播放之前，搶先掌握應該聽到的重點，並對接下來的語音內容有一定程度的了解。**因此培養必要的閱讀技巧也是聽力獲得滿分的關鍵**。

預覽時，不要強迫腦袋記住內容，最好是藉由增加閱讀的次數**自然地將它留在腦海中**。如果遇到難以理解的題目或選項時，請以理解為第一優先，仔細閱讀。藉由不斷的練習，必能體會哪些才是重點。

至於每個題組的語音播放結束之後到開始播放下個題組的這段時間，平均約有30秒（語音朗讀題目2秒 × 3題＋各題之間的空檔8秒 × 3題＝30秒），若作答完有剩餘的時間，就可以趕緊用來預覽下一題組。讓我們依照以下的步驟試著練習看看吧！

以題組**32.～34.**為例：
①只閱讀**32.～34.**的題目。
②閱讀**32.**的題目＋選項（＋圖表）。
③閱讀**33.**的題目＋選項（＋圖表）。
④閱讀**34.**的題目＋選項（＋圖表）。
⑤只閱讀**32.～34.**的題目。
⑥在下個題組的語音開始播放前，不斷重複⑤。

如果時間充裕，不妨在步驟①也加上「選項（＋圖表）」。最終的理想目標是，在**30秒內將題組內的題目與選項（＋圖表）都預覽三次以上**。在正確掌握各題及選項（＋圖表）的意思後，如果還可以預覽三次以上，我們將會實際感受到那些內容留在我們的腦海中。一旦達到這樣的境界，就可以將**99%的注意力集中在聽語音播放上，只需要看一下題目和選項（＋圖表），一邊聽語音的同時就能夠選出正確答案**。

以下將藉**例題1**來解說如何從閱讀題目和選項的過程中收集聽力重點。這一題組雖然是「3人對話」，但即使是2人對話的情形也不會改變作答的步驟及方法。另外，**33.**題是在詢問說話者的意圖（本書稱為「意圖問題」）。意圖問題的作答技巧，**就是「廣泛」略聽並理解這句話附近的內容，以及對話前後的「狀況」**。

例題1

32. What does Louie want to know about?
(A) The right time to register for a convention
(B) His co-workers' thoughts about a convention
(C) An effective way to start up a new convention
(D) The official profiles of speakers at a convention

路易（Louie）想知道什麼？
（A）適合登記參加會議的時間
（B）他的同事對會議的想法
（C）著手舉辦新會議的有效方法
（D）會議上演說者的官方簡介

33. Why does the woman say, “I'm considering it”?
(A) She probably will not attend.
(B) She has not made up her mind yet.
(C) She has not gotten a confirmation e-mail.
(D) She has to get her boss' permission.

這名女性為何說「I'm considering it」？
（A）她可能不會參加。
（B）她還沒下定決心。
（C）她沒有收到確認電郵。
（D）她必須取得老闆的許可。

34. What does the woman imply about the convention?

(A) Employees should go as a team.

(B) This year's presenters are excellent.

(C) Only one day of participation is necessary.

(D) Most of the attendees are not very serious.

關於會議，這名女性暗指什麼？

（A）員工應該組隊一起參加。

（B）今年的演說者很優秀。

（C）只有一天的參與是必要的。

（D）大多數出席者都不是很認真。

預覽題目和選項時，我會將以下的聽力重點放在腦海裡，並直接以英文原文記下關鍵字（請參考以上畫底線處）。

32.「路易想知道什麼？登記的時間、同事的想法、有效的方法、官方簡介？」

33.「I'm considering it、不參加、沒有下定決心、沒有收到電郵、未得到許可？」

34.「女性說了會議什麼？組隊參加、演說者優秀、一天的必要參與、出席者不認真？」

只要透過這種方式「重點預覽」題目和選項，接下來就能專心於該聽的部分並「主動出擊」。接著，讓我們來實際練習聽這一題組的語音播放吧！

例題 1 MP3 57

Questions 32 through 34 refer to the following conversation with three speakers.

試題 32-34 請參考以下 3 人對話。

M1: Hey, Leslie, Eric. Q32 Are you going to the Rapmill Convention?

M2: Q32 I registered yesterday, Louie.

W: I'm considering it. Q33 I'd like to see the full line-up of presenters first because I don't want to waste time. I don't have time to go if the presentations don't pertain to my work. Why do you ask?

M1: My boss wants someone to go as a representative of our team, but I'm not sure if it's worthy of my time either, so Q32 I thought I'd get your perspectives.

M1: 嘿，萊絲莉（Leslie）、艾利克（Eric）。你們要參加拉普米爾（Rapmill）會議嗎？

M2: 我昨天登記了，路易（Louie）。

W: 我還在考慮中。我想先看到所有演說者的陣容，因為我不想浪費時間。如果演講內容與我的工作無關，我就沒有時間去。為什麼你要問這個呢？

M1: 我的老闆想要有人代表我們團隊參加，但我也不確定它是否值得我花時間去，所以想聽看看你們的看法。

M2:	Just networking with the presenters can be beneficial. They're usually phenomenal.	M2:	光是和演說者建立關係就可以很有利。他們通常極為傑出。
W:	Eric's right. Q34 But don't expect much out of the other participants. Many are there to have fun. They're more like…well, college students than colleagues.	W:	艾利克說的對。但是不要對其他參加者期望太高。許多人都是去好玩的。與其說他們是同事……嗯，不如說更像是大學生。
M2:	Sad but true. But some of the presenters have turned out to be great mentors for me.	M2:	很遺憾但確實如此。不過有些演說者已變成是我的良師了。

答案 **32.** (B) **33.** (B) **34.** (D)

字彙 □ pertain to～ 與～有關 □ perspective 看法 □ phenomenal 傑出的、不凡的 □ turn out to be～ 成為～

32. 預覽時先將「路易想知道什麼？登記的時間、同事的想法、有效的方法、官方簡介？」等重點記起來後，務必積極地聽語音內容。從第二位男性的首次發言可知，第一位男性是Louie（路易）。再從路易的第一次和第二次的發言中判斷（B）His co-workers' thoughts about a convention（他的同事對會議的想法）是正確答案。

33. 預覽時將「I'm considering it、不參加、沒有下定決心、沒有收到電郵、未得到許可？」等重點記起來。「大範圍地」聆聽女性說這句話的前後內容，判斷出最能表示這句話所說的「情況」的選項，就是正確答案。針對第一位男性向同事們提問是否參加會議，女性回答了I'm considering it（我還在考慮中），並進一步說「想知道演說者有誰」、「如果演講內容與工作無關就不打算參加」。可知女性尚未決定是否參加，因此正確答案是（B）。

34. 在等待語音中出現女性對會議闡述了什麼想法的同時，還要理解其發言的內容。女性在第二次的發言提到「不要指望其他參加者」、「與其說他們是同事還不如說更像是大學生」。選項（D）將該想法簡潔地換個說法，所以是正確答案。

❷ 破解「單一線索」題型

所謂「單一線索」題型，指的是**正確答案只在對話或獨白中出現一次的問題**（相對地，像Where does this conversation most likely take place?（這篇對話最有可能發生在哪裡？）這類的題型，因為在整個對話內容到處都留有答題線索，我將它稱為「多重線索」題型）。「單一線索」這種題型，就是只要一閃神，**便可能錯失聽到只會出現一次的關鍵字的題型**。接著，就來看看例題2（Part 3）、例題3（Part 4）的具體範例吧！此外，35.和72.是看圖作答的題型（本書稱之為「圖表問題」），藉由這兩道例題，希望大家可以學到圖表問題的解題技巧。

例題 2 MP3 58

Questions 35 through 37 refer to the following conversation and coupon.

試題 35-37 請參考以下對話及優惠券。

W1: Hi there, ma'am. My name is Amy, and I'll be your server for today. Can I start you off with a drink right away?

W2: Q35 Did I make it in time to use this coupon?

W1: Sure, there's a little time left. And Q36 if I put in your whole drink order now, the coupon will work for all of them.

W2: That's great, thanks. I've got some work to do, so I'll be here for a while. So put me down for a lemonade, an iced tea, and a coffee. I'll take the lemonade first.

W1: Sure thing. Any appetizers?

W2: In a little bit. By the way, Q37 I'd like to use your free Wi-Fi for my work, but I don't have the password.

W1: Oh, give me just a second, and I'll come right back with that information and your lemonade.

W1: 嗨，您好，女士。我叫艾咪（Amy），今日由我為您服務。我能現在就先幫您點一杯飲品嗎？

W2: 我還來得及使用這張優惠券嗎？

W1: 當然，還剩一點時間。如果我現在幫您點完所有要買單的飲品，這張優惠券將適用於它們全部。

W2: 太好了，謝謝。我有一些工作要做，所以我會在這裡待上一段時間。麻煩幫我點檸檬水、冰茶和咖啡。我要先上檸檬水。

W1: 當然沒問題。要什麼開胃菜嗎？

W2: 晚一點再說好了。順便問一下，我想要用你們的免費Wi-Fi工作，但是我沒有密碼。

W1: 喔，請等我一下，我很快就會帶著那個資訊和您的檸檬水回來。

字彙 ☐ work for～ 適用於～ ☐ appetizer 開胃菜

35. Look at the graphic. Why is the customer questioning the validity of her coupon?

(A) It is a Friday.

(B) It is only for drinks.

(C) It is just before 4 P.M.

(D) It is May 14.

請看圖。客人為何會詢問優惠券的有效性？

（A）當天是週五。

（B）它僅供飲料使用。

（C）因為快接近4 P.M.了。

（D）當天是5月14日。

36. What will Amy do for the customer?
(A) Apply a discount to all her drinks
(B) Bring her a free appetizer
(C) Give her another coupon
(D) Make the lemonade without ice

艾咪會幫客人做什麼？
（A）將她的所有飲料打折
（B）給她一份免費的開胃菜
（C）給她另一張優惠券
（D）做一份去冰的檸檬水

37. What does the customer need to do her work?
(A) A bigger table for spreading out her things
(B) A code for using the Internet
(C) Another writing utensil
(D) A quieter corner of the restaurant

客人需要什麼來進行她的工作？
（A）更大的桌子來分散擺放她的東西
（B）上網的密碼
（C）另一個書寫用具
（D）餐廳裡更安靜的角落

答案 **35.** (C) **36.** (A) **37.** (B)

對於含有圖表問題的題組，**在預覽選項時，也要一併看圖表內容**。掌握圖表內容與選項內容的關聯性，**作答時也要一邊看圖表一邊聽語音**。

35. 預覽時，記得先確認選項與圖表內容的共通點。因為女性客人詢問「（可以使用優惠券的時間）來得及嗎？」，由此可知她要確認目前的用餐時間是否適用優惠券上Happy Hour（快樂時光）的優惠。所以正確答案是（C）。

36. 從兩人的交談可知，艾咪是服務人員。（A）將紅色底線處簡潔地換個說法，所以是正確答案。

37. 仔細聽女性客人的需求。（B）將紅色底線處提及的password（密碼）換成code（密碼）的說法，所以是正確答案。

例題 3 MP3 59

Questions 71 through 73 refer to the following telephone message and blueprint.

試題 71-73 請參考以下電話留言及設計圖。

Hi, Jake. This is Heidi Vincent. I've been thinking about what you said the other day. Q72 I know you suggested that we put the new laundry room between the kitchen and the bathroom, but I'd really like to have it on the end of that row instead, by the garage. So if you wouldn't mind figuring that into the plans, I'd appreciate it. Q71 Anyway, um, just wanted to tell you that. Q73 I look forward to meeting with you on Monday to discuss start dates and how things will proceed from one part of the project to the next.

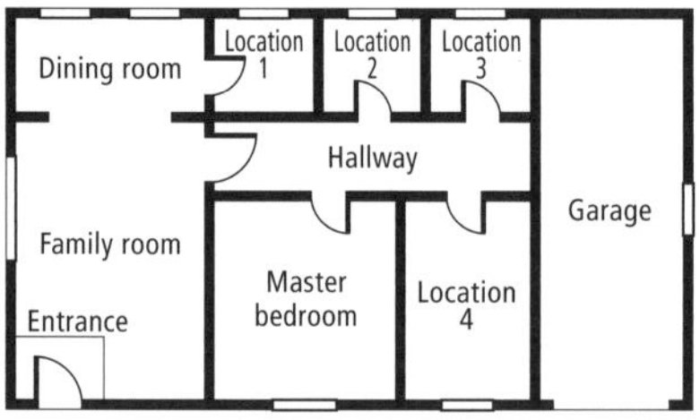

嗨，傑克（Jake）。我是海蒂．文森（Heidi Vincent）。我一直思考著你前幾天說的話。我知道你建議我們把新的洗衣間放在廚房和浴室之間，但是我真的很想把它放在那一排的最後面，就在車庫旁。所以如果你不介意而將它列入計畫，我會很感激的。無論如何，嗯，我只想告訴你那個想法。我很期待週一與你會面，討論開工日期以及如何將計畫從一個部份依序進行到下一階段。

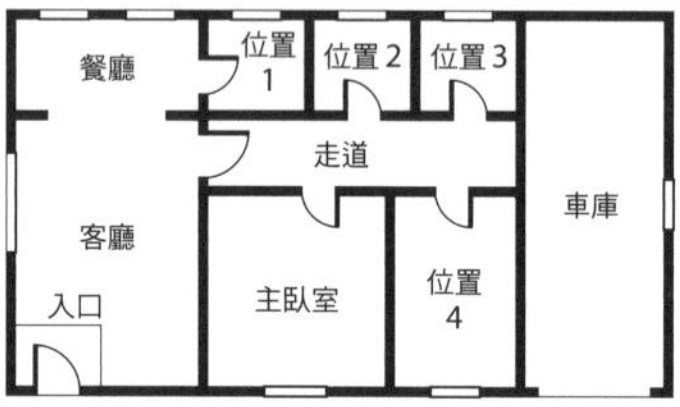

字彙 ☐ figure *A* into *B* 將A列入B ☐ proceed from *A* to *B* 從A進行到B

71. Why is the speaker making the call? 為什麼說話者打這通電話？

(A) To convey a decision （A）為了傳達一項決定

(B) To set up an appointment （B）為了約定見面時間

(C) To request some information （C）為了要求提供一些資訊

(D) To officially hire the listener （D）為了正式僱用聽留言的人

72. Look at the graphic. Where does the speaker plan to put her new laundry room? 請看圖。說話者計畫將她新的洗衣間放置在何處？

(A) Location 1 （A）位置1

(B) Location 2 （B）位置2

(C) Location 3 （C）位置3

(D) Location 4 （D）位置4

73. What will the speaker and the listener do on Monday?
(A) Draw up a blueprint of her idea
(B) Talk about a schedule
(C) Choose materials for a project
(D) Discuss an estimate for a job

說話者和聽者週一要做什麼？
（A）畫出她構想的藍圖
（B）談論時間表
（C）選擇工程的材料
（D）討論工作的估價

答案 **71.** (A) **72.** (C) **73.** (B)

除了選項中提供的資訊之外，圖表上一定會寫出某些字彙、人名等。我將這類的資訊稱為「組合資訊」，這類題型需要邊聽語音，邊看圖表來輔助作答。以例題3這一題組來說，要注意的是garage（車庫）、hallway（走道）、family room（客廳）等。

71. 這題是問打電話的原因。從紅色底線處可知，正確答案是（A）。雖然這題絕不難，但也不能輕忽，要小心作答。

72. 面對圖表問題，**眼睛在注意圖表中「組合資訊」的同時，耳朵也要專心聽語音**。從紅色底線處可聽出，聽者希望將Location 1和3作為廚房和浴室，Location 2作洗衣間，但是說話者從but後面表示希望將洗衣間放在那一排最後，也就是車庫旁。因此正確答案是Location 3的（C）。

73. 若有確實預覽就知道，當在語音中聽到Monday（週一）時，就要注意聽兩人要做什麼事。（B）將紅色底線處的語意簡潔地表達出來，所以是正確答案。

贏得990分之路

對於Part 3&4，請大家練習在語音播放之前將每一題組的題目和選項預覽數次並記住關鍵內容。終極目標是，要達到每一題組的題目和選項都能在30秒內預覽三次的水準。**「預覽能力」的養成，將讓你在Part 3 和 4得以完全制霸。**

接下來的Training基礎練習，是在訓練預覽能力並練習如何收集聽力重點。如此一來，不僅可以養成聆聽語音播放時所需的專注力，讓你面對各種題型都能邊聽邊作答，即使選項將語音內容的意思換個說法來表達，你也能保持記憶力，進而選出正確答案。

總結

Part 3&4，要先預覽題目和選項（＋圖表），然後掌握該聽（該看）的重點。同時也要提升自己，在面對「單一線索」題型時的專注力。

Part 3 Training 基礎練習

MP3 60

（1）請先閱讀以下的題目及選項，並預測對話的重點。

1. Why is the woman visiting the eye clinic?
(A) She has lost one of her lenses.
(B) She wants to replace the frames of her glasses.
(C) Her glasses do not fit right.
(D) Her glasses are scratched.

2. What does Jennifer say about the new lens?
(A) Ms. Ellison will not have to pay for it.
(B) It will not arrive for another week.
(C) It will have a new one-year warranty.
(D) She will inspect it upon arrival.

3. Why couldn't Ms. Ellison see the scratch?
(A) It just happened now.
(B) It was out of her line of vision.
(C) She was not used to her glasses.
(D) She was not wearing her glasses.

（2）請聽語音播放，並針對上述題目從（A）、（B）、（C）、（D）四個選項中選出最正確的答案（答案卡在全書最後）。

（3）最後，請練習盡可能準確地寫出正確答案在對話中的出處。

HUMMER老師小重點

1. 這題應該可以立刻聽懂是問「女性為什麼到眼科診所？」。而選項內容全部都是和「調整眼鏡」有關。且讓我們預測這是一篇有關女性對眼鏡提出的相關問題吧！
2. 雖然上一題提到了The woman（女性），但是這題又出現了另一位叫Jennifer（珍妮佛）的女性。選項（A）更是提到了Ellison（艾莉森），所以聽對話時要特別留意有哪些女性、她們分別扮演什麼角色。
3. 這題是問為什麼艾莉森無法看到the scratch（刮痕）。（C）的was not used to～是指「不習慣～」。注意不要和used to *do*（過去經常～）混淆。

Questions 1 through 3 refer to the following conversation with three speakers.

試題1-3 請參考以下3人對話。

W1: Hi. The other day I got some glasses from your clinic, but since then Q1 they keep sliding down my nose.

M: I'm sorry about that, ma'am. I can adjust them for you right away. Whoa! There's a big scratch in one of your lenses.

W2: Oh, hi, Ms. Ellison. Is there a problem with your glasses?

M: Jennifer, was this scratch here when you fitted her the other day?

W2: I don't think so. But either way, Q2 they're under warranty, so let's order a replacement now so they come in this week.

W1: Strange. I didn't see a scratch.

M: Q3 It's toward the top of the lens, so you probably can't see it while wearing them.

W1: 嗨，前幾天我在你們診所買了眼鏡，但是從那時候開始，它們一直從我的鼻子滑下來。

M: 很抱歉，女士。我可以馬上為您調整。哇！你的一片鏡片有個大刮痕。

W2: 喔，嗨，艾莉森（Ellison）女士。妳的眼鏡有什麼問題嗎？

M: 珍妮佛（Jennifer），前幾天你為她配戴時就有刮痕了嗎？

W2: 我不這麼認為。但不論是哪種方式造成的，它們都在保固期內，所以我們現在就來訂替換品，讓它們這週就可以送來。

W1: 奇怪。我沒有看到刮痕。

M: 它在靠鏡片上方，所以妳戴著它們時可能不會看到。

1. 女性為什麼到眼科診所？

（A）她遺失了一片鏡片。

（B）她想要換鏡框。

（C）她的眼鏡不合適。

（D）她的眼鏡被刮傷。

答案 **(C)**

解析 從紅色底線處可知（C）是正確答案。They是指glasses（眼鏡），keep sliding down（一直滑下來）在選項中被換成do not fit right（不合適）的說法。

2. 對於新鏡片，珍妮佛說了什麼？

（A）艾莉森女士不需支付費用。

（B）要再過一週才會送達。

（C）它將會有新的一年保固期。

（D）送達後她會立刻檢查。

答案 **(A)**

解析 從紅色底線處可知艾莉森女士的眼鏡仍在保固期間，所以正確答案是（A）。

3. 為什麼艾莉森當時沒有辦法看到刮痕？

（A）剛剛才發生。

（B）因為在她的視線之外。

（C）她還不習慣戴她的眼鏡。

（D）她當時沒有戴眼鏡。

答案 **(B)**

解析 從紅色底線處可知（B）是正確答案。因為是It's toward the top of the lens「在靠鏡片上方（邊緣）」，所以才沒有看到。選項將該句換個說法為out of her line of vision（視線之外＝死角）。

字彙 □ *be* used to～ 習慣～

Training 基礎練習

MP3 61

（1）請先閱讀以下的題目及選項，並預測對話的重點。

4. Why can't Lucca go to a concert on Friday?
(A) He has to work for Sherry.
(B) He has to fix some machines.
(C) He has to go out of town.
(D) He has to have some training.

5. What does Lucca suggest Pete do?
(A) Ask the boss for the day off
(B) Talk to a certain co-worker
(C) Change with a first-shift worker
(D) Apply for a different position

6. What does Pete say about Sherry?
(A) She is not very reliable.
(B) She forgets things she promises.
(C) She complains about work.
(D) She already works too much.

（2）請聽語音播放，並針對上述題目從（A）、（B）、（C）、（D）四個選項中選出最正確的答案（答案卡在全書最後）。

（3）最後，請練習盡可能準確地寫出正確答案在對話中的出處。

HUMMER老師小重點

4. 注意聽盧卡（Lucca）週五無法去音樂會的原因。每個選項的前半句都是He has to，所以重點放在to之後，邊聽語音，邊看這部分有何不同就好。

5. 聆聽盧卡建議佩特（Pete）做什麼。從4.和5.的題目和選項內容至少可以判斷出這是盧卡（Lucca）、雪莉（Sherry）及佩特（Pete）等3人的對談內容。

6. 讓我們做好準備，等著聽佩特說了什麼有關雪莉的事吧！

Questions 4 through 6 refer to the following conversation.

試題 4-6 請參考以下對話。

M1: Hey, Lucca. Is there any way you can work for me this Friday? I need someone for the second half of my shift.

M2: Sorry, Pete. Q4 They've scheduled me for training on the new machines then. I had to give concert tickets away because of it. Q5 Anyway, ask Sherry. She's always wanting to trade shifts.

M1: Q6 I've never had any luck trading shifts with her. Last time I tried, she changed her mind a day later. And the time before, she didn't make up her mind until the last minute.

M2: I didn't know that.

M1: Maybe someone on the first shift will switch with me.

M2: That might work. And the boss might know if anyone has requested more hours.

M1: 嘿，盧卡（Lucca）。你這週五有什麼方法可以幫我代班嗎？我需要有人幫我代後半的輪班。

M2: 抱歉，佩特（Pete）。他們已安排我那時候上新機器的培訓。我也因為它而必須放棄音樂會門票。總之，你問看看雪莉（Sherry）。她總是希望換班。

M1: 我和她換班的經驗總是不順利。上次我嘗試（和她換班），她一天之後就改變心意。再更前一次，她到最後一刻才下定主意。

M2: 我都不知道有這種事。

M1: 或許會有上第一班的人跟我換。

M2: 這或許有用。而且老闆可能會知道是否有人希望上更多的班。

字彙 □ trade shifts 換班 □ make up *one*'s mind 下定主意

4. 為什麼盧卡週五無法去音樂會？

（A）他必須幫雪莉上班。 （B）他必須修理機械。

（C）他必須出城。 （D）他必須接受一些培訓。

答案 **(D)**

解析 從紅色底線處可知（D）是正確答案。schedule *A* for *B* 意為「安排A做B」。不妨把主詞they（他們）視為是公司。

5. 盧卡建議佩特做什麼？

（A）向老闆要求請假一天 （B）和一位特定的同事談

（C）找第一班的人換 （D）申請不同的職位

答案 **(B)**

解析 從紅色底線處可知盧卡建議佩特「問看看雪莉」。選項（B）的a certain co-worker（一位特定的同事）是指雪莉。

6. 佩特說了什麼有關雪莉的事？

（A）她不太能信賴。 （B）她忘記她所承諾的事。

（C）她抱怨工作。 （D）她已經做太多工作。

答案 **(A)**

解析 從紅色底線處可知，佩特詳細述說以前他曾向雪莉拜託換班的事。（A）將該情形簡潔地表達出來，所以是正確答案。

Training 基礎練習

MP3 62

（1）請先閱讀以下的題目及選項，並預測對話的重點。

7. Why is the man upset about the meeting?
(A) The boss rescheduled it.
(B) It was cancelled suddenly.
(C) It took place without him.
(D) Several people did not attend.

8. What does the man mean when he says, "Do you know what's up"?
(A) He has some news to share.
(B) He is asking how the woman is today.
(C) He wonders about the state of the company.
(D) He is looking for an explanation.

9. What does the woman suggest about Mr. Leech?
(A) He may just be very busy.
(B) He could be out sick.
(C) He is away seeing clients.
(D) He left on vacation last Friday.

（2）請聽語音播放，並針對上述題目從（A）、（B）、（C）、（D）四個選項中選出最正確的答案（答案卡在全書最後）。

（3）最後，請練習盡可能準確地寫出正確答案在對話中的出處。

HUMMER老師小重點

7. 這題要聽懂男性對於會議的什麼事感到不高興。
8. 確實理解男性說「Do you know what's up?（你知道怎麼回事嗎？）」這句話的前、後內容，並思考說這句話當時的「狀況」後再作答。
9. 這題的 suggest 是「暗示、間接傳達」之意，千萬不要和「提議」的意思相混淆。What is suggested about ～則是「關於～（我們）得知了什麼？」之意。

Questions 7 through 9 refer to the following conversation.

試題7-9 請參考以下對話。

M: Ellen, I just read the e-mail about the meeting. I can't believe it! I've been waiting a week to discuss several important things with the group!	M: 艾倫（Ellen），我剛看了有關會議的電子郵件。太令我無法相信了！我已經等了一週要與小組討論幾個重要的事情。
W: Yeah, and Q7 Q8 Mr. Leech just called it off without setting a new date.	W: 是啊，而且李奇（Leech）先生並沒有訂新的日期就取消會議了。
M: Do you know what's up?	M: 你知道怎麼回事嗎？
W: Q8 No. But I haven't seen Mr. Leech at the office since last Friday, and I know he's not scheduled for any business trips right now. Q9 I just hope he's feeling okay.	W: 不知道。但是從上週五以來我就沒有在辦公室看到李奇先生了，而且我知道他目前沒有安排任何出差。我只希望他身體無恙。

字彙 □ what's up 怎麼回事

7. 為什麼男性對於會議的事感到不高興？

（A）老闆將會議改期。　（B）突然被取消了。

（C）沒有他（的參與）就舉行了。　（D）有幾個人沒有參加。

答案 **(B)**

解析 對話一開頭即可推斷男性表現出不高興的樣子，並具體描述原因，接下來紅色底線處標示的是女性說的關鍵句。call～off意為「取消～」，意指會議被李奇先生取消了。雖然無法判斷李奇先生是否為老闆，但他僅是取消會議，沒有另定日期，所以（A）不正確。

字彙 □ take place 舉行

8. 當男性說「Do you know what's up?」這句話時，代表什麼意思？

（A）他有些消息要分享。　（B）他要問女性今天過得如何。

（C）他好奇公司的狀況。　（D）他正在尋求說明。

答案 **(D)**

解析 理解男性說「Do you know what's up?（你知道怎麼回事嗎？）」這句話的前、後內容，並思考當時的「狀況」後再作答。女性在這句話之前提到李奇先生突然取消會議，之後則回答男性「不知道。但是從上週五以來我就沒有在辦公室看到李奇先生了」。因此依前後句的關聯性可知答案就是選項（D）。男性因會議緊急取消而向女性尋求相關的說明。

字彙 □ wonder about～ 對～感到好奇

9. 關於李奇先生，女性暗指什麼？

（A）他可能只是很忙。　（B）他可能請了病假。

（C）他正外出見客戶。　（D）他上週五就去度假了。

答案 **(B)**

解析 紅色底線處，女性最後說 I just hope he's feeling okay.（我只希望他身體無恙。），所以正確答案是（B）。could是「有可能」，*be* out sick是「請病假」之意。

Training 基礎練習

MP3 63

（1）請先閱讀以下的題目及選項，並預測對話的重點。

10. What is Melanie's current task?
(A) Assigning new projects
(B) Scheduling a window cleaner
(C) Researching new computers
(D) Rearranging the office layout

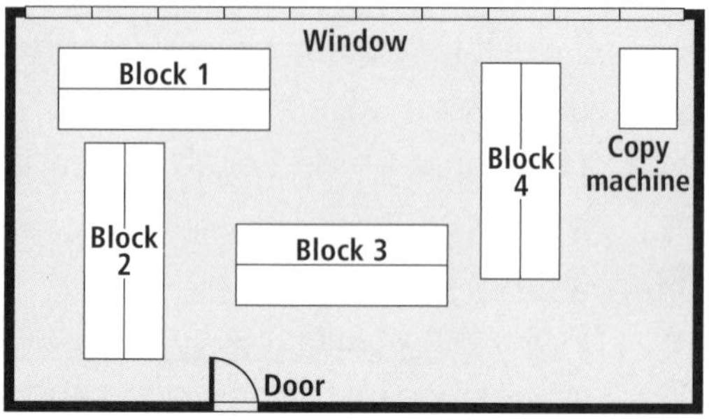

11. What is the B Team's problem with their current desk location?
(A) They dislike the breeze.
(B) They are bored with it.
(C) The sunlight bothers them.
(D) The view outside is distracting.

12. Look at the graphic. Where does Soodi suggest putting the B Team?
(A) In Block 1
(B) In Block 2
(C) In Block 3
(D) In Block 4

（2）請聽語音播放，並針對上述題目從（A）、（B）、（C）、（D）四個選項中選出最正確的答案（答案卡在全書最後）。

（3）最後，請練習盡可能準確地寫出正確答案在對話中的出處。

HUMMER老師小重點

10.（A）的assign是「指定～、分派」之意。（B）的cleaner是「清潔人員、洗淨機」之意，可以用來表示人或物。這類的單字出現在對話中時，要從前後句來判斷是哪一種意思。

11. 這題要聽懂B組對於「現在的辦公桌位置」有什麼抱怨才會解答。

12. 這題需要邊看圖邊作答。看著「組合資訊（僅出現在圖表上，而選項內沒有的字彙）」的同時，耳朵專心聽語音吧！這題的組合資訊是「門．窗戶．印表機」。

Questions 10 through 12 refer to the following conversation and map.

試題 10-12 請參考以下對話及配置圖。

W1: Soodi, Q10 I've been asked to reposition the desks on our floor Q11 because the B Team keeps complaining about the windows being behind them. Apparently it's hard to see their computer screens with the reflections from outside.

W2: Why don't you put them by the door so the windows aren't a problem?

W1: They don't like the distraction of people coming and going.

W2: Okay, Melanie, I've got it! Q12 They're the ones who print the most documents, so put them next to the photocopier. That would be convenient and take care of all their complaints.

W1: 索迪（Soodi），我被要求改變我們這一樓層的辦公桌位置，因為B組一直抱怨窗戶在他們身後。外面的反射顯然讓他們很難看到電腦螢幕。

W2: 為什麼你不把他們安排在門口，這樣窗戶就不是問題了？

W1: 他們不喜歡人們進出而分心。

W2: 好的，梅蘭妮（Melanie），我知道了！他們是印最多文件的人，那就把他們安排在印表機旁。那將會（對他們）很方便且處理到他們所有的抱怨。

字彙 □ reposition 改變～的位置 □ reflection 反射 □ distraction 分心 □ I've got it! 我知道了！

10. 梅蘭妮目前的任務是什麼？

（A）分配新計畫
（B）安排窗戶清潔人員
（C）研究新的電腦
（D）重新安排辦公室佈局

答案 **(D)**

解析 從紅色底線處可知（D）是正確答案。reposition是動詞，意為「改變～的位置」，梅蘭妮被要求「改變辦公桌的位置」，也就是Rearrange the office layout（重新安排辦公室佈局）的意思。

11. B組目前辦公桌位置的問題是什麼？

（A）他們不喜歡微風。
（B）他們厭煩了。
（C）陽光使他們感到困擾。
（D）外面的景色令人分心。

答案 **(C)**

解析 （C）將紅色底線處的第二句it's hard to see their computer screens with the reflections from outside（外面的反射讓他們很難看到電腦螢幕）簡潔地換成The sunlight bothers them.（陽光使他們感到困擾。）的說法，所以是正確答案。

字彙 □ distracting 令人分心的

12. 請看圖。索迪建議將B組安排在哪裡？

（A）區塊1
（B）區塊2
（C）區塊3
（D）區塊4

答案 **(D)**

解析 紅色底線處是索迪在建議對方將B組安排在印表機旁邊。由圖看來，印表機旁邊是區塊4。因此正確答案是（D）。

Part 3 Practice Test 實戰試題

MP3 64～68

請仔細聆聽2人或3人的簡短對話，再針對題目從（A）、（B）、（C）、（D）中選出最適合的答案（答案卡在全書最後）。

1. What does the woman need help with?
(A) Recruiting people for a committee
(B) Selecting some office equipment
(C) Writing complaints about desk chairs
(D) Presenting an idea to the Board of Directors

2. Why will the men help the woman?
(A) They are not busy this week.
(B) They enjoy making decisions.
(C) They are returning a past favor.
(D) They feel it will aid in their comfort.

3. What does the woman say about the committee?
(A) There is already a budget to work from.
(B) The deadline for its decision is soon.
(C) It must start meeting this week.
(D) She needs three more volunteers.

4. What does Julie want to know?
(A) How to get good deals on suits
(B) What styles to wear to the office
(C) Where to buy business attire
(D) When the latest fashions arrive in stores

5. What does Karen say about her J. J. Bell coupon?
(A) It is for 30 percent off only on Saturday.
(B) It can be used multiple times.
(C) She plans on using it.
(D) She just got it in the mail today.

6. What does Julie suggest she will do on Monday?
(A) Wear a new outfit
(B) Return the coupon
(C) Check out the sale at Branson's
(D) Visit J. J. Bell with Karen

7. What is the man unable to find?
(A) An optical instrument
(B) A hand tool
(C) A protective device
(D) Cleaning gear

8. What did the man do last weekend?
(A) He purchased a small vehicle.
(B) He visited an art gallery.
(C) He obtained an old object.
(D) He worked in the garden.

9. Why most likely is the woman surprised?
(A) She has met the man before.
(B) She thought the item was too heavy.
(C) She was not aware of the announcement.
(D) She discovered that they live near each other.

---

10. Why hasn't the woman seen the man lately?
(A) He is busy with projects.
(B) He started a new position.
(C) He is training a co-worker.
(D) He travels to many seminars.

11. What does the woman mean when she says, "Oh, that's right"?
(A) She is looking forward to working with the man.
(B) She had forgotten about the man's situation.
(C) She remembers her time working in sales.
(D) She failed to finish her assignment on time.

12. What doesn't the man like about his job?
(A) Staying in hotels
(B) Working with his co-workers
(C) Getting to know clients
(D) Learning new things

Current Price List—Brochures

Number	Price
500	$110
1,000	$140
2,000	$180
3,000	$210

13. What does Bob point out to Mr. Hartley?
(A) A modification to a company's product prices
(B) A greater need for advertisement distribution
(C) A mistake on some newly printed brochures
(D) A change in a printing company's ownership

14. Look at the graphic. How much did the company pay for brochures the last time?
(A) $55
(B) $70
(C) $90
(D) $105

15. What does Mr. Hartley want Bob to do in the future?
(A) Restock certain items earlier
(B) Make their brochure more effective
(C) Try to negotiate a discounted price
(D) Find a more suitable printing company

Part 3 Practice Test 實戰試題 解答與解析

MP3 64

Questions 1 through 3 refer to the following conversation with three speakers.

試題 1-3 請參考以下 3 人對話。

W: Q1 Are either of you guys interested in being on a committee with me to look into purchasing some new chairs for our desks? The Board of Directors has finally approved our request after years of complaining.

M1: Committees aren't really my thing, but if it means Q2 I'll have a say in something that'll make my back feel better, I'm in.

M2: Q2 I agree. How many people do you need for the committee?

W: Actually, just three. I wasn't expecting you both to commit. Thanks!

M2: Q3 Do you have all the details about how many chairs we can buy and how much we can spend?

W: Q3 Yes. Are you both able to meet this week?

M1: Let's wait until Monday. I've got a lot on my plate this week.

W: No problem. Monday at four?

M2: I'm there.

W: 你們其中哪一位有興趣和我一起參加委員會來討論購買我們的辦公桌專用的新椅子？經過多年的抱怨，董事會終於批准我們的請求了。

M1: 委員會真的不適合我，不過如果它意味著，我對於那些讓背部更舒服的事能擁有發言權的話，我就加入。

M2: 我同意。你需要多少人進委員會？

W: 事實上，只要三個人。我沒想到你們兩位都承諾加入。謝謝！

M2: 你有關於我們可以購買多少椅子以及我們可以花費多少的所有細節嗎？

W: 有的。你們兩位這週可以開會嗎？

M1: 我們等到週一吧！我這週該做的事已堆積如山。

W: 沒問題。週一四點？

M2: 我會在的！

字彙 □ *be one's* thing 適合～ □ have a say 有發言權
□ I've got a lot on my plate 我該做的事已堆積如山

1. What does the woman need help with?
(A) Recruiting people for a committee
(B) Selecting some office equipment
(C) Writing complaints about desk chairs
(D) Presenting an idea to the Board of Directors

女性需要幫助來做什麼事情？
（A）為委員會招募人員
（B）選擇一些辦公設備
（C）寫有關辦公桌椅的投訴
（D）向董事會提出想法

答案 **(B)**

解析 從紅色底線處可知，女性想要找人一起討論購買辦公桌專用的新椅子一事。（B）將它簡潔地換個說法，所以是正確答案。各位作答時要特別留意的重點就是，有不少題目雖然問得是對話中明確描述的內容，在選項中卻以「概括・抽象化」的用法來表達。而這題雖然有提到「委員會需要三個人」，但它的意思並不是「希望幫忙募集人員」，所以（A）是錯誤的。

2. Why will the men help the woman?
(A) They are not busy this week.
(B) They enjoy making decisions.
(C) They are returning a past favor.
(D) They feel it will aid in their comfort.

男性為什麼會幫女性？
（A）他們這週不忙。
（B）他們樂於做決定。
（C）他們回報以往的幫忙。
（D）他們認為這有助於（提高）他們的舒適程度。

答案 **(D)**

解析 首先，看到題目中有the men, the woman，在聽語音播放之前就可以預測到這一組是2名男性與1名女性的「3人對話」可能性很高。一開始出現的男性提到，為了使背部更舒服，如果讓他擁有這方面發言權的話，他就加入女性建議的委員會，第二位男性隨後跟著回答I agree表示同意。因此正確答案是（D）。

字彙 □ past favor 以往的幫忙

3. What does the woman say about the committee?
(A) There is already a budget to work from.
(B) The deadline for its decision is soon.
(C) It must start meeting this week.
(D) She needs three more volunteers.

關於委員會，女性說了什麼？
（A）已有預算可供使用。
（B）決定的最後期限很快就到了。
（C）這週必須開始開會。
（D）她還需要再三名志願者。

答案 **(A)**

解析 從紅色底線處可知要購買的椅子張數及可用的金額已確定，因此正確答案是（A）。（B）的deadline（期限）在對話中並未被提到。（C）和（D）是故意用對話中提到的this week和three來混淆的陷阱選項。

Part 3

MP3 65

Questions 4 through 6 refer to the following conversation.

試題4-6 請參考以下對話。

W1: Karen, I always like your fashion sense, and Q4 I'm in need of a new work wardrobe. Do you have any suggestions on stores?	W1: 凱倫（Karen），我一直很喜歡妳的時尚品味，而我正需要換新一批的工作服裝。妳有什麼商店可以建議嗎？
W2: Actually, Julie, Branson's is having a great sale right now.	W2: 其實，茱莉（Julie），布蘭森（Branson's）現在正進行大促銷。
W1: You know, I've gone there, but things don't seem to fit me right.	W1: 妳知道嗎，我去過那裡，不過它的商品似乎不適合我。
W2: What about J. J. Bell? In fact, I've got a coupon for 30 percent off your whole purchase there valid from this Saturday.	W2: 那麼傑傑貝爾（J.J. Bell）如何？事實上，我有一張優惠券從這週六起生效且購買的所有商品都可獲得30%的折扣優惠。
W1: I'd like to check it out. But won't you use the coupon?	W1: 我想去看看。不過妳不用優惠券嗎？
W2: Q5 You can use it as many times as you want during the one-week period. So just take it, and if I need it back, I'll let you know.	W2: 妳可以在一週的時間內不限次數使用它。所以你就拿去吧，如果我需要拿回使用，我會讓妳知道。
W1: Thanks! Q6 Hopefully I'll be able to show you what my purchases look like on me on Monday! Get ready to see a new me!	W1: 謝謝！但願週一時，我能向你展示我購入的商品穿在我身上的樣子！做好準備看看全新的我吧！

字彙 □ wardrobe 衣櫃、（某人的）一批衣服 □ hopefully 但願

4. What does Julie want to know?
(A) How to get good deals on suits
(B) What styles to wear to the office
(C) Where to buy business attire
(D) When the latest fashions arrive in stores

茱莉想知道什麼？
（A）如何用好價格購得服裝
（B）在辦公室該穿什麼樣的款式
（C）在哪裡買職場服裝
（D）最新的流行款何時到貨

答案 (C)

解析 一開始先說話的女性向凱倫說 I'm in need of a new work wardrobe（我正需要工作上的新服裝），並詢問對方有無建議的商店。接著回應的女性稱呼對方Julie（茱莉），所以正確答案是（C）。business attire是指「職場服裝」。

字彙 □ good deal 好的交易、便宜的價格

5. What does Karen say about her J. J. Bell coupon?
(A) It is for 30 percent off only on Saturday.
(B) It can be used multiple times.
(C) She plans on using it.
(D) She just got it in the mail today.

有關傑傑貝爾優惠券，凱倫說了什麼？
（A）只有週六才有30%的折扣優惠。
（B）可以多次使用。
（C）她打算使用它。
（D）她今天才剛收到它用郵件寄來。

答案 **(B)**

解析 從紅色底線處可知正確答案是（B）。（A）的only on Saturday（只有週六）與對話中的valid from this Saturday（從這週六起生效）矛盾。（C）與if I need it back, I'll let you know（如果我需要拿回使用，我會讓妳知道）不符合。（D）的說法在對話中完全沒有提到。

字彙 □ multiple times 多次 □ mail 郵件

6. What does Julie suggest she will do on Monday?
(A) Wear a new outfit
(B) Return the coupon
(C) Check out the sale at Branson's
(D) Visit J. J. Bell with Karen

茱莉說週一她將做什麼？
（A）穿上新的全套服裝
（B）歸還優惠券
（C）去逛逛布蘭森的促銷特賣
（D）和凱倫一起去傑傑貝爾

答案 **(A)**

解析 茱莉最後向凱莉表示show you what my purchases look like on me（向你展示我購入的商品穿在我身上的樣子），那就是a new me（全新的我），意即穿著新買的服裝來給對方看。因此，正確答案是（A）。

字彙 □ outfit 全套服裝

Part 3

MP3 66

Questions 7 through 9 refer to the following conversation.

試題 7-9 請參考以下對話。

M: Hi. Q7 I'm looking for a claw hammer but I can't find one. Aren't they in the gardening section?

W: No, they're over there in aisle 5. If you follow me, I'll show you exactly where they are. Are you doing a little handiwork?

M: Well, Q8 last weekend I picked up a beautiful antique mirror at a garage sale and now I need to hang it up. It's big and heavy so it's quite challenging. I had a hard time carrying it to my house in a wheelbarrow, even though it was only two blocks away.

W: Q9 You're kidding! Do you mean the garage sale on Elm Street? We live right next to that house!

M: 嗨！我正在尋找一把羊角錘，但我找不到。它們不是在園藝區嗎？

W: 不是，它們在第五走道那邊。如果你跟我來，我會帶你看它們確切在哪裡。你正在做一些手工嗎？

M: 這個嘛，上週末我在車庫拍賣裡買了一個漂亮的古董鏡子，現在我需要把它掛起來。它很大又很重，所以非常具挑戰性。即使僅距離兩條街，我用手推車把它帶回我家時還是很費勁。

W: 你在開玩笑吧！你是指榆樹街上（Elm Street）的車庫拍賣嗎？我們就住在那間房子的隔壁。

字彙 □ claw hammer 羊角錘 □ handiwork 手工、手工製作 □ antique 古董的 □ wheelbarrow 手推車

7. What is the man unable to find?

(A) An optical instrument

(B) A hand tool

(C) A protective device

(D) Cleaning gear

男性找不到什麼？

（A）光學儀器

（B）用手操作的工具

（C）保護裝置

（D）清潔用具

答案 **(B)**

解析 從題目可判斷，男性正在找某樣東西，而且找不到。（B）只是將男性一開始就提到的claw hammer換成hand tool的說法，所以是正確答案。其他的選項很明顯地都不符合描述，就算用刪去法也可以判斷喔！

字彙 □ optical instrument 光學儀器 □ hand tool 用手操作的工具 □ gear 用具、設備

8. What did the man do last weekend?
(A) He purchased a small vehicle.
(B) He visited an art gallery.
(C) He obtained an old object.
(D) He worked in the garden.

男性上週末做什麼事？
（A）他買了一輛小型車。
（B）他參觀了一間藝術畫廊。
（C）他取得一個舊物品。
（D）他在花園裡工作。

答案 **(C)**

解析 這題延續7.，題目和選項中的主詞都是男性，所以邊聽語音要想到解題的關鍵在於男性的說話內容。last weekend是帶出正確答案的關鍵字。男性第二次發言時提到last weekend I picked up a beautiful antique mirror at a garage sale（上週末我在車庫拍賣裡買了一個漂亮的古董鏡子），而（C）將antique mirror換成old object（舊物品）的說法，所以是正確答案。

9. Why most likely is the woman surprised?
(A) She has met the man before.
(B) She thought the item was too heavy.
(C) She was not aware of the announcement.
(D) She discovered that they live near each other.

女性驚訝的原因最有可能為下列何者？
（A）她以前見過這名男性。
（B）她認為這個物品太重。
（C）她不知道有這個公告。
（D）她發現他們彼此住得很近。

答案 **(D)**

解析 女性第二次發言時說You're kidding! Do you mean the garage sale on Elm Street? We live right next to that house!（你在開玩笑吧！你是指榆樹街上（Elm Street）的車庫拍賣嗎？我們就住在那間房子的隔壁。）。that house就是男性在女性說這句話之前提到a garage sale（車庫拍賣）舉辦的地方，且由之前男性提到的訊息可知，男性的住所離那間房子僅距離兩條街，所以正確答案是（D）。雖然男性第二次發言的後半段內容和（B）很接近，但是女性並不是針對鏡子的重量表示驚訝。

Questions 10 through 12 refer to the following conversation.

試題 10-12 請參考以下對話。

W: Hey, Albert. I haven't seen you around much lately. Q11 Are you working on a new assignment or something?	W: 嘿，艾伯特（Albert）。我最近怎麼都不常見到你。你是在經手新的工作任務還是什麼嗎？
M: No. Q10 They've got me traveling weekly now that I'm in the sales department. There's still a lot to learn, but so far the relationships I'm forming with our customers are very rewarding.	M: 不是。因為現在我在銷售部門，他們讓我每週出差。雖然仍有很多東西要學習，但是到目前為止我與客戶建立起來的關係是很值得的。
W: Oh, that's right! Q11 It's quite a change for you.	W: 喔，對喔！這對你來說是一個很大的變化呢！
M: Yes, but a good one. I'm much happier now coming to work each day. Q12 The hotels and time away from family is already getting old, but at least it feels like my work is different every day.	M: 是的，但它是好事。我現在每天工作快樂多了。雖然飯店及長時間遠離家人已變得乏味，但至少它讓我感覺工作每天都不一樣。

字彙 ☐ assignment 作業、（工作上的）任務 ☐ rewarding 值得的

10. Why hasn't the woman seen the man lately? 為什麼女性最近沒有見到男性？

(A) He is busy with projects. （A）他忙於企劃。

(B) He started a new position. （B）他開始新職務。

(C) He is training a co-worker. （C）他正在培訓一位同事。

(D) He travels to many seminars. （D）他去很多研討會。

答案 **(B)**

解析 從紅色底線處可知男性（經歷職務變動）現在任職銷售部門。而判斷男性最近有經歷職務變動的根據，就在男性提到now that，意為「因為現在～」的這個口吻。因此正確答案是（B）。

字彙 ☐ travel to～ 去～

11. What does the woman mean when she says, "Oh, that's right"?
(A) She is looking forward to working with the man.
(B) She had forgotten about the man's situation.
(C) She remembers her time working in sales.
(D) She failed to finish her assignment on time.

當女性說「Oh, that's right」時，代表什麼意思？
（A）她期待和男性一起工作。
（B）她已忘了男性的狀況。
（C）她想起她擔任銷售工作的（那段）期間。
（D）她無法及時完成她的工作任務。

答案 **(B)**

解析 這題要從女性說這句話的前後語意來確實循線追細節。女性一開始問「你經手新的工作任務嗎？」，而男性回應「進入銷售部門出差頻繁、與客戶接觸的工作是很值得的」，對此，女性又表示「喔，對喔」→「是一個很大的變化呢」。由此可知，女性想起她忘了發生在男性身上的事，而回答Oh, that's right。選項（B）符合上述狀況也不會發生矛盾，所以是正確答案。

字彙 □ fail to *do* 無法～

12. What doesn't the man like about his job?
(A) Staying in hotels
(B) Working with his co-workers
(C) Getting to know clients
(D) Learning new things

對於他的工作，男性不喜歡下列何者？
（A）住飯店
（B）和同事一起工作
（C）認識客戶
（D）學習新事物

答案 **(A)**

解析 從紅色底線處可知，男性對「住在飯店」表示already getting old（已變得乏味），因此正確答案是（A）。

MP3 68

Questions 13 through 15 refer to the following conversation and list.

試題 13-15 請參考以下對話及清單。

M1: Mr. Hartley, I was about to put in the order for our newest brochure on the printer's Web site when Q13 I noticed that they have changed the price.

M2: What kind of a difference are we talking about?

M1: Q14 The price has doubled! So...do you want me to still get 2,000 like always?

M2: Wow. You know, Bob, our budget hasn't changed. So since we need some immediately, let's get half this time. But Q15 please start looking into places that can do the job cheaper for next time.

Current Price List—Brochures

Number	Price
500	$110
1,000	$140
Q14 2,000	$180
3,000	$210

M1: 哈特利（Hartley）先生，當我正打算在印刷業者網站訂購我們最新的小冊子時，我注意到他們已經變更價格了。

M2: 如何不同呢？

M1: 價格已經加倍了！所以……你希望我仍然像往常一樣印製2000份嗎？

M2: 哇！你知道的，鮑伯（Bob），我們的預算沒有改變。因為我們馬上需要一些，所以我們這次就訂一半的量吧！但是下次要印時，請開始尋找可以做得更便宜的廠商。

目前價格一覽表—小冊子

數量	價格
500	$110
1,000	$140
2,000	$180
3,000	$210

字彙 □ printer 印刷業者

13. What does Bob point out to Mr. Hartley?
(A) A modification to a company's product prices
(B) A greater need for advertisement distribution
(C) A mistake on some newly printed brochures
(D) A change in a printing company's ownership

鮑伯向哈特利先生指出什麼事？
（A）某公司產品價格的變更
（B）對廣告發佈的需求擴大
（C）一些新印好的小冊子有錯誤
（D）印刷公司所有權變動

答案 **(A)**

解析 先開口的男性提到I noticed that they have changed the price（我注意到他們已經變更價格）。雖然他叫對方為Mr. Hartley（哈特利先生），但當下還無法判斷說話者是Bob（鮑伯），所以聽到紅色底線這句時不妨先猜測（A）是正確答案，先輕輕地用筆頭在該題答案卡空格上做記號。之後從對方叫這位男性Bob時就可確認答案無誤並填滿該空格。changed the price（變更價格）在選項內換成modification to a company's product prices的說法。

字彙 □ ownership 所有權

14. Look at the graphic. How much did the company pay for brochures the last time?
(A) $55
(B) $70
(C) $90
(D) $105

請看圖。這家公司最後一次付多少小冊子的費用？
（A）$55
（B）$70
（C）$90
（D）$105

答案 **(C)**

解析 圖表問題要注意圖表與選項相異之處（＝組合資訊）。這題的每個選項都是金額，而且都是圖表中列出金額的一半。所以要一邊注意左邊的數量一邊聽語音播放內容。從紅色底線這句可知目前金額已是之前的雙倍，且上回已印了2,000份小冊子。因此正確答案是（C）。

15. What does Mr. Hartley want Bob to do in the future?
(A) Restock certain items earlier
(B) Make their brochure more effective
(C) Try to negotiate a discounted price
(D) Find a more suitable printing company

哈特利先生希望鮑伯日後要做什麼？
（A）提前補貨特定品項
（B）讓他們的小冊子更有效果
（C）嘗試交涉折扣價格
（D）尋找更合適的印刷公司

答案 **(D)**

解析 從紅色底線處可知正確答案是（D）。至於（A）～（C），在對話內容中都沒有被提到。像這種整篇對話中都未提及的錯誤選項，我將它們統稱為「無理可證」；另外，連主詞、動詞、受詞、時態及地點等都與對話情況完全不吻合的錯誤選項，我則稱之為「完全偏差」。這題的（A）～（C）即是「無理可證」的選項。

Part 4 Training 基礎練習

MP3 69

（1）請先閱讀以下的題目及選項，並預測獨白的重點。

1. What problem does the speaker mention?
(A) An overload of jobs piling up
(B) A difficulty in keeping contractors
(C) A leak of information to competitors
(D) A lack of new project ideas

2. What does the speaker mean when she says, "and these are my words"?
(A) Her words should not be taken seriously.
(B) She did not understand the exact meaning.
(C) She will give her interpretation.
(D) Her words are trademarked.

3. What does the speaker suggest her company do?
(A) Raise their compensation amounts
(B) Research other companies more often
(C) Become stricter with their illustrators
(D) Charge more for their products

（2）請聽語音播放，並針對上述題目從（A）、（B）、（C）、（D）四個選項中選出最正確的答案（答案卡在全書最後）。

（3）最後，請練習盡可能準確地寫出正確答案在對話中的出處。

HUMMER老師小重點

1. 選項都是「（帶有負面含意的）問題」。若能事先深入預覽，就能夠更清楚區分（A）～（D）全部的選項。
2. 為了想像出and there are my words這段語句的前、後「情況」，請專注聽語音內容吧！這是要依照前後句關係及敘述內容，才能選出正確答案的題目。不能光憑選項的字面就亂猜測，必須在預覽內容的階段，就徹底的理解才行。
3. 專心聆聽「什麼是公司該做的事」。像這些以動詞為首的選項，要邊看著動詞（選項的前半段）邊聽語音內容才容易作答。與其他詞性相比，動詞最有鑑別性，更能有效判別句意有何不同。

Questions 1 through 3 refer to the following excerpt from a meeting.

試題 1-3 請參考以下部分會議內容。

I wanted to talk to you all about something I'm noticing lately. In the last year, Q1 the illustrators we've independently contracted have quit on us several times. Q2 They say they have too many jobs piling up, and ours is…and these are my words…not as important as the other ones. You see, when I investigated other companies to see how much they're paying their illustrators, I found that we're…well, still paying what our competitors paid ten years ago. And that's hurting us. Q3 I think we need to seriously reconsider what we offer so we can stop spending our time ironing out wrinkles!

我想跟你們大家談談我最近注意到的事情。在過去一年裡，與我們個別簽約的插畫家們已多次和我們臨時終止合約。他們說手上已累積太多的工作，而我們公司的工作……再來這些是我的解讀……不像其他公司的那麼重要。你們知道嗎，當我調查其他公司並了解他們付給插畫家多少錢的時候，我發現我們……嗯，仍然在支付我們的競爭對手十年前支付的數字。那對我們造成了傷害。我認為我們需要認真地重新思考我們提供的報酬，這樣就可以停止花時間去解決細碎的難題！

1. 說話者提到了什麼問題？

（A）過多的工作不斷累積　（B）留住契約工作者有困難

（C）有資訊洩漏給了競爭業者　（D）缺乏新的企劃案點子

答案 **(B)**

解析 從紅色底線處可知，公司簽約的插畫家們去年已頻繁終止契約。選項（B）將該狀況換成difficulty in keeping contractors的說法，所以是正確答案。

字彙 □ contractor 契約工作者、立契約者

2. 當說話者說「and these are my words」時，代表什麼意思？

（A）不該認真地看待她的話。　（B）她不懂確切的含意。

（C）她將提出她個人的解釋。　（D）她的話被註冊為商標。

答案 **(C)**

解析 說話者敘述了「插畫家們說他們已累積太多的工作」這句話之後說and these are my words（這些是我的解讀），接著表示「我們公司的工作不像其他公司的那麼重要」。my words可比喻為「自己的解讀」，意即這個見解是說話者自己的見解，所以正確答案是（C）。

字彙 □ trademarked 登記為註冊商標

3. 說話者建議她的公司做什麼？

（A）提高他們的報酬金額　（B）更頻繁地研究其他公司

（C）對他們的插畫家們更嚴格　（D）對他們的產品收更多的費用

答案 **(A)**

解析 從紅色底線處可知，說話者認為「公司一定要認真地重新思考我們提供的報酬」。另外，從前一句的內容可知這家公司付的報酬是其他公司10年前的金額，也就是報酬比其他公司低。而為了解決這個問題，最好的辦法就是如選項（A）所說的提高報酬，所以（A）是正確答案。

Training 基礎練習

MP3 70

（1）請先閱讀以下的題目及選項，並預測獨白的重點。

4. How long will the event last?
(A) A month
(B) Two months
(C) Ten months
(D) A year

5. Who is Eleanor De Marco?
(A) A swimming coach
(B) A gym receptionist
(C) A movie star
(D) A yoga teacher

6. What are participants advised to do?
(A) Put on sunblock
(B) Book a place in advance
(C) Check the activities calendar
(D) Bring a towel and sandals

（2）請聽語音播放，並針對上述題目從（A）、（B）、（C）、（D）四個選項中選出最正確的答案（答案卡在全書最後）。

（3）最後，請練習盡可能準確地寫出正確答案在對話中的出處。

HUMMER老師小重點

4. 句首是How long～?（多久？），所以要掌握住這是問期間的問題。選項中用數字表達出具體期間，但在語音中有可能是用其他的說法，建議要先把這些數字記在腦海裡。

5. 聽語音時，需注意Eleanor De Marco（伊雷諾・迪・馬可）是誰。除了（C）以外都是與健身俱樂部相關的工作，因此要仔細分辨各種職業間的差異。

6. 這題是問參加者，也就是此篇語音的目標聽眾，被建議要做的事，這和do next（下一步動作）系列的題型雷同，要再度提醒自己集中精神聽到全文結束。

Questions 4 through 6 refer to the following advertisement.

試題4-6 請參考以下的廣告。

With luxurious guest rooms and impeccable guest services, Northman Hotel is where you want to be. This summer, Northman Hotel will collaborate with Hilary's Gym to make sure guests get the most out of the summer months. Every Saturday from 8 A.M. to 10 A.M. Q4 during July and August, hotel guests and also those not staying at the hotel can participate in Q5 a free group yoga lesson instructed by gym instructor and professional dancer, Eleanor De Marco. Q6 Remember to bring your own mat and wear sunscreen as the lessons will take place outside in the garden beside the swimming pool.	擁有豪華的客房和無可挑剔的客服，諾斯曼（Northman）飯店正是您想去的地方。今年夏天，諾斯曼飯店將與希拉里（Hilary's）健身房合作，確保客人得以好好利用夏季的這幾個月。在7月和8月期間每週六8 A.M.到10 A.M.，飯店房客以及未入住飯店的客人可以參加由健身教練暨專業舞者伊雷諾・迪・馬可（Eleanor De Marco）指導的免費團體瑜珈課。記得帶著自己的墊子並擦防曬乳，因為課程會在戶外進行，就在泳池旁的花園裡。

字彙 □ impeccable 無可挑剔的 □ wear sunscreen 擦防曬乳

4. 這項活動會持續多久？

（A）1個月 （B）2個月 （C）10個月 （D）1年

答案 **(B)**

解析 廣告中段提到活動期間是during July and August（在7月和8月期間）。（B）換個說法用數字表達，所以是正確答案。雖然在更前面時說了get the most out of the summer months.（得以好好利用夏季的這幾個月），但是描述具體期間的只有中段這個部分，要仔細聆聽不能錯過。

5. 伊雷諾・迪・馬可（Eleanor De Marco）是誰？

（A）游泳教練 （B）健身房接待人員

（C）電影明星 （D）瑜珈老師

答案 **(D)**

解析 Eleanor De Marco在後半段內容有介紹：a free group yoga lesson instructed by gym instructor and professional dancer, Eleanor De Marco.（由健身教練暨專業舞者伊雷諾・迪・馬可指導的免費團體瑜珈課），所以正確答案是（D）。這位人物雖然也是professional dancer（專業舞者），但是沒有符合該身分的選項。

6. 參加者被建議做什麼事？

（A）擦防曬霜 （B）提前預約

（C）查閱活動日程表 （D）帶毛巾和涼鞋

答案 **(A)**

解析 Part 4常出現詢問有關聽者「做什麼」、「被要求做什麼」的題型。這篇廣告的最後有提到wear sunscreen，不過這題正確答案的依據僅出現在這一瞬間，所以稍有難度。wear sunscreen意為「擦防曬乳」，選項是將它換成put on sunblock的說法，所以正確答案是（A）。

字彙 □ put on sunblock 擦防曬霜

Training 基礎練習

MP3 71

（1）請先閱讀以下的題目及選項，並預測獨白的重點。

7. Where does the speaker probably work?
(A) At a human resource agency
(B) At a pharmaceutical company
(C) At an electronics manufacturer
(D) At a telecommunications provider

8. What does the speaker say about the Coral-2000?
(A) It just came out on the market.
(B) It weighs less than the BG-3000.
(C) It is more expensive than the BG-3000.
(D) It has functions not available on the BG-3000.

9. Who most likely is the listener?
(A) A veteran employee
(B) A job candidate
(C) A new recruit
(D) A mobile phone salesperson

（2）請聽語音播放，並針對上述題目從（A）、（B）、（C）、（D）四個選項中選出最正確的答案（答案卡在全書最後）。

（3）最後，請練習盡可能準確地寫出正確答案在對話中的出處。

HUMMER老師小重點

7. 有關詢問場所的題型，出現在正式測驗的機率很高。就算選項裡面，各個答案都不相似，也不能輕忽，更要確實地作答。

8. 選項中有3項是特定機型Coral-2000和其他機型BG-3000互相比較的內容。注意聽語音中有無「重量」、「價格」、「功能」等相關內容。

9. Who most likely is the listener? 放在題組的第3題，對進階學習者而言可能會覺得怪怪的吧！因為通常這類試題大多放在最前面，答案出處也大多出現在文章的前段。這次我將這題放在最後，就是希望大家一邊想像著，獨白的後半段，會不會出現正確答案，然後好好地聽。這是個別具一格的好試題，希望各位仔細地聆聽並了解細節直到最後。注意不要把（B）的job candidate和（C）的new recruit互相混淆。

Questions 7 through 9 refer to the following telephone message.

試題 7-9 請參考以下的電話留言。

Hello. Q7 This is Sam Houser from the human resources department of Clark-Myers Pharmaceuticals with a message for Ms. Teresa Fisher. Ms. Fisher, I received your e-mail about your choice of company-issued mobile phones. Unfortunately, we ran out of the model of your choice. So you have two options: you can wait for us to restock and receive the phone a little later, or you can choose another model. Personally, Q8 I recommend the Coral-2000 since it is similar to the BG-3000 that you chose, but is newer and lighter. If you choose the latter option, you will receive the phone Q9 on your first day at Clark-Myers.	哈囉。我是克拉克－梅爾斯製藥公司（Clark-Myers Pharmaceuticals）人力資源部的山姆．豪瑟（Sam Houser），以下留言給泰瑞莎．費雪（Teresa Fisher）女士。費雪女士，我收到了您的電子郵件，有關您選擇的公司發放的手機。遺憾的是，您選擇的型號已缺貨。所以您有兩個選擇：一是您可以等我們重新進貨並晚點收到手機，或是您可以選擇其他型號。就個人而言，我推薦使用Coral-2000，因為它和您選擇的BG-3000類似，但更新且更輕。如果您選擇後者，您將在克拉克－梅爾斯上班的第一天收到手機。

字彙 □ company-issued 公司發放的 □ restock 補充～、重新進貨

7. 說話者可能在哪裡工作？

（A）在人力資源機構 （B）在製藥公司 （C）在電子製造商 （D）在電信業

答案 **(B)**

解析 詢問說話者任職公司的題型，出現在正式測驗的機率很高。這類的試題在語音前半段大多會提到答案出處。所以如果一開始即聽懂This is Sam Houser from the human resources department of Clark-Myers Pharmaceuticals（我是克拉克－梅爾斯製藥公司人力資源部的山姆．豪瑟），就知道要選（B）。

字彙 □ telecommunications provider 電信業者

8. 關於Coral-2000，說話者說了什麼？

（A）它剛剛上市。 （B）它的重量較BG-3000輕。

（C）它的價錢比BG-3000高。 （D）它擁有BG-3000沒有的功能。

答案 **(B)**

解析 後半段的留言提到Coral-2000。I recommend the Coral-2000 since it is similar to the BG-3000 that you chose, but is newer and lighter.（我推薦使用Coral-2000，因為它和您選擇的BG-3000類似，但更新又更輕。），所以（B）是正確答案。雖然Coral-2000比BG-3000新，但是並未提到是否剛上市，因此（A）不正確。

字彙 □ come out on the market 上市

9. 誰最有可能是聽留言的人？

（A）資深員工 （B）求職者 （C）新進員工 （D）手機銷售員

答案 **(C)**

解析 留言者一開始就自稱是人事部的人，但是並未出現相關資訊特別提及誰是聽留言的人。關鍵就在最後的on your first day at Clark-Myers.（您在克拉克－梅爾斯上班的第一天）。從這個部分可判斷，聽留言的人要開始在留言者的公司上班，所以（C）是正確答案。

Training 基礎練習

MP3 72

（1）請先閱讀以下的題目及選項，並預測獨白的重點。

10. Look at the graphic. During which registration period should the listener sign up?
(A) Early-bird registration
(B) Regular registration
(C) Late registration
(D) Registration at the door

Registration	Fee
Early-bird registration	$469
Regular registration	$519
Late registration	$619
Registration at the door	$800

11. Why does the speaker want the listener to attend the symposium?
(A) To represent their company
(B) To learn about giving presentations
(C) To hear talks related to her work
(D) To check out the venue

12. What does the speaker suggest the listener do at the symposium?
(A) Check out products offered by various businesses
(B) Invite some of the presenters to dinner
(C) Host one of the optional events
(D) Join the symposium committee

（2）請聽語音播放，並針對上述題目從（A）、（B）、（C）、（D）四個選項中選出最正確的答案（答案卡在全書最後）。

（3）最後，請練習盡可能準確地寫出正確答案在對話中的出處。

HUMMER老師小重點

10. 先找出圖表與選項相異之處（＝組合資訊），也就是圖表右半邊的金額，一邊對照該資訊、一邊聽語音播放內容。

11. 先聽懂留言者希望對方參加研討會的理由再作答。（B）的presentations和（C）的talks幾乎是同義詞，因此要小心，不要搞混，好好理解所有選項的內容，並記起來。

12. 這題是要選出留言者希望聽留言的人在研討會做什麼事。選項若是留言中完全未提及的「無理可證」內容，用刪除法最簡單，不過為了讓只有部份內容是錯誤的「完全偏差」選項也能採刪除法，最重要的就是做好準備、確實預覽到試題的細節。

Questions 10 through 12 refer to the following telephone message and list.

試題 10-12 請參考以下的電話留言及清單。

Hi, Angela. This is Darren getting back to you about the symposium which is only three weeks away. Q10 It looks like we can't attend it for $469 anymore. But if you sign up right now, we won't miss the next deadline. Q11 I want you to do it because the theme for this year's symposium is along the same lines as the work you're doing these days. Also, Q12 it would be beneficial for you to attend the optional events, like the exhibitors' forum. Many companies are working on devices and tools that aren't on the market yet, and getting a hands-on demonstration of how they work can be invaluable.

嗨，安琪拉（Angela）。我是達倫（Darren），要回覆你有關只剩三週後就要舉辦的研討會一事。看起來我們是無法以469美元參加了。但是如果妳現在登記報名，我們就不會錯過下一個截止日期。我希望妳去是因為今年的研討會主題與妳目前正在做的工作有關。而且，參加自選活動如參展商座談會等，對妳將會很有幫助的。很多公司正在開發尚未上市的設備和工具，若能看到他們親手實地示範如何操作，那是非常寶貴的。

字彙 □ get back to～ （過了一段時間後）回覆～的詢問、話題
□ early-bird registration 早鳥登記 □ regular registration 正常登記
□ late registration 延遲登記 □ registration at the door 當日登記

10. 請看圖表，聽留言的人應該在哪個登記期間報名？

（A）早鳥登記 （B）正常登記 （C）延遲登記 （D）當日登記

答案 **(B)**

解析 從紅色底線處前半句可知他們錯過了469美元可參加的早鳥登記（Early-bird registration）。但是後半句提到「如果現在報名，就來得及下次的期限」，所以正確答案是（B）。

11. 為什麼留言者希望聽留言的人參加研討會？

（A）以代表他們的公司 （B）以學習發表演說
（C）以聽取與她的工作有關的演講 （D）以實地看看場地

答案 **(C)**

解析 從紅色底線the theme for this year's symposium is along the same lines as the work you're doing these days.這段話可知正確答案是（C）。the same *A* as *B*意為「與B是相同的A」，along the same line as～則是「與～有關、是相同的性質」之意。

字彙 □ related to～ 與～有關

12. 留言者建議聽留言的人在研討會做什麼？

（A）了解看看各家企業提供的產品 （B）邀請一些主講人共進晚餐
（C）主辦其中一項自選活動 （D）加入研討委員會

答案 **(A)**

解析 從紅色底線處可知，留言者建議聽留言的人參加自選（非強制出席的）活動，去看設備及工具的實際操作示範，所以正確答案是（A）。host意為「主辦～」，因此（C）是錯誤的。

Part 4 Practice Test 實戰試題

MP3 73～77

請仔細聆聽各種類別的簡短獨白，再針對題目從（A）、（B）、（C）、（D）中選出最適合的答案（答案卡在全書最後）。

1. What does the speaker say about the last few months?
(A) They have been lowering prices of goods.
(B) They have not been selling many products.
(C) They have been using a new strategy.
(D) They have been developing a new product.

2. What will happen at the launch party?
(A) Books will be signed by Susan Derkins.
(B) Free gift bags will be distributed to clients.
(C) A store gift card will be given to attendees.
(D) A coupon may be used to purchase drinks.

3. When will the report be given?
(A) Today
(B) On Friday
(C) At the end of the month
(D) In a few months

4. What does the speaker say about the documents?
(A) Mr. Rockman needs them to be agreed by everyone.
(B) The listeners will receive them next week.
(C) Mr. Rockman will discuss them personally.
(D) They should be reviewed by a lawyer.

5. What does the speaker mean when he says, "he's making this happen"?
(A) Mr. Rockman will not give up shutting down the company.
(B) Mr. Rockman often buys other companies.
(C) Mr. Rockman requires more investments.
(D) Mr. Rockman is moving fast with the purchase plan.

6. Why does the speaker most likely recommend supporting the plan?
(A) He feels Mr. Rockman will work well with the CEO.
(B) He thinks Mr. Rockman can save the company.
(C) He wants Mr. Rockman to rename the company.
(D) He believes Mr. Rockman can create a better product.

7. Why did the caller purchase the item?
(A) He read positive reviews about the item.
(B) He previously owned the same item.
(C) His friends recommended the item.
(D) He wanted to make it a gift for someone.

8. What did the caller do last week?
(A) He tried to repair a vehicle.
(B) He participated in a cycling race.
(C) He purchased a product from a store.
(D) He called the customer service department.

9. What is the listener asked to do?
(A) Refund the cost to the caller's credit card
(B) Fix the product and send it back to the caller
(C) Exchange the product for another item
(D) Replace the product with the same model

---

10. What is the reason for the change?
(A) The office is getting too crowded.
(B) The management has changed.
(C) The business is failing.
(D) The company is expanding.

11. What did Mordica traditionally produce?
(A) Computer supplies
(B) Electronic equipment
(C) Cleaning products
(D) Athletic clothing

12. What does the speaker say about the company?
(A) Its products are exceptional.
(B) Its e-mail system stopped working.
(C) It will reopen its business next year.
(D) Some of its services will be discontinued.

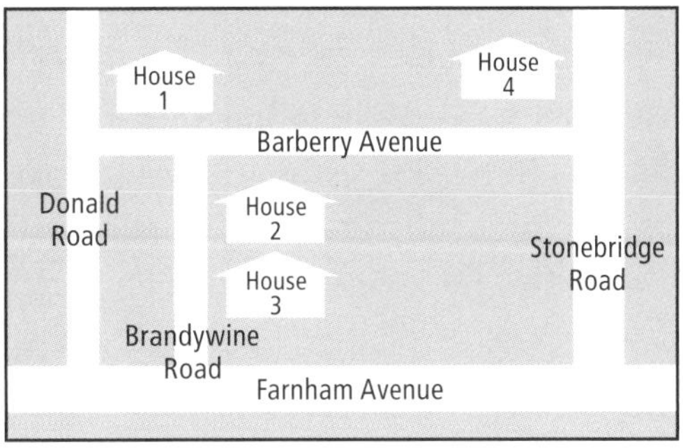

13. What is indicated about the speaker?
(A) She does not own a GPS.
(B) She is a very private person.
(C) She is a member at Gray's Fitness.
(D) She lives in a newly constructed area.

14. Look at the graphic. Where does the speaker live?
(A) In House 1
(B) In House 2
(C) In House 3
(D) In House 4

15. What type of business is the speaker calling?
(A) A plant nursery
(B) A fitness club
(C) A repair shop
(D) An electronics store

Part 4 Practice Test 實戰試題 解答與解析

MP3 73

Questions 1 through 3 refer to the following excerpt from a meeting.

試題 1-3 請參考以下部分會議內容。

Good afternoon, everyone. As you know, Q1 sales have been slow during the last few months, so we need something that will turn the tides. After much discussion, the marketing team has decided to use a new promotional strategy. Instead of spending $1,000 on paper advertising, the team believes it would be more effective to give out a $10 store gift card to 100 customers. To test this, Q2 the gift cards will be given away to customers who attend the launch party of the new novel by Susan Derkins this Friday. The effectiveness will then be measured by how many people return to the store. Q3 Lena Gaul will report on the results at the end of the month.

各位午安。如你們所知，過去幾個月銷售低迷，所以我們需要某些助力來扭轉局勢。經過多次討論之後，行銷團隊已決定採用新的促銷策略。與其花1,000美元在紙類廣告上，團隊認為發給100位顧客價值10美元的商店禮券會更有效果。為了測試這一點，禮券將被贈送給本週五出席蘇珊・德金斯（Susan Derkins）新小說發表派對的顧客們。然後將根據有多少人返回商店來衡量有效性。麗娜・古阿爾（Lena Gual）會在月底報告結果。

字彙 □ slow （銷售）低迷 □ turn the tides 扭轉局勢 □ give out～ 分發～ □ give away～ 贈送～ □ launch party 新品發布派對

1. What does the speaker say about the last few months?
(A) They have been lowering prices of goods.
(B) They have not been selling many products.
(C) They have been using a new strategy.
(D) They have been developing a new product.

關於過去幾個月，演說者說了什麼？
（A）他們一直在降低商品價格。
（B）他們沒有銷售很多產品。
（C）他們一直在採用新策略。
（D）他們一直在開發新產品。

答案 **(B)**

解析 從紅色底線處可知正確答案是（B）。這裡的slow是形容詞，意為「（銷售）低迷」。請注意，紅色底線的內容雖然是肯定句，但正確答案選項卻是用否定句表達相同的意思。至於其他選項，（A）是錯在並非價格降低，而是銷售量。（C）是錯在new strategy（新策略）是今後才要採用的解決方法。（D）是錯在該話題並未出現在演說中。

字彙 □ lower 降低～

2. What will happen at the launch party?
(A) Books will be signed by Susan Derkins.
(B) Free gift bags will be distributed to clients.
(C) A store gift card will be given to attendees.
(D) A coupon may be used to purchase drinks.

新書發表派對上將會發生什麼事？
（A）書籍將由蘇珊・德金斯簽名。
（B）免費禮品袋將被發給客戶。
（C）商店禮券將被發給參加者。
（D）優惠券可用於購買飲料。

答案 **(C)**

解析 這裡提到的the launch party是指「新書發表派對」。從紅色底線處可知商店禮券是要發給出席派對的人，因此正確答案是（C）。至於其他選項，（A）是錯在雖然是新書發表派對，但並未提到有簽名會。而（B）和（D）都是演說中完全未提及的「無理可證」內容，所以都不正確。各位在答題時，務必以演說中有提及的資訊為依據，不可擅自延伸想像。

3. When will the report be given?
(A) Today
(B) On Friday
(C) At the end of the month
(D) In a few months

報告將於何時被提出來？
（A）今天
（B）週五
（C）月底
（D）數個月後

答案 **(C)**

解析 這題是問報告完成的時間。從紅色底線處可知（C）是正確答案。（B）的Friday是舉辦蘇珊・德金斯新小說發表派對的日期。

Questions 4 through 6 refer to the following talk.

試題4-6 請參考以下演說。

So, as we investors know, this company we started a few years ago has failed to get off the ground. Instead of abandoning our wonderful product, I have found someone who has the business sense and contacts to get us in the black within a year. Terri Rockman has a plan to buy the company but keep us as investors. Q4 Legally, however, he can't move forward without our unanimous approval of the documents for the sale, and Q5 he'd like to officially acquire the company by the start of next month. Actually, he's making this happen. And he's not wasting time. He'll present us with the documents for the sale for review tomorrow. Q5 I recommend that everyone support this plan. Q6 Terri has already found an interested buyer for our product, which is more than our previous CEO ever did.

所以，正如我們投資者所知，我們幾年前創辦的這家公司無法順利上軌道。與其放棄我們這麼棒的產品，我找了一位具有商業頭腦及人脈的人選讓我們公司在一年內轉虧為盈。泰利．洛克曼（Terri Rockman）有一個收購該公司、但讓我們繼續當投資者的計畫。然而在法律上，如果沒有我們全體一致核准出售的文件，他就無法進展下去，而且他希望從下個月開始正式收購該公司。事實上，他決心要實現這個目標。而且他不浪費時間。明天他將向我們提出出售文件。我建議大家支持這個計畫。泰利已經找到一位對我們的產品有興趣的買家，這已經遠比我們前任執行長（CEO）做到的多更多了。

字彙 ☐ get off the ground 順利上軌道 ☐ abandon 放棄～ ☐ in the black 有盈餘 ☐ legally 法律上 ☐ unanimous 全體一致的

4. What does the speaker say about the documents?

(A) Mr. Rockman needs them to be agreed by everyone.
(B) The listeners will receive them next week.
(C) Mr. Rockman will discuss them personally.
(D) They should be reviewed by a lawyer.

關於文件，演說者說了什麼？

（A）洛克曼先生需要它們得到每個人的同意。
（B）聽眾將於下週收到它們。
（C）洛克曼先生將親自討論它們。
（D）它們應該經由律師審查。

答案 **(A)**

解析 從紅色底線處可知（A）是正確答案。如果文件沒有得到unanimous approval（全體一致的同意），洛克曼先生就無法進行公司收購的商議。

5. What does the speaker mean when he says, "he's making this happen"?

當演說者說「he's making this happen」時，代表什麼意思？

(A) Mr. Rockman will not give up shutting down the company.
(B) Mr. Rockman often buys other companies.
(C) Mr. Rockman requires more investments.
(D) Mr. Rockman is moving fast with the purchase plan.

（A）洛克曼先生不會放棄關閉這家公司。
（B）洛克曼先生經常收購其他公司。
（C）洛克曼先生需要更多投資。
（D）洛克曼先生正在迅速進行收購計畫。

答案 (D)

解析 這句話的前後過程是「洛克曼先生預定下個月開始收購公司」→「he's making this happen（他決心要實現這個目標）」→「（演說者）向聽眾表示希望大家支持洛克曼先生的計畫」。this是指「收購公司一事」，making this happen是指「決心要實現收購公司一事」。因此正確答案是（D）。

字彙 □ give up 放棄～

Part 4

6. Why does the speaker most likely recommend supporting the plan?

演說者建議支持這項計畫，最有可能的原因為何？

(A) He feels Mr. Rockman will work well with the CEO.
(B) He thinks Mr. Rockman can save the company.
(C) He wants Mr. Rockman to rename the company.
(D) He believes Mr. Rockman can create a better product.

（A）他認為洛克曼先生將與CEO合作愉快。
（B）他認為洛克曼先生可以拯救這家公司。
（C）他想讓洛克曼先生重新命名這家公司。
（D）他相信洛克曼先生可以創造更好的產品。

答案 (B)

解析 這題是問most likely（最有可能），所以最好的方式是收集完演說中的「間接出處」後，再選出正確答案。從紅色底線處可知，演說者想到傳達給聽眾的訊息是「洛克曼先生比前任執行長更盡力開拓對公司有益的路線」。因此，正確答案是以概括簡略的方式表達該想法的（B）為正確答案。

Questions 7 through 9 refer to the following telephone message.

試題7-9 請參考以下電話留言。

Hello. My name is Daniel Weaver and I purchased the Lockman XT-65 Multi-tool two weeks ago from your online store. Q7 I bought the product since so many people wrote good things about it in the review section. However, Q8 when I used it for the first time last week to repair my bicycle, one of the blades snapped in two. I am appalled by the low quality of the item, and would like to return it. If possible, Q9 I would like it replaced with a multi-tool from a different maker, namely the HG-3000 from Tendon International. Since they are both the same price, I believe this should not be a problem. Please call me back to confirm. Thank you.

哈囉，我的名字是丹尼爾．威佛（Daniel Weaver），兩週前我從你們的網路商店購買了Lockman（拉克曼）XT-65的多功能工具。我買這項產品是因為很多人在評論區寫了關於它的好話。然而，當我上週第一次使用它來修理我的自行車時，其中一個刀片斷成兩半。我對這項商品的低品質感到震驚，希望將它退回。如果可能的話，我想改換不同製造商的多功能工具，也就是天東國際（Tendon International）的HG-3000。因為它們都是一樣的價格，我相信這應該不是問題。請回我電話以便確認。謝謝。

字彙 □ multi-tool 多功能工具 □ blade 刀片、片狀物 □ snap 突然折斷
□ *be* appalled by～ 對～感到震驚 □ namely 換句話說、也就是

7. Why did the caller purchase the item? 為什麼留言者購買該項商品？

(A) He read positive reviews about the item. （A）他看了有關該商品的正面評論。

(B) He previously owned the same item. （B）他以前有過一樣的商品。

(C) His friends recommended the item. （C）他的朋友推薦了這項商品。

(D) He wanted to make it a gift for someone. （D）他想把它當作給某人的禮物。

答案 **(A)**

解析 留言一開始便提到 I bought the product since so many people wrote good things about it in the review section.（我買這項產品是因為很多人在評論區寫了關於它的好話。）。since（因為）後面的內容即談到購買產品的理由是「很多人誇讚該商品」。符合這種說法的正確答案是（A）。

8. What did the caller do last week?

(A) He tried to repair a vehicle.

(B) He participated in a cycling race.

(C) He purchased a product from a store.

(D) He called the customer service department.

留言者上週做了什麼？

（A）他試著修理車輛。

（B）他參加自行車比賽。

（C）他從商店買了一項產品。

（D）他致電到客服部門。

答案 **(A)**

解析 紅色底線處提到when I used it for the first time last week to repair my bicycle（當我上週第一次使用它來修理我的自行車時），it是指留言的主題「拉克曼（Lockman）XT-65多功能工具」。選項（A）符合該描述，所以是正確答案。請注意選項把bicycle（自行車）換成vehicle（車輛、交通工具）的說法。（C）的內容是兩週前的事。（B）和（D）是留言中完全未提及的「無理可證」選項，所以不正確。

9. What is the listener asked to do?

(A) Refund the cost to the caller's credit card

(B) Fix the product and send it back to the caller

(C) Exchange the product for another item

(D) Replace the product with the same model

聽留言的人被要求做什麼？

（A）將費用退還到留言者的信用卡

（B）修理商品並將它寄回給留言者

（C）將產品換成另一種商品

（D）用同一型號的產品作替換

答案 **(C)**

解析 預覽階段先認清楚（C）和（D）的差異，再等著聽語音來區別是（C）「另一種商品」或是（D）「同一型號的產品」。留言的後半段談到 I would like it replaced with a multi-tool from a different maker（我想改換不同製造商的多功能工具）。由此可知是希望改換為different maker的產品，所以正確答案是（C）another item。

MP3 76

Questions 10 through 12 refer to the following announcement.

試題 10-12 請參考以下公告。

We are proud to announce that Mordica is changing its name to MD Services. Q10 The name change is due to the significant improvements in our business activities. Today, Q11 our services stretch far beyond the production of traditional Mordica cleaning sprays and detergents. But don't be alarmed, our current structure and contacts will remain the same. Most of our services will also continue to operate as usual, but Q12 a small portion will be discontinued. At the same time, all e-mail addresses will be changed to lastname@MD.com. The old e-mail addresses will be operational until the end of this year. We look forward to growing side by side with our valued customers under the new company name.

我們很自豪地宣布摩蒂卡（Mordica）將更名為摩蒂服務（MD Services）。之所以變更名稱是因為我們的業務有顯著成長。現今，我們服務的項目迅速擴張，已遠不只是生產摩蒂卡傳統的清潔噴霧和清潔劑。但是不用擔憂，我們目前的結構和聯絡方式將保持不變。我們大部分的服務也將繼續像往常一樣運作，不過一小部分的服務將會被終止。同時，所有電子郵件地址將全部變更為姓氏@MD.com（lastname@MD.com）。而舊的電子郵件地址可以使用到今年年底。我們期待以新的公司名稱和我們尊貴的客戶並肩成長。

字彙 ☐ stretch 擴張、延伸 ☐ far beyond～ 遠遠超過～ ☐ detergent 清潔劑 ☐ don't be alarmed 不用擔憂 ☐ structure 結構 ☐ as usual 像往常一樣 ☐ operational 可以使用的

10. What is the reason for the change?
(A) The office is getting too crowded.
(B) The management has changed.
(C) The business is failing.
(D) The company is expanding.

這項變更的理由是什麼？
（A）辦公室變得太擁擠。
（B）管理階層已經改變。
（C）業績下滑。
（D）公司正在擴展。

答案 **(D)**

解析 從一開始的公告內容就知道變更的是公司名稱。後面接著提到The name change is due to the significant improvements in our business activities.（之所以變更名稱是因為我們的業務有顯著成長。），而（D）是將「業務活動有顯著成長」改成The company is expanding.（公司正在擴展）的說法，所以是正確答案。

字彙 ☐ fail 失敗、不順利

11. What did Mordica traditionally produce?
(A) Computer supplies
(B) Electronic equipment
(C) Cleaning products
(D) Athletic clothing

摩蒂卡傳統上生產什麼？
（A）電腦用品
（B）電子設備
（C）清潔用品
（D）運動服

答案 (C)

解析 這題是詢問有關摩蒂卡的產品，所以要一邊聽語音、一邊等待選項的說明出現。公告的前半段提到our services stretch far beyond the production of traditional Mordica cleaning sprays and detergents.（我們服務的項目迅速擴張，已遠不只是生產摩蒂卡傳統的清潔噴霧和清潔劑。），可知摩蒂卡原本是生產清潔噴霧及清潔劑，因此正確答案是（C）。

12. What does the speaker say about the company?
(A) Its products are exceptional.
(B) Its e-mail system stopped working.
(C) It will reopen its business next year.
(D) Some of its services will be discontinued.

關於公司，說話者說了什麼？
（A）它的產品優秀。
（B）它的電子郵件系統停止運作。
（C）它將於明年重新開業。
（D）部分服務即將被終止。

答案 (D)

解析 紅色底線處提到a small portion will be discontinued（一小部分的服務即將被終止），由此可知公司將停止提供現行的部份業務。符合該說法的（D）即為正確答案。（A）和（C）都是公告文中完全未提及的「無理可證」內容，所以都不正確。（B）是錯在電子郵件系統雖有變更，但原有的郵件地址仍然可使用到年底。

字彙 □ exceptional 優秀的

MP3 77

Questions 13 through 15 refer to the following telephone message and map.

試題 13-15 請參考以下電話留言和地圖。

Hi, this is Leslie McIntire returning your call. Yes, you're right that Q13 my neighborhood was recently built, so you can't find my address on the GPS yet. Anyway, if you know where Gray's Fitness is on Stonebridge Road, I'm right behind that. Q14 Just drive north on Donald Road and take a right on Barberry Avenue. My house is on the corner of Barberry and Brandywine. If you hit Stonebridge, you've gone too far. Q15 I'm so excited for my new tree to be delivered!

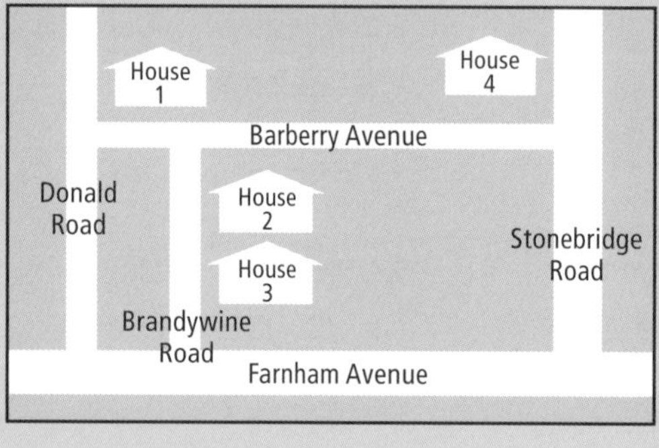

嗨，我是回電給你的萊絲莉．麥克林泰爾（Leslie McIntire）。是的，如你所言，我家所在的社區是最近才新建的，所以你還無法用導航系統（GPS）找到我的地址。總之，如果你知道葛雷健身房（Gray's Fitness）在石橋路（Stonebridge）上的所在位置，我家就在它的正後方。你只要在唐納德路（Donald Road）上往北行駛，於巴寶利大街（Barberry Avenue）右轉。我家就在巴寶利和白蘭地酒路（Brandywine）的街角處。如果你走到石橋路，就表示已經走超過了。很高興我的新樹就要被送來了！

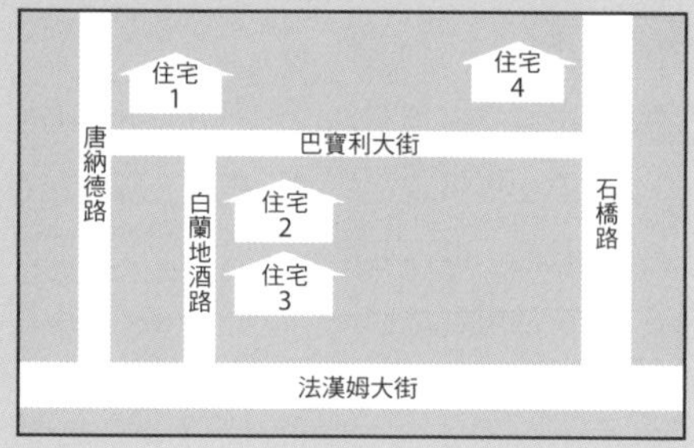

13. What is indicated about the speaker?
(A) She does not own a GPS.
(B) She is a very private person.
(C) She is a member at Gray's Fitness.
(D) She lives in a newly constructed area.

哪一項是有關留言者的描述？
（A）她沒有導航系統。
（B）她是個很內向的人。
（C）她是葛雷健身房的會員。
（D）她住在一處新建好的區域。

答案 **(D)**

解析 從紅色底線處可知留言者自家所在的社區最近剛興建完工。所以正確答案是（D）。

字彙 □ private person 內向的人

14. Look at the graphic. Where does the speaker live?
(A) In House 1
(B) In House 2
(C) In House 3
(D) In House 4

請看圖。留言者住在哪裡？
（A）住宅1
（B）住宅2
（C）住宅3
（D）住宅4

答案 **(B)**

解析 選項和地圖的共同資訊是「住宅編號」。地圖上另外還寫著道路名，這才是正確答案的關鍵所在。邊看著道路名邊聽語音播放，應該就可以了解留言者住在哪裡。在唐納德路上往北（以地圖上方為北）行駛，再根據語音指示的路線走就會抵達留言者的家。正確答案是（B）。

15. What type of business is the speaker calling?
(A) A plant nursery
(B) A fitness club
(C) A repair shop
(D) An electronics store

留言者打電話給哪一類型的公司？
（A）園藝苗圃
（B）健身俱樂部
（C）維修商店
（D）電子產品商店

答案 **(A)**

解析 從紅色底線的句子I'm so excited for my new tree to be delivered!（很高興我的新樹就要被送來了！）可知，聽留言的一方要送「樹」到留言者的家。因此正確答案是（A）。

字彙 □ plant nursery 園藝苗圃

認真持續挑戰，肯定得到佳績。

如何提高聽力技巧

重複練習（重複播放）、保持記憶、跟讀、聽寫等，都是提高聽力技巧的練習方法。其中，我覺得對提高分數最有效的是跟讀，以及我在多益初階程度時採行的斜線分段式閱讀（**slash reading**）。

斜線分段式閱讀與「簡化模式表達」

在剛開始練習時（多益聽力分數約400分左右），我先採取「斜線分段式閱讀」。以分段式「閱讀」並理解文章的內容來當作聽力的初步準備。事先讓自己沒有不懂的單字或句子，再從頭依序理解英文。當時，我以所謂「簡化模式表達」的方法，也就是將大量長串的英文句子替換為簡潔的中文來理解。例如，將這句what time of day is this announcement being made?（這項公告是什麼發布的？）替換成「何時的公告？」。持續這種訓練模式，終會達到一聽英文就能瞬間理解的程度。此外，若能鍛鍊「依照語順，來理解、記憶英文原文的內容」這種能力，那麼對Part 3 & 4中「預覽試題和選項，並將它留在記憶中」這件事，將大有助益。

善用空檔時間跟讀！

反覆上述的訓練，在不知不覺中就能擺脱把中文當做「輔助工具」來思考，直接用英文理解英文。所以，我將一份模擬試題用跟讀方式作為每天的日常功課，利用做家事的時間或是從家裡往返車站等空檔時間進行。耳朵習慣聽英文，自然對TOEIC L&R多益聽讀測驗的語音，以及CNN英文新聞等的理解有更高的精確度。

本書試題完成後，希望各位使用隨書附贈的MP3音檔每天試著跟讀練習。更可將全書音檔分前、後兩半交替使用，每日無休。相信3個月後，各位對自身聽力技巧的明顯提升勢必有所感覺。

Part

5

句子填空

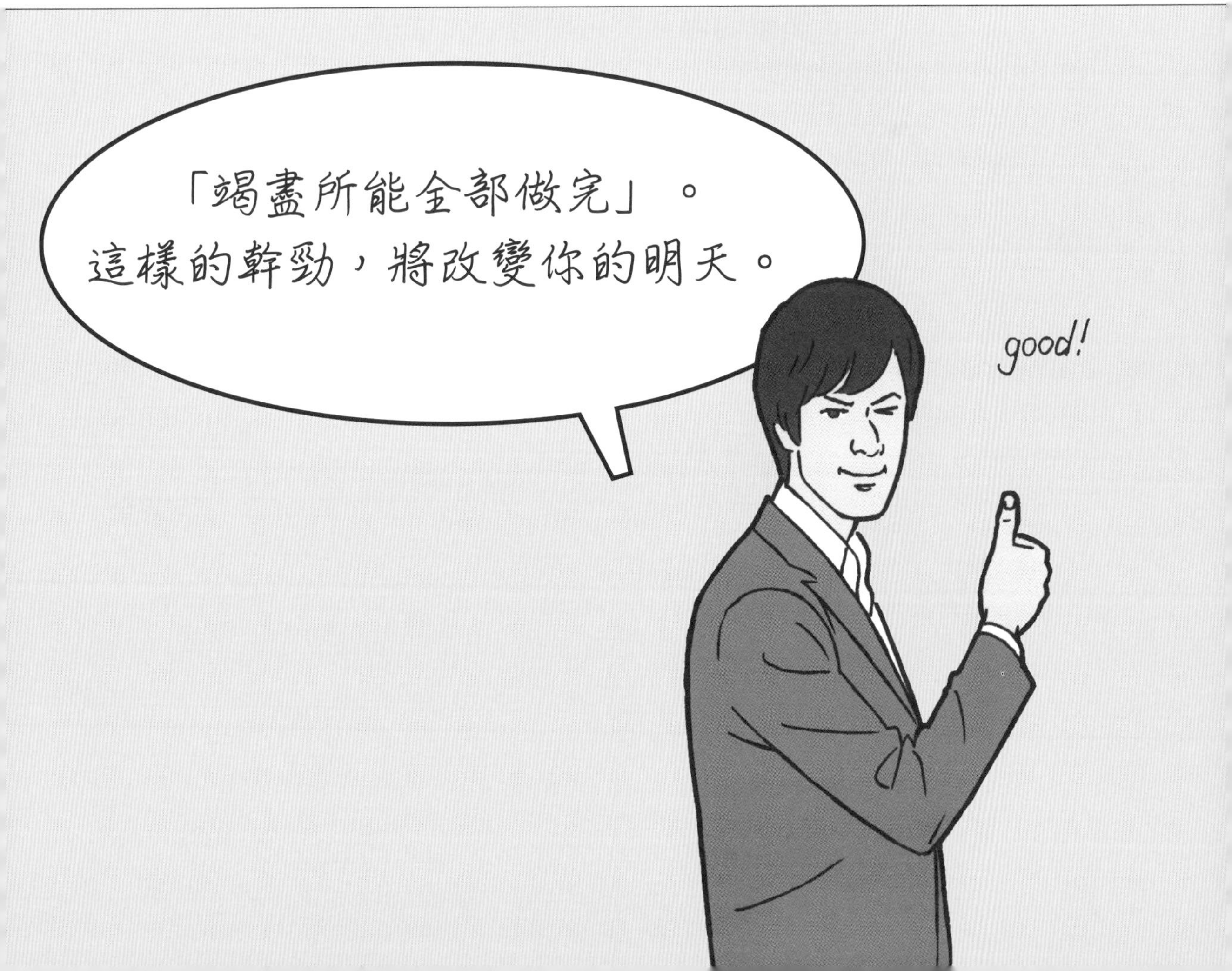
「竭盡所能全部做完」。
這樣的幹勁，將改變你的明天。
good!

Part

5 句子填空

贏得990分的解題技巧及攻略法

連與990分僅有些微差距的學習者，都需要花時間堅持到最後的單元，那就是Part 5。這個單元在正式測驗時每次約出現1～2個難題，其中大多數是**詞彙問題和文法問題**。本章就來教大家學習對應難題的能力！

贏得990分的解題技巧

即使是程度很好的人也容易落入陷阱的「詞彙問題和文法問題」大攻略

先試著寫以下例題。

例題 1

The head of the ward ------- resources to restore the proper and stable supply of electricity after the heavy typhoon had passed the region.

(A) allocated
(B) abbreviated
(C) asserted
(D) delegated Ⓐ Ⓑ Ⓒ Ⓓ

例題 2

Scientists at MLJ Pharmaceuticals are conducting ------- on a promising new drug for cancer.

(A) survey
(B) study
(C) deliberation
(D) research Ⓐ Ⓑ Ⓒ Ⓓ

HUMMER式密技！

即使是程度很好的人也容易落入陷阱的「詞彙問題和文法問題」大攻略

例題 1

The head of the ward ------- resources to restore the proper and stable supply of electricity after the heavy typhoon had passed the region.

強烈颱風經過這個地區後，區長分配資源以修復應有且穩定的電力供應。

(A) allocated (B) abbreviated
(C) asserted (D) delegated

答案 **(A)**

字彙 □ the head of the ward 區長 □ resource（一般加s） 資源 □ restore 修復～
□ proper 適當的、應有的 □ stable 穩定的 □ supply 供應 □ electricity 電力
□ allocate 分配 □ abbreviate 縮減、簡稱～ □ assert 聲稱～、強烈主張
□ delegate 委派～為代表、委派

首先要看選項，判斷這題是問詞彙、結構、時態、主被動語態、主詞動詞一致性、數量或是詞性等其中哪一項。但是，不論是哪一類型的試題都**從頭看完一整句再來作答吧！**

以**例題1**為例，先確認每個選項都是相同的詞性（動詞的過去式或過去分詞），再將句子從頭看到最後。雖然句中看似有restore和had passed等動詞，但由於整句缺少「主要動詞」，因此可判斷全部選項都是「動詞的過去式」。The head（首長）為了restore the proper and stable supply of electricity（修復應有且穩定的電力供應）而採取了什麼行動？選項中只有allocate resources（分配資源）的語意連貫，所以（A）為正確答案。

如果不懂abbreviate這個單字，或許會猶豫不決認為「可能這個答案更合適」，但是如果你正確掌握了allocate的意思和用法，就不會選（B）為答案。因此平常自我練習的時候，每當發現自己因不懂的單字出現在題目或選項中而猶豫不決，就要馬上作標記，並在練習完試題後查找意思及用法，才能**確實學到詞彙能力**。

為了贏得滿分990分，在閱讀部分勢必要拿下495分的滿分才行。不僅對做完試題的速度要有自覺，也不容許失敗。雖然有1～2題錯誤當然也有機會拿下495分，唯有專心一致毫不妥協地讓自己培養全部答對的實力才是王道。

例題 2

Scientists at MLJ Pharmaceuticals are conducting ------- on a promising new drug for cancer.

(A) survey (B) study

(C) deliberation (D) research

MLJ製藥公司的科學家們正在對一種有前景的癌症新藥進行研究。

答案 (D)

字彙 □ promising 有前景的 □ survey 調查 □ study 調查、研究 □ deliberation 細想、深思熟慮 □ conduct research 進行研究

確認每個選項都是意思相近的單字後，接著看題目。從空格前面的conducting判斷，如果是「進行研究」的話則語意連貫，再繼續回頭看選項。因為含「研究、調查」之意的單字有3個，所以我們改用**文法的角度**來重新思考。（A）的survey和（B）的study皆為「研究、調查」之意的可數名詞，前面需要加a。因此正確答案是不可數名詞的（D）research。

超越！進階技巧

累積一定程度的訓練後，讓我們試著練習不假思索、全憑空格前後的資訊和選項來選出正確答案吧！不過，在這種情形下將空格選填後，必須要把試題讀到最後，並確認整句的內容。這是為了避免不要掉入以下這類問題的陷阱。

The ------- of the road will be much more convenient for the people living in the region.

(A) widens

(B) width

(C) widen

(D) widening

（對於居住在這個地區的人們來說，道路拓寬將更加便利。）

the和of之間的空格應該填入名詞，因此應該有不少學習者認為答案是（B）。但是這題還有另一個名詞，那就是（D）widening。將width（寬度）代入句中可知，「道路的寬度」不會帶給附近的居民方便；而將widening（拓寬）代入後得出「道路的拓寬」，才會讓他們的生活更加便利。因此，正確答案是（D）。

這題的錯誤選項（B）width雖然放在正確選項（D）widening的上面，但是預覽選項時如果有先發現（D）是動名詞，判斷出空格應填入名詞後就不會被（B）誤導。最重要的是，事前瀏覽選項，不要輕忽選項代入後的整句意思。

贏得990分之路

例題1是詞彙問題，要理解前後關係，選出語意適當的動詞來連接主詞和受詞，**例題2**則是文法問題，光憑前後關係來判斷是無法解題的。像後者的題型每回都會出現1～2題。如果無法從前後關係來解題，請試著從文法、語法等其他角度來思考，保持隨時切換問題看法的柔軟性。

下一頁開始的Training基礎練習，請大家來挑戰匯集正式測驗最大難度的30題練習試題。另外，我也利用相同的句子設計了不同答案和選項，當作基礎練習的複習篇（Review of Training），以便讓各位將已作答一次的試題再次累積，終成為基本資料庫。希望大家在體驗「TOEIC L&R多益聽讀測驗最高難度填空題」的同時，將它們化為自身穩固的實力。

總結

作答Part 5時，務必在填入選項後，再次確認句子完整的意思，從前後關係、文法及語法等全面的角度來面對問題吧！

Training 基礎練習

請從（A）、（B）、（C）、（D）四個選項中，選出最適合填入空格的正確答案（答案卡在全書最後）。

1. That Yurika Kubo picked up the award for New Salesperson of the Year ------- no surprise to her department.
(A) gets into
(B) makes for
(C) goes through
(D) comes as

2. HM Electronics Corporation is the ------- largest manufacturer of farm machine parts in the country.
(A) every
(B) each
(C) single
(D) all

3. Our company and J.K. Airport Terminal Co., Ltd. agreed to work ------- one another to construct a big mall at the airport.
(A) overtime
(B) below
(C) alongside
(D) together

4. The board of directors has been ------- since last month about expanding into Canada's big market next year.
(A) deliberating
(B) marketing
(C) approving
(D) transforming

5. We are planning a music festival to ------- with the peace conference taking place in the area next summer.
(A) adapt
(B) tally
(C) adjust
(D) coincide

6. Mr. Robinson was ------- responsible for the great success of this product without relying on his staff.
(A) intimately
(B) intensely
(C) principally
(D) solely

7. A ------- in product quality would produce great dissatisfaction followed by a drop in consumer confidence.
(A) parcel
(B) lapse
(C) novice
(D) development

8. If we want to compete in this tough industry, we need to implement a ------- training program as soon as possible.
(A) remediable
(B) hectic
(C) rigorous
(D) various

9. We can hardly afford to pay our present staff's wages at this time, ------- take on new workers.
(A) more or less
(B) no less than
(C) much less
(D) more than

10. The city council was dedicated to ------- the course of the river to reduce the risk of flooding.
(A) forwarding
(B) diverting
(C) reversing
(D) widening

11. The new business venture was found to be only ------- profitable and thus deemed unworthy of further financial support by the backers.
(A) newly
(B) summarily
(C) marginally
(D) implausibly

12. I have no ------- in recommending Charles Laine for the position of CFO of the company.
(A) malfunction
(B) abrasion
(C) residue
(D) hesitation

13. The chairperson spoke ------- to the rest of the commission, and persuaded them to endorse his plan at the last minute.
(A) apprehensively
(B) delicately
(C) outstandingly
(D) convincingly

14. As is the ------- with using your laptop computer, you need to pay attention to the battery life when you use this portable device.
(A) way
(B) action
(C) portal
(D) case

15. Though the doctors' salaries are low and the work is tough, they are devoted to curing the disease ------- long the process may take.
(A) as far as
(B) whereas
(C) no matter how
(D) no wonder

16. The anti-asthmatic drug Theophylline-Z has yet to be approved for use in ------- with pharmaceuticals that treat kidney disease.
(A) conjunction
(B) compliance
(C) accordance
(D) alliance

17. Our company has hired several experts to determine whether the company's growth is -------.
(A) sustainable
(B) suspensive
(C) susceptible
(D) suspensory

18. A person from the architectural firm measured the ------- of the second floor and made a price quote yesterday.
(A) dividers
(B) expenses
(C) styles
(D) dimensions

19. The flight was ------- delayed due to a mechanical problem on the aircraft.
(A) immediately
(B) soon
(C) briefly
(D) shortly

20. Last night, Mr. Anderson ------- left a list of important clients in a taxi, but the driver delivered it this morning.
(A) nervously
(B) inadvertently
(C) previously
(D) accordingly

21. It is expected to take a few years, ------- a decade, to repair the historical building which was damaged by the storm last night.
(A) nevertheless
(B) if not
(C) while
(D) after all

22. You can attend over 20 different events ------- the renowned author's intriguing workshop.
(A) in addition
(B) above all
(C) even though
(D) aside from

23. To achieve ------- performance, Precision Machine 3200 must be kept within a temperature range of 10 to 20 degrees centigrade.
(A) comparative
(B) consecutive
(C) optimal
(D) optimistic

24. Our stock has already been -------, so we need you to ship as many smartphones as possible right away.
(A) inspired
(B) increased
(C) depleted
(D) completed

25. Executing tasks for teams in each of the 12 departments, Ms. McKechnie has proven herself to be quite -------.
(A) insignificant
(B) lively
(C) general
(D) versatile

26. There were complaints that the manufacturer's directions were too ------- and did not provide enough product assembly information for the average consumer.
(A) elaborate
(B) surrealistic
(C) vague
(D) exhaustive

27. This scholarship is designed for disadvantaged students who may ------- not be able to get an education.

(A) rarely
(B) otherwise
(C) seldom
(D) scarcely

28. Ms. Morgan was modestly attired at the celebration yesterday, but she ------- wears flashy clothes.

(A) customarily
(B) amazingly
(C) literally
(D) immensely

29. ------- in the costs of building materials have made it almost impossible for construction companies to forecast their spending.

(A) Tolerances
(B) Fluctuations
(C) Vulnerabilities
(D) Proposals

30. The institute has announced the rising number of part-time workers may have an ------- effect on our economy.

(A) adventive
(B) advanced
(C) adventitious
(D) adverse

Training 基礎練習　解答與解析

1. That Yurika Kubo picked up the award for New Salesperson of the Year ------- no surprise to her department.

(A) gets into　(B) makes for
(C) goes through　(D) comes as

久保百里香（Yurika Kubo）獲得年度最佳新人銷售員獎，對她的部門來說並不感到驚訝。

答案 (D)

解析 從句首的That到Year這段是這題的主詞部分。「久保百里香獲得年度最佳新人銷售員獎」，而她的部門對此並不驚訝，符合這樣前後關係的，是（D）come as～（感到～）。（A）get into～意為「參加～、對～有興趣」。（B）make for～意為「有助於～、促進」。（C）go through意為「經歷～」。

字彙 □ pick up～ 獲得～

2. HM Electronics Corporation is the ------- largest manufacturer of farm machine parts in the country.

(A) every　(B) each
(C) single　(D) all

HM電子公司在這個國家是唯一最大的農業機械零件製造商。

答案 (C)

解析 空格填入single（唯一的），變成the single largest manufacturer（唯一最大的製造商）後，正好符合前後關係。形容詞（A）every（全部的）和（B）each（各自的）雖可用於修飾manufacturer，但兩者語意不合邏輯。（D）all（全部的）也不正確。

字彙 □ manufacturer 製造商、廠商

3. Our company and J.K. Airport Terminal Co., Ltd. agreed to work ------- one another to construct a big mall at the airport.

(A) overtime　(B) below
(C) alongside　(D) together

我們公司和J.K.機場航站有限公司同意與彼此並肩合作在機場建一座大型商場。

答案 (C)

解析 這題是有難度的。從「兩家公司同意 ------- 建造」的前後關係來看，符合語意的選項範圍可縮小為（C）alongside（與～並肩）和（D）together（一起）。但為了連接空格後面的相互代名詞one another（彼此），所以詞性為介係詞的（C）是正確答案。（D）是副詞，所以不正確。（A）overtime意為「超時地」。（B）below意為「在～下面」。

4. The board of directors has been ------- since last month about expanding into Canada's big market next year.

(A) deliberating　(B) marketing
(C) approving　(D) transforming

從上個月以來，董事會已經在仔細討論明年擴展到加拿大的大市場。

答案 (A)

解析 這是現在完成進行式〈have been＋現在分詞〉。可與介係詞about搭配使用的動詞只有選項（A）deliberate（商議、仔細討論）。各位也一起記住deliberate當形容詞時，意為「故意的、慎重的」。（B）market意為「（在市場上）銷售～」。（C）approve意為「贊成」。（D）transform意為「使變形、改變」。

5. We are planning a music festival to ------- with the peace conference taking place in the area next summer.

(A) adapt (B) tally
(C) adjust (D) coincide

我們正在籌畫一個音樂節以期與明年夏天在該地舉行的和平會議同時發生。

答案 (D)

解析 將（D）coincide（同時發生）填入空格後的完整句意為「籌畫一個音樂節以期與和平會議同時發生」，其語意最正確。請牢記coincide with～是「與～同時發生、與～互相一致」。（A）adapt意為「使適應」。（B）tally意為「一致、符合～」。（C）adjust意為「調整」。

6. Mr. Robinson was ------- responsible for the great success of this product without relying on his staff.

(A) intimately (B) intensely
(C) principally (D) solely

羅賓森（Robinson）先生不靠他的員工，獨自負責這項產品的大成功。

答案 (D)

解析 句子後半的without relying on his staff（不靠他的員工）是正確答案所依據的線索。如果沒有這個部分，（C）principally（主要）和（D）solely（獨自）都可以成為正確答案。因為羅賓森先生「不靠他的員工」，可由此判斷是「一個人負責這項產品的成功」，所以正確答案是（D）。（A）intimately意為「親密地」。（B）intensely意為「極度、強烈地」。

字彙 □ *be* solely responsible for～ 獨自負責～

7. A ------- in product quality would produce great dissatisfaction followed by a drop in consumer confidence.

(A) parcel (B) lapse
(C) novice (D) development

產品品質的降低勢必引起很大的不滿，消費者的信心下降隨之而來。

答案 (B)

解析 因為「產品品質的 -------」而「引起很大的不滿，消費者的信心下降」，所以必須選擇含有負面意味且符合前後語意的選項。其中以（B）lapse（過失、降低）最正確。它還有另一個意思是「（時間的）流逝」，希望大家也一併記住。其他選項也是TOEIC L&R多益聽讀正式測驗常出現的單字。（A）parcel意為「包裹」。（C）novice意為「新手、初學者」。（D）development意為「發展、開發」。

8. If we want to compete in this tough industry, we need to implement a ------- training program as soon as possible.

(A) remediable　(B) hectic
(C) rigorous　(D) various

如果我們想在這個艱難的產業中競爭，我們需要儘快實行嚴格的培訓計畫。

答案 (C)

解析 應該實行什麼樣的「培訓計畫」呢？從「在艱難的產業中競爭」的前後關係可想而知，空格是含有「嚴謹、艱難」語意的字彙。因此正確答案是（C）rigorous。請一併將意為「（規則）嚴格的」且經常出現於多益考題的單字stringent背起來。（D）various（各式各樣的）不適合用來形容單數型態的program（計畫）。（A）remediable意為「可治療的、可矯正的」。（B）hectic意為「忙亂的」。

9. We can hardly afford to pay our present staff's wages at this time, ------- take on new workers.

(A) more or less　(B) no less than
(C) much less　(D) more than

我們幾乎付不起現有員工的薪資，更不用說僱用新人員了。

答案 (C)

解析 前半段提到can hardly afford to pay（幾乎付不起），可知連our present staff's wages（現有員工的薪資）都無法支付。在這樣的狀況下更無法僱用新人員。因此正確答案是（C）much less～（更不用說～）。各位要儘量將這類由比較級單字構成的片語整理出來。（A）more or less意為「或多或少」。（B）no less than～意為「不少於～」。（D）more than～意為「超過～、比～更多」。

字彙 □ afford to *do* 付得起～　□ take on～ 僱用

10. The city council was dedicated to ------- the course of the river to reduce the risk of flooding.

(A) forwarding　(B) diverting
(C) reversing　(D) widening

市議會致力於河川改道，以減少（發生）洪水的風險。

答案 (B)

解析 為了「減少（發生）洪水的風險」，應該針對河道做什麼呢？（B）diverting的原形是divert，意為「使～轉向、使～改道」，它適合當the course（路線）的動詞。至於其他三個選項，都不適合與受詞the course搭配使用。（A）forward意為「轉寄、促進～」。（C）reverse意為「將～倒轉、反向」。（D）widen意為「將～加寬」。

字彙 □ city council 市議會　□ flooding 洪水

11. The new business venture was found to be only ------- profitable and thus deemed unworthy of further financial support by the backers.

(A) newly　(B) summarily
(C) marginally　(D) implausibly

新的創業公司被發現只有些微地獲利，因此被贊助者認為不值得（投入）進一步財務支持。

答案 (C)

解析 從deemed unworthy of further financial support（被認為不值得進一步財務支持）可推測這家創業公司不太有利潤。因此，（C）marginally（些微地）為正確答案。（A）newly意為「最近、重新」。（B）summarily意為「立刻」。（D）implausibly意為「難以置信地、不合情理地」。

字彙 □ business venture 創業公司 □ deem *A B* 認為、以為A是B □ unworthy of～ 不值得～
□ backer 贊助者

12. I have no ------- in recommending Charles Laine for the position of CFO of the company.
(A) malfunction (B) abrasion
(C) residue (D) hesitation

我毫不猶豫地推薦查理斯・萊恩（Charles Laine）擔任公司的財務長職位。

答案 (D)

解析 正確答案是（D），have no hesitation in *doing*是「毫不猶豫地做～」的意思。（B）abrasion意為「磨損、磨耗」，要注意這個單字常出現在正式測驗中。（C）的residue（殘餘、剩餘）和remainder（殘餘、餘留物）為同義字，請一併記起來。（A）malfunction意為「故障」。

字彙 □ CFO（= Chief Financial Officer） 財務長

13. The chairperson spoke ------- to the rest of the commission, and persuaded them to endorse his plan at the last minute.
(A) apprehensively (B) delicately
(C) outstandingly (D) convincingly

主席對委員會其他的成員令人信服地發表談話，並在最後一刻說服他們贊成他的計畫。

答案 (D)

解析 從後半段的persuaded them to endorse his plan at the last minute（在最後一刻說服他們贊成他的計畫）可知，主席說服了委員會其他的成員，因此正確答案是（D）convincingly（令人信服地）。（A）apprehensively意為「擔心地、憂慮地」，也請大家一併把它的形容詞apprehensive（擔心的）記起來。（B）delicately意為「精緻地、優美地」。（C）outstandingly意為「明顯地、特別地」。

字彙 □ persuade＋人＋to *do* 說服某人做～ □ endorse 贊成～、背書

14. As is the ------- with using your laptop computer, you need to pay attention to the battery life when you use this portable device.
(A) way (B) action
(C) portal (D) case

與使用筆記型電腦的情況一樣，使用這種手提式裝置時（也）需要注意電池的壽命。

答案 (D)

解析 as is the case with～意為「與～（的情況）一樣」，所以正確答案是（D）。請一併將as is often the case with～「如同（～情況）常發生的」記起來。（A）way意為「方法」。（B）action意為「行動」。（C）portal意為「門」。

字彙 □ laptop computer 筆記型電腦

Part 5

15. Though the doctors' salaries are low and the work is tough, they are devoted to curing the disease ------- long the process may take.

(A) as far as (B) whereas
(C) no matter how (D) no wonder

儘管醫生的薪資低且工作辛苦，但他們都致力於治好疾病，不管過程需要多久。

答案 (C)

解析 正確答案（C），〈no matter how＋形容詞或副詞〉意為「不管有多麼～」。請一併記住*be* devoted (committed) to *doing*（致力於～）也是常見的用法，且介係詞to後須接動名詞（-ing）。（A）as far as～意為「就～而言」。（B）whereas～意為「反觀～」。（D）no wonder～意為「難怪～」。

16. The anti-asthmatic drug Theophylline-Z has yet to be approved for use in ------- with pharmaceuticals that treat kidney disease.

(A) conjunction (B) compliance
(C) accordance (D) alliance

抗氣喘藥茶鹼-Z（Theophylline-Z）尚未被核准與治療腎臟病的藥物一起使用。

答案 (A)

解析 選項內的單字都能符合in～with的片語結構，所以要從前後意思來判斷。這句的意思是「抗氣喘藥茶鹼-Z尚未被核准與治療腎臟病的藥物 ------- 使用」，如果是填in conjunction with～（與～一起）的話，則語意連貫。因此正確答案是（A）。（B）compliance意為「依照、順從」。（C）accordance意為「依據、一致」。（D）alliance意為「同盟、結盟」。

字彙 □ anti-asthmatic drug 抗氣喘藥 □ have yet to *do* 尚未～ □ pharmaceuticals 藥物
□ kidney disease 腎臟病

17. Our company has hired several experts to determine whether the company's growth is -------.

(A) sustainable (B) suspensive
(C) susceptible (D) suspensory

我們公司已聘請幾位專家來判斷公司的成長是否可持續下去。

答案 (A)

解析 「我們公司已聘請幾位專家」的目的是要「判斷公司的成長是否 -------」。語意上適合與growth（成長）搭配使用的選項是（A）sustainable（可持續下去）或（C）susceptible（易受影響的），但需要請專家判斷的應該是「成長是否可持續下去」。（B）suspensive意為「中止的」。（D）suspensory意為「懸吊的、暫時中止的」。

18. A person from the architectural firm measured the ------- of the second floor and made a price quote yesterday.

(A) dividers (B) expenses
(C) styles (D) dimensions

昨天一位建築公司的人來測量二樓的尺寸，並做了一份報價單。

答案 (D)

解析 「測量二樓的 -------」，選項中符合語意的單字只有（D）dimension「（長、寬、高等）尺寸、大小」。而（A）divider（隔板）在聽力測驗中也常出現，所以請各位一併記住。（B）expense意為「費用」。（C）style意為「樣式」。

字彙 □ price quote 報價單

19. The flight was ------- delayed due to a mechanical problem on the aircraft.

(A) immediately (B) soon
(C) briefly (D) shortly

由於飛機的機械問題，航班被短暫延誤。

答案 (C)

解析 這句的意思是「由於飛機的機械問題，航班被 ------- 延誤」，選項中以修飾delayed的副詞（C）briefly（短暫地）為正確答案。（A）immediately、（B）soon、（D）shortly都是「馬上、立刻」的意思，用於修飾下一步要進行的動作，所以都不正確。

字彙 □ *be* delayed 被延誤

20. Last night, Mr. Anderson ------- left a list of important clients in a taxi, but the driver delivered it this morning.

(A) nervously (B) inadvertently
(C) previously (D) accordingly

昨晚，安德森（Anderson）先生不慎把重要的客戶名單遺留在計程車內，但是司機今早將它送（回）來了。

答案 (B)

解析 先從一整句來了解，大致內容是「安德森先生把名單留在計程車內，但是司機將它送回來了」。空格是要填入副詞來修飾left（遺留），因此由前後關係可知（B）inadvertently（不慎地）是最適當的。（A）nervously意為「緊張地」。（C）previously意為「以前」。（D）accordingly意為「因此」。

21. It is expected to take a few years, ------- a decade, to repair the historical building which was damaged by the storm last night.

(A) nevertheless (B) if not
(C) while (D) after all

昨晚被暴風雨破壞的歷史建築，若非10年，預計也要花數年才能修復。

答案 (B)

解析 整句的內容是「------- 10年，也要花數年修復該棟歷史建築」。空格填入（B）if not～（若非～）即是if not a decade「若非10年」的意思，這樣的口吻更能凸顯a few years（數年）至少要花費的時間。decade＝ten years的替換說法也常見於多益正式測驗，請一併記起來。（A）nevertheless意為「儘管如此」。（C）while意為「當～時候」。（D）after all意為「畢竟、終究」。

字彙 □ decade 10年

22. You can attend over 20 different events ------- the renowned author's intriguing workshop.

(A) in addition (B) above all

(C) even though (D) aside from

除了那位有名作家引人入勝的研討會之外，你還可以參加超過20種不同的活動。

答案 (D)

解析 整句的內容是「------- 那位有名作家引人入勝的研討會，你還可以參加超過20種不同的活動」。（D）的aside from～和besides是一樣的用法，意為「除了～以外」，所以是正確答案。（A）in addition意為「此外」。（B）above all意為「尤其」。（C）even though～意為「儘管～」。

字彙 □ renowned 有名的 □ intriguing 吸引人的、引人入勝的

23. To achieve ------- performance, Precision Machine 3200 must be kept within a temperature range of 10 to 20 degrees centigrade.

(A) comparative (B) consecutive

(C) optimal (D) optimistic

為了達到最佳性能，精密機械3200型號（Precision Machine 3200）必須維持在攝氏10到20度的溫度範圍內。

答案 (C)

解析 正確答案為（C），optimal performance意為「最佳性能」。（B）consecutive（連續的）也常見於多益正式測驗，如 the third consecutive day（連續3天中的第3天）／three consecutive days（連續三天）。（A）comparative意為「比較的、相對的」。（D）optimistic意為「樂觀的」。

24. Our stock has already been -------, so we need you to ship as many smartphones as possible right away.

(A) inspired (B) increased

(C) depleted (D) completed

我們的庫存已經用完，所以需要你馬上運送智慧型手機過來，越多越好。

答案 (C)

解析 整句大意是「因為沒有庫存，所以希望運送過來」。沒有庫存，可以用deplete（用完～）來表達，所以正確答案是（C）。（A）inspire意為「賦予靈感」。（B）increase意為「增加～」。（D）complete意為「完成～」。

25. Executing tasks for teams in each of the 12 departments, Ms. McKechnie has proven herself to be quite -------.

(A) insignificant (B) lively

(C) general (D) versatile

為12個部門的每個團隊執行任務，麥克妮（Mckechnie）女士證明自己是相當多才多藝的。

答案 (D)

解析 從Executing tasks for teams in each of the 12 departments這句可知，麥克妮女士一手負責12個部門每個團隊的工作。空格需要填入能表達「她有能力」的字彙，所以正確答案是（D）versatile（多功能的、多才多藝的）。（A）insignificant意為「無足輕重的」。（B）lively意為「活潑的、生氣勃勃的」。（C）general意為「一般的」。

字彙 □ execute 執行～ □ prove oneself to be～ 證明自己是～

26. There were complaints that the manufacturer's directions were too ------- and did not provide enough product assembly information for the average consumer.

(A) elaborate (B) surrealistic
(C) vague (D) exhaustive

有人抱怨製造商的指示太過含糊，並沒有為一般消費者提供足夠的產品組裝資訊。

答案 (C)

解析 the manufacturer's directions were too -------（製造商的指示太過 -------）是抱怨的內容，依照前後的關係來看，可以成為directions（指示）的補語是（C）vague（含糊的、模糊不清的）。（D）的exhaustive（徹底的、全面的）是exhaust（用完～、使精疲力盡）的衍生字。另外也請一併記住它的形容詞exhausting（使人精疲力竭的、費力的）。（A）elaborate意為「精巧的、精心的」。（B）surrealistic意為「超現實主義的」。

字彙 □ assembly 組裝

27. This scholarship is designed for disadvantaged students who may ------- not be able to get an education.

(A) rarely (B) otherwise
(C) seldom (D) scarcely

這筆獎學金是為弱勢學生而設計的，否則他們可能無法接受教育。

答案 (B)

解析 排除空格來思考，整句的內容是「這筆獎學金是為可能無法受教育的弱勢學生設計的」。也就是如果學生沒有接受獎學金的話（如果不設獎學金的話）就無法受教育，從這樣的前後關係來看，（B）的otherwise（否則）是最正確的答案。其他選項全是含有否定意味的單字，無法使前後連貫。（A）rarely意為「很少～」。（C）seldom意為「不常～」。（D）scarcely意為「幾乎不～」。

字彙 □ scholarship 獎學金

28. Ms. Morgan was modestly attired at the celebration yesterday, but she ------- wears flashy clothes.

(A) customarily (B) amazingly
(C) literally (D) immensely

摩根（Morgan）女士昨天在慶祝會上打扮端莊，但她通常穿華麗的衣服。

答案 (A)

解析 對等連接詞but（但是）連接兩個子句。「摩根女士昨天在慶祝會上打扮樸素端莊」，那麼「穿華麗的衣服」是什麼時候呢？如果將（A）的customarily（通常）填入空格，後半子句的意思即是「通常穿華麗的衣服＝向來都做華麗的打扮」，因此語意連貫。（B）amazingly意為「令人驚奇地」。（C）literally意為「按字面上地」。（D）immensely意為「極大地、非常」。

字彙 □ *be* modestly attired 打扮端莊 □ flashy clothes 華麗的衣服

29. ------- in the costs of building materials have made it almost impossible for construction companies to forecast their spending.

(A) Tolerances (B) Fluctuations

(C) Vulnerabilities (D) Proposals

建築材料成本的波動，使建設公司幾乎不可能預測花費。

答案 (B)

解析 想一下建設公司預測花費時的阻力是什麼。由此可知正確答案是（B）fluctuation（波動）。至於（A）tolerance（容忍度）和（C）vulnerability（弱點、易受傷的性質）和成本的關聯性低，都不符合整句語意。（D）proposal（提案）後面的介系詞必須接on而不是in，proposal on～意為「有關～提案」。

字彙 □ forecast 預料～、預測

30. The institute has announced the rising number of part-time workers may have an ------- effect on our economy.

(A) adventive (B) advanced

(C) adventitious (D) adverse

該機構已宣布，持續上升的兼職工人數可能對我們的經濟有不利的影響。

答案 (D)

解析 正確答案是（D）adverse（相反的、不利的）。adverse也常以adverse effect（不利的影響、副作用）及adversely affect～（不利地影響著～）的形式出現在考題中，請大家要記住。（A）adventive意為「外來的」。（B）advanced意為「先進的、高階的」。（C）adventitious意為「外來的、偶然的」。

字彙 □ institute 機構、協會

Review of Training 複習基礎練習

請從（A）、（B）、（C）、（D）四個選項中，選出最適合填入空格的正確答案（答案卡在全書最後）。

1. That Yurika Kubo ------- the award for New Salesperson of the Year comes as no surprise to her department.
(A) put up
(B) picked up
(C) signed up
(D) tidied up

2. HM Electronics Corporation is the single largest manufacturer of ------- machine parts in the country.
(A) phase
(B) farm
(C) pharmacy
(D) farmhand

3. Our company and J.K. Airport Terminal Co., Ltd. agreed to work alongside ------- to construct a big mall at the airport.
(A) each
(B) another
(C) one another
(D) others

4. The board of directors has been deliberating since last month about ------- into Canada's big market next year.
(A) expanding
(B) extending
(C) ensuring
(D) expiring

5. We are planning a music festival to coincide with the peace conference ------- in the area next summer.
(A) having held
(B) hosting
(C) having organized
(D) taking place

6. Mr. Robinson was solely ------- for the great success of this product without relying on his staff.
(A) charged
(B) unaccountable
(C) obligated
(D) responsible

7. A lapse in product quality would produce great ------- followed by a drop in consumer confidence.
(A) dissatisfactory
(B) dissatisfaction
(C) satisfaction
(D) satisfactory

8. If we want to compete in this tough industry, we need to ------- a rigorous training program as soon as possible.
(A) implore
(B) imply
(C) implement
(D) impress

9. We can hardly afford to pay our present staff's wages at this time, much less take ------- new workers.
(A) on
(B) after
(C) up
(D) along

10. The city council was ------- to diverting the course of the river to reduce the risk of flooding.
(A) decided
(B) diluted
(C) dedicated
(D) declined

11. The new business venture was found to be only marginally profitable and thus ------- unworthy of further financial support by the backers.
(A) remained
(B) compounded
(C) dazzled
(D) deemed

12. I have no hesitation in ------- Charles Laine for the position of CFO of the company.
(A) restructuring
(B) commenting
(C) cooperating
(D) recommending

13. The chairperson spoke convincingly to the rest of the commission, and persuaded them to ------- his plan at the last minute.
(A) endorse
(B) enlarge
(C) extract
(D) encourage

14. As is the case with using your laptop computer, you need to pay attention to the battery life when you use this portable -------.
(A) drapery
(B) device
(C) directory
(D) donation

15. Though the doctors' salaries are low and the work is tough, they are devoted to curing the disease no matter how long the ------- may take.
(A) process
(B) proceeds
(C) proximity
(D) productivity

16. The anti-asthmatic drug Theophylline-Z has yet to be approved for use in conjunction with pharmaceuticals that ------- kidney disease.
(A) deal
(B) handle
(C) address
(D) treat

17. Our company has hired several experts to ------- whether the company's growth is sustainable.
(A) determine
(B) demote
(C) deplete
(D) deserve

18. A person from the ------- firm measured the dimensions of the second floor and made a price quote yesterday.
(A) accountable
(B) accurate
(C) architectural
(D) abundant

19. The flight was briefly delayed ------- a mechanical problem on the aircraft.
(A) thanks for
(B) due to
(C) in addition to
(D) hence

20. Last night, Mr. Anderson inadvertently left a list of important clients in a taxi, but the driver ------- it this morning.
(A) delighted
(B) demolished
(C) delivered
(D) deteriorated

21. It is expected to take a few years, if not a -------, to repair the historical building which was damaged by the storm last night.
(A) demeanor
(B) detergent
(C) decade
(D) diagnosis

22. You can attend over 20 different events aside from the renowned author's ------- workshop.
(A) inaccurate
(B) intriguing
(C) intact
(D) inactive

23. To ------- optimal performance, Precision Machine 3200 must be kept within a temperature range of 10 to 20 degrees centigrade.
(A) achieve
(B) adhere
(C) decrease
(D) focus

24. Our stock has already been depleted, so we need you to ship as ------- smartphones as possible right away.
(A) soon
(B) much
(C) many
(D) far

25. Executing tasks for teams in each of the 12 departments, Ms. McKechnie has ------- herself to be quite versatile.
(A) abided
(B) illustrated
(C) established
(D) proven

26. There were complaints that the manufacturer's directions were too vague and did not provide enough product ------- information for the average consumer.
(A) assembled
(B) assembly
(C) assembler
(D) assemble

27. This scholarship is ------- for disadvantaged students who may otherwise not be able to get an education.
(A) demoted
(B) depicted
(C) designed
(D) deprived

28. Ms. Morgan was ------- attired at the celebration yesterday, but she customarily wears flashy clothes.
(A) consistently
(B) voluntarily
(C) respectively
(D) modestly

29. Fluctuations in the costs of building materials have made it almost impossible for construction companies to ------- their spending.
(A) foreclose
(B) forerun
(C) forecast
(D) forestall

30. The institute has announced the rising number of part-time workers may have an adverse ------- on our economy.
(A) affect
(B) effect
(C) effector
(D) affection

Review of Training 複習基礎練習 解答與解析

1. 久保百里香（Yurika Kubo）獲得年度最佳新人銷售員獎，對她的部門來說並不感到驚訝。

答案 (B)

解析 只有（B）的pick up～（獲得（獎賞等）、拿起）讓語意連貫。（A）put up～意為「建造～、提供」。（C）sign up意為「（署名）參加」。（C）tidy up～意為「使～整潔」。

2. HM電子公司在這個國家是唯一最大的農業機械零件製造商。

答案 (B)

解析 farm machine parts是「農業機械零件」的意思。（A）phase意為「階段」。（C）pharmacy意為「藥局」。（D）farmhand意為「農場工人」。

3. 我們公司和J.K.機場航站有限公司同意與彼此並肩合作在機場建一座大型商場。

答案 (C)

解析 work alongside one another意為「彼此並肩工作」。請各位把work alongside～（與～並肩工作、共同行動）記起來。（A）each意為「每一個」。（B）another意為「另一個」。（D）others意為「其他的」。

4. 從上個月以來，董事會已經在仔細討論明年擴展到加拿大的大市場。

答案 (A)

解析 （A）expand和（B）extend都有「擴大」的意思，不過expand是往立體空間擴大的動詞，而extend是往平面方向延伸的動詞。這題可當不及物動詞接into表示「向市場發展、業務擴大」的是（A）expand。（C）ensure意為「保證～」。（D）expire意為「到期」。

5. 我們正在籌畫一個音樂節以期與明年夏天在該地舉行的和平會議同時發生。

答案 (D)

解析 和主詞conference或meeting（會議）等字配合的動詞是有「主動舉行」意味的（D）take place。（A）hold意為「舉行」。（B）host意為「主辦～」。（C）organize意為「組織～」。

6. 羅賓森（Robinson）先生不靠他的員工，獨自負責這項產品的大成功。

答案 (D)

解析 從前後關係可知，填入（D）成為*be* responsible for～（對～負責）才是正確答案。（A）charged意為「充滿強烈感情的」。（B）unaccountable意為「沒有責任的」。（C）obligated意為「有義務的」。

7. 產品品質的降低勢必引起很大的不滿，消費者的信心下降隨之而來。

答案 (B)

解析 空格由形容詞great修飾，應填入名詞來表達因lapse（降低、失誤）而產生的負面內容。（B）的dissatisfaction（不滿）為正確答案。（A）dissatisfactory意為「不滿意的」。（C）satisfaction意為「滿意」。（D）satisfactory意為「令人滿意的」。

8. 如果我們想在這個艱難的產業中競爭，我們需要儘快實行嚴格的培訓計畫。

答案 (C)

解析 「實行」嚴格的培訓計畫語意最適當。（A）implore意為「懇求～」。（B）imply意為「暗示～」。（D）impress意為「使驚豔」。

9. 我們幾乎付不起現有員工的薪資，更不用說僱用新人員了。

答案 (A)

解析 空格需與take搭配成為「僱用」的意思，才能讓語意連貫。因此正確答案是（A）的 take on～。（B）take after～意為「與～（相貌、性格等）相似」。（C）take up～意為「吸收、佔用」。（D）take along～意為「將～帶去、帶著」。

10. 市議會致力於河川改道，以減少（發生）洪水的風險。

答案 (C)

解析 能成為片語*be*～to *do*ing的是（C）dedicated，be dedicated to *do*ing是「致力於～」的意思。（A）decide意為「決定～」。（B）dilute意為「稀釋～」。（D）decline意為「拒絕～」。

11. 新的創業公司被發現只有些微地獲利，因此被贊助者認為不值得（投入）進一步財務支持。

答案 (D)

解析 正確答案是（D），deem *A B*意為「認為A（是）B」，在句中以被動語態呈現。A即是句中被動語態的主詞The new business venture。（A）remain意為「保持～」。（B）compound意為「使惡化～、混和」。（C）dazzle意為「使～眼花撩亂」。

12. 我毫不猶豫地推薦查理斯・萊恩（Charles Laine）擔任公司的財務長職位。

答案 (D)

解析 recommend *A* for *B*意為「推薦A做B」，因此正確答案是（D）。其他選項都和前後不連貫。（A）restructure意為「重組～」。（B）comment意為「評論～」。（C）cooperate意為「合作」。

13. 主席對委員會其他的成員令人信服地發表談話，並在最後一刻說服他們贊成他的計畫。

答案 (A)

解析 能連貫前後關係，將 his plan（他的計畫）當受詞的是（A）endorse意為「贊成～」。（B）enlarge意為「擴大～」。（C）extract意為「抽出～」。（D）encourage意為「鼓勵～」。

14. 與使用筆記型電腦的情況一樣，使用這種手提式裝置時（也）需要注意電池的壽命。

答案 (B)

解析 使用時需要注意battery life（電池壽命）的是（B）的device（裝置）。portable device是「手提式裝置」的意思。（A）drapery意為「帷幔」。（C）directory意為「名冊」。（D）donation意為「捐贈」。

15. 儘管醫生的薪資低且工作辛苦，但他們都致力於治好疾病，不管過程需要多久。

答案 (A)

解析 從前後關係可判斷may take（會需要）的主詞是（A）process（過程）。（B）proceeds意為「收益」。（C）proximity意為「鄰近」。（D）productivity意為「生產力」。

16. 抗氣喘藥茶鹼-Z（Theophylline-Z）尚未被核准與治療腎臟病的藥物一起使用。

答案 (D)

解析 從空格前、後的pharmaceuticals（藥物）和kidney disease（腎臟病）的關係可看出，有「治療～」之意的（D）treat是正確答案。（A）deal意為「處理、經營」。（B）handle意為「處理」。（C）address意為「處理～、對人攀談」。

17. 我們公司已聘請幾位專家來判斷公司的成長是否可持續下去。

答案 (A)

解析 從句子的前後關係可知空格應該填入有「判斷、確實了解後決定～」之意的（A）determine。（B）demote意為「被降級為～」。（C）deplete意為「用盡～」。（D）deserve意為「值得～」。

18. 昨天一位建築公司的人來測量二樓的尺寸，並做了一份報價單。

答案 (C)

解析 「建築公司」就是architectural firm。（A）accountable意為「負有責任的」。（B）accurate意為「準確的」。（D）abundant意為「豐富的」。

19. 由於飛機的機械問題，航班被短暫延誤。

答案 (B)

解析 空格後面說明了航班被延誤的原因。因此正確答案是表達原因的（B）due to。（A）thanks for～意為「感謝～」。（C）in addition to～意為「除～之外還有」。（D）hence意為「因此」。

20. 昨晚，安德森（Anderson）先生不慎把重要的客戶名單遺留在計程車內，但是司機今早將它送（回）來了。

答案 (C)

解析 這句若是指司機將安德森先生不慎遺留在計程車內的it（＝list）「送回」，則整句意思完整。因此（C）deliver是正確答案。（A）delight意為「令人高興～」。（B）demolish意為「破壞～」。（D）deteriorate意為「使～惡化」。

Part 5

21. 昨晚被暴風雨破壞的歷史建築，若非10年，預計也要花數年才能修復。

答案 (C)

解析 a few year（數年）的對照對象是a decade（＝a period of 10 years）。（A）demeanor意為「行為、態度」。（B）detergent意為「清潔劑」。（D）diagnosis意為「診斷」。

22. 除了那位有名作家引人入勝的研討會之外，你還可以參加超過20種不同的活動。

答案 (B)

解析 應選擇形容詞來修飾「有名作家的研討會」。因此將intrigue（激起～的興趣）的形容詞型態intriguing（吸引人的、引人入勝的）填入空格最適當。（A）inaccurate意為「不正確的」。（C）intact意為「未受損傷的」。（D）inactive意為「不活躍的」。

23. 為了達到最佳性能，精密機械3200型號（Precision Machine 3200）必須維持在攝氏10到20度的溫度範圍內。

答案 (A)

解析 從前後關係可知有「達成、得到～」之意的（A）achieve為正確答案。（B）adhere意為「遵守」。（C）decrease意為「減少～」。（D）focus意為「聚焦於～」。

24. 我們的庫存已經用完，所以需要你馬上運送智慧型手機過來，盡可能越多越好。

答案 (C)

解析 雖說是as ------- as possible（盡可能越～越好）的句型，但是要注意不要輕易地選soon（即將）。因為句中已有right away（馬上），所以選soon意思重複。而且，要選形容詞來修飾空格後面的smartphones（智慧手機）。從前後來判斷，如果是as many smartphones as possible就是「盡可能越多智慧型手機越好」，語意連貫。smartphone是可數名詞，所以（B）much（許多的）不適合。

25. 為12個部門的每個團隊執行任務，麥克妮（Mckechnie）女士證明自己是相當多才多藝的。

答案 (D)

解析 prove oneself to be～意為「證明自己是～」。（A）abide意為「容忍～」。（B）illustrate意為「說明～」。（C）establish意為「設立～」。

26. 有人抱怨製造商的指示太過含糊，並沒有為一般消費者提供足夠的產品組裝資訊。

答案 (B)

解析 從前後關係可知空格是指「產品組裝的資訊」，所以（B）的assembly（組裝）是正確答案。（A）assembled意為「已組裝的」。（C）assembler意為「組裝員」。（D）assemble意為「組裝～」。

27. 這筆獎學金是為弱勢學生而設計的，否則他們可能無法接受教育。

答案 (C)

解析 *be* designed for～意為「為～而設計的」。（A）demote意為「使降級為～」。（B）depict意為「描寫～」。（D）deprive意為「剝奪～」。

28. 摩根（Morgan）女士昨天在慶祝會上打扮端莊，但她通常穿華麗的衣服。

答案 **(D)**

解析 兩個子句用but（但是）連結，後句描述通常是「華麗的」，所以前句應該是指「非華麗的」。因此（D）的modestly（端莊的）是正確答案。（A）consistently意為「一貫地」。（B）voluntarily意為「自願地」。（C）respectively意為「分別地」。

29. 建築材料成本的波動，使建設公司幾乎不可能預測花費。

答案 **(C)**

解析 想想價格的波動，會讓建築公司很難對花費做什麼動作，即可知正確答案是（C）forecast（預測）。（A）foreclose意為「妨礙～」。（B）forerun意為「超越～、在～前面」。（D）forestall意為「搶先阻止～行動」。

30. 該機構已宣布，持續上升的兼職工人數可能對我們的經濟有不利的影響。

答案 **(B)**

解析 adverse effect的意思是「不利的影響」。（A）affect意為「影響～」。（C）effector意為「（對刺激）作出反應者」。（D）affection意為「喜愛」。

Practice Test 實戰試題

請從（A）、（B）、（C）、（D）四個選項中，選出最適合填入空格的正確答案（答案卡在全書最後）。

1. The fact that the Canadian real estate sector has grown ------- in the last two decades is amazing.
(A) exemplarily
(B) exponentially
(C) candidly
(D) meticulously

2. The doctors have warned ------- activities in this weather can cause heat exhaustion or heat stroke in healthy individuals.
(A) strenuous
(B) versatile
(C) feasible
(D) stranded

3. Miracle Co., Ltd. has introduced steam mopping as an alternative to ------- customers who are accustomed to the conventional mop and bucket.
(A) lucrative
(B) integral
(C) commensurate
(D) janitorial

4. The Singapore retail giant might be famous for its cheap designer furniture, but it's almost as well-known as a ------- of pineapple juice.
(A) demeanor
(B) drapery
(C) splendor
(D) purveyor

5. We heard there were ------- in the unemployment statistics between the government figures and those of the private agencies.
(A) jargon
(B) affiliations
(C) outages
(D) discrepancies

6. As the view at night is so amazing, people are eating dinner at a ------- pace.
(A) rapidly
(B) leisurely
(C) strategically
(D) slowly

7. Reportedly, the U.S. government is going to implement ------- laws to regulate the pharmacy profession.
(A) avid
(B) abrupt
(C) stringent
(D) exquisite

8. The managing editor always says the real mission of journalists is to report events ------- as well as to work publicly.
(A) mistakenly
(B) provisionally
(C) impartially
(D) cursorily

9. The manager opted to ask workers to stay late, questioning the ------- of convincing the board to hire part-timers.
(A) continuity
(B) likelihood
(C) approximation
(D) admittance

10. The Taiwanese government said that it was dedicated to increasing the number of tourist arrivals in the country in this fiscal year by ------- the visa process.
(A) invigorating
(B) depleting
(C) expediting
(D) demolishing

11. Throughout her 20-year -------, Katie inspired numerous graduate students to pursue work in the academic areas that fascinated them most.
(A) turnout
(B) norm
(C) momentum
(D) tenure

12. The forecast showed hot weather, but in fact, we actually experienced a severe cold ------- last week.
(A) ventilation
(B) gala
(C) proximity
(D) spell

13. It is still ------- at local small shops that customers make their purchases on weekends in this region.
(A) predominantly
(B) inadvertently
(C) radically
(D) hourly

14. The tourist center to which we are heading is ------- indicated on the brochures we have so that we can easily find it.
(A) unanimously
(B) enthusiastically
(C) prominently
(D) proficiently

15. The weekly magazine that I am reading says stretching before and after exercise can ------- improve your health.
(A) exclusively
(B) concisely
(C) markedly
(D) unfavorably

16. My doctor said to me that eating too much salt could ------- to high blood pressure in the near future.
(A) commit
(B) support
(C) devote
(D) contribute

17. The deadline for the project is next Monday so if you need an ------- you should request permission from your supervisor immediately.
(A) extinction
(B) excursion
(C) expansion
(D) extension

18. A lot of parents around me ------- their children to daycare centers to have them cared for during the day.
(A) impart
(B) entrust
(C) relegate
(D) assign

19. A lot of observers participated in the viewing even though the meteor shower was ------- less intense than specialists had anticipated.
(A) predictably
(B) preferably
(C) environmentally
(D) somewhat

20. The property that got an estimate last week was ------- five times more than its initial price.
(A) worthy
(B) worthwhile
(C) worthless
(D) worth

21. According to today's newspaper, the oldest ------- in that competition was 68 years old.
(A) contestability
(B) contest
(C) contestation
(D) contestant

22. The guest house in the seminar house has three rooms, six beds and a ------- kitchen.
(A) common
(B) retrieved
(C) neglected
(D) prohibited

23. In the eastward sky, the group of clouds remained ------- for half an hour.
(A) stationery
(B) station
(C) stationary
(D) stationer

24. The old computer in this room has been ------- for two years, so it will be disposed of at the end of this month.
(A) null
(B) idle
(C) void
(D) invalid

25. This old apartment is now vacant and can be ------- for sale or lease as of next month.
(A) arranged
(B) lined
(C) listed
(D) pretended

26. Would you check with Mr. Yoshida or one of his ------- to see if they have any extra paper for printing flyers?
(A) submissions
(B) subordinates
(C) subjects
(D) subscriptions

27. The supplier packages every item very carefully to ------- nothing is damaged in transit.
(A) assure
(B) ensure
(C) censure
(D) unsure

28. The factory director ------- his assistants to inspect the factory thoroughly because some inspectors were coming the next day.
(A) commenced
(B) commented
(C) commanded
(D) commended

29. It is important to give the person in charge a clear ------- for choosing equipment when you make a presentation at an unfamiliar place.
(A) rationale
(B) fraction
(C) outfit
(D) inception

30. Everyone in our company knows that Ms. Shirakawa is the ------- behind the company's marketing strategy.
(A) masterstroke
(B) mastery
(C) masterpiece
(D) mastermind

Practice Test 實戰試題　　解答與解析

1. The fact that the Canadian real estate sector has grown ------- in the last two decades is amazing.
(A) exemplarily　(B) exponentially
(C) candidly　(D) meticulously

加拿大不動產業界在過去二十年以指數方式成長的這一事實令人驚嘆。

答案 (B)

解析 這句是在形容the Canadian real estate sector has grown -------（加拿大不動產業界已經 ------- 成長）的這件事是amazing（令人驚嘆的），選項中能正確修飾has grown的是（B）exponentially（以指數方式）。其他選項的單字在TOEIC L&R聽讀正式測驗中也是出現機率很高，請大家一併記住它們的形容詞型態（exemplary, candid, meticulous）。（A）exemplarily意為「作為模範地」。（C）candidly意為「率直地」。（D）meticulously意為「極細心注意地、一絲不苟地」。

2. The doctors have warned ------- activities in this weather can cause heat exhaustion or heat stroke in healthy individuals.
(A) strenuous　(B) versatile
(C) feasible　(D) stranded

醫生們已經警告過，在這種天氣下激烈的活動會造成健康的人熱衰竭及熱中暑。

答案 (A)

解析 思考一下究竟in this weather（在這種天氣下）做什麼樣的活動會引起熱衰竭及熱中暑呢？空格若是填入（A）strenuous（激烈的）成為strenuous activities（激烈的活動），則前後語意連貫。（B）versatile意為「多功能的、多才多藝的」，如versatile device（多功能裝置）。（C）feasible意為「可行的」，如feasible design（可行的設計）。（D）stranded意為「觸礁、受困的」，如*be* stranded at the station（被困在車站）。

字彙 □ heat exhaustion 熱衰竭　□ heat stroke 熱中暑

3. Miracle Co., Ltd. has introduced steam mopping as an alternative to ------- customers who are accustomed to the conventional mop and bucket.
(A) lucrative　(B) integral
(C) commensurate　(D) janitorial

奇蹟（Miracle）有限公司已經推出蒸氣拖把，讓習慣用傳統拖把和水桶的門管清潔的客戶們作為另一項選擇。

答案 (D)

解析 從who後面內容可知，customers（客戶們）是使用傳統拖把和水桶的人，因此空格需填入符合該敘述的形容詞。選擇（D）的janitorial（門管清潔的）讓整句語意連貫，請大家也把它的名詞型態janitor（清潔人員）記起來。（A）lucrative意為「賺錢的」。（B）integral意為「不可缺的」。（C）commensurate意為「相稱的、成比例的」。

字彙 □ steam mopping 蒸氣拖把、以蒸氣拖地（的方式）　□ alternative 可替代的東西
□ conventional 傳統的、慣用的

4. The Singapore retail giant might be famous for its cheap designer furniture, but it's almost as well-known as a ------- of pineapple juice.

(A) demeanor (B) drapery
(C) splendor (D) purveyor

這家新加坡大型零售商可能是因其廉價的設計師家具而聞名，但它身為鳳梨汁供應商的身份也幾乎一樣地眾所周知。

答案 (D)

解析 想一下大型零售商經營家具的同時，其身兼果汁的「什麼」是眾所周知的。空格填入（D）purveyor（供應商）後就是「鳳梨汁供應商」，整句語意連貫。（A）demeanor意為「舉止、態度」。（B）drapery意為「帷幔」。（C）splendor意為「光彩、壯麗」。

字彙 □ retail giant 大型零售商 □well-known 眾所周知的

5. We heard there were ------- in the unemployment statistics between the government figures and those of the private agencies.

(A) jargon (B) affiliations
(C) outages (D) discrepancies

我們聽說在失業統計上，政府和私人機構之間的數字有差異。

答案 (D)

解析 從between the government figures and those of the private agencies（政府和私人機構之間的數字）可知，空格應填入兩者之間數字上的「什麼」。將（D）的discrepancy填入後就是指雙方公布的數字有「差異」，語意連貫。（A）jargon意為「專門術語」。（B）affiliation意為「隸屬（關係）、聯繫」。（C）outage意為「中斷、停電」。

6. As the view at night is so amazing, people are eating dinner at a ------- pace.

(A) rapidly (B) leisurely
(C) strategically (D) slowly

由於夜晚的景色令人讚嘆，人們都以悠閒的步調吃著晚餐。

答案 (B)

解析 這題是有難度的。基本上修飾名詞pace（步調）的應該是形容詞，但是選項單字全都以-ly結尾，看似全是副詞，需要小心分辨。正確答案（B）leisurely可作副詞或形容詞使用，意為「悠閒地、悠閒的」。而（A）rapidly（迅速地）、（C）strategically（戰略上）、（D）slowly（慢慢地）都是副詞，不能修飾pace。

7. Reportedly, the U.S. government is going to implement ------- laws to regulate the pharmacy profession.

(A) avid (B) abrupt
(C) stringent (D) exquisite

據說，美國政府將實施嚴格的法律來規範藥劑師業。

答案 (C)

Part 5

解析 思考一下，為了regulate the pharmacy profession（規範藥劑師業）而將要implement（實施～）什麼樣的law（法律）。將（C）stringent（嚴格的）填入空格後，全句語意連貫。其他的選項（A）avid（熱心的）、（B）abrupt（突然的）、（D）exquisite（精湛的、精緻的）都不適合修飾law。這些單字的常見用法如avid reader（熱心的讀者）、abrupt change（突然的改變）、exquisite meal（精緻的佳餚），請一起將它們記起來。

字彙 □ reportedly 據說 □ regulate 規範～ □ pharmacy profession 藥劑師業

8. The managing editor always says the real mission of journalists is to report events ------- as well as to work publicly.

(A) mistakenly (B) provisionally
(C) impartially (D) cursorily

總編輯總是說新聞記者的真正使命是公正地報導事件以及公開地工作。

答案 **(C)**

解析 從says後的內容「新聞記者的真正使命是 ------- 報導事件」可知，空格填入（C）impartially（公正地）最適當，其相關字partially意思為「部分地」，請一併記起來。（A）mistakenly意為「錯誤地」。（B）provisionally意為「暫時地」。（D）cursorily意為「草率地」。

字彙 □ publicly 公開地、公然地

9. The manager opted to ask workers to stay late, questioning the ------- of convincing the board to hire part-timers.

(A) continuity (B) likelihood
(C) approximation (D) admittance

經理選擇要求工人加班，對於說服董事會僱用兼職人員的可能性表示質疑。

答案 **(B)**

解析 這是以現在分詞（-ing）引導的分詞構句，question的主詞是manager（經理）。從逗點前後的關係可知，如果空格填入likelihood（可能性）就是指「對於說服董事會僱用兼職人員的可能性表示質疑」，語意連貫。（C）approximation（接近）的相關字有approximate（大約的）、approximately（大概）。（D）admittance（入場）的相關字有admission（入學許可、入會許可），請都一併記住。（A）continuity意為「連續性」。

字彙 □ opt to *do* 選擇～ □ question 對～表示疑問、質疑 □ convince＋人＋to *do* 說服人做～

10. The Taiwanese government said that it was dedicated to increasing the number of tourist arrivals in the country in this fiscal year by ------- the visa process.

(A) invigorating (B) depleting
(C) expediting (D) demolishing

透過加速簽證的程序，台灣政府表示致力於增加本財政年度抵達該國的觀光客人數。

答案 **(C)**

解析 思考一下要如何發簽證才能增加觀光客人數。如果是by expediting visa process（透過加速簽證的程序）則語意連貫，所以正確答案是（C）。（B）deplete意為「使～衰減、用盡」，常見用法如deplete customer confidence（失去顧客的信心）。（A）invigorate意為「讓～振奮人心」。（D）demolish意為「破壞～」。

11. Throughout her 20-year -------, Katie inspired numerous graduate students to pursue work in the academic areas that fascinated them most.

(A) turnout (B) norm
(C) momentum (D) tenure

在她20年的任職期間之內，凱蒂（Katie）啟發了許多的研究生去追求他們最著迷的學術領域方面的工作。

答案 **(D)**

解析 在20-year這段具體時間後填入（D）tenure（任職期間），即是「20年的任職期間」，語意連貫。（A）turnout意為「（活動的）到場人群、投票人數」，如a large turnout（許多人出席）。（B）norm意為「規範、基準」，如an accepted social norm（被認可的社會規範）（C）momentum意為「氣勢」，如add momentum to～（為～增加氣勢、動力）。

字彙 □ throughout 遍及～、始終 □ inspire 鼓舞～、啟發～ □ numerous 許多的 □ fascinate 著迷～

12. The forecast showed hot weather, but in fact, we actually experienced a severe cold ------- last week.

(A) ventilation (B) gala
(C) proximity (D) spell

預報顯示天氣炎熱，但事實上，我們上週其實經歷了一陣寒流。

答案 **(D)**

解析 請記住（D）的spell在這裡是指「（天氣現象）一段短暫持續的時間」。（A）ventilation意為「通風」。（B）gala意為「慶典、盛會」。（C）proximity意為「鄰近、接近」。

13. It is still ------- at local small shops that customers make their purchases on weekends in this region.

(A) predominantly (B) inadvertently
(C) radically (D) hourly

在這個地區，客人主要仍然在當地小型商店做週末的購買。

答案 **(A)**

解析 這題用強調的句型將still～shops放在前面。空格要填入副詞來修飾後面的形容詞片語 at local small shops（在當地小型商店）。選項中能使語意連貫的副詞是（A）predominantly（主要地）。（B）的inadvertently（不經意地）用於修飾表達「實際動作」的動詞。（C）radically意為「徹底地、激進地」。（D）hourly意為「每小時地」。

14. The tourist center to which we are heading is ------- indicated on the brochures we have so that we can easily find it.

(A) unanimously　(B) enthusiastically

(C) prominently　(D) proficiently

我們要前往的遊客中心被明顯地標示在我們的指南上，以便我們可以很容易地找到它。

答案 (C)

解析 思考一下tourist center（遊客中心）是怎麼被標示在brochures（指南）上。選（C）prominently（明顯地）表示被明顯標示所以容易找得到，語意連貫。（A）unanimously意為「全體一致地」。（B）enthusiastically意為「滿腔熱情地」。（D）proficiently意為「熟練地、精通地」。

15. The weekly magazine that I am reading says stretching before and after exercise can ------- improve your health.

(A) exclusively　(B) concisely

(C) markedly　(D) unfavorably

我正在閱讀的週刊說，在運動前、後做伸展可以明顯地改善你的健康。

答案 (C)

解析 這題要填入副詞來修飾空格後面的動詞improve（改善）。（A）exclusively（獨佔地）、（B）concisely（簡潔地）及（D）unfavorably（不利地），雖然都是副詞卻不適合與improve一起搭配使用。正確答案是（C），markedly improve是「明顯地改善」的意思。

16. My doctor said to me that eating too much salt could ------- to high blood pressure in the near future.

(A) commit　(B) support

(C) devote　(D) contribute

我的醫生跟我說，吃太多的鹽在不久的將來可能會造成高血壓。

答案 (D)

解析 這題如果只記得contribute to～是「有貢獻於～」的正面意思就會很難作答。就像Smoking contributes to the deterioration of health.（抽菸是造成健康惡化的原因之一。）一樣，請記住該片語也有「造成～的原因之一」這種帶負面意思的用法。（A）也有commit *oneself* to～的用法，意為「使自己承諾～、投身於～」。（B）support意為「支持」。（C）devote意為「投入於～、奉獻」。

17. The deadline for the project is next Monday so if you need an ------- you should request permission from your supervisor immediately.

(A) extinction　(B) excursion

(C) expansion　(D) extension

這個計畫案的截止日期是下週一，所以如果你需要延期，你應該立刻請求你主管的許可。

答案 (D)

解析 從「截止日期接近」因此「有 ------- 必要的話應該請求主管許可」來看，空格應填入有「延期」之意的（D）extension。extension在TOEIC L&R聽讀正式測驗中也常取其「電話分機」的意思。（A）extinction意為「熄滅、絕種」。（B）excursion意為「短途旅行」。（C）expansion意為「擴展」。

18. A lot of parents around me ------- their children to daycare centers to have them cared for during the day.

(A) impart (B) entrust
(C) relegate (D) assign

我周圍的很多父母都把孩子託付到日托中心，讓他們在白天得到照顧。

答案 (B)

解析 entrust *A* to *B*是「把A託給B」。請一併記住其他選項與to搭配時用法，（A）是impart *A* to *B*（將A分給B）。（C）是relegate *A* to *B*（把A降級為B）。（D）〈assign＋人＋to do～〉是「指派人去做～」，如The manager assigned me to give a presentation.（經理指派我做簡報。）

字彙 □ care for～ 照顧～

19. A lot of observers participated in the viewing even though the meteor shower was ------- less intense than specialists had anticipated.

(A) predictably (B) preferably
(C) environmentally (D) somewhat

即使流星雨比專家預期的有點不太強烈，很多觀測者還是參與了觀察。

答案 (D)

解析 空格要修飾less intense（不太強烈），同時又要使語意連貫，以（D）副詞somewhat最適合。somewhat less intense是「有點不太強烈」，全句自然又完整地表達出「雖然流星雨沒有比專家預測的強烈，但還是聚集了很多人」。（A）predictably意為「可預見地」。（B）preferably意為「最好是」。（C）environmentally意為「有關環境方面」。

字彙 □ observer 觀測者 □ viewing 觀看、觀測 □ meteor shower 流星雨
□ intense 強烈的、劇烈的

20. The property that got an estimate last week was ------- five times more than its initial price.

(A) worthy (B) worthwhile
(C) worthless (D) worth

上週得到估價的房地產比其原始價格多出五倍的價值。

答案 (D)

解析 worth～times是「有～倍的價值」。（A）worthy（值得的）基本上要放在名詞前面修飾該名詞，如片語*be* worthy of～，意為「值得～」。（B）worthwhile意為「有價值的」，請各位記起來它常用於It is worthwhile to *do* (*do*ing) 的句型。（C）worthless意為「沒有價值的」。

Part 5

21. According to today's newspaper, the oldest ------- in that competition was 68 years old.
(A) contestability (B) contest
(C) contestation (D) contestant

根據今天的報紙，那項競賽最年長的參賽者是68歲。

答案 (D)

解析 從前後關係可判斷，空格要填入表示「人物」的單字。選項中表示人物的只有（D）contestant（參賽者）。同樣表示人物且以-(t)ant結尾的單字還有assistant（助手）、attendant（服務人員）、participant（參與者）等。（A）contestability意為「可競爭性、可被挑戰性」。（B）contest意為「比賽、競爭」。（C）contestation意為「爭論」。

22. The guest house in the seminar house has three rooms, six beds and a ------- kitchen.
(A) common (B) retrieved
(C) neglected (D) prohibited

研討室的招待所有三個房間，六張床和一個共用的廚房。

答案 (A)

解析 這題的空格不但要修飾後面的kitchen（廚房），同時要符合前後關係。common kitchen意為「共用的廚房」。（B）的retrieve大多被用於「檢索～、取回」的意思，如retrieve a document from a disk（從光碟檢索文件檔）。（C）neglect意為「忽視～」。（D）prohibit意為「禁止～」。

23. In the eastward sky, the group of clouds remained ------- for half an hour.
(A) stationery (B) station
(C) stationary (D) stationer

東側的天空中，雲團維持不動有半小時。

答案 (C)

解析 從前後關係可知，應該要選雲團是「不動的」才對。選項中是形容詞的只有（C）stationary，意思是「不動的」，所以是正確答案。除了eastward（東側、向東的），請大家也一起把跟方向有關的字如westward（向西的）、northward（向北的），以及southward（向南的）記起來。（A）stationery意為「文具、事務用品」。（B）station意為「車站」。（D）stationer意為「文具店（的老闆）」。

24. The old computer in this room has been ------- for two years, so it will be disposed of at the end of this month.
(A) null (B) idle
(C) void (D) invalid

這個房間的舊電腦已經閒置兩年，因此要在這個月底被處理掉。

答案 (B)

解析 空格是形容The old computer的狀態，應填入一形容詞以符合「這個月底將處理掉該電腦」的前後關係。正確答案是（B）idle（停頓的、閒置的）。（A）null、（C）void、（D）invalid都是「無效的」，請一併記住null and void也是在表達「（法律上）無效的」的意思。

字彙 □ dispose of～ 處理掉～

25. This old apartment is now vacant and can be ------- for sale or lease as of next month.

(A) arranged (B) lined
(C) listed (D) pretended

這棟舊公寓現在是空著的，可以在下個月時列入銷售或出租。

答案 (C)

解析 *be* listed for sale意為「列入銷售」。list是「將～列於表上、列入」，〈arrange for＋人＋to *do*〉是「為人安排～」，這些都一併記起來。（A）arrange意為「安排～」。（B）line意為「排隊、沿～排列」。（D）pretend意為「假裝～」。

字彙 □ vacant 空著的 □ as of～ 自～起、在～時候

26. Would you check with Mr. Yoshida or one of his ------- to see if they have any extra paper for printing flyers?

(A) submissions (B) subordinates
(C) subjects (D) subscriptions

你能詢問吉田（Yoshida）先生或是他的任何一位部屬看看他們是否有多的紙張能用於印刷傳單嗎？

答案 (B)

解析 空格中應填入表示「人物」的單字，並以（B）的subordinate（部屬）最適當。TOEIC L&R聽讀正式測驗常出現以sub-為開頭的單字，如subsidiary（子公司）及subsidy（津貼）等。（A）submission意為「服從、提交」。（C）subject意為「主題、題材、實驗對象」。（D）subscription意為「訂購」。

字彙 □ check with～ 與～核對、詢問 □ extra 多餘的、額外的 □ flyer （廣告）傳單

27. The supplier packages every item very carefully to ------- nothing is damaged in transit.

(A) assure (B) ensure
(C) censure (D) unsure

供應商非常小心地包裝每件物品，為了確保在運送中沒有任何損壞。

答案 (B)

解析 仔細地包裝商品，由此可判斷這是為了「確保」在運送中不會損壞商品。雖然選項（A）assure和（B）ensure都含有「保證、確保～」之意，不過由於空格後面是子句，所以可直接接子句的ensure才是正確答案。請記住assure若接子句的話，要用〈assure＋人＋that...〉，意為「向人保證……」。（C）censure意為「譴責～」。（D）unsure意為「不確定的」。

字彙 □ in transit 在運送中、過境的、通行中

28. The factory director ------- his assistants to inspect the factory thoroughly because some inspectors were coming the next day.

(A) commenced (B) commented

(C) commanded (D) commended

廠長命令他的助手徹底檢查工廠，因為隔天有些督察員要來。

答案 (C)

解析 空格後面是his assistants to inspect，也就是〈人＋to *do*〉，所以要填入符合這種用法的動詞。（C）〈command＋人＋to *do*〉是「命令人做～」的意思，因此是正確答案。（D）的用法是〈commend＋人＋for (on, upon)～〉，意為「稱讚人的～」。（A）commence意為「開始～」。（B）comment意為「評論」。

字彙 □ thoroughly 完全地、徹底地

29. It is important to give the person in charge a clear ------- for choosing equipment when you make a presentation at an unfamiliar place.

(A) rationale (B) fraction

(C) outfit (D) inception

當你要在不熟悉的地方做簡報時，給負責人員一個明確的依據去選擇設備是很重要的。

答案 (A)

解析 （A）的rationale意為「原理（因）、依據」，填入空格後是「給負責人員明確的依據」的意思，語意連貫。（C）的outfit意為「一整套服裝、用具（裝備）」，當動詞時的用法是outfit *A* with *B*（為A配備B）。而（D）的inception意為「開始、開端」，如since its inception in 2013（自2013年創立以來），請一併記起來。（B）fraction意為「碎片、一小部分」。

30. Everyone in our company knows that Ms. Shirakawa is the ------- behind the company's marketing strategy.

(A) masterstroke (B) mastery

(C) masterpiece (D) mastermind

我們公司的每個人都知道白川（Shirakawa）女士是公司行銷策略的幕後策畫者。

答案 (D)

解析 選項都是含有master字首的名詞。從前後關係可知空格應填入表示「人物」的單字，其中只有（D）mastermind（策畫者、指導者）符合該條件。（A）masterstroke意為「絕妙的高招」，如 Her idea was a masterstroke.（她的點子是個絕妙的高招。）。（B）mastery意為「熟練、精通」，如mastery on a skill（技巧的熟練），請都記起來吧！（C）masterpiece意為「名作、傑作」。

Part

6

段落填空

Part 6

段落填空

贏得 990 分的解題技巧及攻略法

Part 6不需要特別的技巧和解題方法，但需要耐力與細心。不僅空格前後，還要從頭到尾閱讀整篇英文，完全理解內容後才能作答。遇到空格時，你可以從**前後句關係**、**文法**、**詞彙**等三個角度來選擇正確的答案。但是，要注意正確答案的出處不一定接近空格，因此各位要時時留意會出現**拖延出處（Delayed Clue）**的題型。另外，面對插入句題型，在作答時還要注意代名詞及（連接）副詞等「**連結空格與前後內容的關鍵字**」，做再次確認喔！相關細節請詳以下例題的解說。

贏得 990 分的解題技巧

① 不僅空格前後，還要從頭到尾閱讀整篇英文

② 時時留意會出現拖延出處（Delayed Clue）的題型

③ 插入句的題型要注意「連結空格與前後內容的關鍵字」

先試著寫以下例題。

例題 **Questions 131-134** refer to the following notice.

> As you know, -------(131.) are scheduled to begin on May 1 and end by May 15. -------(132.) the reduction in the number of usable meeting rooms, our company has created a Web page for reserving meeting rooms. Only a few of our rooms will be accessible during this period at any given time, so please use the reservation page to check for availability and to book a room. -------(133.). Employees will promptly receive a confirmation e-mail for any of these types of requests made. We are aware that both refurbishment of the existing meeting rooms and two weeks without easy access to them can hamper progress on projects. Therefore, we remind you that meeting rooms can be reserved outside of -------(134.) work hours for project teams who arrive at the office early or stay late.

131. (A) interviews
(B) renovations
(C) leadership programs
(D) orientation sessions

132. (A) Now that
(B) Due to
(C) Even if
(D) As though

133. (A) We will discuss the situation and make our decision soon.
(B) Only managers are allowed to make reservations.
(C) Room cancellations can be put in there as well.
(D) Meetings should consist of three or more employees.

134. (A) typical
(B) expected
(C) natural
(D) average

131. Ⓐ Ⓑ Ⓒ Ⓓ
132. Ⓐ Ⓑ Ⓒ Ⓓ
133. Ⓐ Ⓑ Ⓒ Ⓓ
134. Ⓐ Ⓑ Ⓒ Ⓓ

HUMMER式密技！

關於Part 6，建議將整篇英文（含空格在內）先讀過一遍，再來思考空格該填入哪一個選項。讀的同時也請留意拖延出處的試題，其正確解答的出處離空格有段距離。

我將試題的閱讀順序用紅色編號標示如下，並於右側頁面依每個步驟做解說。希望各位從❶看到→❷，再從❷看到→❸，❸看到→❹等依序進行閱讀。

例題

❶❼ As you know, -------(131.) are scheduled to begin on May 1 and end by May 15. →❷→❽❸ -------(132.) the reduction in the number of usable meeting rooms, our company has created a Web page for reserving meeting rooms. →❹❺ Only a few of our rooms will be accessible during this period at any given time, so please use the reservation page to check for availability and to book a room. -------(133.). Employees will promptly receive a confirmation e-mail for any of these types of requests made. We are aware that both refurbishment of the existing meeting rooms and two weeks without easy access to them can hamper progress on projects. →❻❾ Therefore, we remind you that meeting rooms can be reserved outside of -------(134.) work hours for project teams who arrive at the office early or stay late. →❿

如各位所知，翻修工程預定在5月1日開始，並於5月15日結束。由於可用會議室數量的減少，我們公司已經設立了一個預約會議室的網頁。在這段期間內，我們只有幾間會議室隨時可供使用，因此請使用預約網頁查詢可使用的間數及預約會議室。取消（已預約的）會議室也可以在那裡登記。員工將立即收到任何這類請求的確認電子郵件。我們知道，現有會議室的翻新作業和為期兩週的會議室取得不便都會阻礙專案的進展。因此，我們提醒各位，對於提早到辦公室或加班的專案團隊，可以在標準的工作時間之外預約會議室。

131. (A) ❷❽interviews
(B) renovations
(C) leadership programs
(D) orientation sessions→❸→❾

132. (A) ❹Now that
(B) Due to
(C) Even if
(D) As though→❺

133. (A) ⑥We will discuss the situation and make our decision soon.
(B) Only managers are allowed to make reservations.
(C) Room cancellations can be put in there as well.
(D) Meetings should consist of three or more employees.→⑦

134. (A) ⑩typical
(B) expected
(C) natural
(D) average

答案 **131.** (B) **132.** (B) **133.** (C) **134.** (A)

字彙 □ usable 可用的 □ at any given time 在任何時候、隨時 □ hamper 阻礙～

從❶開始閱讀第一句就出現空格「------- 預定在5月1日開始，並於5月15日結束」。讀完這句後，看❷的選項內容，將四個答案選項記在腦中，再回到❸繼續閱讀。

132.空格後面有the reduction（減少）。將這一句完整讀完後，再看❹的選項內容可得知除了（B）的Due to（由於～）之外都是從屬連接詞。因為從屬連接詞後面要接含有主詞和動詞的子句，因此這時候可確認正確答案是（B）。其餘選項分別是（A）的now that（既然～），（B）的even if（即使～），（C）的as though（好像～），都是TOEIC L&R聽讀正式測驗常出現的連接詞。

另外，從the deduction in the number of usable meeting rooms（可用會議室數量的減少）可推測**131.**應填入（B），不過為了再三確認，現在先繼續往下閱讀。

❺的**133.**是插入句問題。要從前後句的關係來判斷正確答案。空格前面是說「在這段期間內，我們只有幾間會議室隨時可供使用，因此請使用預約網頁查詢可使用的間數及預約會議室。」，空格後面則是說「員工將立即收到任何這類請求的確認電子郵件」。也就是說，空格前後是「有關預約網頁的說明」。跟預約相關的選項是（B）和（C），而（B）提到的only manager（只有經理）和前後內容不連貫，所以正確答案是（C）。as well意為「也、同樣地」，因此這句話表達出不僅可以「預約會議室」，而且「也可以取消預約」，前後語意連貫。面對這類插入句的問題作答秘訣就是，對於選項內各句的「關係副詞」、「連接詞」、「連接副詞」、「代名詞」、「轉換說法」、「選項內容和空格前後所指的事物是否一樣」等等要有自覺。要時時注意，這些「空格前後的內容以及連鎖關係（連貫性）」有沒有出現在選項裡，謹慎作答。

接著繼續閱讀**133.**後面的句子，就會出現**131.**的正確答案出處，因此從→❼回到❼。這時就可了解這篇是在敘述refurbishment of the existing meeting rooms（現行會議室的翻新作業）。而**131.**的（B）只是將refurbishment（翻新）換成renovation（翻修）的說法，所以是正確答案。選出正確答案後，再從→❾往❾繼續閱讀。

❾從Therefore（因此）開始，表示前句是「因」，接下來將說明「結果」，而該結果就是「對於提早到辦公室或加班的專案團隊，可以在「------- 工作時間之外預約會議室」，所以能讓整句語意連貫的是（A）typical（標準的）。typical work hours是「標準的工作時間」，也就是「標準的工作時間」。

贏得990分之路

Part 6濃縮了Part 5和Part 7答題技巧。題型分為兩種，一種是只憑著包含空格的英文句子就能作答的「獨立型」，另一種是在測驗是否完全理解空格前後的敘述過程的「前後句關係型」。「獨立型」可以用像Part 5一樣的方式解題。而「前後句關係型」以字彙及時態等問題居多。「拖延出處（**Delayed Clue**）」的題型則可以說是迎戰Part 7多篇閱讀的基礎。

Part 6沒有基礎練習，而是在每篇實戰試題中都特別加入了拖延出處的題型。希望各位不要只做選擇性瀏覽，要從頭讀全部的英文內容做「紮實的閱讀」，進而以全部完勝為目標。

總結

閱讀Part 6的試題文章時，要留意會有拖延出處的題型。基本上要將英文全文做「紮實的閱讀」，而且別忘了要從「前後句關係、文法、詞彙」等三個角度來解題。
對於插入句題型，前後句關係是選擇正確答案的決定性因素，但還是要用「選項和前後句中的連結關鍵字」來再三確認。

Practice Test 實戰試題

請從（A）、（B）、（C）、（D）四個選項中，選出最適合填入空格的正確答案（答案卡在全書最後）。

Questions 1-4 refer to the following advertisement.

Beginner Public Speaking

Learn how to speak in public like a pro! During this continuing education course, discover presentation strategies used by the most brilliant public speakers in the world today. -------- (1.) Dick Branum will reveal his research analyzing more than 500 public speeches and the common features that make them so powerful. -------- (2.), he'll teach you how to embed stories effectively into your speeches and how to connect with your audience and make a lasting impression on them. This course is directed at people with no experience at all who want to develop public speaking -------- (3.) or just learn how to sell themselves better!

The course will run from March 6 until April 10 in Room 8 of Valley Creek College's Hinkley Building. Register online at www.valleycreekeducation.com/register. -------- (4.). We accept credit cards, cash, or checks.

1. (A) Instructor
(B) Instructing
(C) Instruct
(D) To instruct

2. (A) For this reason
(B) Ever since
(C) In a word
(D) Furthermore

3. (A) news
(B) skills
(C) origins
(D) values

4. (A) Please bring these books to your first class.
(B) Mr. Branum will answer questions after each class.
(C) Payment is required in advance for this course.
(D) Videos of speeches will be shown during the course.

試題 1-4 請參考以下廣告。

初學者的公開演說課程
學習如何像專業人士一樣在公開場合談話！在這個成人進修教育課程中，您可以學到當今世界上最出色的公眾演說者使用的演講策略。講師迪克．布朗姆（Dick Branum）將公開他對超過500場公開演講的分析研究以及使它們具如此強大影響力的共同特點。而且，他將教您如何有效地將故事嵌入您的演講中，以及如何與聽眾產生連結並讓他們留下持久的印象。這門課程是針對想要提高公開演說技巧卻完全沒有經驗的人，或者只是學習如何更好地推銷自己！
該課程將於3月6日到4月10日在谷溪學院（Valley Creek College）的辛克利大廈（Hinkley Building）8號廳舉行。請於www.valleycreekeducation.com/register上網註冊。本課程需要預先付款。我們接受信用卡、現金或支票。

字彙 □ continuing 繼續的、進修 □ discover 發現～、（首次）了解 □ brilliant 出色的
□ embed 嵌入～ □ lasting 持久的

1.

答案 (A)

解析 空格後面有人名 Dick Branum，該人物的動作是will reveal his research（將公開他的研究）。如果是Instructor Dick Branum就是「講師Dick Branum」的意思，前後句可以連貫。在文法上雖然空格可填入Instructing及To instruct，不過會變成是「指導Dick Branum一事」之意，無法當will reveal的主詞，語意不連貫。這題要採〈名詞＋名詞〉，也就是「用前面的名詞修飾後面名詞」的結構。

2.

答案 (D)

解析 選項都是副詞（片語）。空格前面的內容是「課程的特色之一」，後面的內容是「課程的特色之二」，可見空格即是追加內容時的連結語，所以正確答案是（D）的Furthermore（而且）。（A）For this reason意為「因為這個原因」。（B）Ever since意為「從那時以來」。（C）In a word意為「總之」。

3.

答案 (B)

解析 到目前為止的內容可知，這套課程是以「想要學好演說的人」為對象。因此，正確答案是（B）的skills（技巧）。develop public speaking skills是「提高公開演說技巧」之意。

4.

答案 (C)

解析 空格前面描述了課程的日期及註冊方法（用網路方式）等。後面則是提到「接受信用卡、現金或支票」。因此選項中能符合前後語意的內容是（C），意思是「課程需要預先付款」，後面再接著敘述具體的支付方式，這是最自然的表達順序。（A）所提到的these books（這些書）在全篇中未提到，（B）和（D）都是與「課程的註冊方法」及「相關付款事宜」無關的內容。

Questions 5-8 refer to the following e-mail.

To: Anita Patel <apatel@hmail.com>
From: Alan Jefferies <info@mail.hedwigcommunity.com>
Date: September 18
Subject: New Statement

Dear Valued Client,

Your -------(5.) statement for your Hedwig Community Bank account ending in 5469 is now available online. To view this statement, covering the period from January 1 to June 30, please log in to your account and go to My Account > History > Statements. -------(6.).

If you have any questions, you have a couple of -------(7.). You can log in to your account and go to the Message Center to write us. -------(8.), you can call Client Services at 888-392-0853. Experienced agents are available seven days a week, 24 hours a day.

Sincerely,

Alan Jefferies
President, Retail Distribution
Hedwig Community Bank

5. (A) weekly
(B) monthly
(C) semi-annual
(D) annual

6. (A) Enroll now to receive paperless statements.
(B) You can see all previous statements on this page as well.
(C) We will upload your most recent statement next Friday.
(D) A representative will look into the mistake on your statement.

7. (A) locations
(B) representatives
(C) weeks
(D) options

8. (A) Primarily
(B) Additionally
(C) Unfortunately
(D) Occasionally

試題 5-8 請參考以下電子郵件。

收信者：阿妮塔．派特爾<apatel@hmail.com>
發信者：亞蘭沃．傑佛瑞<info@mail.hedwigcommunity.com>
日期：9月18日
主旨：最新對帳單

尊敬的客戶：

您的赫丁社區銀行（Hedwing Community Bank）帳戶尾數5469，半年度對帳單現在可在網上查詢。若要查看這份涵蓋1月1日至6月30日期間的對帳單，請上網登入到我的帳戶＞歷史紀錄＞對帳單。您也可以在此頁面查看之前的所有對帳單。

如果您有任何疑問，您有兩種選擇。您可以登入帳戶並進到留言中心寫信給我們。此外，您也可以撥打888-392-0853致電客戶服務部。經驗豐富的專員每週七天，每天24小時提供服務。

謹致問候

亞蘭．傑佛瑞
部長，零售金融業務部
赫丁社區銀行

字彙 □ experienced 有經驗的 □ agent 代理人

5.

答案 (C)

解析 空格後面的statement（對帳單）上所記載的內容是covering the period from January 1 to June 30，也就是半年份的帳款明細，所以正確答案是意為「半年一次」的（C）semi-annual。semi-annual也可換成biannual（每半年的）說法，請當作同義詞記起來。

6.

答案 (B)

解析 空格前面的內容描述了「上網查看銀行帳戶對帳單的步驟」。因為已知可以看到截至6月的明細，所以（A）和（C）都不正確，而（D）是描述有關「銀行對明細有誤的應對做法」，也不適用於此。所以正確答案是（B）。除了前後句關係要符合之外，選項（B）中提到的on this page及as well才是確認為正確答案的關鍵。遇到插入句題型時，要多注意代名詞和副詞片語來幫助作答。

7.

答案 (D)

解析 空格這句內容是「若有任何疑問，您有兩種 -------」。後面提到的You can log in to your account and go to the Message Center to write us.（您可以登入帳戶並進到留言中心寫信給我們。）即是指「對帳單若有問題時的第一種方法」，接著在8.的空格後面又敘述了you can call Client Services（您也可以致電客戶服務部），也就是第二種方法。因為有這兩種方法可以「選擇」，所以正確答案是（D）的options（選擇）。

8.

答案 (B)

解析 這與7.的正確答案出處重複。因為空格位置連接了「對帳單若有問題時的第一種方法」和「第二種方法」，所以正確答案是（B）的Additionally（此外）。（A）Primarily意為「主要地」。（C）Unfortunately意為「遺憾地」。（D）Occasionally意為「偶而」。

Questions 9-12 refer to the following want ad.

NOW HIRING

-------. (9.) In this role, you will be responsible for supporting the store manager in sales and operational management. This includes helping to achieve sales targets, assist customers, and improve visual merchandising.

You must have a passion for retail, customer service, and stock management. Additionally, a proven sales record and experience in a fashion retail environment is -------(10.). The ability to manage a small team is a plus.

The successful candidate will receive excellent remuneration. As an added bonus, by joining our team, the successful candidate will have the opportunity to attend -------(11.) training programs in order to increase skills. These free programs can help -------(12.) who participate to advance rapidly.

Please send your job application to nona@dierbergmenswear.com and include references so we can verify your sales record and experience.

9. (A) Dierberg Menswear will open a new store in Janville this month.
(B) Dierberg Menswear is happy to announce a newly hired manager.
(C) Dierberg Menswear thanks all recent job applicants for their interest.
(D) Dierberg Menswear is looking for a retail assistant to join our team.

10. (A) unnecessary
(B) practical
(C) required
(D) negotiable

11. (A) company-funded
(B) well-mannered
(C) government-issued
(D) fund-raising

12. (A) those
(B) they
(C) them
(D) their

試題 9-12 請參考以下徵人廣告。

招募中

戴爾伯格男裝（**Dierberg Menswear**）正在尋找零售助理加入我們的團隊。在這個職位，您將負責在銷售和營運管理方面支援店經理。包括實現銷售目標、協助客戶和改善店面展示行銷等。

您必須對零售、客戶服務和庫存管理有熱情。此外，需要（提供）經證實過的銷售（成果）紀錄和時裝零售業的工作經驗。有管理小團隊能力者優先。

成功錄取的應徵者將收到優厚的報酬。作為額外的獎勵是，加入我們的團隊後，成功錄取的應徵者將獲得參加公司出資的培訓課程的機會來增加技能。這些免費課程可以幫助那些參加者快速進步。

請將您的工作申請表寄至nona@dierbergmenswear.com並附上推薦信，以便我們可以查證您的銷售（成果）紀錄及工作經驗。

字彙 □ now hiring 招募中 □ role 職務 □ operational management 營運管理
□ visual merchandising 透過店面展示（含商品陳設、店鋪裝潢等）的商品行銷手法

9.

答案 **(D)**

解析 因為標題是NOW HIRING（招募中），空格後面是In this role（在這個職位），所以正確答案當然是要描述「招募的職務」。再看空格後的職務敘述you will be responsible for supporting the store manager in sales and operational management（您將負責在銷售和營運管理方面支援店經理），可知招募中的職務是retail assistant（零售助理）。因此，正確答案是（D）。

10.

答案 **(C)**

解析 從You must have開始的第二段，說明了「應徵者必備的資格、經驗等」。空格的這句話是從Additionally（此外）開始，可判斷a proven sales record and experience in a fashion retail environment（經證實過的銷售（成果）紀錄和時裝零售業的工作經驗）也是應徵者的「必備條件」。因此，（C）以被動語態is required來表達該條件「被需要」，是正確答案。（A）unnecessary意為「不必要的」。（B）practical意為「實際的」。（D）negotiable意為「可協商的」。

11.

答案 **(A)**

解析 從下一句提到的These free programs（這些免費課程）可知，------- training program是「免費的」。換個說法的選項（A）company-funded（公司出資的）是正確答案。（B）well-mannered意為「有禮貌的」。（C）government-issued意為「政府發行的」。（D）fund-raising意為「集資的」。

12.

答案 **(A)**

解析 空格是help（幫助）的受詞，並用後面的who participate（參與的人）來限定說明對象。those who是指「那些～的人們」，語意也能連貫，所以正確答案是（A）。

Questions 13-16 refer to the following information.

RETURN POLICY

Items purchased through Gilliers.com must be returned with a receipt. If you do not have -------(13.), print a Simple Returns Receipt at www.Gilliers.com/SimpleReturns/myaccount. With your Simple Returns Receipt, you can then return the items to a store or by mail.

-------(14.). We recommend that you keep these materials just in case you decide to make a request for a refund.

A full refund -------(15.) to the card used during the original transaction, for returns made within 90 days of the purchase date. -------(16.), we can only give customers Gillier's store credit when returning items after 90 days. Store credit can be used online or in-store.

13. (A) one
(B) them
(C) some
(D) each

14. (A) Items that are damaged must be sent directly to the manufacturer.
(B) You must return items in their original manufacturer's packaging.
(C) Please call Customer Service about shipping costs on returns.
(D) All items can be returned regardless of the department they came from.

15. (A) credit
(B) is crediting
(C) has been credited
(D) will be credited

16. (A) Thus
(B) Likewise
(C) Instead
(D) However

試題 13-16 請參考以下資訊。

退貨條件

透過吉利爾斯網站（Gilliers.com）購買的商品必須與收據一併退回。如果您沒有它，請在www.Gilliers.com/SimpleReturns/myaccount網站上印出簡易退貨收據。有了您的簡易退貨收據，您就可以將商品退回商店或用郵件退回。

您必須以原製造商包裝退回商品。我們建議您保留這些包材，以防您決定要求退款。

如果在購買之日起90天內退貨，全額退款將被存入原始交易時所使用的卡片內。然而，若在超過90天後退回商品，我們只能提供給客戶吉利爾斯的商店抵用金。商店抵用金可在網站或店內使用。

13.

答案　(A)

解析　選項都是代名詞，想想看空格是在指什麼。這句意思是「如果沒有空格內的單字，請print a Simple Returns Receipt（印出簡易退貨收據）」，所以空格要填入表示前句中a receipt（收據）的代名詞。因此，這裡的空格要填入可數名詞的單數代名詞one。

14.

答案　(B)

解析　空格後面提到We recommend that you keep these materials just in case you decide to make a request for a refund.（我們建議您保留這些包材，以防您決定要求退款。）。可見第二段是在做「要求退款」時的說明，所以正確答案是（B）。該句中所說的these materials，即是（B）中提及的their original manufacturer's packaging（原製造商包裝）。其他選項都沒有關於these materials的敘述。

15.

答案　(D)

解析　選項都是動詞credit（將信用額度轉入～）的變化形。主詞是A full refund（全額退款），如果後面接「將被存入帳戶」的未來式被動語態則語意連貫，因此正確答案是（D）。請各位將be credited to（被存入～）記起來。

16.

答案　(D)

解析　選項都是連接副詞，所以要選擇能讓前後句關係連貫的答案。空格前面說的是「購買之日起90天內退回，全額退款」，空格後面則是說「超過90天後退回商品者，提供（等價的）商店抵用金」。因此，用來連貫兩組對照內容的連接副詞However（然而）才是正確答案。（A）Thus意為「因此」。（B）Likewise意為「同樣地」。（C）Instead意為「作為替代地」。

認真持續挑戰，肯定得到佳績。

破解「插入句題型」與「句子歸置題型」

用「前後句關係」來作答，用「連貫性」來確認

在此，我將Part 6每個題組各有一題的「插入句題型」與Part 7的「句子歸置題型」的解題方法進行歸納總結。「從前後句關係進行判斷」來作答是最基本的，但是同時，也要好好確認，那些（填入正確答案後的）空格和前後文，是不是有「連貫性」。而這裡所說的「連貫性」是指常在「插入句」中出現的以下單字及片語。

・代名詞（代指前句中提到的事物或替換說法）
・連接詞
・副詞（特別是連接副詞）
　因果關係：therefore（因此）／thus（如此）／accordingly（於是）／consequently（結果）／in consequence（結果）／as a result（結果）／hence（因此）等
　轉　折：however（然而）／nevertheless（儘管如此）／nonetheless（雖然如此）／still（然而）／all the same（仍然）／even so（即使如此）等
　對　比：on the other hand（在另一方面）／meanwhile（同時）／in contrast（相比之下）等
・呼　應（與插入句放置位子前後所表達的內容互相呼應）
・並　列（於插入句放置位子前後，有數個同類的敘述或舉例）

不論是Part 6選「句子」或Part 7選「位置」，用上述的「連貫性」來協助作答都非常有用。原因就是，所謂的「前後句關係」，其實正是運用上述的「連貫性」加以延伸變化而已。

Part

7

文章理解

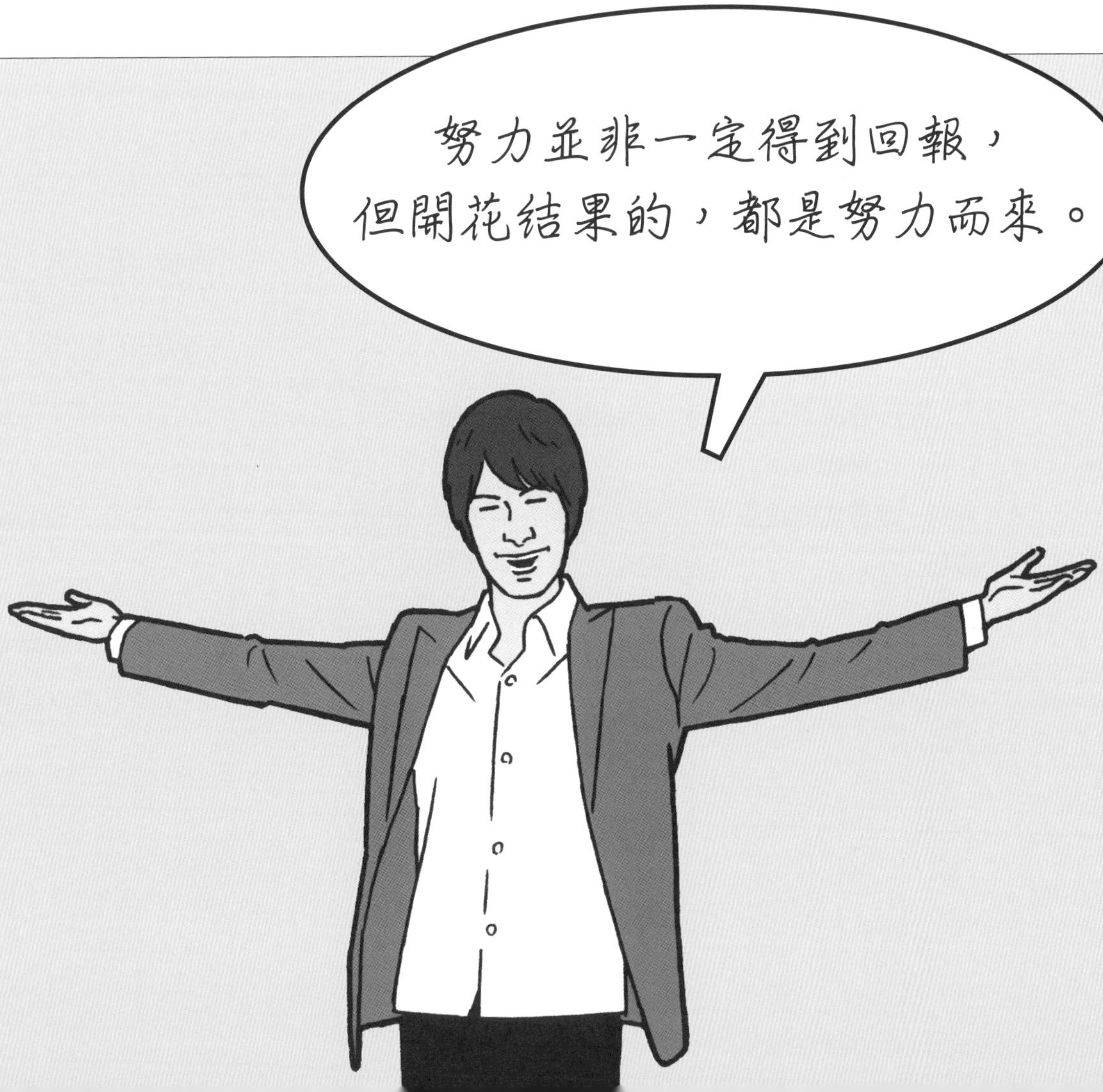
努力並非一定得到回報，
但開花結果的，都是努力而來。

Part 7

文章理解

贏得990分的解題技巧及攻略法

Part 7 需要用正確又快速地閱讀方式來解題。為此，本書特別設計出一套「解題的正確思路（找出正確答案的方式）」，將解題過程自動化並達到有效閱讀，讓考生得以提高解題的準確度和速度。此外，平時自我訓練時，切忌速讀！若能用精讀的方式閱讀全文，且能明確指出正確答案的出處，相信終可達到「正確又快速地閱讀」。希望各位從這一章節中好好地體會。

贏得990分的解題技巧

1 建立「解題的正確思路（找出正確答案的方式）」

2 訓練自己提出正確答案的出處

以下就是Part 7的「解題的正確思路（找出正確答案的方式）」。請先理解這些步驟，再試著寫例題。

（1）先看第一題的題目問什麼，記起來（先不讀選項）。
（2）從頭開始精讀試題文章。
（3）讀到一個適當的段落後（或是找不到正確答案的出處時）就先暫停，往第一題的選項看。
（4）將試題文章內正確答案的出處和選項比對，再將答案畫記在答案卡上。
（5）接著看第二題的題目，從剛才暫停的段落開始，再繼續閱讀試題文章。
（重複這樣的步驟至答完該題組，全部答完後再進入下一篇題組。）

例題　**Questions 147-149** refer to the following article.

Bexi.com to Open New Warehouse

Bexi.com, the world's third largest online retailer, has announced the opening of a new warehouse in Berlin, Germany, in May. Bexi.com currently has forty warehouses strategically placed around the world to fulfill orders from its customers. Last year, Bexi.com sold around 15 million items a day over the holiday season and this winter they expect the figure to rise to 20 million per day.

The new warehouse will be built on the site of an old brewery and will be Bexi.com's biggest shipping center in Europe. Nelly Wilde, who works at Bexi.com's headquarters in Phoenix, says that many people are astonished when they hear that there are no robots within Bexi.com's immense warehouses. Instead, hundreds of workers use bar codes to find and ship the ordered items. According to Wilde, this is more economical than implementing and using automated systems. Reportedly, Bexi.com will need an additional 200 workers to staff its latest warehouse.

147. What is indicated about Bexi.com?
(A) It made 15 million dollars last year.
(B) It runs an Internet shopping business.
(C) It has forty storage buildings in the U.S.
(D) Its head office is located in Berlin.

147. Ⓐ Ⓑ Ⓒ Ⓓ

148. According to Nelly Wilde, what are people surprised by?
(A) The low prices they can find on Bexi.com
(B) The complex machines used at Bexi.com's shipping centers
(C) The lack of robots in Bexi.com's warehouses
(D) The number of items sold by Bexi.com per day

148. Ⓐ Ⓑ Ⓒ Ⓓ

149. What is suggested about the Berlin warehouse?
(A) It will be built next to a brewery.
(B) It will be the largest in the world.
(C) It will create a lot of jobs.
(D) It is the only shipping center in Europe.

149. Ⓐ Ⓑ Ⓒ Ⓓ

HUMMER式密技！

例題

❷ *Bexi.com to Open New Warehouse*

貝西網購（Bexi.com）將啟用新的倉庫

Q147 Bexi.com, the world's third largest online retailer, has announced the opening of a new warehouse in Berlin, Germany, in May. Bexi.com currently has forty warehouses strategically placed around the world to fulfill orders from its customers. Last year, Bexi.com sold around 15 million items a day over the holiday season and this winter they expect the figure to rise to 20 million per day. → ❸

❺ The new warehouse will be built on the site of an old brewery and will be Bexi.com's biggest shipping center in Europe. Nelly Wilde, who works at Bexi.com's headquarters in Phoenix, says that Q148 many people are astonished when they hear that there are no robots within Bexi.com's immense warehouses. → ❻ ❽ Instead, hundreds of workers use bar codes to find and ship the ordered items. According to Wilde, this is more economical than implementing and using automated systems. Reportedly, Q149 Bexi.com will need an additional 200 workers to staff its latest warehouse. → ❾

貝西網購，全球第三大網路零售商，已宣布五月在德國柏林（Berlin）要啟用一間新的倉庫。貝西網購目前在全球已戰略性設點40間倉庫來滿足客戶的訂單。去年，貝西網購在節日期間每日售出約1500萬件物品，且今年冬天他們預計這數字將提高到每天2000萬件。

這間新的倉庫將被建在舊啤酒廠舊址上，並將成為貝西網購在歐洲最大的送貨中心。妮莉．王爾德（Nelly Wilde）在貝西網購於鳳凰城（Phoenix）的總部工作，她表示很多人聽說貝西網購龐大的倉庫裡沒有機器人時都很訝異。反而，數百名員工使用條碼來查找和運送訂購的商品。根據王爾德的說法，這比裝備和使用自動化系統更符合經濟效益。據說，貝西網購將需要配置額外200名員工到最新的倉庫。

147. ❶ What is indicated about Bexi.com? → ❷
(A) ❸ It made 15 million dollars last year.
(B) It runs an Internet shopping business. → ❹
(C) It has forty storage buildings in the U.S.
(D) Its head office is located in Berlin.

關於貝西網購，下列敘述何者正確？
（A）它去年賺了1500萬。
（B）它經營線上購物生意。
（C）它在美國有40家倉庫。
（D）它的總公司位於柏林。

148. ❹ According to Nelly Wilde, what are people surprised by? → ❺
(A) ❻ The low prices they can find on Bexi.com
(B) The complex machines used at Bexi.com's shipping centers
(C) The lack of robots in Bexi.com's warehouses → ❼
(D) The number of items sold by Bexi.com per day

根據妮莉．王爾德的說法，人們對什麼感到驚訝？
（A）他們在貝西網購可以找到的低價。
（B）貝西網購的運輸中心使用的複雜機器。
（C）貝西網購的倉庫沒有機器人。
（D）貝西網購每日的銷售量。

149. ❼ What is suggested about the Berlin warehouse? → ❽
(A) ❾ It will be built next to a brewery.
(B) It will be the largest in the world.
(C) It will create a lot of jobs. → 正確答案，結束這篇題組的作答
(D) It is the only shipping center in Europe.

關於柏林倉庫，下列推論何者正確？
（A）它將蓋在啤酒廠旁邊。
（B）它將是世界上最大的。
（C）它將創造很多的就業機會。
（D）它是歐洲唯一的送貨中心。

答案 **147. (B) 148. (C) 149. (C)**

字彙 □ brewery 啤酒廠、釀造廠 □ immense 龐大的、巨大的 □ storage building 倉儲建築

和Part 6相同，將試題的閱讀順序用紅色編號標示。從❶看到→❷，再從❷看到→❸等依序進行。

❶ 先看第一題的題目問什麼，記起來。不看選項，接著閱讀試題文章。

★最好將題目問什麼換成簡單的語句記起來。以例題來說，雖然**147.**中是用indicate（指示），那我們就換成「什麼與貝西網購有關」。

❷ 從頭開始精讀試題文章。出現像**147.**的indicate、suggest（暗示）、infer（推論）等提問的關鍵字時先不看選項，馬上開始閱讀試題文章至適當的段落後，再與選項比對。若是有分段的試題文章，可以每一道試題讀一個段落；如果文章本身沒分段而有三道試題的話，就先閱讀三分之一的文章內容。

★藉由精讀，就不會猜想「沒有讀到的地方或許有答案出處」而感到不安，因此可以穩定地繼續作答。

★如果採取的方法，是把試題文章讀到最後再作答，不但容易忘記前面一開始的內容，而且要回到有答案出處的地方也很花時間。但是用這個方法，就不會有這些問題，可以避免遺漏。

❸ 從（A）開始依序確認**147.**的選項。（B）的It runs an Internet shopping business（它經營線上購物生意。）符合文章一開頭的Bexi.com, the world's third largest online retailer（全球第三大網路零售商貝西網購），所以是正確答案。這時就在答案卡劃上（B），結束這一題。選項（C）和（D）看一眼確認一下就往❹進行。

★不正確的選項就不需要探索其錯誤原因。把握寶貴的時間最重要。

❹ 看**148.**，記住題目是問「人們為什麼訝異？」，再回頭從暫停處❺接著閱讀文章。

❺ 第二段中間部分似乎出現了正確答案的出處，再換去→❻看**148.**的選項。

❻ 從（A）開始閱讀**148.**的選項就會看到，（C）的The lack of robots in Bexi.com's warehouse（貝西網購的倉庫沒有機器人。）和第二段中間的there are no robots within Bexi.com's immense warehouse（貝西網購龐大的倉庫裡沒有機器人）相符，是正確答案，並往→❼進行。

❼ 看**149.**，記住題目是問「寫了什麼有關柏林倉庫的內容？」，再回到暫停處從❽繼續閱讀完剩下的文章。

★和**147.**一樣，將suggest換成不影響意思的簡單語句。

❽ 讀完文章後至❾看**149.**的選項。

❾（C）It will create a lot of jobs.（它將創造很多的就業機會。）和文章最後說的Bexi.com will need an additional 200 workers to staff its latest warehouse.（貝西網購將需要配置額外200名員工到最新的倉庫）相符，所以是正確答案。從第一段可知，latest warehouse（最新的倉庫）即是指Berlin warehouse（柏林的倉庫）。

贏得990分之路

讓我們再次歸納Part 7正確思路的重點。

（1）先看第一題的題目問什麼，記起來（先不讀選項）。

・為了更容易記住題目問什麼，如有必要，應該換成簡單的語句。

（2）從頭開始精讀試題文章。

・確切做到閱讀全文，可以讓你更有自信地作答。最重要的是要做到「沒有漏掉試題文章中的任何死角」。

（3）讀到一個適當的段落後（或是找不到正確答案的出處時）就先暫停，往第一題的選項看。

・沒有分段的文章，最好用試題數量來分等分閱讀。

・逐題作答，可以避免一次記住全篇文章的負擔，以及回頭尋找正確答案出處的時間耗費。

（4）將試題文章內正確答案的出處和選項比對，再將答案畫記在答案卡上。

・大多數的不正確選項既不用找錯誤之處也不需要看，所以絕對不要浪費時間多停留。

（5）接著看下一題的題目，從剛才暫停的段落開始，再繼續閱讀試題文章。

・每一個段落也可能會出現多道試題的正確答案出處，請務必精讀。

請重複上述（1）～（5）的步驟來迎戰Part 7。因為是精讀，所以要訓練自己達到在時間內可以全部答完的速度。因此，藉由每天的學習來增加閱讀英文的時間和次數是必須的。閱讀英文的速度，是靠反覆練習慢慢掌握而來的。

接下來進行的Training基礎練習，會讓各位有感於要正確地把握答案出處來作答。即使是900分的學習者，能精確地指出所有試題的正確解答出處的人也不多。由於TOEIC L&R聽讀測驗的試題中，正確的選項和不正確的選項區別很清楚，所以如果能夠大致依照前後文關係，大多還是可以答對。

然而，光憑這種準確度的閱讀能力是無法贏得990分的。為了學習精確地找出正確解答的出處，以及有自信跳過不正確選項的能力，請各位利用本書做緊密的練習吧！至於有關「NOT試題（是非題題型）」以及將完整句歸置在正確位置的「句子歸置題型」等一些「耗時的題目」，在接下來的Training和Practice Test（基礎練習和實戰試題）都會討論到，請各位拭目以待。

總結

Part 7最重要的是認真地建立解題的正確思路（找出正確答案的方式）。而且，要能夠明確指出正確答案的出處。

Training 基礎練習

針對以下試題作答，並指出正確答案的出處（答案卡在全書最後）。

Questions 1-4 refer to the following article.

Baruti Wildlife Park

By Dingane Mbeki

For 36 years, Baruti Wildlife Park in South Africa has been providing sanctuary to orphaned and injured animals from South Africa and beyond, including cheetahs, lions, marmosets, and many species of birds. The 1,000-acre park is privately owned and relies heavily on donations from individuals, companies and organizations.

David Seaberg, best known as a director of the popular science fiction series *Solar Adventures*, donated €2 million to the Baruti Wildlife Park after spending a two-week family holiday at the luxurious lodge located within the park's grounds. "I was moved by the passion of the volunteers and employees at the park and wanted to show my support," Seaberg commented.

In an effort to finance the growing maintenance costs, Baruti Wildlife Park also partnered with Sunrise Travels, which now organizes various tours to the park. Besides enjoying the spectacular nature and wildlife, visitors can participate in a wildlife photography course or explore the grounds with a certified field guide to learn about local ecology and culture.

1. The word "sanctuary" in paragraph 1, line 1, is closest in meaning to
(A) medicine
(B) goods
(C) shelter
(D) prayer

2. What is indicated about David Seaberg?
(A) He participated in a volunteer program.
(B) He is famous for his love of animals.
(C) He shot a film about Baruti Wildlife Park.
(D) He took a vacation to South Africa.

3. What is NOT true about Baruti Wildlife Park?
(A) It takes care of animals that got hurt.
(B) It has been operating for more than a decade.
(C) It works together with a travel agency.
(D) It breeds endangered species.

4. According to the article, what can visitors do at Baruti Wildlife Park?
(A) Adopt an orphaned animal
(B) Be certified as a park ranger
(C) Take a guided tour
(D) Study how to paint

Questions 5-6 refer to the following text-message chain.

HELEN UHLMAN (11:45 A.M.)
Hey, I just finished my meeting, so I'll go down and wait for you in the lobby.

MIKE MITCHELL (11:47 A.M.)
Actually, I have to speak with Mr. Gilmore quickly. Wanna just go straight to Treetop Bistro and get a table?

HELEN UHLMAN (11:47 A.M.)
Good idea. It's almost noon, so I'm sure it'll be busy.

MIKE MITCHELL (11:48 A.M.)
Thanks. I'll let you know as soon as I'm on my way.

HELEN UHLMAN (11:58 A.M.)
Oh, is Mr. Gilmore coming?

MIKE MITCHELL (11:59 A.M.)
Not this time. He wants us to get all the preliminary details ready, and then he'll meet with us the day after tomorrow.

HELEN UHLMAN (12:00 P.M.)
Oh, boy. Then we've got our work cut out for us.

MIKE MITCHELL (12:10 P.M.)
Yep. So we'll have to get down to business right away to finish. OK, I'm on my way!

5. What is suggested about Mr. Mitchell?
(A) He has been waiting in the lobby.
(B) He will meet Ms. Uhlman at a restaurant.
(C) He is the owner of the Treetop Bistro.
(D) He got a new assignment from Mr. Gilmore.

6. At 12:00 P.M., what does Ms. Uhlman mean when she writes, "we've got our work cut out for us"?
(A) She is relieved by the schedule change.
(B) She feels they need more information.
(C) She thinks they have a hard task ahead.
(D) She wants to switch to a different project.

Questions 7-10 refer to the following letter.

Lo-Mart

May 15

Mr. Larry Arroyo
78 Candy Lane
Dallas, TX 75982

Dear Mr. Arroyo,

Congratulations!
Your essay has been awarded third prize in the parent category of the Lo-Mart and I Contest sponsored by Lo-Mart. We wish to celebrate your accomplishment at an award ceremony on Sunday, June 1, at Kosting Elementary School. — [1] —. Upon entering the school's North Gate, turn left and walk past the vegetable garden to get to the school's auditorium, where the ceremony will be held. — [2] —.
The winning essays, including yours, will be published in the Lo-Mart Newsletter, which is delivered to members every month, and put on our Web site. Additionally, they will be printed and displayed in every Lo-Mart store. — [3] —. As a third place winner, you will receive a 50-dollar gift voucher redeemable at any Lo-Mart store before December 31. — [4] —.
Again, congratulations on your achievement!

Sincerely,

Arthur Lucero

Arthur Lucero, Manager,
Lo-Mart, Inc.

7. Who most likely is Mr. Arroyo?
(A) A winner of a lucky draw
(B) A teacher at an elementary school
(C) A participant in a competition
(D) An employee of Lo-Mart

8. What is NOT provided in the letter?
(A) The date of an award event
(B) The content of a prize
(C) Directions to the event venue
(D) The names of award winners

9. According to the letter, how can people read the essays?
(A) By obtaining a local newspaper
(B) By visiting a Lo-Mart store
(C) By sending an e-mail request
(D) By going to the school library

10. In which of the positions marked [1], [2], [3] and [4] does the following sentence best belong?
"You can pick it up at the award ceremony, or provide us with an address where you want it to be sent."
(A) [1]
(B) [2]
(C) [3]
(D) [4]

Questions 11-14 refer to the following e-mail.

From: Matt Juliano [Mjuliano@kg.com]
To: Customer Service [customerservice@elecABC.com]
Subject: Alarmio 2109
Date: October 6

I purchased the Alarmio 2109 from your online store after browsing the Internet to find a replacement for my old alarm clock which I accidentally broke a few months ago.

I have no complaints about the alarm clock itself. I always wanted an alarm clock that could project the time on the wall, which is why I bought the Alarmio 2109. I also found the functions which allow me to set two separate wake times and change the intensity of the night light very useful. However, on your Web site, some of the customer reviews for Alarmio 2109 mention how it automatically adjusts to daylight saving time. It is the Alarmio 2110 that has this function and not the Alarmio 2109. I thought this was rather confusing and hope you will take down these reviews from the site, or move them to the reviews for Alarmio 2110.

Matt Juliano

11. The word "browsing" in paragraph 1, line 1, is closest in meaning to
(A) wondering
(B) searching
(C) comparing
(D) connecting

12. According to the e-mail, what happened a few months ago?
(A) An order was delivered.
(B) A device was upgraded.
(C) An item stopped working.
(D) A watch went missing.

13. Which function is indicated as the reason for the purchase?
(A) Time projection
(B) Dual wake time
(C) Night light adjustment
(D) Automatic daylight saving time adjustment

14. What is suggested about the reviews?
(A) Some of them are offensive.
(B) Some of them are misleading.
(C) Some of them are outdated.
(D) Some of them are too long.

Questions 15-19 refer to the following article and e-mail.

NEW YORK — Hudson Air's popular calendar came about due to a digital photography competition for crew members ten years ago. As part of a learning incentive program, Hudson Air let their crews showcase their best photographs taken at its destination cities, with a $50 gift voucher for the best one. The idea of turning the top 13 pictures into a charity calendar followed.

The calendars were printed and sold onboard Hudson Air flights. To the surprise and delight of airline staff, the first 570 copies sold out in just 2 days. Judith Oak, the Managing Director of Hudson Air donated the $6,840 proceeds to Determined Kids, a global charity focusing on children's education, a few months later at a ceremony in New York.

Since then, the airline has been producing the charity calendar every year. This year's calendar features an extra 3 pages containing a map of New York, London and Beijing, the three most frequent destinations of Hudson Air.

Copies are available onboard Hudson Air flights, at hudsonair.com and in Determined Kids' charity shops in the U.S., Canada and Europe.

To: Penelope Ward [pward@hudsonair.com]
From: Deborah Hugh [Hugh@dk.org]
Date: August 3, 11:25 A.M.
Subject: Thank you for your support

Dear Ms. Ward,

Thank you for your continued support of Determined Kids. Because of your company's generous donation, this year our organization was able to offer scholarships to 5 students who face financial difficulties, and help establish two new children's learning centers in India. Please know that your company's efforts have made a big difference in the lives of these children.

On a more personal note, I purchased several copies of your calendar for myself as well as for my friends, and was very impressed. The maps are beautiful, and I have hung them in my living room. I have never traveled much myself, but the pictures truly inspire imagination. Moreover, my friends who travel have found the added bonus to be extremely useful and I hope it will be a recurring feature.

Sincerely,
Deborah Hugh
Determined Kids

15. What does the article imply about the calendar?
(A) It costs $50 for each copy.
(B) It originated from a photo contest.
(C) It contains pictures of flight attendants.
(D) It had been planned for many years.

16. Where are people NOT able to purchase the calendar?
(A) Inside Hudson Air airplanes
(B) At major international airports
(C) From a company's Web site
(D) At an organization's store

17. What is indicated about Determined Kids?
(A) It focuses on adult learning.
(B) It operates domestically.
(C) It runs a business in Beijing.
(D) It provides aid to students.

18. What feature of the calendar did Ms. Hugh's friends find helpful?
(A) City maps
(B) Fridge magnets
(C) Logo stickers
(D) World atlas

19. What can be inferred about Ms. Hugh?
(A) She works at Hudson Air.
(B) She does not fly frequently.
(C) She received a financial reward.
(D) She is interested in local arts.

Questions 20-24 refer to the following e-mails.

To: Astrilla Technologies Staff
From: Human Resources, Madeline Steinhoff
Date: May 12
Subject: Team Building

To all staff,

Astrilla Technologies is excited to offer a day of team building, split up by department, on May 31. The activities will be great for creating and strengthening bonds between co-workers that are long-lasting. Discover each other's unique talents and build relationships that will later make a difference at the office. This event is highly recommended for everyone but certainly not mandatory, especially since it's held on a Saturday. If you are interested in participating, please sign up by Friday, May 16. Just e-mail Lynn Campbell at l-campbell@astrillatechnologies.com and be sure to give her a fun name that everyone can call you during the event. The company will pay for the cost of the team building event. As for lunch, since we're aware that many employees have dietary restrictions, we will leave it up to you. You may bring your own or place an order for a Pitata's Sandwich Meal through us for $8, also due by Friday, May 16. Hope to see you there!

Madeline Steinhoff
Human Resources

To:	Lynn Campbell <l-campbell@astrillatechnologies.com>
From:	Harry Sturgis <h-sturgis@astrillatechnologies.com>
Date:	May 20
Subject:	Team Building

Hi, Lynn,

I'm sorry for my late e-mail—I've been out of the office sick, so I didn't know about the e-mail that you sent last week. I'd love to participate, so please let me know if there's still room. If there is, I'll run my $8 down to you right away. By the way, could you let me know when the event begins and ends? I am free most of the day, but I have a special family event that evening and want to know how much time I'll have in between.

Thanks!

Harry Sturgis
Accounting, Astrilla Technologies

To: Harry Sturgis <h-sturgis@astrillatechnologies.com>
From: Lynn Campbell <l-campbell@astrillatechnologies.com>
Date: May 20
Subject: Re: Team Building

Harry,

Glad you're feeling better. That must have been a bad illness to keep you away from the office for over a week! Actually, the closing date for registration was Friday and I finished all the paperwork on Monday! But...you're in luck. Dylan Phillips had to give up his spot this morning. So bring me your money, and I'll swap your names. Oh, and the day will begin at 9:30 and end around 4:30.

Lynn Campbell
Human Resources, Astrilla Technologies

20. What is indicated about the team building event?
(A) It aims to promote better communications between departments.
(B) The plan is to do a lot of work in one day.
(C) The whole company will participate.
(D) It will take place during the weekend.

21. What piece of information is requested in the first e-mail?
(A) Ideas for events
(B) An amusing nickname
(C) A funny personal story
(D) Dietary restrictions

22. What is inferred about Mr. Sturgis?
(A) He will cancel a family event.
(B) He wants to eat a sandwich during the event.
(C) He has taken part in team building events before.
(D) He helps organize Astrilla Technologies events.

23. In the second e-mail, the word "free" in paragraph 1, line 4, is closest in meaning to
(A) exempt
(B) loose
(C) available
(D) unpaid

24. What does Ms. Campbell say about the event?
(A) One space has just opened up.
(B) Mr. Phillips needs a partner.
(C) She will try to plan another one.
(D) Mr. Sturgis is not well enough to attend.

Training 基礎練習　解答與解析

Questions 1-4 refer to the following article.

試題 1-4 請參考以下文章。

❷Baruti Wildlife Park
By Dingane Mbeki

Q3 (B) For 36 years, Baruti Wildlife Park in South Africa Q3 (A) has been providing sanctuary to orphaned and injured animals from South Africa and beyond, including cheetahs, lions, marmosets, and many species of birds. The 1,000-acre park is privately owned and relies heavily on donations from individuals, companies and organizations. → ❸

❺David Seaberg, best known as a director of the popular science fiction series *Solar Adventures*, donated €2 million to the Baruti Wildlife Park Q2 after spending a two-week family holiday at the luxurious lodge located within the park's grounds. "I was moved by the passion of the volunteers and employees at the park and wanted to show my support," Seaberg commented. → ❻

❾In an effort to finance the growing maintenance costs, Q3 (C) Baruti Wildlife Park also partnered with Sunrise Travels, which now organizes various tours to the park. Besides enjoying the spectacular nature and wildlife, visitors can participate in a wildlife photography course or Q4 explore the grounds with a certified field guide to learn about local ecology and culture. → ❿

巴魯地野生動物園
撰文者：丁甘納．姆貝基

36年來，南非巴魯地野生動物園一直為南非及其他地區失親及受傷的動物提供庇護所，包括獵豹、獅子、狨猴和多種鳥類。這個佔地1,000英畝的園區是私人擁有的，且非常仰賴個人、公司及團體組織的捐款。

大衛．西伯格（David Seaberg），以身為人氣科幻系列電影《太陽冒險》（*Solar Adventures*）的導演最廣為人知，在位於園區境內的豪華客棧度過了為期兩週的家庭假期後，捐贈了200萬歐元給巴魯地野生動物園。「我被園區的志工和員工的熱情所感動，並希望表達我的支持，」西伯格評論道。

為了努力籌措日益增長的維護成本，巴魯地野生動物園也與目前安排各種園區之旅的日出旅行社（Sunrise Travels）合作。除了享受壯觀的大自然和野生動物之外，遊客們還可以參加野生動物攝影課程或與經認證的野外導遊一同探索這片土地，認識當地的生態和文化。

字彙 □ orphaned 失親的　□ marmoset 狨猴（動物）　□ acre 英畝（面積單位）

1. ❶The word "sanctuary" in paragraph 1, line 1, is closest in meaning to → ❷
(A) ❸medicine
(B) goods
(C) shelter 正確答案，往下一題進行 → ❹
(D) prayer

第1段第1行中的單字「sanctuary」，意思最接近下列何者？
（A）藥
（B）商品
（C）避難所
（D）禱告

答案 **(C)**

解析 park對orphaned and injured animals（失親及受傷的動物）提供sanctuary。sanctuary是「庇護所」之意，意思最接近的是（C）的shelter。即使對sanctuary只知道是「聖殿」的意思，從前後句關係也可推測而知。

2. ❹What is indicated about David Seaberg?

記住「有關大衛西伯格的描述是？」後再看文章 → ❺

(A) ❻He participated in a volunteer program.
(B) He is famous for his love of animals.
(C) He shot a film about Baruti Wildlife Park.
(D) He took a vacation to South Africa.

正確答案，往下一題進行 → ❼

關於大衛．西伯格，下列敘述何者正確？

（A）他參加了志工課程。
（B）他以喜愛動物聞名。
（C）他拍了一部有關巴魯地野生動物園的電影。
（D）他到南非度假。

答案 (D)

解析 將第二段的spending a two-week family holiday（度過了為期兩週的家庭假期）換成took a vacation（度假）說法的（D）是正確答案。（A）～（C）都有部分內容與文章有出入。

3. ❼What is NOT true about Baruti Wildlife Park?

遇到是非題題型直接看選項 → ❽

(A) ❽It takes care of animals that got hurt.
(B) It has been operating for more than a decade.
(C) It works together with a travel agency.
(D) ❿It breeds endangered species.

記住四個選項內容再看文章 → ❾

正確答案，往下一題進行 → ⓫

關於巴魯地野生動物園，下列敘述何者為非？

（A）它照顧受傷的動物。
（B）它已經營運10年以上。
（C）它與旅行社合作。
（D）它培育瀕臨絕種動物。

答案 (D)

解析 遇到是非題題型要先看選項，把選項內容記住後再閱讀文章，當確定找到其中3個選項的出處時，剩下的選項就是答案了。從第2題暫停的段落繼續往下看，要到最後一段才會出現（C）的出處。同時，如果記得第一段就有提到（A）、（B）的出處，只要快速地回去確認一下即可。也就是說，若能用心閱讀全文並保持記憶，作答就會很有效率。

4. ⓫According to the article, what can visitors do at Baruti Wildlife Park?

此時，應已在文章中讀過本題正確解答的出處，直接看選項確認 → ⓬

(A) ⓬Adopt an orphaned animal
(B) Be certified as a park ranger
(C) Take a guided tour → 正確答案，結束這篇題組的作答
(D) Study how to paint

根據這篇文章，遊客可以在巴魯地野生動物園做什麼？

（A）領養失親的動物
（B）被認證為園區管理員
（C）參加導覽
（D）學習如何畫畫

答案 (C)

解析 最後一段提到visitors can ... explore the grounds with a certified field guide（遊客們可以……與經認證的專業野外導遊一同探索這片土地）。將該說法換成Take a guided tour的（C）是正確答案。（B）提及的park ranger是「園區管理員、護林員」，經常出現在TOEIC L&R正式測驗，請一併記起來。

Questions 5-6 refer to the following text-message chain.

試題 5-6 請參考以下一連串的文字訊息。

② HELEN UHLMAN (11:45 A.M.) Hey, I just finished my meeting, so I'll go down and wait for you in the lobby.	海倫・尤爾曼 (11:45 A.M.) 嘿，我剛結束會議，所以我會下樓在大廳等你。
MIKE MITCHELL (11:47 A.M.) Actually, I have to speak with Mr. Gilmore quickly. Q5 Wanna just go straight to Treetop Bistro and get a table?	麥克・米歇爾 (11:47 A.M.) 其實，我必須跟吉爾摩（Gilmore）先生很快談一下。你要不要直接去樹頂（Treetop）餐酒館先佔個位子？
HELEN UHLMAN (11:47 A.M.) Q5 Good idea. It's almost noon, so I'm sure it'll be busy.	海倫・尤爾曼 (11:47 A.M.) 好主意。快中午了，所以我相信它那兒會生意很好。
MIKE MITCHELL (11:48 A.M.) Thanks. I'll let you know as soon as I'm on my way. → ③	麥克・米歇爾 (11:48 A.M.) 謝謝。我一出發就會馬上告訴你。
⑤ HELEN UHLMAN (11:58 A.M.) Oh, is Mr. Gilmore coming?	海倫・尤爾曼 (11:58 A.M.) 對了，吉爾摩先生會來嗎？
MIKE MITCHELL (11:59 A.M.) Not this time. He wants us to get all the preliminary details ready, and then he'll meet with us the day after tomorrow.	麥克・米歇爾 (11:59 A.M.) 他這次不會來。他希望我們今天要把所有事前預備的細節都準備好，然後他後天會跟我們見面。
HELEN UHLMAN (12:00 P.M.) Oh, boy. Then we've got our work cut out for us.	海倫・尤爾曼 (12:00 A.M.) 哎呀！看來我們有艱難的工作在等著我們。
MIKE MITCHELL (12:10 P.M.) Yep. Q6 So we'll have to get down to business right away to finish. OK, I'm on my way! → ⑥	麥克・米歇爾 (12:10 A.M.) 是的。所以我們必須立刻開始工作才能完成。好，我在路上了。

字彙 □ preliminary 初步的、預備的 □ Oh, boy. 哎呀 □ yep 是的（口語）

5. ❶What is suggested about Mr. Mitchell?

關於米歇爾先生，下列推論何者正確？

記住「有關米歇爾的描述是？」後再看文章 → ❷

(A) ❸He has been waiting in the lobby.

(B) He will meet Ms. Uhlman at a restaurant.

正確答案，往下一題進行 → ❹

(C) He is the owner of the Treetop Bistro.

(D) He got a new assignment from Mr. Gilmore.

（A）他已經在大廳等候。

（B）他將在餐廳跟尤爾曼女士見面。

（C）他是樹頂餐酒館的老闆。

（D）他從吉爾摩先生那兒得到新的任務。

答案 (B)

解析 11:47 A.M.，米歇爾在訊息裡說Wanna just go straight to Treetop Bistro and get a table?（你要不要直接去樹頂（Treetop）餐酒館先佔個位子？）。尤爾曼對此回答了Good idea.（好主意），由此可知兩人約好要在餐廳會合。

6. ❹At 12:00 P.M., what does Ms. Uhlman mean when she writes, "we've got our work cut out for us"?

12:00 P.M.，尤爾曼女士寫著「we've got our work cut out for us」，這意味著什麼？

記住「說 we've got our work cut out for us 這句話時的狀況是什麼？」後再看文章 → ❺

(A) ❻She is relieved by the schedule change.

(B) She feels they need more information.

(C) She thinks they have a hard task ahead.

→ 正確答案，結束這篇題組的作答

(D) She wants to switch to a different project.

（A）她因行程表的改變而鬆一口氣。

（B）她認為他們需要更多資訊。

（C）她認為他們今後有艱鉅的任務。

（D）她想變更至不同的計畫。

答案 (C)

解析 這是在Part 3和Part 4也會出現的「說話者的目的題型」，在Part 7基本上也是採同樣的解答方法。想一下「這是在什麼狀況下說的」，再依照目標句的前後句關係來判斷。這題的目標句前面是米歇爾說「今天需要做好事前準備。後天再見面」，而目標句後面則是米歇爾說So we'll have to get down to business right away to finish.（所以我們必須立刻開始工作才能完成）。也就是說，她是在認為「沒有太多時間」的狀況下說這句的，所以（C）是正確答案。get *one's* work cut out for *one*是指「排定很多困難的工作、必須要做的事很多」。（A）的is relieved（鬆一口氣）、（B）的後半部分，以及（D）的全部內容都不符合該狀況。

字彙 □ switch to 改變為～

Questions 7-10 refer to the following letter.

試題7-10 請參考以下信件。

❷Lo-Mart May 15 Mr. Larry Arroyo 78 Candy Lane Dallas, TX 75982 Dear Mr. Arroyo, Congratulations! Q7 Your essay has been awarded third prize in the parent category of the Lo-Mart and I Contest sponsored by Lo-Mart. → ❸ ❻ We wish to celebrate your accomplishment at an award ceremony on Sunday, Q8 (A) June 1, Q8 (C) at Kosting Elementary School. — [1] —. Upon entering the school's North Gate, turn left and walk past the vegetable garden to get to the school's auditorium, where the ceremony will be held. — [2] —. The winning essays, including yours, will be published in the Lo-Mart Newsletter, which is delivered to members every month, and put on our Web site. Additionally, Q9 they will be printed and displayed in every Lo-Mart store. — [3] —. As a third place winner, you will receive Q8 (B) Q10 a 50-dollar gift voucher redeemable at any Lo-Mart store before December 31. → ❼ ⓫ — [4] —. → ⓬ Again, congratulations on your achievement! Sincerely, Arthur Lucero Arthur Lucero, Manager, Lo-Mart, Inc.	洛馬超市 5月15日 賴瑞・阿羅約先生 糖果巷78號 達拉斯，德州75982 親愛的阿羅約先生， 恭喜！ 洛馬超市主辦的「洛馬與我比賽」雙親組中，您的短文已獲得第三名殊榮。我們希望在6月1日星期日，在寇斯汀（Kosting）小學舉行頒獎典禮來慶祝您獲獎。進入學校的北門，左轉並走過菜園就到了學校禮堂，典禮將在該場地舉辦。包括您在內的獲獎短文，將被刊登在每個月寄給會員的洛馬超市快訊中，並放在我們的網站上。此外，它們將被印出來並展示在每家洛馬商店。身為第三名獲獎者，您將獲得一張50美元的禮品券，在12月31日之前可至任何一家洛馬超市兌換商品。您可以在頒獎典禮上領取，或是提供給我們您希望寄到的地址。 再次祝賀您獲獎！ 謹致問候， 亞瑟・盧塞羅（簽名） 亞瑟・盧塞羅，經理 洛馬超市公司

字彙 □ auditorium 禮堂、大會堂 □ redeemable 可退現金的、換成商品

7. ❶Who most likely is Mr. Arroyo?

記住「阿羅約是誰？」，從頭開始閱讀文章 → ❷

(A) ❸A winner of a lucky draw

(B) A teacher at an elementary school

(C) A participant in a competition

正確答案，往下一題進行 → ❹

(D) An employee of Lo-Mart

誰最有可能是阿羅約先生？

（A）幸運抽獎的中獎者

（B）小學教師

（C）參賽者

（D）洛馬超市的員工

答案 **(C)**

解析 從Your essay has been awarded third prize（您的短文已獲得第三名殊榮）這句可判斷，阿羅約先生是比賽的獲獎者，所以（C）是正確答案。（A）是錯在a lucky draw（幸運抽獎）。

8. ❹What is NOT provided in the letter?

遇到是非題題型直接看選項 → ❺

(A) ❺The date of an award event

(B) The content of a prize

(C) Directions to the event venue

(D) ❼The names of award winners

記住四個選項內容再看文章 → ❻

正確答案，往下一題進行 → ❽

信中沒有提到什麼？

（A）頒獎活動的日期

（B）獎品的內容

（C）活動會場的路線指引

（D）獲獎者的名字

答案 (D)

解析 看到選項（A）、（C）、（B）是依序出現在信件的資訊，此時即可結束確認。剩下（D）的資訊就不需要確認是否有出現在信件內，馬上可往下一題進行。

9. ❽According to the letter, how can people read the essays?

此時，應已在文章中讀過本題正確答案的出處，直接看選項確認 → ❾

(A) ❾By obtaining a local newspaper

(B) By visiting a Lo-Mart store

正確答案，往下一題進行 → ❿

(C) By sending an e-mail request

(D) By going to the school library

根據這封信，人們如何才能看到這些文章？

（A）要取得當地報紙

（B）要到洛馬超市各店

（C）要用電子郵件傳送請求

（D）要到學校圖書館

答案 (B)

解析 第三段中間提到they will be printed and displayed in every Lo-Mart store.（它們將被印出來並展示在每家洛馬商店。），因此正確答案是（B）。they即是指第三段開頭的the winning essays（獲獎短文）。Lo-Mart Newsletter（洛馬超市快訊）是每月會發送給洛馬超市會員的刊物，並非local newspaper（當地報紙），注意不要誤選（A）。這些得獎文章在Web site（網站）也看得到，不需要用e-mail提出請求，所以（C）是不正確的。

10. In which of the positions marked [1], [2], [3] and [4] does the following sentence best belong?

❿"You can pick it up at the award ceremony, or provide us with an address where you want it to be sent." → ⓫

(A) [1]　(B) [2]　(C) [3]　(D) [4]

→ 正確答案，結束這篇題組的作答（剩下的文章內容不看也無妨）

下面這句應歸置在標記 [1]、[2]、[3]、[4] 的哪一個位置？

「您可以在頒獎典禮上領取，或是提供給我們您希望寄到的地址。」

（A）[1]　（B）[2]　（C）[3]　（D）[4]

答案 (D)

解析 從要歸置的句子You can pick it up...可知，正確位置的前面當然是描述「可pick up的是什麼（可領取什麼）」。如果 [4] 的前一句提到的a 50-dollar gift voucher（50美元的禮品券）就是pick it up的it，則語意連貫，因此正確答案是（D）。要理解歸置處的前後內容能否與句子語意連貫（如這題的連結關鍵字就是代名詞it）再來作答。

Questions 11-14 refer to the following e-mail.

試題 11-14 請參考以下電子郵件。

②From: Matt Juliano [Mjuliano@kg.com] To: Customer Service [customerservice@elecABC.com] Subject: Alarmio 2109 Date: October 6	發信者：麥特·朱利安諾 [Mjuliano@kg.com] 收信者：客服人員 [customerservice@elecABC.com] 主旨：鬧鈴米歐2109 日期：10月6日
I purchased the Alarmio 2109 from your online store after browsing the Internet to find a replacement for Q12 my old alarm clock which I accidentally broke a few months ago. → ③	幾個月前我不小心弄壞我的舊鬧鐘，為了尋找它的替代品而上網瀏覽後，我就從您的網路商店買了鬧鈴米歐2109。
⑦I have no complaints about the alarm clock itself. Q13 I always wanted an alarm clock that could project the time on the wall, which is why I bought the Alarmio 2109. → ⑧ ⑩ I also found the functions which allow me to set two separate wake times and change the intensity of the night light very useful. However, on your Web site, some of the customer reviews for Alarmio 2109 mention how it automatically adjusts to daylight saving time. It is the Alarmio 2110 that has this function and not the Alarmio 2109. Q14 I thought this was rather confusing and hope you will take down these reviews from the site, or move them to the reviews for Alarmio 2110. → ⑪	我對鬧鐘本身沒有不滿意。我一直想要一個可以將時間投影在牆上的鬧鐘，這就是我購買鬧鈴米歐2109的原因。還有它可以讓我設定兩個不同喚醒時間，以及改變夜燈強度的這些功能，我也覺得非常有用。然而，在您的網站上，一些顧客對鬧鈴米歐2109的評論提到它如何地自動調整至日光節約時間。但具有此功能的是鬧鈴米歐2110而不是鬧鈴米歐2109。我認為這是很令人混淆的，希望您從網站上刪掉這些評論，或是將它們移到鬧鈴米歐2110的評論區。
Matt Juliano	麥特·朱利安諾

字彙 □ project 投影~ □ intensity 強度、強烈 □ night light 夜燈
□ daylight saving time 日光節約時間

11. ①The word "browsing" in paragraph 1, line 1, is closest in meaning to → ②
(A) ③wondering
(B) searching 正確答案，往下一題進行 → ④
(C) comparing
(D) connecting

第1段第1行中的單字「browsing」，意思最接近下列何者？
（A）想知道~
（B）搜尋~
（C）比較~
（D）連接~

答案 **(B)**

解析 這題是指after browsing the Internet（在我上網瀏覽後）這段話，這裡的browse是「瀏覽~」之意。（B）的search最接近該字的意思，所以是正確答案。browse在Part 1也以「隨意翻閱（店內商品）」的意思出現過，請一併記起來。

12. ❹According to the e-mail, what happened a few months ago?

根據電子郵件，幾個月前發生了什麼事？

此時，應已在文章中讀過本題正確答案的出處，直接看選項確認 → ❺

(A) ❺An order was delivered.
(B) A device was upgraded.
(C) An item stopped working.
正確答案，往下一題進行 → ❻
(D) A watch went missing.

（A）訂購品交付了。
（B）設備升級了。
（C）一個物件停止運作了。
（D）手錶遺失了。

答案 (C)

解析 各位看到12.的題目，瞬間要想到「剛才答11.時已有讀到相關的內容」。如此一來就不用回頭閱讀文章，可繼續看選項。從my old alarm clock which I accidentally broke a few months ago.（幾個月前我不小心弄壞的舊鬧鐘）可知，（C）An item stopped working.（一個物件停止運作了）是正確答案。

13. ❻Which function is indicated as the reason for the purchase?

下列何種功能是購買的理由？

記住「購買的理由是什麼？」後再看文章 → ❼

(A) ❽Time projection 正確答案，往下一題進行 → ❾
(B) Dual wake time
(C) Night light adjustment
(D) Automatic daylight saving time adjustment

（A）時間投影
（B）雙重喚醒時間
（C）夜燈調光
（D）自動的日光節約時間調整

答案 (A)

解析 這句I always wanted an alarm clock that could project the time on the wall, which is why I bought the Alarmio 2109.（我一直想要一個可以將時間投影在牆上的鬧鐘，這就是我購買鬧鈴米歐2109的原因。）明確地描述了購買的理由，毫無疑問地就該選（A）Time projection（時間投影）。雖然文中有提到（B）和（C）也很方便，但不是最初購買的理由。（D）是他款鬧鐘才有的功能。

字彙 □ dual 雙重的

14. ❾What is suggested about the reviews?

關於（商品）評論，下列推論何者正確？

記住「有關評論的描述是？」後再看文章 → ❿

(A) ⓫Some of them are offensive.
(B) Some of them are misleading.
→ 正確答案，結束這篇題組的作答
(C) Some of them are outdated.
(D) Some of them are too long.

（A）有些是冒犯人的。
（B）有些是使人誤解的。
（C）有些是過時的。
（D）有些篇幅太長。

答案 (B)

解析 應該寫在產品Alarmio 2110的review（評論）被寫在Alarmio 2109的位置，文中也提到I thought this was rather confusing（我認為這是很令人混淆的）。（B）Some of them are misleading.（有些是使人誤解的）只是將它換個說法，所以是正確答案。試題文章內的confusing可換成misleading的說法。

字彙 □ offensive 無禮的、冒犯人的

Questions 15-19 refer to the following article and e-mail.

試題 15-19 請參考以下文章及電子郵件。

❷ NEW YORK— Q15 Hudson Air's popular calendar came about due to a digital photography competition for crew members ten years ago. As part of a learning incentive program, Hudson Air let their crews showcase their best photographs taken at its destination cities, with a $50 gift voucher for the best one. The idea of turning the top 13 pictures into a charity calendar followed. → ❸

❻ The calendars were printed and sold onboard Hudson Air flights. To the surprise and delight of airline staff, the first 570 copies sold out in just 2 days. Judith Oak, the Managing Director of Hudson Air donated the $6,840 proceeds to Q17 Determined Kids, a global charity focusing on children's education, a few months later at a ceremony in New York.

Since then, the airline has been producing the charity calendar every year. Q18 This year's calendar features an extra 3 pages containing a map of New York, London and Beijing, the three most frequent destinations of Hudson Air.

Copies are available Q16 (A) onboard Hudson Air flights, Q16 (C) at hudsonair.com and Q16 (D) in Determined Kids' charity shops in the U.S., Canada and Europe. → ❼

紐約—哈德森（Hudson）航空的人氣日曆是因十年前空勤組員的數位攝影比賽而來的。作為激勵學習計畫的一部份，哈德森航空讓他們的空勤人員展示他們在目的地城市拍攝的最佳照片，並贈予最出色者50美元的禮券。而將最棒的13張照片變成慈善日曆的想法便隨之而來。

當時，這些日曆被印製出來並在哈德森的航班上出售。令航空公司工作人員驚訝和高興的是，首刷570份僅在2天內便銷售一空。幾個月後在紐約的一個典禮上，哈德森航空的常務董事茱迪絲・歐克（Judith Oak），捐贈了6,840美元的收益給底特明德孩童機構（Determined Kids），一家關注兒童教育的全球慈善機構。

從那時候起，該航空公司每年都會製作慈善日曆。今年的日曆特別新增了3頁地圖，包含紐約、倫敦及北京，3個哈德森航空最頻繁飛行的目的地。

哈德森的航班上、哈德森網站（hudsonair.com）以及美國、加拿大和歐洲的底特明德孩童機構的慈善商店均可購得。

⓫ To: Penelope Ward [pward@hudsonair.com]
From: Deborah Hugh [Hugh@dk.org]
Date: August 3, 11:25 A.M.
Subject: Thank you for your support

Dear Ms. Ward,

Thank you for your continued support of Determined Kids. Because of your company's generous donation, this year our organization was able to offer scholarships to 5 students who face financial difficulties, and help establish two new children's learning centers in India. Please know that your

收信者：佩妮洛普・沃德 [pward@hudsonair.com]
發信者：黛博拉・修 [Hugh@dk.org]
日期：8月3日　11:25 A.M.
主旨：感謝您的支持

親愛的沃德女士，

感謝您對底特明德孩童機構的支持。由於貴公司的慷慨捐贈，今年我們的組織得以為面臨經濟困難的5名學生提供獎學金，並協助在印度創辦兩間新的兒童學習中心。在此想讓您知道，貴公司的

company's efforts have made a big difference in the lives of these children.	付出對這些孩子的生活帶來了很大的不同。
On a more personal note, I purchased several copies of your calendar for myself as well as for my friends, and was very impressed. The maps are beautiful, and I have hung them in my living room. Q19 I have never traveled much myself, but the pictures truly inspire imagination. Moreover, Q18 my friends who travel have found the added bonus to be extremely useful and I hope it will be a recurring feature. → ⑫	公事說完，來講點私人的，我為自己和朋友購入了幾份日曆，而且給了我非常深刻的印象。地圖很漂亮，我將它們掛在我的客廳。我自己不常旅行，但是這些照片真的激發了很多想像。而且，我常旅行的朋友們覺得外加的附贈頁面非常有用，我希望這項特色之後還會再次出現。
Sincerely, Deborah Hugh Determined Kids	謹致問候， 黛博拉・修 底特明德孩童機構

字彙 □ showcase 使～亮相、展示 □ make a difference 帶來（正面的）影響、改變
□ recur 重複發生

15. ❶What does the article imply about the calendar? 關於日曆，文中暗示了什麼？

記住「有關日曆的描述是？」後再看文章 → ❷

(A) ❸It costs $50 for each copy. （A）每份50美元。

(B) It originated from a photo contest. （B）它源自於一次的攝影比賽。

正確答案，往下一題進行 → ❹

(C) It contains pictures of flight attendants. （C）它包含空服員的照片。

(D) It had been planned for many years. （D）它已計畫好多年。

答案 (B)

解析 第一篇文章第一段開頭就提到calendar came about due to a digital photography competition（日曆是因數位攝影比賽而來的）。（B）是將came about due to （因～而產生）換成originated from（源自於）的說法，所以是正確答案。（A）的50美元是贈送的禮券金額。而日曆也沒有空服員的照片，所以（C）不正確。

字彙 □ originate from～ 源自於～

16. ❹Where are people NOT able to purchase the calendar? 人們在哪些地方無法買到日曆？

遇到是非題題型直接看選項 → ❺

(A) ❺Inside Hudson Air airplanes （A）哈德森航空的飛機內

(B) ❼At major international airports （B）主要的國際機場

正確答案，往下一題進行 → ❽

(C) From a company's Web site （C）公司網站

(D) At an organization's store （D）機構的商店

記住四個選項內容再看文章 → ❻

答案 (B)

解析 第一篇文章最後一段提到有關可購得日曆的場所訊息。（B）的At major international airport（在主要的國際機場），儘管這個地方有可能販賣這項商品，但是這篇文章中完全沒有提到，所以為正確答案。

17. ❽What is indicated about Determined Kids? 關於底特明德孩童機構，下列敘述何者正確？

此時，應已在文章中讀過本題正確答案的出處，直接看選項確認 → ❾

(A) ❾It focuses on adult learning. （A）它關注成人學習。

(B) It operates domestically. （B）它在國內經營。

(C) It runs a business in Beijing. （C）它在北京經營業務。

(D) It provides aid to students. （D）它為學生提供援助。

正確答案，往下一題進行 → ❿

答案 (D)

解析 有關Determined Kids（底特明德孩童機構）是怎樣的一個組織，在第一篇文章有寫到。（D）將a global charity focusing on children's education（關注兒童教育的全球慈善機構）換個說法，所以正確答案。（A）的adult learning（成人學習）和（B）的domestically（在國內地）說法與試題文章描述相牴觸，而（C）的Beijing（北京）則是日曆上追加地圖的地點。

18. ❿What feature of the calendar did Ms. Hugh's friends find helpful? 記住「修女士的朋友、日曆、特色？」後再看文章 → ⓫

修女士的朋友覺得日曆的哪個特色很有幫助？

(A) ⓬City maps 正確答案，往下一題進行 → ⓭ （A）城市地圖

(B) Fridge magnets （B）冰箱磁鐵

(C) Logo stickers （C）商標貼紙

(D) World atlas （D）世界地圖

答案 (A)

解析 第二篇文章結尾處提到my friends who travel have found the added bonus to be extremely useful（我常旅行的朋友們覺得外加的附贈頁面非常有用），其中added bonus指的是什麼，要回到第一篇文章才能做確認。This year's calendar features an extra 3 pages containing a map of New York, London and Beijing（今年的日曆特別新增了3頁地圖，包含紐約、倫敦及北京，3個哈德森航空最頻繁飛行的目的地。）這句就是bonus（額外的好處），所以（A）是正確答案。希望各位在整個題組全部答完之前，都要牢記文章中所有的內容，才有辦法一一解題。

19. ⓭What can be inferred about Ms. Hugh? 關於修女士，下列推論何者正確？

此時，應已在文章中讀過本題正確答案的出處，直接看選項確認 → ⓮

(A) ⓮She works at Hudson Air. （A）她在哈德森航空工作。

(B) She does not fly frequently. （B）她不常搭飛機。

→ 正確答案，結束這篇題組的作答

(C) She received a financial reward. （C）她獲得金錢獎勵。

(D) She is interested in local arts. （D）她對當地藝術有興趣。

答案 (B)

解析 在第二篇文章的最後一段提到I have never traveled much myself（我自己不常旅行），（B）將它換成She does not fly frequently.（她不常搭飛機）的說法，所以是正確答案。

Questions 20-24 refer to the following e-mails.

試題 20-24 請參考以下電子郵件。

❷ → To: Astrilla Technologies Staff From: Human Resources, Madeline Steinhoff Date: May 12 Subject: Team Building	收信者：阿斯瑞拉科技公司員工們 發信者：人力資源部，瑪德蓮·史汀霍夫 日期：5月12日 主旨：團隊建立活動
To all staff,	致所有員工們，
Astrilla Technologies is excited to offer a day of team building, split up by department, on May 31. The activities will be great for creating and strengthening bonds between co-workers that are long-lasting. Discover each other's unique talents and build relationships that will later make a difference at the office. Q20 This event is highly recommended for everyone but certainly not mandatory, especially since it's held on a Saturday. If you are interested in participating, please sign up by Friday, May 16. Just e-mail Lynn Campbell at l-campbell@astrillatechnologies.com and Q21 be sure to give her a fun name that everyone can call you during the event. The company will pay for the cost of the team building event. As for lunch, since we're aware that many employees have dietary restrictions, we will leave it up to you. You may bring your own or Q22 place an order for a Pitata's Sandwich Meal through us for $8, also due by Friday, May 16. Hope to see you there! → ❸	阿斯瑞拉科技公司很高興能夠在5月31日提供一個分部門的團隊建立活動日。這些活動將非常適合建立和加強同事之間持久的凝聚力。發現彼此獨特的才能，並建立關係使日後的辦公室有不同的氣象。強烈向大家推薦這個活動，但絕非強制性的，特別是因為它在週六舉行。如果你有興趣參加，請在5月16日週五之前報名。只需要發送電子郵件至l-campbell@astrillatechnologies.com給琳恩·坎貝爾（Lynn Campbell），並且一定要給她一個有趣名字，讓大家在活動期間能用來稱呼你。公司將支付團隊建立活動的費用。至於午餐，我們知道很多員工都有飲食上的限制，所以就留給你們決定。你可以帶自己的或是透過我們訂購一份8美元的碧塔塔（Pitata）三明治餐，這也是在5月16日週五前截止。希望能在那兒見到你們！
Madeline Steinhoff Human Resources	瑪德蓮·史汀霍夫 人力資源部

❼ To: Lynn Campbell <l-campbell@astrillatechnologies.com> From: Harry Sturgis <h-sturgis@astrillatechnologies.com> Date: May 20 Subject: Team Building	收信者：琳恩·坎貝爾 [l-campbell@astrillatechnologies.com] 發信者：哈利·斯特吉斯 [h-sturgis@astrillatechnologies.com] 日期：5月20日 主旨：團隊建立活動
Hi, Lynn,	嗨，琳恩，

Part 7

I'm sorry for my late e-mail — I've been out of the office sick, so I didn't know about the e-mail that you sent last week. I'd love to participate, so please let me know if there's still room. If there is, Q22 I'll run my $8 down to you right away. By the way, could you let me know when the event begins and ends? Q23 I am free most of the day, but I have a special family event that evening and want to know how much time I'll have in between.	很抱歉我的郵件來晚了——我因病不在辦公室，所以我不知道妳上週寄的電子郵件。我很樂意參加，所以請讓我知道是否還有名額。如果有的話，我會馬上跑下去把8美元給妳。順便問一下，能讓我知道活動開始和結束的時間嗎？我大部分的時間都有空，但那天晚上我有一場特殊的家庭活動，我想知道我在這兩者之間有多少的時間。
Thanks!	謝謝！
Harry Sturgis Accounting, Astrilla Technologies → ⑧	哈利・斯特吉斯 會計部，阿斯瑞拉科技公司

⑫ To: Harry Sturgis <h-sturgis@astrillatechnologies.com> From: Lynn Campbell <l-campbell@astrillatechnologies.com> Date: May 20 Subject: Re: Team Building	收信者：哈利・斯特吉斯 [h-sturgis@astrillatechnologies.com] 發信者：琳恩・坎貝爾 [l-campbell@astrillatechnologies.com] 日期：5月20日 主旨：回覆：團隊建立活動
Harry,	哈利，
Glad you're feeling better. That must have been a bad illness to keep you away from the office for over a week! Actually, the closing date for registration was Friday and I finished all the paperwork on Monday! Q24 But...you're in luck. Dylan Phillips had to give up his spot this morning. So bring me your money, and I'll swap your names. Oh, and the day will begin at 9:30 and end around 4:30.	很高興你好多了。想必那是嚴重的病狀，才讓你不在辦公室一週以上！其實，登記截止日是週五，而我在週一就完成所有的文書工作了！但……你很幸運。狄倫・菲力普斯（Dylan Phillips）今天早上不得不放棄他的名額。所以把你的錢給我，我把你們倆的名字交換。喔，還有那天我們將在9:30開始，約4:30結束。
Lynn Campbell Human Resources, Astrilla Technologies → ⑬	琳恩・坎貝爾 人力資源部，阿斯瑞拉科技公司

字彙 □ team building 團隊建立活動 □ split up by 依～劃分 □ strengthen 加強～
□ bond 連結、凝聚力 □ mandatory 強制的 □ swap 交換～

20. ❶What is indicated about the team building event?

關於團隊建立活動，下列敘述何者正確？

記住「有關團隊建立活動的描述？」後再看文章。因為第一篇文章不算太長，所以最好閱讀完再看選項內容 → ❷

(A) ❸It aims to promote better communications between departments.
(B) The plan is to do a lot of work in one day.
(C) The whole company will participate.
(D) It will take place during the weekend.

正確答案，往下一題進行 → ❹

（A）活動目的在促進各部門之間更好的溝通。
（B）計畫是在一天內完成大量工作。
（C）全公司都將參與。
（D）將在週末舉行。

答案 (D)

解析 遇到What is indicated about...? 這類題型，一定要自己判斷文章應該先閱讀到哪裡。若是在Part 7多篇閱讀的第一題就遇到這類題型，最好先把第一篇文章全部閱讀完畢後再看選項。這項活動是it's held on a Saturday（它在週六舉行），（D）將Saturday換成weekend（週末）的說法，所以是正確答案。

21. ❹What piece of information is requested in the first e-mail?

第一封電子郵件要求提供哪些資訊？

此時，應已在文章中讀過本題正確答案的出處，直接看選項確認 → ❺

(A) ❺Ideas for events
(B) An amusing nickname

正確答案，往下一題進行 → ❻

(C) A funny personal story
(D) Dietary restrictions

（A）辦活動的點子
（B）有趣的暱稱
（C）有趣的親身故事
（D）飲食上的限制

答案 (B)

解析 郵件中要求大家寄信給坎貝爾女士的敘述中有提到give her a fun name that everyone can call you during the event（給她一個有趣名字，讓大家在活動期間能用來稱呼你）可知，（B）將a fun name換成An amusing nickname（有趣的暱稱）的說法，是正確答案。

22. ❻What is inferred about Mr. Sturgis?

記住「有關斯特吉斯的描述是？」後再看文章 → ❼

(A) ❽He will cancel a family event.

(B) He wants to eat a sandwich during the event.

正確答案，往下一題進行 → ❾

(C) He has taken part in team building events before.

(D) He helps organize Astrilla Technologies events.

關於斯特吉斯先生，下列推論何者正確？

（A）他將取消家庭活動。

（B）他在活動期間想吃三明治。

（C）他以前曾參加過團體建立活動。

（D）他協助規畫阿斯瑞拉科技公司的活動。

答案 **(B)**

解析 第一篇文章提到要參加活動的人可以選擇place an order for a Pitata's Sandwich Meal through us for $8（透過我們訂購一份8美元的碧塔塔（Pitata）三明治餐）。第二篇文章中，斯特吉斯先生針對這點回覆了I'll run my $8 down to your right away（我會馬上跑下去把8美元給妳），所以正確答案是（B）。請各位在作答Part 7多篇閱讀時要一邊閱讀，一邊隨時意識到各篇文章之間是否有「連貫性」。以這題為例，「$8」就是連貫兩篇文章的關鍵字。

23. ❾In the second e-mail, the word "free" in paragraph 1, line 4, is closest in meaning to → ❿

(A) ❿exempt

(B) loose

(C) available 正確答案，往下一題進行 → ⓫

(D) unpaid

在第二封電子郵件中，第1段第4行中的單字「free」，意思最接近下列何者？

（A）被免除的

（B）鬆散的

（C）有空的

（D）未付款的

答案 **(C)**

解析 把free想成是空格，選擇最適合的單字填入空格吧！將I am free most of the day, but I have a special family event that evening（我大部分的時間都有空，但那天晚上我有一場特殊的家庭活動）這句的前段變成I am available most of the day的話，則語意相通。所以正確答案是（C）。

24. ⑪ What does Ms. Campbell say about the event? 關於這項活動，坎貝爾女士說了什麼？

記住「坎貝爾說了什麼跟活動有關的話？」後再看文章 → ⑫

(A) ⑬ One space has just opened up.

→ 正確答案，結束這篇題組的作答

(B) Mr. Phillips needs a partner.

(C) She will try to plan another one.

(D) Mr. Sturgis is not well enough to attend.

（A）剛空出一個名額。

（B）菲利浦斯先生需要一位夥伴。

（C）她會試著計劃另一個（活動）。

（D）斯特吉斯先生還沒恢復到可以參加。

答案 **(A)**

解析 坎貝爾女士在第三篇文章中向斯特吉斯先生說「因為狄倫．菲力普斯（Dylan Phillips）取消，所以你可以繳錢報名參加了」。因此正確答案是（A）。（B）說的夥伴和（C）提到的另一個活動，文章中並未描述。至於（D），雖然從文章描述可看出斯特吉斯先生確實身體不適，但是已經復原，所以坎貝爾女士才會朝著「讓他參加」的方向繼續說明。

Practice Test 實戰試題

閱讀各篇英文，並針對以下試題從（A）、（B）、（C）、（D）四個選項中，選出最適合的答案（答案卡在全書最後）。

Questions 1-3 refer to the following article.

Book of the Month

by Jason Kang

One of the industries most radically transformed by the development of the Internet was investment. Today, many private individuals buy and sell stocks and bonds online with little help from professional brokers. However, with an overwhelming amount of information available at a click of a finger, the average first-time investor is at a loss as to where to start. Such investors will find *The Happy Person's Guide to Investing Online* by Tito Bergman most helpful. The guide provides basic instructions, such as how to choose online banking services and where to get the facts. It is very well-written overall. The chapter on preparation is a must-read for all first-time investors. In this chapter, Bergman warns people to be mindful of investment risks and to safeguard themselves from Internet scams. He also encourages novice investors to practice first, for example, by playing online investment games.

1. What is the purpose of the article?

(A) To advertise a book sale

(B) To review a publication

(C) To rate a Web site

(D) To criticize an opinion

2. What is suggested about investing online?

(A) It is quickly losing popularity.

(B) It should be done by specialists.

(C) It is hard to obtain related information.

(D) It can be confusing for beginners.

3. What is NOT indicated as advice from Tito Bergman?

(A) Save up enough money

(B) Play online games

(C) Protect yourself against fraud

(D) Be aware of possible risks

試題 1-3 參考以下文章。

Q1 本月一書

撰文者：傑森・康

由於網際網路的發展而改變得最徹底的行業之一就是投資業。今天，許多個人在沒有專業仲介的幫助下以網路買賣股票和債券。然而，由於只要用指頭點擊就可獲得大量的資訊，Q2 一般的首次投資者對於從何處開始是茫然不知的。Q1 這類的投資者將會發現，由泰托・柏格曼（Tito Bergman）所著的《快樂人的線上投資指南》（*The Happy Person's Guide to Investing Online*）一書是最有幫助的。這本指南提供基本的教學，例如如何選擇線上的銀行服務以及何處可以獲得有根據的資訊。整體上寫得非常好。對於所有的首次投資者而言，介紹事前準備的章節是必讀的。在該章節中，柏格曼警告人們要Q3 (D) 注意投資風險和Q3 (C) 保護自己免受網路詐騙。他也鼓勵新手投資者先做練習，例如Q3 (B) 玩線上投資遊戲。

字彙 □ radically 徹底地 □ overwhelming 勢不可擋的 □ as to～ 關於～、至於～
□ scam 詐騙 □ novice 新手

1. 這篇文章的目的是什麼？

（A）宣傳書籍特賣 （B）評論出版物 （C）評價網站 （D）批評某項看法

答案 **(B)**

解析 標題是Book of the Month（本月一書），且第4句提到Such investors will find *The Happy Person's Guide to Investing Online* by Tito Bergman most helpful.（這類的投資者將會發現，由泰托・柏格曼所著的《快樂人的線上投資指南》一書是最有幫助的。），所以正確答案是（B）的To review a publication（評論出版品）。因為這篇文章只有一段，所以建議各位在作答這題之前，先讀到全文的一半（本題答案出處）為止，要作答第二題時再接續讀完全篇文章。

2. 與線上投資有關的敘述，何者正確？

（A）它很快失去人氣。 （B）它應該由專家來做。
（C）很難獲得與之相關的資訊。 （D）它對初學者而言可能令人困惑。

答案 **(D)**

解析 文章第3句提到the average first-time investor is at a loss as to where to start.（一般的首次投資者對於從何處開始是茫然不知的。），所以將其換個說法的（D）It can be confusing for beginners.（它對初學者而言可能會覺得困惑。）是正確答案。at a loss（茫然不知的）可以換成confusing（令人困惑的）的說法。

3. 下列何者不是泰托・柏格曼的建議？

（A）存到足夠的錢 （B）玩線上遊戲 （C）保護自己免受欺騙 （D）注意可能存在的風險

答案 **(A)**

解析 文章的最後倒數2句是Bergman warns people to be mindful of investment risks and to safeguard themselves from Internet scams. He also encourages novice investors to practice first, for example, by playing online investment games.（柏格曼警告人們要注意投資風險和保護自己免受網路詐騙。他也鼓勵新手投資者先做練習，例如玩線上投資遊戲。）。（B）～（D）的內容都是本文中出現的建議，但並沒有提到（A）的save up enough money（存到足夠的錢）。

字彙 □ fraud 欺騙、騙局

Part 7

Questions 4-7 refer to the following letter.

March 21

Mr. Jordan White
LTK Corporation
6 York Street, Richmond
Victoria 3887

Dear Sir,

I wish to register my opposition to the proposed Potham Beach Revitalization Project. — [1] —. As a property owner and long-time resident of Potham Beach, I am concerned about the numerous adverse impacts the proposed project may have on our community. — [2] —. Although the construction of a large-scale shopping mall may seem attractive as it brings in more visitors and energizes the community, it may also cause road congestion and impose a serious burden on the town's existing Fire, Police and Medical services that are already operating at maximum capacity as it is.

— [3] —. Further, the nearby Potham Beach Forest which presently supports a variety of birds, snakes and lizards may be adversely affected by the development. I feel we should be working to preserve nature instead of jeopardizing it.

I plan to formally voice my concerns at the resident meeting held by LTK Corporation on April 3. — [4] —.

Sincerely,

Maggy Grant

Maggy Grant

4. What can be inferred about Ms. Grant?
(A) She runs a souvenir store in Potham Beach.
(B) She visits Potham Beach every year.
(C) She recently moved to Potham Beach.
(D) She has lived in Potham Beach for years.

5. What does LTK Corporation plan to do?
(A) Open a resort hotel
(B) Build a shopping center
(C) Develop a golf course
(D) Set up a power plant

6. What is NOT mentioned as a concern of Ms. Grant?
(A) The project may lessen the number of tourists.
(B) The project may increase vehicular traffic.
(C) The project may overload local resources.
(D) The project may negatively affect wildlife.

7. In which of the positions marked [1], [2], [3] and [4] does the following sentence best belong?
"I hope that LTK Corporation will strongly consider on how it can address these issues at that time."
(A) [1]
(B) [2]
(C) [3]
(D) [4]

試題 4-7 請參考以下信件。

3月21日
喬登・白（Jordan White）先生
LTK公司
約克街（York Street）6號，李奇曼（Richmond）
維克多莉亞（Victoria）3887

您好，

我謹表示反對擬議的波塔姆海灘振興計畫（Potham Beach Revitalization Project）。Q4 身為波塔姆海灘的一名地主和長期居民，我擔心擬議的計畫可能對我們的社區造成眾多不利的影響。雖然 Q5 建設大型購物中心可能看似很有吸引力，因它帶來更多的遊客並活化社區，但，Q6 (B) 它也可能導致道路擁塞和 Q6 (C) 對城鎮現有的消防、警察及醫療服務帶來嚴重負擔，這些服務目前已經是以最大限度在營運中。

此外，Q6 (D) 附近的波塔姆海灘森林目前生養著各種鳥類、蛇類和蜥蜴，可能會因開發而負面地受到影響。我覺得我們應該努力保護大自然而不是危及它。

我計畫於4月3日由LTK公司舉行的居民會議上正式表達我的擔憂。我希望LTK公司將好好考慮貴公司屆時會如何回應這些議題。

謹致問候，

瑪吉・格蘭特（簽名）
瑪吉・格蘭特（Maggy Grant）

字彙 □ energize 使～精力充沛 □ lizard 蜥蜴 □ adversely 負面地、不利地 □ jeopardize 危及～

4. 關於格蘭特女士，下列推論何者正確？
（A）她在波塔姆海灘經營一家紀念品商店。
（B）她每年都會去波塔姆海灘。
（C）她最近搬到了波塔姆海灘。
（D）她在波塔姆海灘住了多年。

答案 **(D)**

解析 因為文中提到了long-time resident of Potham Beach（波塔姆海灘的長期居民），所以換個說法的（D）She has lived in Potham Beach for years.（她在波塔姆海灘住了多年。）是正確答案。請將（C）的move to～（搬到～）和同義詞relocate to～都一併記起來。

5. LTK 公司計畫做什麼？

（A）開度假酒店。

（B）蓋購物中心。

（C）開發高爾夫球場。

（D）蓋發電廠。

答案 **(B)**

解析 格蘭特女士寫了一封反對LTK公司的海灘振興計畫，從the construction of a large-scale shopping mall可知，振興計畫包含了建設購物中心。因此正確答案是（B）。

6. 下列何者不是格蘭特女士關注的問題？

（A）這項計畫可能會減少遊客數量。

（B）這項計畫可能會增加車流量。

（C）這項計畫可能使當地資源超過負荷。

（D）這項計畫可能負面地影響野生動物。

答案 **(A)**

解析 第1段和第2段都提到了正確答案的出處。cause road congestion（導致道路壅塞）即是（B），impose a serious burden on the town's existing Fire, Police and Medical services（對城鎮現有的消防、警察及醫療服務帶來嚴重的負擔）即是（C），a variety of birds... may be adversely affected by the development（各種鳥類……可能會因開發而負面地受到影響）即是（D）。

7. 下面這句應歸置在標記 [1]、[2]、[3]、[4] 的哪一個位置？

「我希望 LTK 公司將好好考慮貴公司屆時會如何回應這些議題。」

（A）[1]

（B）[2]

（C）[3]

（D）[4]

答案 **(D)**

解析 文章內容全部讀完後再看這句時，應該就會發現「用前後關係來看，當然要放在這一段」。句中包含了做為連結關鍵字的代名詞these issues（這些問題）。these issues就是指第1段和第2段描述的各種問題點，而第3段開頭則用my concerns（我的擔憂）來代表那些問題。因此（D）是正確答案。

Questions 8-11 refer to the following online discussion.

Turner, Fay (9:15 A.M.)
So, guys, what are we going to do about the keynote speaker for our conference?

Nicholson, Adam (9:17 A.M.)
Well, we couldn't help that something important came up for Mr. Lehman.

Turner, Fay (9:18 A.M.)
Sure, so what's Plan B? It took a while to make sure we could satisfy all of his requirements.

Madigan, Rachel (9:20 A.M.)
I know, but we'll just have to contact the others that were on our original list. And we have to hurry since the programs need to go to the printer soon.

Nicholson, Adam (9:21 A.M.)
I guess we should call rather than send e-mails then. Which one of us do you want working on that, Rachel?

Madigan, Rachel (9:24 A.M.)
Since you're in the office the next two days, I'd like you to make that your top priority. I want to have someone lined up by the time Fay's back. And once that's taken care of, I'll e-mail all the attendees to let them know of the change.

Nicholson, Adam (9:24 A.M.)
No problem.

Turner, Fay (9:25 A.M.)
Thanks, Adam. But, Rachel, what happens in the event that no one on our list can do it?

Madigan, Rachel (9:26 A.M.)
Then I'll have to pull a few strings. I've got a friend who's the CEO at A & F Packaging Technologies. He's so knowledgeable about the industry that he wouldn't have to prepare much.

Turner, Fay (9:27 A.M.)
I just hope he'd do it for us.

Madigan, Rachel (9:28 A.M.)
He'd have to. He's always extremely busy, but he owes me.

8. According to the discussion, what is implied about the keynote speaker?
(A) He is going to be late to the conference.
(B) He has not confirmed his participation.
(C) He has backed out of his obligation.
(D) He is now asking for more compensation.

9. What is NOT suggested about the conference?
(A) The printed material will be ordered soon.
(B) It will be held over two days.
(C) Participants can be contacted by e-mail.
(D) Ms. Madigan is in charge.

10. At 9:24 A.M., what does Mr. Nicholson mean when he writes, "No problem"?
(A) He will get a phone call from Mr. Lehman.
(B) He will contact people who are on a list.
(C) He is pleased that programs will be printed earlier than planned.
(D) He permits Ms. Turner to become a keynote speaker.

11. Why does Ms. Madigan feel her friend would do a favor for her?
(A) He enjoys leaving the office.
(B) He needs little preparation.
(C) He has a lot of experience.
(D) He is indebted to her.

試題 8-11 請參考以下線上討論。

費伊・特娜（Turner, Fay）　　　　　（9:15 A.M.）
Q8 所以，各位，我們要怎麼處理有關會議主講人一事呢？

亞當・尼克森（Nicholson, Adam）　　　　（9:17 A.M.）
Q8 這個嘛，雷曼（Lehman）先生臨時發生了重要的事，我們也沒辦法。

費伊・特娜（Turner, Fay）　　　　　（9:18 A.M.）
當然，那麼B計畫是什麼？我們當初可是花了好一段時間才確認可以滿足他的所有要求。

瑞秋・馬迪根（Madigan, Rachel）　　　　（9:20 A.M.）
我知道，但我們也只能聯繫原始名單上的其他人了。Q9 (A) 而且我們必須要快，因為日程表需要盡快拿去列印。

亞當・尼克森（Nicholson, Adam）　　　　（9:21 A.M.）
那我想我們應該用電話聯絡而不是發電子郵件。那妳想讓我們當中誰來做這個工作，瑞秋？

瑞秋・馬迪根（Madigan, Rachel）　　　　（9:24 A.M.）
Q10 由於接下來兩天你在辦公室，我希望你把聯絡事宜作為首要任務。 我想在費伊回來之前就安排好人選。Q9 (C) 一旦確定，我會傳電子郵件給所有參加者讓他們知道這個改變。

亞當・尼克森（Nicholson, Adam）　　　　（9:24 A.M.）
Q10 沒問題。

費伊・特娜（Turner, Fay）　　　　　（9:25 A.M.）
謝謝，亞當。但是，瑞秋，如果我們的名單上沒有人可以來幫忙，那怎麼辦？

瑞秋・馬迪根（Madigan, Rachel）　　　　（9:26 A.M.）
到時候我就得利用一些私人關係了。我有個朋友是A & F包裝技術公司的執行長（CEO）。他對這個行業非常了解，因此他不需要做太多準備。

費伊・特娜（Turner, Fay）　　　　　（9:27 A.M.）
我真的希望他會幫我們的忙。

瑞秋・馬迪根（Madigan, Rachel）　　　　（9:28 A.M.）
他必須得幫忙的。Q11 他一直非常忙碌，但他欠我的。

字彙　□ pull a few strings 利用一些私人關係　□ owe 欠～

8. 關於（原）主講人，討論中暗示了什麼？

（A）會議他會遲到。

（B）他沒有確認是否參與。

（C）他已無法履行合約義務。

（D）他現在要求更高的報酬。

答案　**(C)**

解析　從一開始特娜女士和尼克森的對話可看出主講人雷曼發生了某些事而無法出席會議。因此正確答案是（C）。back out of～是表達「不履行～」的意思。

9. 關於會議的推論，何者不正確？

（A）印刷品即將被訂購。

（B）過兩天舉行。

（C）參與者將接到電子郵件聯繫。

（D）馬迪根女士是負責人。

答案 **(B)**

解析 因為是是非題題型，所以先來選出3個符合文章內容的選項吧！And we have to hurry since the programs need to go to the printer soon.（而且我們必須要快，因為日程表需要盡快拿去列印。）是（A）。And once that's taken care of, I'll e-mail all the attendees to let them know of the change.（一旦確定，我會傳電子郵件給所有參加者讓他們知道這個改變。）是（C）。（D）則是從馬迪根女士的整個發言內容可判斷出來。因此，剩下的（B）選項是正確答案。

字彙 □ be in charge 負責

10. 9:24 A.M.，尼克森先生寫著「No problem」這意味著什麼？

（A）他將接獲雷曼先生的電話。

（B）他將聯繫名單上的人。

（C）他很高興日程表將比計畫的還早印製。

（D）他允許特娜女士成為主講人。

答案 **(B)**

解析 這篇的主要目的是要找到主講人人選，而馬迪根女士在9:20 A.M.的發言中說了「我們也只能聯繫原始名單上的其他人」。對此，尼克森先生問了馬迪根女士「應該用電話連繫（名單上的人），但妳想讓我們當中的誰來做這個工作？」。而尼克森先生被馬迪根女士請託做這項任務時回答了「No problem（沒問題）」，由此可知尼克森先生接受這項任務。所以，（B）是正確答案。

11. 為什麼馬迪根女士覺得她的朋友會幫她忙？

（A）他喜歡離開辦公室。

（B）他幾乎不需要準備。

（C）他有很多經驗。

（D）他欠她人情。

答案 **(D)**

解析 9:28 A.M.馬迪根女士說he owes me（他欠我的）。這個he即是指她在前面提到的the CEO at A & F Packaging Technologies（A & F包裝技術公司的執行長），對話的過程中提到萬一找不到任何人選時要拜託這位人物。而這位人物因欠了馬迪根女士人情（也就是說，如果拜託他來主講一定會答應），所以正確答案是（D）。

字彙 □ be indebted to 對～很感激、欠～人情

Questions 12-16 refer to the following letters.

March 21

Kix Outing Center

Ms. Aditi Baboor
MT Exchange Bank
8 Bridge Street, Cavendish
Newfoundland

Dear Madam,

Thank you for considering Kix Outing Center for your event this year. We are confident that your guests and employees will enjoy a memorable day at the Center.

Below are the plans we offer:

Included in your private site:	Plan 1	Plan 2	Plan 3	Plan 4
Pavilion	✓	✓	✓	✓
Swimming pool			✓	✓
Sand volleyball court		✓		✓
Miniature golf course	✓		✓	✓
Tennis court	✓	✓	✓	✓
Max. number of guests	120	120	240	240
Max. price	$1,500	$2,000	$3,200	$3,800

All private sites are available for rent from 9 A.M. to 5 P.M. Please ask about our free usage of game equipment. We are also happy to arrange a disk jockey service, pony rides and air bounces to meet your outing themes for a minimal fee. For your safety, we also provide lifeguards at the pools at no extra cost. All plans are available Tuesday through Sunday. Every Monday, the Center is closed for maintenance.

Kind regards,
Jing Malm
Jing Malm, Director of Operations

March 29

Kix Outing Center

Ms. Aditi Baboor
MT Exchange Bank
8 Bridge Street, Cavendish
Newfoundland

Dear Ms. Baboor,

Thank you for choosing Kix Outing Center! We have received your signed contract with a deposit of $2,000. The remaining balance can be paid on the day of the outing. Please note that the plan you have chosen does not include a sand volleyball court. As you have requested that we include pony rides, an extra $300 will be added to the total.

We understand that your corporate outing theme for this year is "Family Fun". Although Kix Outing Center is suitable for people of all ages, we excel at providing an enjoyable occasion to families. This is why, with your permission, we will set up a crafts corner for free for your event. Crafts corner is an attraction for children where they can create paper hats, friendship bracelets and egg carton animals.

Sincerely,

Jing Malm

Jing Malm, Director of Operations

12. Who most likely are the letters addressed to?
(A) An organizer of an exhibtion
(B) A captain of a local sports team
(C) An employee at a financial institution
(D) A member of a luxury fitness club

13. What is NOT true about Kix Outing Center?
(A) Some music can be arranged.
(B) An employee will watch over swimmers.
(C) Maintenance is performed on weekends.
(D) Visitors can borrow game equipment.

14. What is the purpose of the second letter?
(A) To confirm a receipt of first payment
(B) To ask a customer to sign a contract
(C) To provide a client with a quote
(D) To give an overview of Kix Outing Center

15. Which plan did Ms. Baboor choose?
(A) Plan 1 (B) Plan 2 (C) Plan 3 (D) Plan 4

16. What can be inferred about the event?
(A) The entrance fee will be charged at the gate.
(B) The pony rides will be provided for free.
(C) The children of staff members are invited.
(D) The drinks will be catered by a different company.

試題 12-16 請參考以下 2 封信件。

3月21日

基克斯（Kix）戶外活動中心

Q12 亞迪蒂．巴布爾（Aditi Baboor）女士

MT外匯銀行

橋街8號（8 Bridge Street），卡文狄希（Cavendish）

紐芬蘭（Newfoundland）

親愛的女士，

感謝您今年為您的活動考慮基克斯戶外活動中心。Q16 我們有信心讓您的客人和員工在中心度過難忘的一天。

以下是我們提供的方案：

私人包場包括：	Q15 方案1	方案2	Q15 方案3	方案4
大型帳篷	✓	✓	✓	✓
游泳池			✓	✓
沙灘排球場		✓		✓
迷你高爾夫球場	✓		✓	✓
網球場	✓	✓	✓	✓
容納人數上限	120	120	240	240
收費上限	Q15 $1,500	$2,000	Q15 $3,200	$3,800

所有包場均可從9 A.M.到5 P.M.租用。請向我們詢問有關 Q13 (D) 能免費使用的遊戲設備。我們也很樂意以極低的費用為您安排 Q13 (A) DJ（唱片音樂播放）服務、騎乘迷你馬和大型充氣遊具，來滿足您的戶外活動主題。Q13 (B) 為了您的安全，我們也在游泳池提供無須額外費用的救生員。所有方案在每週二至週日提供。Q13 (C) 每週一，中心會為維修保養而關閉。

親切問候，

晶．馬爾姆（簽名）

晶．馬爾姆（Jing Malm），營運總監

3月29日

基克斯戶外活動中心

Q12 亞迪蒂．巴布爾女士

MT外匯銀行

橋街8號，卡文狄希

紐芬蘭

親愛的巴布爾女士，

感謝您選擇基克斯戶外活動中心！Q14 Q15 我們已收到您簽署的合約以及訂金2,000美元。餘額可以在戶外活動的當天支付。Q15 請注意您選擇的方案不包括沙灘排球場。由於您要求我們包括騎乘迷你馬，因此額外的300美元會再加入總金額中。

我們了解到 Q16 您今年的公司戶外活動主題是「家庭同樂（Family Fun）」雖然基克斯戶外活動中心適合所有年齡層的人，但我們尤其擅長為家庭提供愉快的聚會時光。這就是為什麼，在您許可的情況下，我們將為您的活動免費設置一個工藝品角落。Q16 工藝品角落對兒童們來說很具吸引力，他們可以在這裡創作紙帽、友誼手鍊及用紙蛋盒做成動物。

謹致問候，
晶・馬爾姆（簽名）
晶・馬爾姆，營運總監

12. 這封信最有可能是寫給誰的？

(A) 展覽的組織者　(B) 當地體育隊的隊長
(C) 金融機構的員工　(D) 豪華健身俱樂部的會員

答案 **(C)**

解析 兩封信的收件人都是Ms. Aditi Baboor, MT Exchange Bank（MT外匯銀行的亞迪蒂・巴布爾女士），（C）將其換個說法為An employee at a financial institution（金融機構的員工），所以是正確答案。正式測驗時，也會出現像這種在信頭就有關鍵字的情形，記得一定要瀏覽一下喔！

13. 有關基克斯戶外活動中心，下列敘述何者為非？

(A) 可以安排一些音樂。　(B) 一名員工會照看游泳的人。
(C) 維修保養在週末執行。　(D) 訪客可以借用遊戲設備。

答案 **(C)**

解析 第一封信的最後段落總括了正確答案的出處。free usage of game equipment（免費使用的遊戲設備）是（D）。arrange a disk jockey service（安排DJ服務）是（A）。we also provide lifeguards at the pools at no extra cost.（我們也在游泳池提供無須額外費用的救生員）是（B）。而從Every Monday, the Center is closed for maintenance（每週一，中心會為維修保養而關閉）可得知維修保養日是週一，因此，正確答案是（C）。

14. 寫第二封信的目的是什麼？

(A) 確認收到第一筆付款。　(B) 要求客戶簽訂合約。
(C) 向客戶提供報價。　(D) 提供基克斯中心的概況。

答案 **(A)**

解析 第二封信開頭提到了We have received your signed contract with a deposit of $2,000.（我們已收到您簽署的合約以及訂金2,000美元）。表示已收取2,000美元的訂金，（A）只是將它簡潔地換個說法，因此是正確答案。

15. 巴布爾女士選擇哪個方案？

(A) 方案1　(B) 方案2　(C) 方案3　(D) 方案4

答案 **(C)**

解析 這二封信的首段第3行提到Please note that the plan you have chosen does not include a sand volleyball court.（請注意您選擇的方案不包括沙灘排球場。）。而不含sand volleyball court（沙灘排球場）的方案是第一封信的1和3。因為巴布爾女士已付了2,000美元訂金，所以收費上限為1,500美元的方案1可刪除不用考慮。因此，正確答案是（C）的方案3。

16. 關於這項活動，下列推論何者正確？

(A) 入場費將在門口被收取。　(B) 迷你馬騎乘將被免費提供。
(C) 邀請職員的子女被邀請。　(D) 飲料將由不同的公司供應。

答案 **(C)**

解析 從第一封信的前半段可知，這項活動是以銀行的客戶及員工為對象，第二封信的後段則提到活動的主題是「家庭同樂（Family Fun）」，由此可知是會讓大人小孩都開心的事。而從這句再往下2行則提到設立工藝品角落來吸引孩子的建議，所以（C）是正確答案。

Questions 17-21 refer to the following article, schedule, and e-mail.

DANTON — When Danton native Kendra Fellars was just 2 years old, her grandfather recognized her talent on the piano. Three years later, Fellars was enrolled at the Lander City Music Academy to study classical music. At age 6, after her schooling at the academy, she debuted at the Mackler Festival. By the time she was 7, Fellars had composed more than 200 pieces. Now just 13 years old, Fellars has already won several distinguished awards and played for the President and other special audiences around the world as well as on various talk shows. Fellars is now based in Graveltown and composing for TV, film, and commercials.

Fellars tries to appear before audiences here in her hometown each year, so keep an eye out for details. We will print information when we get it.

MAGELLAN THEATER OCTOBER EVENTS

Aljaz Dance Troupe **October 8** **6 P.M.**

Enjoy a unique performance by the Slovenian dance troupe on tour in America! You'll be awed by these youths, age 13 to 24, and their merging of the spirit and energy of Slovenia's modern and traditional dance forms.

Kendra Fellars **October 15** **6 P.M.**

Danton's very own child piano prodigy will perform multiple pieces, all from the collection she composed during her year in music school. This talented young woman won't return to the Magellan until next year, so don't miss this opportunity to enjoy her masterpieces!

Centennial Oaks **October 22** **7 P.M.**

This musical comedy is full of song and dance and tells the story of a young dancer who goes to Broadway in hopes of starting a successful career on stage.

The Googles **October 29** **4 P.M.**

This is a brand-new children's stage performance based on the hit TV show on Maxim Junior and the popular children's book series!

To: info@magellantheater.org
From: Denise Rewerts drew@peacemail.com
Subject: Seats with disability access
Date: October 17

Dear Magellan Theater,

I am in a wheelchair, and I had never been to your theater because I didn't know how well I'd be able to view the performances. But I took a chance this past weekend and attended the wonderful performance. I am happy to say that I was pleasantly surprised. Not only could I see and hear well from my seats, but the aisle had a nice amount of space for entering and exiting. I also appreciated that the seats were to the side of the theater so I didn't have to compete with the traffic in the main aisle in the middle of the theater. I am sorry that I didn't try to attend one of your performances until now because I would have liked to see the Slovenian dancers. I will be getting tickets soon for the upcoming evening performance you're offering, and I'm looking forward to frequenting your theater during the winter months, too.

Thank you,
Denise Rewerts

17. What is indicated about Ms. Fellars?
(A) She lived with her grandfather.
(B) She studied music formally since age 2.
(C) She is now appearing in commercials.
(D) She no longer lives in Danton.

18. How old was Ms. Fellars when she composed the pieces she played at the Magellan?
(A) 2
(B) 5
(C) 7
(D) 13

19. In the e-mail, the word "sorry" in paragraph 1, line 7, is closest in meaning to
(A) apologetic
(B) regretful
(C) concerned
(D) offended

20. What does Ms. Rewerts NOT mention about her seat at the theater?
(A) There was easy access to it.
(B) There were no audio or visual problems.
(C) It had plenty of room for her legs.
(D) It was not in a central location.

21. Which performance does Ms. Rewerts plan to attend?
(A) Aljaz Dance Troupe
(B) Kendra Fellars
(C) Centennial Oaks
(D) The Googles

試題 -17-21 請參考以下文章、時間表和電子郵件。

丹頓（Danton）——丹頓出身的坎卓拉．費勒斯（Kendra Fellars）在2歲時，她的祖父認出她在鋼琴方面的天分。Q18 三年後，費勒斯入學蘭德城（Lander City）音樂學院學習古典音樂。6歲時，她在該學院的教育結束之後，於麥克勒節（Mackler Festival）上首次亮相。到了她7歲時，費勒斯已經作了超過200多首的曲子。現在才13歲，費勒斯已經贏得了數個傑出獎項，並為總統、世界各地的特別觀眾演奏，以及在許多脫口秀節目上表演。Q17 她目前長駐格瑞費爾鎮（Graveltown），為電視、電影和商業廣告作曲。

費勒斯試著每年都回來為家鄉的觀眾演出，所以隨時注意（演出）細節。當我們取得消息時，將會印出資訊。

麥哲倫劇場十月活動（MAGELLAN THEATER OCTOBER EVENTS）

阿札茲舞蹈團（Aljaz Dance Troupe）　10月8日　6 P.M.

享受一場由斯洛維尼亞舞蹈團在美國巡迴演出的獨特表演！您將被這些年齡在13到24歲的年輕人，以及他們融合斯洛維尼亞現代和傳統舞蹈形式的精神與活力所震憾。

坎卓拉．費勒斯（Kendra Fellars）　10月15日　6 P.M.

Q18 出身自丹頓的鋼琴神童將演出多首作品，所有曲目都是她在音樂學院就學期間的創作。 這位才華洋溢的年輕女子明年才會再回到麥哲倫，所以別錯過這場享受其傑作的良機！

Q21 百年的橡樹（Centennial Oaks）　10月22日　7 P.M.

這部音樂喜劇充滿歌舞，講述一位年輕舞者懷抱著在舞台上開始成功職業生涯的希望前往百老匯。

古歌思（The Googles）　10月29日　4 P.M.

這是根據麥克希姆．喬立爾（Maxim Junior）的熱門電視節目和受歡迎的兒童書系列結合而成的一個全新兒童舞台表演。

收信者：麥哲倫劇場客服（info@magellantheater.org）
發信者：丹妮絲．李沃茲（Denise Rewerts）（drew@peacemail.com）
主旨：無障礙座位
Q21 日期：10月17日

致麥哲倫劇場，

我是坐輪椅者，以前因為我不知道是否能好好地觀看演出，所以我從未去過　貴劇場。但是上週末我做了一次嘗試並觀賞了很精彩的表演。我要很高興地說我非常驚喜。Q20 (B) 我不但可以好好地從我的座位上看到和聽到表演，Q20 (A) 而且走道有很大的進出空間。我也很感謝 Q20 (D) 座位是在劇場的側邊，所以我不需要和劇場中間主要走道的人們往來相競。Q19 很遺憾我在這之前從未嘗試去看一場演出，因為我想我那個時候應該會很想去看斯洛維尼亞舞者的表演。Q21 我很快地就會為你們即將上檔的晚間演出購入門票，也期待於冬季期間經常到劇場觀看演出。

謝謝，
丹妮絲．李沃茲

17. 關於費勒斯女士，下列敘述何者正確？
（A）她曾和她的祖父住在一起。
（B）她從2歲開始正式學習音樂。
（C）她現在在廣告中露臉。
（D）她不再住丹頓了。

答案 **(D)**

解析 第一篇文章第一段結尾提到，Fellars is now based in Graveltown and composing for TV, film, and commercials.（她目前長駐格瑞費爾鎮，為電視、電影和商業廣告作曲。）。可知費勒斯女士雖生長於Danton（丹頓），但現在已搬到Graveltown（格瑞費爾鎮）。因此，正確答案是（D）。因為文中只提到her grandfather（她的祖父）「認出她的天分」，所以（A）不正確。而正式的音樂學習是從5歲開始，所以（B）不符合。雖然她有製作廣告歌曲，但文中沒有提到有在廣告中露臉，所以（C）也是錯誤的。

18. 費勒斯女士在麥哲倫劇場演奏的曲目是幾歲時創作的？
（A）2
（B）5
（C）7
（D）13

答案 **(B)**

解析 第一篇文章第一段開頭就提到，費勒斯女士5歲時進入音樂學校，6歲時完成學業。而且，第二篇文章的第二段介紹了費勒斯女士，描述了她在麥哲倫劇院演奏的曲目是composed during her year in music school（創作於她在音樂學院的就學期間）。因此，正確答案是（B）。

19. 在電子郵件中，第 1 段第 7 行中的單字「sorry」意思最接近下列何者？

（A）抱歉的

（B）後悔的

（C）擔心的

（D）被冒犯的

答案 **(B)**

解析 從I am sorry that I didn't try to attend one of your performances until now because I would have liked to see the Slovenian dancers.（很遺憾我在這之前從未嘗試去看一場演出，因為我想我那個時候應該會很想去看斯洛維尼亞舞者的表演。）這句可知，李沃茲女士對於之前從未去麥哲倫劇院是「後悔的」。因此，正確答案是（B）的regretful。

20. 關於她的戲院座位，李沃茲女士沒有提到下列何者？

（A）出入容易。

（B）沒有音響或視線上的問題。

（C）有足夠的放腳空間。

（D）不是在中間的位置。

答案 **(C)**

解析 第三篇電子郵件的中間總括了正確答案的出處。the aisle had a nice amount of space for entering and exiting（走道有很大的進出空間）是（A）。Not only could I see and hear well from my seats（我不但可以好好地從我的座位上看到和聽到表演）是（B）。還有the seats were to the side of the theater so I didn't have to compete with the traffic in the main aisle in the middle of the theater（座位是在劇場的側邊，所以我不需要和劇場中間主要走道的人們往來相競）是（D）。

21. 李沃茲女士計畫觀賞哪一場表演？

（A）阿札茲舞蹈團

（B）坎卓拉．費勒斯

（C）百年的橡樹

（D）古歌思

答案 **(C)**

解析 發送電子郵件的日期是10月17日。在信中，李沃茲女士表達了I will be getting tickets soon for the upcoming evening performance you're offering（我很快地就會為你們即將上檔的晚間演出購入門票）。也就是說，這時候要確認下一次晚上的表演是什麼。從時間表來看，可知接下來是10月22日的Centennial Oaks（百年的橡樹）。因此，正確答案是（C）。

認真持續挑戰，肯定得到佳績。

Part 7 的「最進階」解題步驟

Part 7的解題步驟依學習者的程度不同而有多種方式。我想在此說明的，就是本書推薦的「如何更上一層樓」的解題步驟。

「先閱讀」全篇文章

不論是SP（Single　Passages單篇閱讀）或是MP（Multiple　Passages多篇閱讀），作答步驟都是先閱讀全篇文章，把所有的內容記在腦中，再針對每個題組的2～5道試題，**「僅憑記憶」一口氣作答**。如果你的程度能完全掌握並記住文章的內容，這將是最有效率的解題步驟。多篇閱讀採行這種方式，需要非常精確的記憶力，所以不熟悉者最好先從單篇閱讀累積練習。不過，不論是SP或MP，都是以**「全部聽取／全部閱讀」為基礎**。這是為了攻下990分的鐵則。雖然有很多例子是即使不全部閱讀而只看部分內容也能把所有的試題答完，我還是希望大家能具備速讀力＋精讀力，讓自己不僅全部讀完，還能有充裕的作答時間。

讀完「一篇文章」再解一道試題

如果覺得閱讀全篇文章後再作答有困難度，最好先試著從**讀完一篇文章再解一道試題**的方式開始為佳。若是SP，就依上述的作答步驟；若是MP，其步驟就是先讀完第一篇文章再解一道試題，要寫第二題時再讀第二篇文章。用這個方法，在答完第2題時應可讀完全部的文章內容了，因此做第3～5題時就「憑記憶」作答了。如果使用這種步驟重複練習「記住文章的內容」，相信達成「先閱讀全篇文章再一次性解題」的水準是指日可待的。可以記憶的分量，將會日積月累一點一滴慢慢增加。如果可能的話，希望各位將「每日1題組」的閱讀解題訓練視為每日的課題。

結語

本書前身《新TOEIC®テスト990点攻略》（新TOEIC®測驗990分攻略）承蒙眾多學習者的支持，由衷向各位表示感謝。

而這本是獻給今後將目標定在「猶如高不可攀之金字塔頂端」的900分、950分，以及990分的各位！

「滿分」，就是「990分」，絕不是一條簡單的路，但也不是絕對不可能。

沒有什麼可以保證努力就一定有結果。

然而，有結果的人必定是盡了一切的努力。

我希望各位務必相信自己的能力，繼續追逐你的夢想而堅持到最後不放棄。

至今，我依然參加每次的多益正式測驗，並且持續拿下990分，在此還是要再次表達，這樣的成果是任何人都無法模仿的努力，但也不是「遙不可及的努力」。

以學習素材來說，單靠這本TOEIC L&R試題對策的教材，是可以完全致勝、拿下滿分的。

只要確實掌握每單元不同的解題技巧及攻略法，這就足夠了。

而且，如果你每天，能以每個人都能做到的最大程度持續努力的話，我可以斷言，你即將「圓夢」了。

「夢想真的能成真嗎？」

這就得看你了，「人生，由自己決定」。

相信自己，相信並挑戰自己的能力，我相信這是人生的真正樂趣。

既然生於此世，你更應該要好好體會生命存在的證明，以及真實生命的感覺。

煞費苦心認真挑戰990分的過程，應該讓你對此更有所體驗。

對於使用本書來學習的各位，不管現在的你是否過著幸福生活，我都希望不論男女老少有朝一日都能幸福。

藉由這個機會，我真誠地希望這本書可以讓各位完成夢想。

同時，我在此誓言會繼續為持續挑戰的你加油打氣。

我也不會輸給各位，今後我會繼續全力以赴！

濱崎潤之輔

Final Test

終極模擬測驗

Listening Test
Reading Test

※ 答案卡在全書最後

LISTENING TEST

MP3 1～7

In the Listening test, you will be asked to demonstrate how well you understand spoken English. The entire Listening test will last approximately 45 minutes. There are four parts, and directions are given for each part. You must mark your answers on the separate answer sheet. Do not write your answers in your test book.

PART 1

Directions: For each question in this part, you will hear four statements about a picture in your test book. When you hear the statements, you must select the one statement that best describes what you see in the picture. Then find the number of the question on your answer sheet and mark your answer. The statements will not be printed in your test book and will be spoken only one time.

Statement (C), "They're sitting at a table," is the best description of the picture, so you should select answer (C) and mark it on your answer sheet.

1.

2.

GO ON TO THE NEXT PAGE

3.

4.

5.

6.

GO ON TO THE NEXT PAGE

PART 2

MP3 8～33

Directions: You will hear a question or statement and three responses spoken in English. They will not be printed in your test book and will be spoken only one time. Select the best response to the question or statement and mark the letter (A), (B), or (C) on your answer sheet.

7. Mark your answer on your answer sheet.

（8.～30. 省略）

31. Mark your answer on your answer sheet.

PART 3

MP3 34～47

Directions: You will hear some conversations between two or more people. You will be asked to answer three questions about what the speakers say in each conversation. Select the best response to each question and mark the letter (A), (B), (C), or (D) on your answer sheet. The conversations will not be printed in your test book and will be spoken only one time.

32. Who most likely is the man?
(A) A secretary
(B) A mechanic
(C) A store clerk
(D) A car salesman

33. What is Ms. Scott asking for?
(A) Use of a rental car
(B) A discount on the price
(C) Expedited service
(D) A quote for repairs

34. What does the man recommend?
(A) Recharging the battery
(B) Changing a bad part
(C) Replacing the car
(D) Getting a second opinion

35. What is the advantage of the recently available apartment?
(A) It is in a quiet neighborhood.
(B) It has many lighting fixtures.
(C) It is within Ms. Short's budget.
(D) It has lots of space.

36. What does Lisa offer?
(A) To fax an application form
(B) To take Ms. Short for a viewing
(C) To stop by Ms. Short's home
(D) To reserve the property on Augustus Lane

37. What does Ms. Short want to confirm?
(A) If she can play the piano
(B) If she can have two vehicles
(C) If she can have pets
(D) If she can renovate

---

38. Where is the conversation most likely taking place?
(A) At a driver's license facility
(B) At the man's office
(C) At a grocery store
(D) At a bank

39. Why couldn't the man use his debit card?
(A) His account balance was too low.
(B) It had expired the day before.
(C) He forgot his PIN number.
(D) He used the wrong card.

40. What did the man learn about his monthly pay?
(A) It happens later than he thought.
(B) It was lower than he expected for this month.
(C) It is in different amounts each month.
(D) The date of payment is not fixed.

---

41. Where does the man most likely work?
(A) At an elementary school
(B) At a kitchen appliance store
(C) At a hotel
(D) At a muffin shop

42. What problem does the woman mention?
(A) An item is currently out of stock.
(B) A product is no longer available.
(C) A worker is temporarily occupied.
(D) A client is making unreasonable demands.

43. Why does the woman discourage self-installation?
(A) To protect the equipment
(B) To avoid injuries
(C) To secure employment
(D) To speed up the process

GO ON TO THE NEXT PAGE →

44. Where does the man most likely work?
(A) At a city service department
(B) At a construction company
(C) At a landscaping company
(D) At a telephone company

45. What is the problem?
(A) Employees have taken the day off.
(B) A company's driveway is blocked.
(C) Fallen trees have ruined a company's lawn.
(D) A tree was fallen onto a company building.

46. What will the man do for the woman?
(A) Find another company to assist her right away
(B) Put her on the schedule for Wednesday
(C) Help her call workers to clean up the area
(D) Send someone to her company today

---

47. Why is the man pessimistic?
(A) He doesn't have enough qualifications.
(B) He thinks he won't get the job.
(C) He failed an important exam.
(D) He received a bad evaluation.

48. What does the woman say about a follow-up call?
(A) It gives a good impression.
(B) It is better than sending an e-mail.
(C) It should be made as soon as possible.
(D) It demonstrates his responsibility.

49. What does the man say he has done?
(A) Phoned the employer
(B) Sent a recommendation letter
(C) Applied to other places
(D) Consulted a professional

---

50. What are the speakers mainly discussing?
(A) Moving up in a company
(B) Financing extra schooling
(C) Satisfying work requirements
(D) Teaching business classes

51. What does the man suggest the woman do?
(A) Check her company's policy
(B) Get special training at work
(C) Apply for a federal scholarship
(D) Ask her boss for a raise

52. What does the woman imply when she says, "I'll see what the case is with my company"?
(A) She will pay for her school by herself.
(B) She doubts her company will help her.
(C) She hopes her company can support her.
(D) She will ask the company to educate employees.

---

53. What is the problem?
(A) A delivery of office supplies was delayed.
(B) A wrong type of material has been used.
(C) A device is not working properly.
(D) An office supplies store has been closed.

54. Where does Mark most likely work?
(A) At an electronics store
(B) At a school office
(C) At a school cafeteria
(D) At a stationery company

55. What will the technician most likely do?
(A) Visit the office tomorrow
(B) Bring another kind of paper
(C) Replace old components
(D) Order a new unit

---

56. What will probably happen next month?
(A) An employee will be transferred.
(B) A staff member will go on holiday.
(C) Some duties will be outsourced.
(D) Some departments will be merged.

57. What does the woman say about her department?
(A) It is heavily cluttered.
(B) It lacks sufficient manpower.
(C) It will get some new recruits.
(D) It will move to another location.

58. How did the man know payroll associated tasks would be outsourced?
(A) He heard rumors about it.
(B) He saw a notice on the bulletin board.
(C) He read about it in a publication.
(D) He received a memo from his boss.

GO ON TO THE NEXT PAGE

59. Why can't the woman do the meeting in person?

(A) She did not get any work done last night.

(B) She is getting her laptop repaired.

(C) She had trouble with her vehicle.

(D) She double-booked for half of the meeting.

60. What does the man mean when he says, "It happens to all of us at some point"?

(A) The woman has entered a new stage in life.

(B) The woman had to make a difficult decision.

(C) The woman should be much more careful.

(D) The woman should not worry about it.

61. What was the woman supposed to do last night?

(A) Write down her ideas about an e-mail

(B) Work on a document

(C) Speak to someone about a warranty

(D) Negotiate a contract with a company

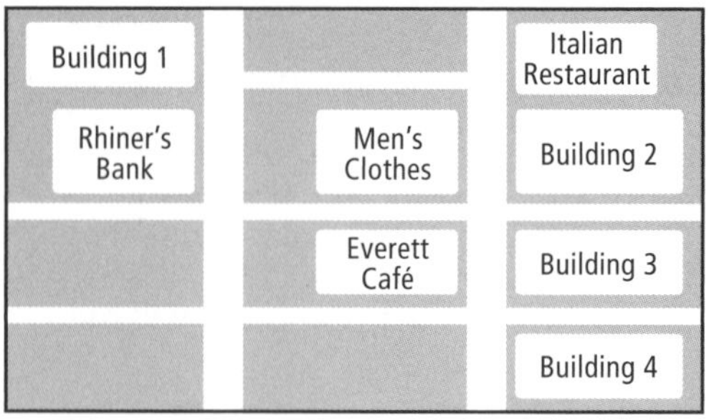

62. What is indicated about the man?

(A) He has an account at Rhiner's Bank.

(B) He is new to the area.

(C) He needs to buy a new suit.

(D) He is not very observant.

63. Look at the graphic. Which building is the post office?

(A) Building 1

(B) Building 2

(C) Building 3

(D) Building 4

64. Why will the man be gone for a while?

(A) He will probably get lost.

(B) He wants to get to know the town.

(C) He wants to try the Italian restaurant.

(D) He has plans to meet someone.

Employee Training Program Times
8:00 A.M.-10:00 A.M.
10:00 A.M.-12:00 P.M.
1:00 P.M.-3:00 P.M.
3:00 P.M.-5:00 P.M.

65. What is the woman trying to do?
(A) Establish a more effective daily routine
(B) Find someone to teach a program
(C) Decide on a temporary work schedule
(D) Choose days to be away from the office

66. Why is the woman consulting the man?
(A) They often have lunch together.
(B) They share some responsibilities.
(C) He generally gives good advice.
(D) He is the department manager.

67. Look at the graphic. When will the woman most likely take the training program?
(A) 8:00 A.M.-10:00 A.M.
(B) 10:00 A.M.-12:00 P.M.
(C) 1:00 P.M.-3:00 P.M.
(D) 3:00 P.M.-5:00 P.M.

AMHERST AEROSPACE
125 Lowry Ln, Amherst, RI (865) 555-1000

Theodore Dubrovka
President

*meetings must be in person, by appointment, 1-4 P.M.; contact secretary at: sec@amherstaerospace.com

68. What are the speakers mainly discussing?
(A) A friend's new idea
(B) Recent job offers
(C) Investing in a company
(D) A business referral

69. What does the man want to do?
(A) Become self-employed
(B) Invest in the friend's company
(C) Invent something for Amherst Aerospace
(D) Collaborate with the woman

70. Look at the graphic. Why can't the man consult with the woman's friend over the phone?
(A) This company only accepts calls in the afternoon.
(B) The company secretary meets with everyone first.
(C) Discussions are conducted face-to-face.
(D) The woman's friend is often out of the office.

GO ON TO THE NEXT PAGE

PART 4

MP3 48~58

Directions: You will hear some talks given by a single speaker. You will be asked to answer three questions about what the speaker says in each talk. Select the best response to each question and mark the letter (A), (B), (C), or (D) on your answer sheet. The talks will not be printed in your test book and will be spoken only one time.

71. Why is the speaker calling the man?
(A) He failed to meet a deadline.
(B) He missed a meeting.
(C) He performed poorly on a test.
(D) He has not returned a message.

72. What will the man most likely do next week?
(A) Take a business trip
(B) Present a report
(C) Have an interview
(D) Go on vacation

73. According to the woman, what will happen to the forms?
(A) They will be reviewed by the board of directors.
(B) They will be sent to headquarters.
(C) They will be used at a performance.
(D) They will be handed to Erik Cole.

74. What type of business is being advertised?
(A) A hotel chain
(B) A textile corporation
(C) A food delivery service
(D) A laundry company

75. According to the speaker, what is flexible?
(A) Payment method
(B) Delivery time
(C) Service costs
(D) Pick-up location

76. What does the speaker suggest about the cleaning process?
(A) It only takes a short time.
(B) It is fully automated.
(C) It involves using cutting-edge computers.
(D) It is environmentally friendly.

77. What is the talk mainly about?
(A) Reducing employee turnover
(B) Improving compliance to rules
(C) Communicating effectively
(D) Meeting deadlines

78. What does the speaker mean when he says, "you'd be surprised to know this"?
(A) He will talk about what he thinks few people know.
(B) It is not difficult to communicate well.
(C) He decided to hold the training session suddenly.
(D) Changes in the workplace may suddenly occur.

79. Why will the speaker e-mail the listeners after a week?
(A) To send all the handouts
(B) To get their feedback
(C) To respond to their questions
(D) To remind them about the next session

80. What is the purpose of the telephone message?
(A) To make a reservation
(B) To give details about a booking
(C) To change an order
(D) To provide a cost estimate

81. How much is the penalty charge?
(A) 10 dollars
(B) 15 dollars
(C) 24 dollars
(D) 40 dollars

82. What can the listener obtain from the Web site?
(A) A form for making an inventory
(B) A worksheet to calculate the total cost
(C) A timetable to facilitate moving
(D) A copy of the rental agreement

GO ON TO THE NEXT PAGE

83. What is the news broadcast about?
(A) Increased international shipping costs
(B) Global environmental protection programs
(C) New promotional strategies for companies
(D) Relocation of employees to foreign countries

84. What does Mr. Chang say about last year?
(A) Demand for Glomore's products increased.
(B) Business was slow for Glomore.
(C) Glomore had to lay off some employees.
(D) Glomore had to close down its overseas office.

85. Which area is Glomore increasingly involved with?
(A) Asia
(B) The United States
(C) Western Europe
(D) Africa

---

86. Where does the caller most likely work?
(A) At a tent rental company
(B) At a bakery
(C) At an ice cream shop
(D) At a party supply store

87. What does the listener need desserts for?
(A) A work event
(B) A birthday party
(C) A graduation party
(D) A family reunion

88. What does the caller mean when she says, “it's always best to try these things first”?
(A) The listener should try baking a gluten-free cake.
(B) The listener should buy some desserts to test out.
(C) The listener should bring a good recipe.
(D) The listener may not like the gluten-free items.

---

89. What is the broadcast mainly about?
(A) Technical difficulties at an airport
(B) Bad weather approaching an area
(C) The decline of a city's tourism
(D) Major delays during construction season

90. How are hotels in the area affected?
(A) Stranded travelers are sleeping in the ballrooms.
(B) Reservations are rapidly being canceled.
(C) Rooms are being shared by strangers.
(D) All of them are completely booked.

91. What does the speaker mean when he says, "rental car agencies aren't faring so well"?
(A) They cannot fulfill all of their reservations.
(B) They are losing a lot of customers.
(C) Their cars are being ruined.
(D) There are complaints about their customer service.

92. What is the talk about?
(A) Customer relations
(B) Security measures
(C) Emergency procedures
(D) Wellness guidelines

93. What happened last week?
(A) An updated version of a product was released.
(B) Construction of some buildings began.
(C) Electronic devices were installed.
(D) A professional assessment was conducted.

94. What are employees asked to do?
(A) Attend a photo session
(B) Back up important files
(C) Lock the break room doors
(D) Keep the office tidy

GO ON TO THE NEXT PAGE

José Martinez	
First user	$15 off
Frequent user	$5 off
Family user	$7 off
Premium member	$20 off

95. Why is the speaker's service special?
(A) He does not use any equipment.
(B) He takes people to and from salons.
(C) He specializes in styles for the elderly.
(D) He goes to clients' houses.

96. What do we learn about the speaker?
(A) He is bilingual.
(B) He sees more people in a day than usual.
(C) He has an assistant to help clean up.
(D) He works very quickly.

97. Look at the graphic. Which amount of discount is the speaker talking about?
(A) $5 off
(B) $7 off
(C) $15 off
(D) $20 off

Delivery Schedule
Orders placed by noon
→ Next morning delivery (9 A.M.)
Orders placed after noon
→ Next afternoon delivery (1 P.M.)

98. What do we learn about some of the listeners?
(A) They often work with customers.
(B) They arrived late to the office.
(C) They used to be contractors.
(D) They are new to the company.

99. Look at the graphic. When was Michael's order most likely processed?
(A) Thursday before noon
(B) Thursday after noon
(C) Friday before noon
(D) Friday after noon

100. What does the speaker ask the listeners to do?
(A) Order extra items to have on hand
(B) Take care of orders right away
(C) Expedite all special orders
(D) Learn project managers' order patterns

This is the end of the Listening test. Turn to Part 5 in your test book.

READING TEST

In the Reading test, you will read a variety of texts and answer several different types of reading comprehension questions. The entire Reading test will last 75 minutes. There are three parts, and directions are given for each part. You are encouraged to answer as many questions as possible within the time allowed.

You must mark your answers on the separate answer sheet. Do not write your answers in your test book.

PART 5

Directions: A word or phrase is missing in each of the sentences below. Four answer choices are given below each sentence. Select the best answer to complete the sentence. Then mark the letter (A), (B), (C), or (D) on your answer sheet.

101. A restructuring of the major divisions will end up taking place after SO & T ------- Supersoft next month.
(A) foresees
(B) acquires
(C) rests
(D) merges

102. The annual shareholders' meeting will be held in the Hamptons in ------- with company tradition.
(A) connecting
(B) keeping
(C) realizing
(D) concluding

103. For being a senior partner at Berizon and Rukoil Law Firm, frequent travel to other countries is one of the -------.
(A) recoupment
(B) requirements
(C) reflections
(D) refurbishment

104. Mr. Moskovitz reviewed the latest proposal and ------- it to the manager for approval.
(A) continued
(B) extinguished
(C) forwarded
(D) converted

GO ON TO THE NEXT PAGE

105. Von Vai Industry's new fall line of siding for houses is guaranteed to ------- the look of your house.
(A) quicken
(B) depict
(C) exemplify
(D) enhance

106. Please write your name on the label in the space provided and ------- it to the top of the bottle.
(A) abide
(B) affix
(C) detach
(D) confine

107. Donations to the Takashi Tanaka & Family Home will be greatly appreciated, yet are only -------.
(A) optional
(B) usable
(C) individual
(D) candid

108. The new attorneys must be under the supervision of a senior manager for several months before they are ------- any clients.
(A) garnered
(B) assumed
(C) incurred
(D) assigned

109. Due to the ------- of a self-development training program at Ballmer Company, staff absenteeism has been reduced to 10 percent.
(A) implementation
(B) temptation
(C) independency
(D) indemnity

110. Follow the ------- of steps to unlock the emergency exit door, or you will not be able to open it again.
(A) orbit
(B) sequence
(C) instruction
(D) expertness

111. Bale Energy is seeking an alternative lubricant that is ------- in quality to the brand that they have been using over the past decade.
(A) quantity
(B) comparable
(C) pilot
(D) substantial

112. Tokyo has an ------- public transit system with many subway, train and bus lines.
(A) attachable
(B) ensuing
(C) assertive
(D) extensive

113. Fortunately, the readings for the chemical analysis were well ------- the acceptable range for safety.
(A) within
(B) slight
(C) amid
(D) mutually

114. The manager spoke most ------- about focusing on customer satisfaction, although he failed to address several topics during the last meeting.
(A) independently
(B) previously
(C) eloquently
(D) evasively

115. The area has the largest ------- of coffee plants in the country due to the favorable climate in the southern hills.
(A) concentration
(B) conversion
(C) compost
(D) correspondence

116. ------- of consumers who bought Berizon's new laptop were not entirely satisfied with the quality.
(A) Some
(B) Any
(C) A large number
(D) A few

117. On November 20, the sales department is going to ------- a new policy that will take effect as soon as the current one expires.
(A) chaperon
(B) introduce
(C) derive
(D) command

118. Unless oak doors are treated with a chemical stabilizer, they have a tendency to ------- in a humid climate.
(A) append
(B) intensify
(C) expand
(D) inflate

119. All the recipes in this book are ------- enough to be adjusted to individual preferences.
(A) miscellaneous
(B) versatile
(C) prototypical
(D) unabridged

120. The amber grapes are used to make ice wine, the most ------- and expensive wine in the world.
(A) renowned
(B) utter
(C) seasoned
(D) devoted

GO ON TO THE NEXT PAGE

121. Actually, ------- all the applications reviewed, Mr. Persson's is by far the most impressive one.
(A) out
(B) toward
(C) of
(D) onto

122. In preparation for the arrival of the DM25, the older version, the DM20 will be ------- phased out over the next three months.
(A) sufficiently
(B) excessively
(C) gradually
(D) inadvertently

123. Most of the workers may find the daily tasks ------- due to the intrinsic nature of the work.
(A) disposed
(B) repetitive
(C) unfortunate
(D) preceding

124. Students who have yet to submit their plans for their next research project must submit those documents ------- after the completion of them this evening.
(A) exceptionally
(B) particularly
(C) promptly
(D) inwardly

125. The Italian food festival downtown has become so popular that almost all local residents avoid going into the city -------.
(A) never
(B) slightly
(C) scarcely
(D) altogether

126. Before we make a decision on purchasing the property, we are currently having an ------- undertaken to determine the true value of it.
(A) advantage
(B) appraisal
(C) aggregate
(D) absorption

127. The extra 30-minute break time added to the workday may explain the facility's high ------- over the last year.
(A) entry
(B) induction
(C) mandate
(D) output

128. City officials ------- to widen the road in order to ease traffic congestion in this area.
(A) proposed
(B) braced
(C) advocated
(D) asserted

129. Several industry analysts predict the market is heading into the worst recession ------- the last decade.
(A) for
(B) in
(C) during
(D) to

130. Berkshire Group will try to offer consumers more accurate information on a wide range of goods so that they can make an ------- decision.
(A) informal
(B) informed
(C) informative
(D) informing

GO ON TO THE NEXT PAGE →

PART 6

Directions: Read the texts that follow. A word, phrase, or sentence is missing in parts of each text. Four answer choices for each question are given below the text. Select the best answer to complete the text. Then mark the letter (A), (B), (C), or (D) on your answer sheet.

Questions 131-134 refer to the following advertisement.

-------. (131.) We specialize in helping business professionals enhance core skills and keep up on evolving trends through our business seminars, which we have ------- (132.) over the years to meet today's challenges. We offer more than 120 training seminars in dozens of subject areas of business management and staff development, ------- (133.) interpersonal skills, time management, and supervisory skills. Our seminars are conducted in person at 40 executive conference centers around the country. Register today and join the tens of thousands of managers, leaders, and professionals ------- (134.) careers and organizations have been strengthened by their participation in LPL's seminars.

131. (A) Read the following testimonials from LPL's satisfied professional participants.
(B) Thank you for participating in LPL's recent employee training seminar.
(C) LPL has been a leader in management and employee training since 1949.
(D) An online consulting company called LPL has just opened.

132. (A) refined
(B) authorized
(C) surpassed
(D) approved

133. (A) on the whole
(B) regardless of
(C) by the way
(D) for instance

134. (A) who
(B) whose
(C) whom
(D) who's

Questions 135-138 refer to the following letter.

Mr. Edward Walton
207 Elkhorn Drive
Wheaton, IL 60189

Dear Mr. Walton,

This is it, your last chance to sign up for another year of *Industry Robots* magazine at the low price of $34.99, the best rate offered to date. Plus, respond now and get your ------- (135.) copy of *Robotic Trends Guidebook*! Don't risk missing a single issue. Go online to renew now, or send us the ------- (136.) Renewal Request!

Last year, *Industry Robots* featured the Biennial International Robot Classic. We promise that this year will be ------- (137.) fascinating in the robotics world! We won't offer this low rate again, so hurry! Renew today! And don't pass up this opportunity to get our special guidebook for robotic trends at no cost to you!

Sincerely,
Betty Lundin

P.S. ------- (138.). Make sure the mailing address above is correct so that all 12 issues arrive on time.

135. (A) digital
(B) award-winning
(C) complimentary
(D) instant

136. (A) dispatched
(B) enclosed
(C) outlined
(D) combined

137. (A) exactly
(B) properly
(C) uniformly
(D) equally

138. (A) Help us deliver your magazines to your door without fail.
(B) We have a 100% money-back guarantee if you're not satisfied.
(C) Have us give a free subscription of our magazine to a colleague.
(D) Your first issue of the year is scheduled to arrive in a few days.

GO ON TO THE NEXT PAGE

Questions 139-142 refer to the following notice.

NOTICE

Employee parking permits will -------(139.) on August 3. All employees must reapply for a permit for the upcoming year, as a valid parking permit is required for every vehicle that parks on campus. This can be done online at www.fsu.edu/parking. Employees are entitled to a -------(140.) permit sticker only.* However, those with unpaid parking citations are not eligible to receive a new parking permit until outstanding citations -------(141.). Employees will be sent an e-mail to inform them of their outstanding fine amount.

A brochure containing information about university parking and traffic policies will be sent along with each renewed parking permit. The permit holder is responsible for understanding the policies for parking on campus. -------(142.). They are always happy to provide assistance.

*Since multiple permit stickers are not issued, employees who drive more than one vehicle to campus must contact the Parking Office to register the extra license plates.

139. (A) expire
(B) renew
(C) arrive
(D) change

140. (A) discounted
(B) temporary
(C) single
(D) congenial

141. (A) paid
(B) be paid
(C) will be paid
(D) have been paid

142. (A) You must visit the Web site to print your own copy.
(B) Please contact the Parking Office with any questions.
(C) Thank you for responding to our notice so quickly.
(D) Employees may park in any available space on campus.

Questions 143-146 refer to the following article.

SEATTLE — -------. (143.) Because of this, Amber Richards, vice president of client services at Barkley, Inc., will now have the opportunity to contribute articles to *Fremd Magazine* and share her decades of business insight with tens of millions of readers. The Council is an ------- (144.) only community for successful professionals who have been recognized publicly by organizations or in publications. The Council searched dozens of qualified candidates and then hand-selected Richards before offering her a position. Richards looks forward to telling a wider ------- (145.) about the special programs and technology developed by Barkley, Inc. Moreover, she feels she can gain a better understanding of ------- (146.) other professionals are thinking through their comments on her articles on Fremd.com. *Fremd Magazine* can be read in print and on the Internet in over 10 languages. Find more information at www.fremdagencycouncil.com.

143. (A) The Fremd Agency Council is happy to announce the formation of a new group.
(B) The Fremd Agency Council is on the lookout for new members for their community.
(C) Amber Richards was selected as a member of the Fremd Agency Council.
(D) Amber Richards is a candidate vying for a position on the Fremd Agency Council.

144. (A) online
(B) English
(C) administrator
(D) invitation

145. (A) turnout
(B) market
(C) gathering
(D) audience

146. (A) whom
(B) what
(C) where
(D) when

GO ON TO THE NEXT PAGE

PART 7

Directions: In this part you will read a selection of texts, such as magazine and newspaper articles, e-mails, and instant messages. Each text or set of texts is followed by several questions. Select the best answer for each question and mark the letter (A), (B), (C), or (D) on your answer sheet.

Questions 147-148 refer to the following text-message chain.

Manning, Alex (8:33 A.M.)
How's it going with sponsorship for the charity walk?

Frey, Theresa (8:35 A.M.)
I have to figure everything out myself. I wish Mr. Elliot had written up a manual before he left the company.

Manning, Alex (8:36 A.M.)
I understand. But at the same time, are you learning a lot in the process?

Frey, Theresa (8:38 A.M.)
Absolutely. And while I think our booklet with information about our organization, charity, and sponsors is great, I think we need to do more.

Manning, Alex (8:38 A.M.)
Like what?

Frey, Theresa (8:40 A.M.)
We could easily have an area at the charity walk where our sponsors could set up tables.

Manning, Alex (8:41 A.M.)
What are you saying?

Frey, Theresa (8:42 A.M.)
It would give them an in-person presence. They could hang their company banners, give out information, and maybe even have a quick activity to engage kids.

Manning, Alex (8:43 A.M.)
I like it. It could help us get more sponsors and therefore more money for the charity.

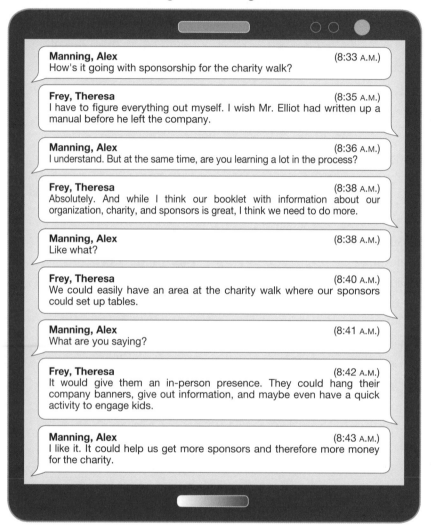

147. What is the discussion mainly about?
(A) Hiring a new organization leader
(B) Raising funds for an event
(C) Advertising for a nonprofit organization
(D) Ms. Frey's recent training

148. At 8:41 A.M., what does Mr. Manning most likely mean when he writes, "What are you saying"?
(A) He does not like the idea.
(B) He is feeling insulted.
(C) He wants Ms. Frey to give another example.
(D) He wants an explanation.

Questions 149-150 refer to the following article.

Density-2000 Wins Again

Globe-biz.net has released its list of top-selling mobile phones for this month. According to the list, Density-2000 by Bensen is in first place for the third consecutive month. In second place is Hyuwa-90 by Hyuwa Electronics.

It has been quite a year for Bensen, with its Density-2000 selling 35 million units worldwide. Bensen also overtook Hyuwa, becoming the biggest mobile phone manufacturer in January this year.

More details on Density-2000 are available on page 27 — find out if the features that attract thousands are suitable for you.

149. Where would the article most likely appear?
(A) In a technology magazine
(B) In a historical novel
(C) In a scholarly journal
(D) In a business report

150. What is indicated in the article?
(A) Hyuwa-90 has sold more than Density-2000.
(B) Hyuwa is the largest mobile phone manufacturer.
(C) Density-2000 has been a best-selling product for 3 months.
(D) Bensen sold less than 35 million mobile phones last year.

GO ON TO THE NEXT PAGE

Questions 151-152 refer to the following advertisement.

Get the Professional Look with MP Solutions!

How can MP Solutions improve your business?
The way in which you present your material says a lot about your company. Create sophisticated, professional-looking documents by using our thermal binding system. We offer only the highest performance machines in the market.

We provide:
Fast delivery
The machines are normally delivered and are ready for use within 2-3 days from the time of your call.

User support
Customers will be provided with an exclusive phone number where an expert will answer any questions you may have.

Flexible lease terms
Our machines are available for short or long-term lease. At this time, items are not available for retail purchases.

151. What type of service does MP Solutions offer?
(A) Document shipping service
(B) Equipment rental service
(C) Printer maintenance service
(D) Fashion consultation service

152. What is suggested in the advertisement?
(A) Orders are delivered to destinations overnight.
(B) A support service is available to customers.
(C) Payment can be made in installments.
(D) Support is offered to users 24 hours a day.

Questions 153-155 refer to the following Web page.

Pinecone Entertainment

Home
About us
Rates
DJs

Our entertainment division offers tailor-made packages to suit functions of up to 300 people. Our four DJs devote an enormous amount of time to music research and meet with clients beforehand to discuss requests. Our goal is your satisfaction! With our lighting and audio-visual effects, we can create just the mood you are looking for!

Mr. Enzo Rankin of Dacota Financial Institute says,

"Thank you for your performance at our gala dinner. Judging from the fact that you were able to extend your services for a few hours and from the compliments we received from guests, I must say hiring you was a great idea. Our guests came from all walks of life and all of them were happy."

153. What is indicated about Pinecone Entertainment's service?
(A) It is customized for each client.
(B) It guarantees 100 percent satisfaction.
(C) It is suitable for events of all sizes.
(D) It must be reserved one week in advance.

154. What is NOT provided by Pinecone Entertainment?
(A) Lighting adjustment
(B) Market research
(C) Audio-visual effects
(D) Pre-event meeting

155. What is mentioned in Mr. Rankin's comment?
(A) The event ended earlier than expected.
(B) The attendants were happy with the food quality.
(C) The guests came from a variety of backgrounds.
(D) The company had been recommended by a guest.

GO ON TO THE NEXT PAGE

Questions 156-159 refer to the following e-mail.

From: Margaret Klimov [Mklimov@lonetech.com]
To: Jim Barros [Jbarros@lonetech.com]
Subject: Ice Hockey Event
Date: Wednesday, March 7

Hi Jim,

I wonder if you got the message I left on your desk on Monday. Have you already reserved the bus to Yolanda Ice Hockey Stadium? If so, please notify me of the pick-up time and meeting point as I am making the final copy of the itinerary of the event to distribute to staff members at tomorrow's meeting.

Incidentally, there are a few dozen sheets of name tag stickers in the storage room if you need them for the event. I thought there were some paper cups and napkins left over from last year's picnic but didn't find any. The storage room is usually open on weekdays, but if it's locked, you can get the key from Elena in the accounting department.

I read in the newspaper that the weather will be nice on Friday. I hope you will all enjoy yourselves, and I look forward to hearing all about it when you return!

Margaret

156. What is the purpose of the e-mail?
(A) To inform a colleague of an office clean-up
(B) To reserve a bus for a sports team
(C) To obtain missing information
(D) To ask about existing stocks

157. What can be found in the storage room?
(A) Adhesive labels
(B) Disposable cups
(C) Picnic baskets
(D) Paper towels

158. When will the outing take place?
(A) Monday
(B) Wednesday
(C) Friday
(D) Sunday

159. What is probably NOT true about the event?
(A) Transportation will be arranged.
(B) Schedules will be handed out beforehand.
(C) All employees will participate.
(D) The weather is expected to be sunny.

GO ON TO THE NEXT PAGE →

Questions 160-162 refer to the following e-mail.

From: Jimmy Chang [Jchang@ssf.com]
To: Colin Peters [Cpeters@osc.org]
Subject: GMT Technologies
Date: April 29

Dear Mr. Peters,

Following the near miss incident at the Abo factory last week, I was assigned to conduct an assessment of worker safety in twelve GMT factories. Upon careful inspection, I found all safety equipment at the factories in good working condition. — [1] —. However, twenty-five accidents and ten near misses were reported within GMT facilities last year. This year, there have so far been a total of five accident reports. The analysis of incidents shows that 40 percent of the injuries were caused by falling. — [2] —. Regrettably, many of the reported incidents could have been avoided if workers followed basic safety rules, such as using ladders to reach higher shelves, wiping any spills on the floor and not leaving unnecessary tools lying around.

My conclusion is that the number of accidents can be significantly lowered by reinforcing workplace safety through rewarding workers who demonstrate safe behavior, encouraging workers to participate in developing safety programs, and placing signs and guidelines in appropriate locations. — [3] —. My full report is attached to this e-mail for the review of the Oakland Safety Commission. — [4] —.

Jimmy Chang
SSF, Inc.

160. What is indicated as the main reason for the incidents?
(A) A malfunction in the machinery
(B) Failure to follow regulations
(C) Lack of human resources
(D) Too much overtime work

161. What is NOT a suggestion made by Mr. Chang?
(A) Putting up signs on site
(B) Getting workers involved in some programs
(C) Making stricter rules to protect confidentiality
(D) Rewarding employees who act safely

162. In which of the positions marked [1], [2], [3] and [4] does the following sentence best belong?
"This included falling from steps, chairs, stools and slipping on wet or uneven surfaces on the floor."
(A) [1] (B) [2] (C) [3] (D) [4]

Questions 163-164 refer to the following book review.

Book of the Month

Reviewed by Michael Gottenberg

Meals and Magic

By Lorenzo Carreras
Illustrated. 258 pages
Don Juan Publishing. £19.99

Bookstores today are filled with stacks of books dedicated to helping you with creating great healthy dishes in no time. But have you ever wondered how those images of steaming home-cooked pasta or lamb curry that make your mouth water are taken?

Wonder no more — Lorenzo Carreras takes you behind the scenes in his new book *Meals and Magic.* A self-confessed food enthusiast, Carreras interviews chefs, photographers and editors to discover the secret behind creating magnificent food photographs.

The book is filled with tricks experienced photographers use to make the dishes look fresh, such as brushing oil over finished food to add shine, and hiding hot towels behind the plate to create steam. Even if you are not a professional cook, it will be simple to apply the tips in the book to take amazing snapshots of your own culinary handiwork.

163. What is indicated about Mr. Carreras?
(A) He is a skilled photographer.
(B) He works with Michael Gottenberg.
(C) He is passionate about food.
(D) He cooks delicious meals.

164. What is suggested about the photographic techniques described in the book?
(A) They were developed over many years.
(B) They determine the sales of a product.
(C) They require professional equipment.
(D) They can easily be adopted by amateurs.

GO ON TO THE NEXT PAGE

Questions 165-168 refer to the following online chat.

FRANCIS BOHR (3:42 P.M.)
Have you noticed that some of our cooks' and waiters' uniforms seem to have food on them even when they start their shift?

ED KAEHLER (3:44 P.M.)
Yeah. Sometimes I see them leaving their uniforms here when they go home, so I guess they're not laundering them regularly.

FRANCIS BOHR (3:45 P.M.)
Hmm, I'm thinking it might be worth it to invest in a uniform service.

ED KAEHLER (3:45 P.M.)
What would that entail?

FRANCIS BOHR (3:46 P.M.)
We would no longer buy uniforms for workers. The service would own them, so they'd pick them up, launder them, and deliver clean ones. I know it would be more expensive, but it would help with cleanliness and our image in general.

ED KAEHLER (3:48 P.M.)
Oh, that's an idea. So workers would change their clothes before and after their shifts. They'd have to come to work a bit early then, but I'm sure they'd get used to that.

FRANCIS BOHR (3:49 P.M.)
Right. But I think most workers would be happy with the change, especially the high schoolers who probably don't like doing laundry at all!

165. For what type of business does Ms. Bohr most likely work?
(A) Food service
(B) A laundry service
(C) A delivery company
(D) A retail clothing company

166. What is Ms. Bohr considering?
(A) Checking workers' uniforms daily
(B) Requiring workers to buy their own uniforms
(C) Cleaning uniforms at the workplace
(D) Renting uniforms for the staff

167. At 3:48 P.M., what does Mr. Kaehler mean when he writes, "Oh, that's an idea"?
(A) He feels the plan will help them keep workers longer.
(B) He is unsure about the cost.
(C) He is thinking favorably about the idea.
(D) He believes the change will not help.

168. What is indicated about the company?
(A) It has expanded outside the city.
(B) It employs young workers.
(C) It is dealing with financial problems.
(D) It needs to reduce its employee numbers.

Questions 169-171 refer to the following article.

Drought Hurts Milk Production

The drought over much of the south-eastern region is putting pressure on dairy farmers. Over the last seven months, the region has experienced a 35 percent decrease in the production of crops such as corn and soybeans. This has resulted in the doubling of crop prices, which in turn has impacted the price of animal feed.

Compared to last year, the cost of animal feed has increased by 20 percent and many farmers are being forced to use cheaper, less nutritious cattle feed. Not only has this led to a drop in the total production of milk, but it is affecting the density and creaminess of the product.

Those who refuse to compromise on quality are driven to take on more debt, or to simply leave the field. Analysts say many of the small dairy farmers will be forced out of business while larger farms and corporate milking operations may have to go through major restructuring.

169. What is indicated about animal feed?
(A) It is mainly manufactured in the south-eastern region.
(B) It is in low supply across the world.
(C) It generally does not contain a lot of vitamins.
(D) It has gotten more expensive than before.

170. The word "affecting" in paragraph 2, line 4, is closest in meaning to
(A) continuing
(B) surrendering
(C) influencing
(D) concerning

171. What is suggested by analysts?
(A) Larger corporations should help small farmers.
(B) Both small and large farmers will have a hard time.
(C) Small farmers will need to make more products.
(D) Large farms will be hit the hardest by the drought.

GO ON TO THE NEXT PAGE

Questions 172-175 refer to the following letter.

March 28

Mr. Jonathan Lee
767 Kensington Drive
Springfield, VT 05465

Dear Mr. Lee,

After house hunting for several months, I was delighted to discover your beautiful home located at 767 Kensington Drive. Since I enjoy hiking as a hobby, the wooded surroundings near the house is perfect for me. — [1] —. Moreover, I was impressed by the consideration given to the floor layout. The location of the two bedrooms on the upper floor gives a lot of privacy and shuts out noise from the living room on the first floor. — [2] —.

I have carefully considered my offering price and have decided to offer $139,000. — [3] —. My reason for not offering the asking price of $143,000 is because I noticed that the floorboards in several rooms need to be fixed, and the living room wall needs a new paint job. I think it is a fair offer compared to local housing prices. — [4] —. For example, a similar two-bedroom house just one block away on Dexter Avenue sold for $128,000.

Thank you for considering my offer. I look forward to hearing from you.

Sincerely,
Russ Taylor
Russ Taylor

172. Who most likely wrote the letter?
(A) A property owner
(B) A real estate agent
(C) A home buyer
(D) A next-door neighbor

173. What is NOT indicated about the house?
(A) It has a well thought-out layout.
(B) It is surrounded by woods.
(C) It has more than one floor.
(D) It has been soundproofed.

174. What is suggested about the asking price of the house?
(A) It has been reduced.
(B) It is comparatively high.
(C) It is similar to others on the market.
(D) It is not negotiable.

175. In which of the positions marked [1], [2], [3] and [4] does the following sentence best belong?
"It is rare to find such nature and calm so close from downtown Springfield, where incidentally my office is located."
(A) [1]
(B) [2]
(C) [3]
(D) [4]

GO ON TO THE NEXT PAGE →

Questions 176-180 refer to the following e-mails.

To: Joanna Flore [jflore@lgar.com]
From: Erika Smith [SmithE@joosta.com]
Date: November 1, 10:25 A.M.
Subject: Introducing Joosta, Inc.

Dear Ms. Flore,

Hello! I am writing to introduce you to our company, Joosta, Inc. We are a German company which designs and produces top quality wooden toys. Our products have been widely enjoyed in Germany for over fifteen years. All our toys are made from safe, premium quality material and each one is crafted by hand by an expert toymaker in Germany. Within the country, our products are sold in such reputable department stores as Axi and Rian Guus.

Currently, we are working to develop our clientele in the North American region. This is why we have prepared a sample package which you, as a retailer in North America, can receive for free by filling out the attached form and sending it back to us. It is important that you fill out all the entries on the form to ensure a swift delivery. Included in the package are a few of our most popular toys and some items from our brand-new children's apparel line. After you experience our products first-hand, you can then decide whether to place further orders with us.

We look forward to working with you.

Sincerely,
Erika Smith, Manager
Joosta, Inc.

To: Joanna Flore [jflore@lgar.com]
From: Adrian Appel [AppelA@joosta.com]
Date: November 7, 9:00 A.M.
Subject: Sample Pack

Dear Ms. Flore,

We are delighted to hear of your interest in our products. A sample package is on its way! Should you decide to place an order, simply fill out and return the order sheet enclosed in the package.

In an effort to reduce our carbon footprint, we no longer provide printed literature with our sample packs. However, detailed product information and technical documentation can be downloaded from our Web site.

Regarding your question concerning high-volume order discount, the manager will get back to you with details in a separate e-mail which will be sent shortly.

Thank you.

Adrian Appel, Customer Representative
Joosta, Inc.

176. What can be inferred about Joosta, Inc.?
(A) It is a family-owned company.
(B) It is expanding its business.
(C) Its products are manufactured abroad.
(D) Its main customer base is in North America.

177. Who most likely is Ms. Flore?
(A) A representative of a manufacturing company
(B) A customer of a department store
(C) A store owner in North America
(D) A wood supplier based in Germany

178. What is Ms. Flore encouraged to do?
(A) Let customers try out Joosta, Inc. products
(B) Return a document to receive complimentary samples
(C) Complete and send a form to enter a contest
(D) Read customer reviews on Joosta, Inc.'s Web site

179. What is NOT included in the package?
(A) Some garments
(B) Handmade toys
(C) A product catalogue
(D) An order form

180. What is indicated about high-volume orders?
(A) A separate price list will be sent.
(B) The toy designs do not allow for mass production.
(C) Joanna Flore will need to meet with the manager.
(D) Erika Smith will provide more information.

GO ON TO THE NEXT PAGE →

Questions 181-185 refer to the following article and letter.

NEWPORT — Potential visitors to the Newport Flower Show are not the only ones hoping for better summer weather. As the unusually rainy summer forces many flower shows to be canceled, organizers hope the same won't happen to their show which brings in approximately 40,000 visitors to the town each year. The show, which is hosted by the Newport Horticultural Society and costs £300,000 to stage, is a big boost to Newport's economy.

"I don't think the event will be canceled totally, but I'm afraid it will be severely curtailed like the flower shows at Stony Shade or Templeton," said Rolf Kelly, a Newport business owner.

This year at the Newport Flower Show, on top of the usual display of various flowers and over 100 fantastic English-style gardens, a demonstration by the rescue dog team will take place. Also, a glass pavilion has once again been set up to house the many species of roses.

Bob Martin, President of the Newport Horticultural Society says, "We have prepared a stunning range of events with the help of the local community. For example, this is our first attempt to incorporate animals into our show, which we hope will be appreciated by people of all ages but especially by our younger guests."

August 31

Mr. Bob Martin
Newport Horticultural Society
287 Bane Street
Newport, South Wales
NP18 6G5

Dear Mr. Martin,

I would like to congratulate you on the success of last week's flower show. I'm happy to hear that you had a turnout of around 40,000 visitors despite adverse weather conditions. I visited the show twice during its opening days myself. I loved the glass pavilion section last year and the roses were magnificent this year as well.

I deeply appreciate the kind suggestion by the Newport Horticultural Society of donating flowers and plants for the Newport Hospital playground. Unfortunately, however, at this time we do not have enough funds or manpower to plant and maintain them. Nevertheless, we thank you for thinking of us.

Sincerely,

Jing Wong

Jing Wong, Director

181. Why is Mr. Kelly concerned?
(A) A major town event has been canceled.
(B) The water shortage has damaged plants.
(C) Business has been slow in Newport.
(D) Some other flower shows were cut short.

182. What feature is new to this year's show?
(A) Glass pavilion
(B) English gardens
(C) Rescue dog demonstration
(D) Children's playground

183. What can be inferred about the turnout?
(A) It was poorer than expected.
(B) It was more than usual.
(C) It was less than last year.
(D) It was about the same as usual.

184. What is the purpose of the letter?
(A) To congratulate an award winner
(B) To report on the outcome of an event
(C) To give thanks for a monetary donation
(D) To decline a proposed offer

185. What type of organization does Mr. Wong most likely work for?
(A) A regional committee
(B) A local school
(C) A health service
(D) A charity organization

GO ON TO THE NEXT PAGE

Questions 186-190 refer to the following itinerary, information, and comment.

ITINERARY

Day 1: Jandara - Arrival

Arrival and welcome meeting at 7 P.M. Feel free to explore the city or join the optional tour of the Galli Temple ($15).

Day 2: Jandara

Enjoy an orientation walk of Jandara. Visit your leader's favorite spots around the city, including the spice market, Leroni Palace, Souvenir Alley, and a rooftop lunch which offers a great view of the city. Then take an afternoon cruise down the Anderly River and have an ethnic dinner with the group.

Day 3: Nalan

Transfer to Nalan in the morning. Spend a slow day with a host family and experience the way of life in this quaint village. Enjoy home-cooked meals and stay the night as a guest in your family's dwelling.

Day 4: Nalan / Rudapi / Achad

Bid farewell to your host family after breakfast and head to the city of Rudapi. Rudapi was an important stop on the Turley Trail thousands of years ago and is home to some of the most unique architecture in the country. During your free time today, join an optional tour around this streetless city ($10) or wander around by yourself. Sleep in nearby Achad.

Day 5: Achad / Marnitka / Nidapolis

Take a morning stroll through this charming seaside town and enjoy the cobbled streets and outdoor cafés. Meet at 10 A.M. for a tour of the Achad Museum. Then, head to Marnitka for an up-close view of the famous white cliffs. Stay the night in the ancient village of Nidapolis.

Day 6: Nidapolis / Bendalay

Start the morning with a local cooking class and visit Nidapolis' ancient ruins before transferring to Bendalay. View the city's modern architecture during a walk along the waterfront, and stop at a café for a chat with one of the city's many university students. Stay overnight in a converted palace built in 1838.

Day 7: Bendalay / Jandara

Take an optional morning tour of the famous Bendalay battlefield ($10) before heading back to Jandara for some free time. Consider visiting the Jandara Handicraft Co-op for souvenirs. A group goodbye dinner will be held at the hotel.

Day 8: Jandara - Departure

Depart any time today.

Style of travel : **Classic**

See the highlights of the region and experience the culture, all at a great price.

Physical rating : **2**

Generally, the walking on this tour is light and not too challenging for most fitness levels. However, the optional tour on Day 1 includes many steps.

Age requirement : **None**

All travelers under 18 years of age must be accompanied by an adult.

Service level : **Standard**

Accommodations are tourist-class and comfortable. Travelers will experience a mix of public and private transport.

Trip type : **Small group**

This tour provides a small group experience with a maximum of 16 travelers but an average of 12.

EXPLORE TOURS

Comment

Name: Raj Singh

I love getting a feel for what a country is really like, in both the big city and the countryside. This tour did not disappoint. I think the highlight of my trip was the time I spent in Nalan. I also enjoyed the other travelers, and I often look affectionately at the wonderful picture taken with everyone. The only thing I wish we had more time for was getting gifts to bring home.

GO ON TO THE NEXT PAGE

186. What kind of accommodation will travelers sleep in on Day 6?
(A) A historical building
(B) A hotel on the waterfront
(C) A university dormitory
(D) A dwelling in ancient ruins

187. What is NOT indicated about the tour?
(A) People in any physical shape can join.
(B) The entire itinerary is included in the price.
(C) Travelers can see the country's main sights.
(D) Local transportation will be utilized.

188. In the information, the word "light" in paragraph 2, line 1, is closest in meaning to
(A) bright
(B) easy
(C) small
(D) pleasant

189. What does Mr. Singh indicate he liked best about the tour?
(A) The size of the group
(B) The homestay
(C) Walking the Turley Trail
(D) Seeing unique architecture

190. What did Mr. Singh feel was missing from the tour?
(A) Ample shopping opportunities
(B) Cultural experiences
(C) A group photograph
(D) A visit to the countryside

Questions 191-195 refer to the following e-mail, Web page, and memo.

To:	Ignacio Ortiz <ortiz-i@hemingwayfinancial.com>
From:	Fiona Hoople <hoople-f@hemingwayfinancial.com>
Subject:	A thought
Date:	July 18

Ignacio,

Take a look at this Web site I came across: www.jobmatch.com. It's funny how a solution to the problem you and I were just talking about appeared. I think with this new tool, you're going to find that you have a lot more time and a lot fewer headaches in the winter! Anyway, hope this helps.

Fiona

www.jobmatch.com

JOB MATCH

Log in | Create a FREE account

HOME | Post a Job | Search Résumés | Employer FAQs

Recruiting has never been as easy as 1-2-3...until now. Create a FREE account with Job Match, post a job, and have résumés at your fingertips in no time. When you send us information about a job using our site, we save you time by automatically posting it to hundreds of job boards for you. And customize a questionnaire for applicants to answer to help the screening process go quickly and smoothly. No more sifting through résumé after résumé to find appropriate applicants for your specific job! We will analyze your requests and send you the best candidates. Finally, with one click, give those applicants a thumbs up or a thumbs down, and we will send replies on behalf of your company updating the applicants on their status. Want more? Make use of our premium tools for a minimal monthly fee. You can't go wrong with Job Match. So go on, click the button below and try ALL of our tools for free during a 7-day trial!

FREE TRIAL

GO ON TO THE NEXT PAGE

MEMO

Dear Staff:

Interview season is approaching! I know I'm giving this memo to you early this year—a new tool has helped streamline the process of choosing candidates. A big thank you to Fiona Hoople for introducing me to it. Anyway, interviews will still take place next month, and we'll have 15 candidates and two interviewers for each session like usual. The whole process usually takes about a week. If you are interested in volunteering to help me, please e-mail me at ortiz-i@hemingwayfinancial.com. I appreciate your consideration.

Ignacio Ortiz
Human Resources

191. What is implied about Mr. Ortiz?
(A) He has started a recruiting business.
(B) He is looking for new employment.
(C) He has more work than he can handle.
(D) He has the job of hiring new employees.

192. In the Web page, the word "appropriate" in paragraph 1, line 7, is closest in meaning to
(A) significant
(B) definite
(C) suitable
(D) accurate

193. What type of Job Match users pay a fee?
(A) Those creating applicant questionnaires
(B) Those who have found good job candidates
(C) Those using high-quality features
(D) Those posting to many job sites

194. What is NOT suggested about interviews this year?
(A) They are taking place now.
(B) The number of applicants per session are the same as before.
(C) A tool is making the process faster.
(D) Two people will be involved in giving each interview.

195. What does Mr. Ortiz mention about the process of selecting applicants?
(A) He must recruit volunteers this week.
(B) Ms. Hoople will take charge of it this year.
(C) It will last about seven days.
(D) It will not utilize Job Match.

GO ON TO THE NEXT PAGE →

Questions 196-200 refer to the following article, information, and review.

Ways to Move Through Airports Faster

Airports are busy, and there are often long lines due to staff reductions. Since wait times are unpredictable, it helps to save a few minutes here and there. Try these five tips to speed your way through the airport the next time you travel:

- Check in online and print your boarding pass before you leave for the airport. This can save a lot of time if there are lines at the check-in kiosks.
- Before you leave for the airport, weigh your bags and make sure they are not above the maximum limit. It takes a lot of time to rearrange bags or to pay extra fees.
- Have your ID and boarding pass in an easily accessible location like a pocket or a special place in your wallet or purse. This way, you can get them quickly when you need them.
- Apply for the Airport Pre-Check program. If approved, you will be considered a "safe traveler" and will be awarded access to a special line at security checkpoints whenever you use any airport nationwide. In this line, the procedures are less strict than the procedures in regular lines.
- If you go through regular security lines, wear slip-on shoes, have liquids in clear bags, and buy an airport-friendly laptop bag.

AIRPORT PRE-CHECK

Frequently Asked Questions

Q What are the allowed methods of payment for the $100 Airport Pre-Check application fee?

A We accept credit cards or money orders from a bank.

Q I usually book flights through third-party Web sites or travel agencies. How can I make sure my tickets reflect my authorized Airport Pre-Check status?

A When you are approved for the Airport Pre-Check program, you will receive an Authorized Traveler Number (ATN). Input this number when booking tickets online or give it to your travel agent so that it is indicated on your ticket.

Q I am traveling with family. Are they allowed to use the special line with me?

A People who are not authorized under the Airport Pre-Check program are not allowed to pass through the special security line unless they are 12 years of age or below and accompanying an authorized family member.

https://www.airportexperience.com/top-five-ways-to-move-through-airports-faster /reviews

June 25

I have found that these top five tips save time in varying degrees. When I don't check bags, the first one saves me a lot of time since I can go straight to security. When I do check bags, I still have to wait in a line, and often the airport worker prints out a new boarding pass anyway. What I find really speeds me through the airport is the tip about security. While it requires a lot of effort to get approved, including an in-person interview, background check, finger-printing, and $100, it is worth it. Not only is there a special line for approved travelers, which is definitely shorter than the regular lines, but we also don't have to take off our shoes, belts, or coats, and we don't have to take our laptops out of our bags. The one complaint I have with the system is that when the regular lines are very busy, airport workers often allow non-approved travelers to go through the special line. At many times, these are the elderly, who move slowly and must have the procedures for the special line explained to them, which holds up the line. It also doesn't speed things up when traveling with family if they haven't all gone through the same approval process. I was traveling with my 14-year-old daughter recently and was very annoyed because, while I got through security quickly, I had to wait a long time for her to get through.

196. In the article, the word "awarded" in paragraph 5, line 2, is closest in meaning to
(A) transferred
(B) donated
(C) decorated
(D) granted

197. What is indicated about travelers who are Airport Pre-Check approved?
(A) They carry a special pre-check card.
(B) They are assigned a special number.
(C) They must be 12 years old or older.
(D) They must buy tickets through special agents.

198. How is the special line different from the regular line?
(A) There are more employees working there.
(B) It exists specifically for elderly travelers.
(C) Travelers do not have to remove clothing.
(D) No one has to go through metal detectors.

199. Which tip does the reviewer feel saves time when traveling with carry-ons only?
(A) Online check-in
(B) Weighing bags at home
(C) Placing certain items in a pocket
(D) Wearing specific clothing

200. What is implied about the daughter of the person writing the review?
(A) She traveled at a different time than her parent.
(B) She preferred to use the regular line.
(C) She did not apply for the pre-check program.
(D) She had too many bags for the pre-check line.

Stop! This is the end of the test. If you finish before time is called, you may go back to Part 5, 6, and 7 and check your work.

Final Test 解答與解析

正確答案一覽表

題號	答案	題號	答案	題號	答案	題號	答案	題號	答案
1	B	41	C	81	D	121	C	161	C
2	B	42	C	82	A	122	C	162	B
3	C	43	A	83	D	123	B	163	C
4	C	44	C	84	B	124	C	164	D
5	B	45	B	85	D	125	D	165	A
6	C	46	D	86	B	126	B	166	D
7	A	47	B	87	A	127	D	167	C
8	A	48	A	88	D	128	A	168	B
9	C	49	C	89	B	129	B	169	D
10	A	50	B	90	D	130	B	170	C
11	B	51	A	91	B	131	C	171	B
12	C	52	C	92	B	132	A	172	C
13	C	53	C	93	C	133	D	173	D
14	B	54	B	94	D	134	B	174	B
15	A	55	C	95	D	135	C	175	A
16	B	56	B	96	A	136	B	176	B
17	C	57	B	97	C	137	D	177	C
18	A	58	C	98	D	138	A	178	B
19	A	59	C	99	B	139	A	179	C
20	C	60	D	100	B	140	C	180	D
21	A	61	B	101	B	141	D	181	D
22	A	62	B	102	B	142	B	182	C
23	B	63	B	103	B	143	C	183	D
24	C	64	D	104	C	144	D	184	D
25	B	65	C	105	D	145	D	185	C
26	C	66	B	106	B	146	B	186	A
27	A	67	D	107	A	147	B	187	B
28	B	68	D	108	D	148	D	188	B
29	B	69	A	109	A	149	A	189	B
30	A	70	C	110	B	150	C	190	A
31	B	71	A	111	B	151	B	191	D
32	B	72	A	112	D	152	B	192	C
33	D	73	B	113	A	153	A	193	C
34	B	74	D	114	C	154	B	194	A
35	C	75	B	115	A	155	C	195	C
36	C	76	D	116	C	156	C	196	D
37	C	77	C	117	B	157	A	197	B
38	D	78	A	118	C	158	C	198	C
39	A	79	B	119	B	159	C	199	A
40	A	80	B	120	A	160	B	200	C

預測成績換算表

各位在完成終極模擬測驗後，可參考下表，將答對題數換算為分數，試著算出預測成績吧！本換算表和實際TOEIC聽讀測驗的計算方式不同，所以請把它當作推算目前實力的一種標準即可。

聽力（Listening）

答對題數	預測分數	答對題數	預測分數
100	495	74	395
99	495	73	390
98	495	72	385
97	495	71	380
96	495	70	375
95	495	69	370
94	495	68	365
93	490	67	360
92	485	66	355
91	480	65	350
90	475	64	345
89	470	63	340
88	465	62	335
87	460	61	330
86	455	60	325
85	450	59	320
84	445	58	315
83	440	57	310
82	435	56	305
81	430	55	300
80	425	54	295
79	420	53	290
78	415	52	285
77	410	51	280
76	405	50	275
75	400		

閱讀（Reading）

答對題數	預測分數	答對題數	預測分數
100	495	74	380
99	495	73	375
98	495	72	370
97	495	71	365
96	490	70	360
95	485	69	355
94	480	68	350
93	475	67	345
92	470	66	340
91	465	65	335
90	460	64	330
89	455	63	325
88	450	62	320
87	445	61	315
86	440	60	310
85	435	59	305
84	430	58	300
83	425	57	295
82	420	56	290
81	415	55	285
80	410	54	280
79	405	53	275
78	400	52	270
77	395	51	265
76	390	50	260
75	385		

聽力	+	閱讀	=	預測分數
答對題數（　　） ／分		答對題數（　　） ／分		答對題數（　　） ／分

PART 1

MP3 1～7

1.

2

(A) Some plants are being watered in a flower bed.
(B) Some shrubs are being trimmed in a yard.
(C) Some water hoses are being sold at an open-air market.
(D) Some flowers are being planted in a garden by the man.

（A）花圃內一些植物正被澆著水。
（B）庭院裡一些矮樹正被修剪著。
（C）露天市場裡一些水管正被出售。
（D）花園裡一些花正由男性栽種著。

答案　(B)

解析　這是男性正在庭院剪樹枝的照片。（B）用現在進行式被動語態「正在被～」描述照片的實際情形，所以是正確答案。其他選項雖然是現在進行式被動語態，也包括照片內相關物品的用語，但是描述內容不符合照片的情況。

字彙　☐ flower bed　花圃　☐ shrub　矮樹　☐ trim　修剪　☐ open-air market　露天市場

2.

3

(A) The man is gathering up some electrical wires on the ground.
(B) Some boxes are being loaded in the back of the truck.
(C) The man is labeling the packages.
(D) Some storage warehouses have been constructed in the field.

（A）男性正在地上收拾電線。
（B）一些箱子正被裝進卡車後車廂。
（C）男性正在包裹上貼標籤。
（D）一些倉庫已經被蓋在田裡。

答案　(B)

解析　照片中看到的是箱子正被裝進卡車的後車廂內。（B）用現在進行式被動語態表示該狀況，所以是正確答案。請注意，不管是做什麼動作的人物照片，大多會以事物為主詞的被動語態來出題。因此在聽語音播放內容之前，最好先意識到這一點。

字彙　☐ electrical wire　電線

3.

4

(A) Some pottery is being cleared from the rack.

(B) Some pots have fallen on the ground.

(C) Various kinds of pots are being displayed on the shelves.

(D) Some mirrors are being hung on the wall.

（A）一些陶器正被從架上清除。

（B）一些花盆已掉在地上。

（C）各式各樣的花盆正被陳列在架上。

（D）一些鏡子正被掛在牆上。

答案 (C)

解析 選項（A）～（C）都出現了表達照片中「缽、盆」的字彙pottery和pot。（A）的be being cleared是「正在被清除」的意思，必須要拍到正在工作中的人，因此描述不正確。（B）是現在完成式，表示花盆已掉在地上的狀態。（C）雖然也是現在進行式被動語態，但是用be being displayed來表示持續陳列著的「狀態」，因此是正確答案。

字彙 □ pottery 陶器

4.

5

(A) A woman is looking at some trees outdoors.

(B) Some chairs remain empty on the terrace.

(C) There are some potted plants sitting on the ledge side by side.

(D) A woman is turning off a bedside lamp.

（A）一名女性正在看戶外的一些樹木。

（B）陽台上的椅子仍是空的。

（C）有一些盆栽植物並排在窗台上。

（D）一名女性正在關床頭燈。

答案 (C)

解析 ledge是指突出牆面的窗台。（C）形容盆栽植物（potted plants）並排在ledge的樣子，所以是正確答案。從（A）和（D）提到的a woman（一名女性），以及（B）的chairs（椅子）都可以判斷不符合照片的情況。

字彙 □ ledge 突出牆面的窗台、棚架

5.

6

(A) The women are relaxing under some umbrellas near the water.

(B) Some bicycles are under the lamppost.

(C) Some bicycles are parked next to each other at the beach.

(D) The lampposts are casting shadows on the road.

（A）女性們正在靠近水邊的傘下放鬆。

（B）一些腳踏車在街燈下。

（C）一些腳踏車在海灘上相鄰停放。

（D）路燈柱的影子投射在路上。

答案 **(B)**

解析 照片上的腳踏車就在街燈下，所以（B）是正確答案。從（A）提到的The women（女性們）就知道描述錯誤。而（C）描述海灘的樣子，還有（D）形容數支街燈投影的狀況都不符合照片內容，所以不是正確答案。像遠景照片的題型，除了一邊聽語音描述，也要一邊感受照片中的背景喔！

6.

7

(A) Some waiters are carrying some menus to the customers.

(B) The woman is taking something out of the backpack.

(C) A pair of customers is examining the menus at the restaurant.

(D) The couple is reading a sign by the entrance.

（A）一些服務生正在拿一些菜單給顧客們。

（B）女性正從背包裡取出某物。

（C）餐廳裡一對顧客正在詳閱菜單。

（D）這對夫婦正在讀著入口處旁的標語。

答案 **(C)**

解析 照片是一對男女在餐廳看著菜單的模樣。Part 1偶爾會使用動詞examine來確切表達照片的狀況，所以（C）是正確答案。雖然examine含有「檢查、診察、測驗」等意思，但也可以用於像Part 1這類看書或菜單等的照片，請大家要記住。

7.

9

New notices will soon be posted on the message board, won't they?
(A) Yes, I think so.
(B) Thank you so much for calling me on such short notice.
(C) Due to the bad weather.

新的公告很快就會公佈在留言板上，是吧？
（A）是的，我認為是。
（B）非常感謝你在這麼短的時間內打電話給我。
（C）由於天氣不好。

答案 (A)

解析 這題是在確認新的公告是否即將被公佈，（A）直接回答對方，所以是正確答案。（B）雖然用題目中提到的notice（公告、通知）來回答，不過內容完全不符題意，所以錯誤。（C）回答的是原因或理由，不適合用在這題。

8.

10

All your new laptops come with some free software, right?
(A) Several of the new models we carry do.
(B) It'll be set up on February 16.
(C) Mr. Smith will fix the broken one as soon as possible.

你們所有新的筆記型電腦都附帶一些免費軟體，對吧？
（A）我們帶來的新型號中有幾個是這樣沒錯。
（B）它預計在2月16日被安裝。
（C）史密斯（Smith）先生會盡快將壞掉的修復。

答案 (A)

解析 對於「所有的筆記型電腦是否都附帶一些免費軟體」的提問，以（A）「有一些是這樣沒錯」的回應最自然，所以是正確答案。do代指提問中的come（with some free software）。（B）和（C）的用語雖然與電腦相關，但沒有針對提問來回答，所以是錯的。

9.

11

The concert was really awful, wasn't it?
(A) Yes, it's a very successful film.
(B) No, I'm very struck by your work.
(C) It wasn't good at all, I think.

音樂會真的很糟糕，不是嗎？
（A）是的，它是一部非常成功的電影。
（B）不，我被你的作品感動了。
（C）它一點都不好，我覺得。

答案 (C)

解析 這題是以徵求同意的附加疑問句來詢問對音樂會的感想。（C）用not～at all（一點都不～）來強調「音樂會不好」的感受，所以是正確答案。（A）的film（電影）和（B）針對work（作品）的感想，都是錯誤的。

字彙 □ awful 很糟的 □ *be* struck by～ 被～感動

10.

12

That company's earnings should be recalculated by next week.

(A) I have no idea if that can be done by next week.

(B) Heavier paper will work better, I think.

(C) They work at a large legal office, I heard.

那家公司的盈餘應該在下週前被重新計算。

（A）我不知道下週前是否可以完成。

（B）我認為較重的紙會更好。

（C）我聽說他們在一家大型律師事務所上班。

答案 (A)

解析 由於陳述句的回答很難預測，所以必須小心作答。針對「下週前應該要重新計算盈餘」的陳述，（A）回答「不知道是否可以完成」，所以是正確答案。（B）的回答完全不符合前後內容，（C）提到的office（辦公室、事務所）雖然與company（公司）相關，但是語意與陳述句內容無關，所以都不適當。

字彙 □ recalculate 重新計算～

11.

13

Everyone seemed to make it to the conference on time.

(A) No, it's in the filing cabinet in the corner, isn't it?

(B) I just heard that Ms. Wilson was slow in arriving.

(C) Did you miss the conference yesterday?

每個人似乎都準時參加會議。

（A）不，它在角落的檔案櫃裡，不是嗎？

（B）我剛聽說威爾森（Wilson）女士遲到了。

（C）你昨天是否錯過了會議呢？

答案 (B)

解析 make it to～意為「到達～」。針對「每個人似乎都準時參加會議」的陳述，以（B）「剛聽說威爾森女士遲到了」的回答最自然。（A）是在表達某物品擺放的位置，（C）是在確認對方沒有參加會議，兩者都不正確。

12.

14

His team's new product is being unveiled next month.

(A) He'll renew his membership next month.

(B) It's the second largest assembly facility around there.

(C) They're excited to show it.

他的團隊的新產品將於下個月亮相。

（A）他將在下個月更新他的會員資格。

（B）它是那附近第二大的組裝工廠。

（C）他們很興奮能展示它。

答案 (C)

解析 針對「他的團隊的新產品下個月要亮相」的陳述，以（C）they're excited（他們很興奮）的回答最正確。雖然（A）和（B）的內容似乎與陳述句中的product（產品）及next month（下個月）有關，不過卻無法構成合理的對話，因此兩者都不正確。（B）的the second largest意為「第二大的」，請牢記這類的用法。

13.

15

We'll be able to inspect the facility tomorrow.
(A) I'll buy you a novel tomorrow.
(B) No, they'll shut down the facility next year.
(C) OK, what time should I go there?

我們明天可以檢查設備了。
（A）我明天買一本小說給你。
（B）不，明年他們將停用該設備。
（C）好的，我應該什麼時間到那裡？

答案 **(C)**

解析 針對明天要一同檢查設備的確認事宜，（C）回答OK並提問了會合時間，所以是正確答案。像這類用提問來回答陳述句的類型也會出現在選項中，希望各位要經常練習一邊聽語音內容，一邊記住當下所掌握到的句子含意。

14.

16

The novel by Ignazio Fellini got terrific reviews.
(A) You can get a great view of the ocean from the terrace.
(B) Oh, have you already read his book?
(C) Actually, I've been working at the publishing company.

伊格納奇歐·費里尼（Ignazio Fellini）的小說獲得很棒的評論。
（A）你可以從陽台看到不錯的海景。
（B）哦，你看過他的書了嗎？
（C）事實上，我一直在出版公司上班。

答案 **(B)**

解析 這是在陳述某個作家的書獲得非常好的評價。（B）對此回問了「你看過他的書了嗎？」，所以是正確答案。（A）的view（景色）和terrace（陽台）是使用題目中單字的類似發音，故意設的陷阱。（C）是故意使用與novel（小說）相關的字彙publishing company（出版公司）讓作答者混淆。

字彙 □ terrific 很棒的

15.

17

The insurance on your car expired last month, didn't it?
(A) That reminds me, I need to renew it as soon as possible.
(B) No, our company guarantees you are getting the lowest price.
(C) The expiration date can be found at the bottom of the bottle.

你的汽車保險上個月到期了，不是嗎？
（A）這提醒了我，我需要盡快更新它。
（B）不，我們公司保證你獲得最低的價格。
（C）有效日期可以在瓶底找到。

答案 **(A)**

解析 這是在確認對方的汽車保險到期一事。（A）在被人問及後，想起了保險要更新，所以是正確答案。（B）是在向客人保證最低價格。（C）是描述如何得知有效日期的方法。

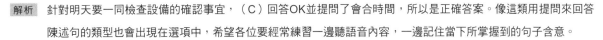

16.

18

They're flying to Sydney via Singapore today.
(A) They had a nice time in Sydney.
(B) I heard they're looking forward to it so much.
(C) I tried to buy some travel guidebooks.

他們今天要經由新加坡（Singapore）飛往雪梨（Sydney）。
（A）他們在雪梨度過美好的時光。
（B）我聽說他們非常期待。
（C）我試著要買幾本旅遊指南。

答案 (B)

解析 題目簡潔地陳述第三方的預定行程，（B）簡單地回應有關第三方的資訊，所以是正確答案。由於（A）和（C）的內容也都與旅行有關，因此必須對題目要有正確的理解和記憶。

17.

19

What should we name our new mountaineering boots?
(A) You'd better put yourself in his shoes.
(B) We never knew you had mountaineering boots.
(C) Something fashionable.

我們應該把新的登山靴命名為什麼呢？
（A）你最好站在他的立場想。
（B）我們從不知道你有登山靴。
（C）取個時髦一點的名字。

答案 (C)

解析 這是詢問如何命名新產品。（C）簡單地說出意見，所以是正確答案。單憑這麼簡短的選項就做出選擇並不容易，但如果把（A）和（B）合在一起考慮，應該就不成問題了。（A）的put *oneself* in *someone*'s shoes是「站在～的立場想」。

字彙 □ mountaineering boots 登山靴

18.

20

The presentation will be about forty minutes long.
(A) Probably, but it might be a little longer.
(B) Yes, for about four hours.
(C) My colleague did it yesterday at the conference.

簡報大約會是40分鐘。
（A）有可能，但或許會再久一點。
（B）是的，大約4個小時。
（C）我的同事昨天在會議上做過了。

答案 (A)

解析 這是在談論有關簡報所需的時間。選項（A）「或許會再久一點」才是正確的回應。（B）雖然回答Yes，但是所需的時間卻不一樣。（C）描述的時態與題目不同，無法成為正確答案。

19. 21

I'll give you some time to go over the terms and conditions of the contract.
(A) OK, I'll call you again in a few minutes.
(B) Sorry, I don't have any contact with the attorney.
(C) Yes, it was discussed at the last meeting.

我會給你一些時間詳閱合約的條款和條件。
（A）好的，我再過幾分鐘後再打給你。
（B）對不起，我跟律師沒有任何聯繫。
（C）是的，在上次會議討論過它了。

答案 (A)

解析 說話者給聽者一些時間去詳閱合約，而聽者以（A）的回答「幾分鐘後再打（電話）給你」最正確。（B）除了故意使用跟contract（合約）發音相似的contact（聯繫）之外，還使用與contract有關的單字attorney（律師），不過這樣的應答無法構成合理對話。（C）描述的時態與題目不一致，對話也連不起來，所以是錯的。

字彙 □ attorney 律師

20. 22

Tom, some fluorescent lights are dead and need to be replaced now.
(A) Dinner will need to be served promptly at 9 P.M.
(B) I think you are missing Jack.
(C) OK, I'll get them fixed right away.

湯姆（Tom），一些日光燈不亮了，需要現在更換。
（A）晚餐將必須在9 P.M.立刻提供。
（B）我認為你想念傑克（Jack）了。
（C）好的，我馬上把它們修好。

答案 (C)

解析 題目中的fluorescent light是「日光燈」的意思，因為dead（熄滅），也就是不亮了、必須更換。〈get＋受詞＋過去分詞〉是「讓～成為⋯⋯的狀態」，正確答案（C）正是這樣的用法。（A）的〈promptly at＋時間〉是「在～點整立刻」的意思，也可以替換為〈at 時間＋sharp〉。

字彙 □ fluorescent light 日光燈

21. 23

I should have caught some sleep because it was a long flight.
(A) You can get some sleep now.
(B) I'd like you to show me your passport.
(C) For about eight hours.

因為是趟長途飛行，我當時應該要睡一下的。
（A）你現在可以睡一會。
（B）我希望你出示護照讓我看。
（C）大約8小時。

答案 (A)

解析 題目陳述自己應該睡個覺，（A）提議現在可以睡了，是最適當的回答。（B）和（C）的內容雖然也是跟飛行有關，但是前後語意不符合，所以是錯的。

22.

24

I've lost the combination for my locker.

(A) Why don't you tell Ms. Brown at the security office about that?

(B) Please pass this document to Ms. Jones.

(C) I'm so sorry, she's on another line now.

我把我的置物櫃密碼弄不見了。

（A）你何不告訴安全室的布朗（Brown）女士呢？

（B）請將這份文件交給瓊斯（Jones）女士。

（C）很抱歉，她現在電話中。

答案 (A)

解析 對於沒有開鎖密碼而很困擾的陳述，（A）提出了解決方案「你何不告訴布朗女士」，所以是正確答案。（B）和（C）完全是不相關的回應，所以是錯的。

字彙 ☐ combination（用來解除鎖定的）文字或數字組合的密碼鎖

23.

25

Mr. Rodriguez's speech is supposed to start at ten o'clock, right?

(A) During the teleconference last weekend.

(B) I have no idea, so I'll find out and let you know.

(C) We'll hire ten new employees as soon as we can.

羅德里格斯（Rodriguez）先生的演說應該要在10點開始，對吧？

（A）在上週末的視訊期間。

（B）我不曉得，所以我會查清楚並讓你知道。

（C）我們會盡快僱用10名新的員工。

答案 (B)

解析 對於提問者在確認演講的時間，（B）回答「不知道」是最適當的答案。be supposed to *do*～（應該要～），對於描述未來計畫時，這是常見的用法。（A）的回答適用在when（何時）的提問下，（C）的回答則適用在人手不足時的話題，所以這兩個選項都無法成為正確答案。

24.

26

We have to talk about making some changes to the new personnel system.

(A) It's in this year's general budget report.

(B) I have to convert the local currency into Australian dollars.

(C) Is there something wrong with it?

關於對新的人事系統做一些改變，我們必須談談。

（A）它在今年的總預算報告中。

（B）我必須將當地的貨幣兌換成澳幣。

（C）有什麼不妥之處嗎？

答案 (C)

解析 對於需要變更人事制度之提議，（C）回答「有什麼不妥之處嗎？」是最適當的答案。選項（B）的convert *A* into *B*（將A換成B），經常被用作「兌換～（貨幣等）」的意思，請大家要牢記。

字彙 ☐ convert 兌換～

25.

27

You're going to the company picnic, aren't you?
(A) I took her to the picnic last week.
(B) I'd like to go, but I'm not sure yet.
(C) She went on an outing last Saturday.

你會去公司野餐，不是嗎？
（A）我上週帶她去野餐了。
（B）我想去，但還不確定。
（C）她上週六去郊遊了。

答案 (B)

解析 這題是在確認是否參加日後舉辦的野餐，（B）表示「想去，但還不確定」才是正確答案。（A）和（C）雖然也是跟野餐有關的內容，但是時態和題目不符合，所以都是錯的。

字彙 □ outing 遠足、郊遊

26.

28

I've been to Rio de Janeiro three times.
(A) Oh, where was that?
(B) That'll be during your next vacation.
(C) So have I, but twice.

我去過里約熱內盧（Rio de Janeiro）三次了。
（A）喔，那是哪裡？
（B）那會在你下次的度假期間。
（C）我也去過，但兩次而已。

答案 (C)

解析 對於經驗的陳述，以So have I（＝I have been to Rio de Janeiro, too.「我也去過里約熱內盧。」）來表示自己也有經驗的（C）回答最適當。（A）是在詢問地點，（B）是說明某件事情的時間，但是都無法成為正確的對話。

27.

29

My thesis is about five hundred pages long.
(A) Ms. Hernandez's is much longer, I heard.
(B) Did you report it to the front desk?
(C) She said that the year-end sale will begin next week.

我的論文長達500頁。
（A）我聽說赫爾南德斯（Hernandez）女士的更長。
（B）你向櫃台報告了嗎？
（C）她說年終拍賣將於下週開始。

答案 (A)

解析 對於thesis（論文）的頁數陳述，以（A）「聽說赫爾南德斯女士的（論文）更長」回答最適當。（B）報告的對象如果是professor（教授）等和論文相關的人，就可能是正確答案，不過這裡的報告對象是櫃台就顯得不自然。（C）是錯在與題目的陳述內容毫無關連。

字彙 □ thesis 論文

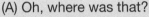

28.

30

The department manager notified you of the sales goals, didn't she?
(A) I read the parking notice last Friday.
(B) We were told about them at the meeting yesterday.
(C) They are all working toward the same goal.

部門經理通知你銷售目標了，對吧？
（A）我上週五看過停車公告了。
（B）我們昨天在會議上被告知了。
（C）他們都朝著同一個目標努力。

答案 (B)

解析 這是在向對方確認所表達的資訊是否無誤。（B）直言「昨天在會議上被告知了」，所以是正確答案。（A）故意使用跟notified（通知）發音相似的notice（公告），（C）也是試圖誤導作答者將same goal（同一個目標）聽成sales goal（銷售目標），因此這兩個選項都是錯的。

29.

31

The entrance ticket is ten dollars, isn't it?
(A) We'll offer you better quality products at reasonable prices.
(B) The sign at the box office says it costs twelve.
(C) You had to pay for it before entering the movie theater.

門票是十美元，不是嗎？
（A）我們將以合理的價錢提供給您更優質的產品。
（B）售票處招牌寫著12美元。
（C）在進電影院之前你必須付錢。

答案 (B)

解析 這題是用附加疑問句來確認票價。（B）表達正確的資訊「box office（售票處）的sign（招牌）寫著12美元」，是最適當的回答。雖然（A）提及的reasonable prices（合理的價格）跟價錢有關，但是回答內容與提問毫不相關，所以是錯的。（C）雖然是跟入場有關的內容，不過卻在陳述相關手續而不是價錢本身，因此是不適當的回答。

字彙 □ box office 售票處

30.

32

Ms. Ortiz will order office supplies this afternoon.
(A) She already did yesterday, I heard.
(B) She's older than she looks.
(C) That's not so expensive, right?

歐帝斯（Ortiz）女士今天下午要訂購辦公用品。
（A）我聽說她昨天已經訂了。
（B）她比看起來的年齡大些。
（C）那不是很貴，對吧？

答案 (A)

解析 這是在陳述歐帝斯女士要訂購辦公用品的資訊。（A）對此表示「昨天已經做（訂購）了」，回答最自然。（B）是故意使用跟order（訂購）發音相似的older（較老的）來混淆，（C）是使用和order相關的單字expensive（貴的），都是典型的陷阱選項。

31.

33

Our team's weekly profits have decreased by three percent.

(A) I heard the outlet sold it at a discount.

(B) Oh, that's unfortunate.

(C) In three weeks.

我們團隊的每週利潤已下降了3%。

（A）我聽說它在暢貨中心有打折。

（B）喔，那真是遺憾。

（C）在3週後。

答案 **(B)**

解析 對於團隊利潤下降的陳述，（B）簡潔地表達感想，因此回答最適當。簡單的選項常常最容易錯過，所以隨著每個選項的語音播放，請調整呼吸，專注掌握100%的內容。

字彙 □ outlet 暢貨中心、批發商店

PART 3

MP3 34～47

Questions 32 through 34 refer to the following conversation with three speakers.

試題 32-34 請參考以下 3 人對話。

35

W1: Hi. Q33 I'm Elena Scott. Q32 You have my Celcius in the shop right now. Q33 I stopped in to see if you had an estimate for me.
W2: Frank just handed it to me. Q32 Your battery was the culprit. Because it was basically dead, a light must've been left on. So a replacement will be $315.48.
W1: It can't be recharged?
W2: Frank? Can you talk to Ms. Scott about her Celcius battery?
M: Sure. Q32 We can recharge an extremely low battery, but once a battery is drained to a certain level, it never runs the same again.
W1: I certainly don't want more problems anytime soon...
M: Q34 Your car is 8 years old, and batteries generally only last about 5. So you've gotten a lot out of this one.

W1：嗨，我是伊蓮娜．史考特（Elena Scott）。我的賽爾修斯（Celcius）現在正在你店裡。我過來看一下你是否幫我估好價了。
W2：法蘭克（Frank）剛把它交給我。你的電池是罪魁禍首。因為基本上它已經耗盡，一定是有燈忘記關了。你得花315.48美元來更換了。
W1：它不能再充電嗎？
W2：法蘭克？你可以跟史考特女士說明她的塞爾修斯電池嗎？
M： 當然。我們可以為極低電量的電池進行充電，但是電池一旦耗盡到一定的程度，就沒辦法再像之前一樣運作了。
W1：我確實不希望在短期內遇到更多問題……
M： 妳的車齡8年了，而且電池一般只持續5年，所以這個電池已經被用到底了。

字彙 □ hand 交給～ □ culprit 罪魁禍首、犯人 □ *be* drained to～ 被耗盡到～

32. Who most likely is the man?
(A) A secretary
(B) A mechanic
(C) A store clerk
(D) A car salesman

誰最有可能是男性的角色？
（A）秘書
（B）機械師
（C）店員
（D）汽車銷售員

答案 **(B)**

解析 讓我們來仔細聽對話內容，從間接證據來推測這個男性是誰。雖然女性第一句說You have my Celcius in the shop right now.（我的賽爾修斯現在正在你店裡），但是我們在這個時候還不知道女性說的Celcius是指什麼。接著換另一名女性出現，告訴前面那名女性車子的電池有問題。這時，一名似乎是女性同事的男性，叫Frank，他說了We can recharge an extremely low battery（我們可以為極低電量的電池進行充電）後，也針對（車子發生的）問題做說明及表達因應的方式。由此可知男性是處於檢查並修理故障車子的立場，所以正確答案是（B）。

33. What is Ms. Scott asking for?
(A) Use of a rental car
(B) A discount on the price
(C) Expedited service
(D) A quote for repairs

史考特女士要求什麼？
（A）租用車子
（B）價格折扣
（C）急件服務
（D）維修報價

答案 **(D)**

解析 第一位出現的女性就是自稱為Elena Scott的史考特女士。她接著說 I stopped in to see if you had an estimate for me.（我過來看一下你是否幫我估好價了）。這時雖然還不確定待估價的物品Celcius是指什麼，但是和估價有關的敘述只有（D），所以是正確答案。大家把estimate（估價）和quote（報價）當作一組近義詞，記起來吧！兩者都是可數名詞。

字彙 □ ask for～ 要求～ □ expedited 加快的

34. What does the man recommend?
(A) Recharging the battery
(B) Changing a bad part
(C) Replacing the car
(D) Getting a second opinion

男性建議什麼？
（A）讓電池再充電
（B）更換壞的零件
（C）更換車子
（D）取得第二個意見

答案 **(B)**

解析 男性第二次發言時說Your car is 8 years old, and batteries generally only last about 5. So you've gotten a lot out of this one.（妳的車齡8年了，而且電池一般只持續5年，所以這個電池已經被用到底了）。雖然未直接講明「該換電池了」，但由此可知是指「已經用盡了」，也就是建議「因為已經用到底，最好更換」。所以正確答案是（B）。

Questions 35 through 37 refer to the following conversation.

試題 35-37 請參考以下對話。

36

W1: Hello, Ms. Short. This is Lisa Green calling from Tyler Real Estate Agency. An apartment on Augustus Lane just became available for rent. It's in the same building as the one we went to look at on Saturday. Although it's a little smaller than the one we saw, it's cheaper and it has more windows so you get plenty of sunlight. I hope you received the details I faxed you earlier.

W2: Yes, I'm very interested. Q35 I liked the apartment we saw last week, but unlike this one it was too expensive for me. Shall I come to your office to sign the application?

W1: Well, I'm showing a property in your neighborhood to some clients this morning, so Q36 I can stop by afterward with the papers.

W2: That's great. Q37 By the way, I just want to make sure that the apartment allows cats, as I have two tabbies.

W1：哈囉，修特（Short）女士，我是泰勒（Tyler）房產代理公司的麗莎·格林（Lisa Green）。奧古斯特（Augustus）巷有一間公寓剛好空出待租。它和我們週六去看的那間是同一棟大樓。雖然它比我們看的那間小一點，但比較便宜，而且有更多的窗戶讓您有充足陽光。我希望您收到了我早些時候傳真給您的詳細內容。

W2：是的，我很感興趣。雖然我喜歡上週看到的物件，但是它不像今天這間，那物件對我來說太貴了。我該去你的辦公室簽署申請文件嗎？

W1：這個嘛，我今天早上要向一些客戶介紹您住處附近的房產，所以之後我可以帶著文件順路去您那兒。

W2：太好了！對了，我只想確認一下公寓是否允許養貓，因為我有兩隻虎斑貓。

字彙 □ afterward 之後、以後 □ tabby 虎斑貓、大花貓

35. What is the advantage of the recently available apartment?

(A) It is in a quiet neighborhood.

(B) It has many lighting fixtures.

(C) It is within Ms. Short's budget.

(D) It has lots of space.

最近空出的公寓有什麼優點？

（A）它在一個安靜的社區。

（B）它有許多照明裝置。

（C）它在修特女士的預算範圍內。

（D）它有很多空間。

答案 **(C)**

解析 聽著對話的同時，就要密切注意有關公寓房間的優點資訊。第一位女性雖然提到房租便宜及陽光充足，但是並沒有符合該條件的選項，因此就繼續聽下去。第二位女性說 I liked the apartment we saw last week, but unlike this one it was too expensive for me.（雖然我喜歡上週看到的物件，但是它不像今天這間，那物件對我來說太貴

了。），可知她雖然喜歡上週看的物件，但是它比這次要看的租金還要貴。由此可以推斷這次提到的新物件是在預算範圍內，所以（C）是正確答案。

字彙 □ lighting fixture 照明裝置

36. What does Lisa offer? 麗莎提議了什麼？

(A) To fax an application form （A）傳真一份申請表

(B) To take Ms. Short for a viewing （B）帶修特女士去看房

(C) To stop by Ms. Short's home （C）順路去修特女士的家

(D) To reserve the property on Augustus Lane （D）預留奧古斯特巷的物件

答案 **(C)**

解析 一開始說話的人就是麗莎。她在第二次發言時說 I can stop by afterward with the papers.（我可以帶著文件順路去您那兒）。stop by意思是「順路造訪」，也就是她之後要帶著申請書順路造訪，因此正確答案是（C）。其他選項的內容是在這種情況下可能延伸的話題，如果理解這篇對話的內容，作答時就不會被混淆。

字彙 □ viewing 調查、視察、觀看

37. What does Ms. Short want to confirm? 修特女士想要確認什麼？

(A) If she can play the piano （A）她是否可以彈鋼琴

(B) If she can have two vehicles （B）她是否可以有兩輛車

(C) If she can have pets （C）她是否可以有寵物

(D) If she can renovate （D）她是否可以翻新裝潢

答案 **(C)**

解析 第一位出現的女性跟對方說Hello, Ms. Short.，由此可知Ms. Short就是第二位女性。遇到同性之間的對話，一定要努力弄清楚誰是誰。從修特女士第二次發言時說By the way, I just want to make sure that the apartment allows cats, as I have two tabbies.（對了，我只想確認一下公寓是否允許養貓，因為我有兩隻虎斑貓）可知，（C）是正確答案。

Questions 38 through 40 refer to the following conversation.

試題 38-40 請參考以下對話。

37

M: Hi. Q38 I tried to use my debit card at the supermarket today, but it was declined. I didn't even get to punch in my PIN number. Thankfully I had my checkbook with me.

W: I see. Q38 Let's check your account. Can I have your name and ID, please?

M: It's Jack Ridges, and here's my driver's license.

W: Thank you, Mr. Ridges. Q39 It looks like there were insufficient funds in your account when you tried to use your card.

M: That's odd. My salary should've been deposited today.

W: Q40 That transaction took place at 10:30 A.M. and seems to each month.

M: Q40 Oh, that explains it. I always thought the transaction occurred right after midnight, and I was shopping first thing this morning.

M：嗨，我今天試著在超市使用我的簽帳卡，但遭到拒絕。甚至無法輸入個人識別碼。幸好我帶著支票簿。

W：了解。讓我們查看一下您的帳戶。能麻煩您提供大名和身分證字號嗎？

M：我叫傑克．里奇斯（Jack Ridges），這是我的駕照。

W：謝謝您，里奇斯先生。看起來，在您試著使用卡片時，您的帳戶似乎資金不足。

M：那很奇怪。我的薪資應該今天就存入了才對。

W：該項交易發生在10:30 A.M.，而且似乎每個月都如此。

M：哦，那就解釋一切了。我一直以為該交易在午夜過後就會發生，而我今天早上做的第一件事就是購物。

字彙 □ debit card 簽帳卡（立即結帳卡） □ punch in～ 輸入～ □ PIN number 個人識別碼 □ thankfully 幸好 □ checkbook 支票簿 □ insufficient 不足的

38. Where is the conversation most likely taking place?

(A) At a driver's license facility

(B) At the man's office

(C) At a grocery store

(D) At a bank

這篇對話最有可能發生於何處？

（A）駕駛執照中心

（B）男性的辦公室

（C）食品雜貨店

（D）銀行

答案 **(D)**

解析 題目出現most likely時，大多必須要從間接證據來判斷正確答案。對於「簽帳卡不能用」，女性向對方回答Let's check your account.（讓我們查看一下您的帳戶）。會出現類似對話的場所應該是銀行，所以正確答案是（D）。

39. Why couldn't the man use his debit card? 為何男性無法使用他的簽帳卡？

(A) His account balance was too low. （A）他的帳戶餘額過低。

(B) It had expired the day before. （B）卡片在前一天已到期。

(C) He forgot his PIN number. （C）他忘記個人識別碼。

(D) He used the wrong card. （D）他用錯卡。

答案 **(A)**

解析 注意聽男性為何無法使用簽帳卡的原因。女性第二次發言時說It looks like there were insufficient funds in your account（您的帳戶似乎資金不足），（A）簡潔地將其換個說法，所以是正確答案。

字彙 ☐ account balance 帳戶餘額 ☐ expire 到期

40. What did the man learn about his monthly pay? 關於他的每月薪資，男性得知了什麼資訊？

(A) It happens later than he thought. （A）比他原先想的還晚進行。

(B) It was lower than he expected for this month. （B）本月收入比預期的還低。

(C) It is in different amounts each month. （C）每個月的金額不同。

(D) The date of payment is not fixed. （D）支付日不固定。

答案 **(A)**

解析 女性第三次的發言時提到，男性的薪資匯入是在上午10點30分。對此，男性回答Oh, that explains it.（哦，那就解釋一切了），還表達了他原先所想的the transaction occurred right after midnight（交易在午夜過後就會發生）。所以正確答案是（A）。

Questions 41 through 43 refer to the following conversation.

試題 41-43 請參考以下對話。

38

M: This is Lionel Donovan Q41 from Paradise Grand Resort. I'd like to order a new convection oven for our kitchen, please. The product number is WA789S.

W: Certainly, Mr. Donovan. Oh, but Q42 Tom, our installation specialist, is working for another client until Thursday. Is it all right if he comes to install the product on Friday?

M: Can't one of our staff install it? It seems pretty straightforward.

W: We strongly recommend that our customers do not attempt to install the equipment themselves. Q43 It can seriously damage the product.

M：我是天堂渡假村（Paradise Grand Resort）的萊恩內爾．多諾凡（Lionel Donovan）。我想替我們的廚房訂購一台新的對流型烤箱。產品編號是WA789S。

W：沒問題，多諾凡先生。喔，不過我們的安裝專員，湯姆（Tom），正在為另一位客戶工作，要到週四為止。如果他在週五前往安裝產品，可以嗎？

M：我們的員工不能安裝嗎？它看起來非常簡單。

W：我們強烈建議客戶不要嘗試自行安裝設備。那有可能會嚴重損害產品。

字彙 □ convection oven 對流型烤箱 □ straightforward 簡單的、易懂的

41. Where does the man most likely work?

(A) At an elementary school

(B) At a kitchen appliance store

(C) At a hotel

(D) At a muffin shop

男性最有可能在哪裡工作？

（A）小學

（B）廚房用品店

（C）飯店

（D）瑪芬蛋糕店

答案 **(C)**

解析 男性一開始就說from Paradise Grand Resort.（是天堂渡假村）。由此可知男性工作的地方是飯店，所以正確答案是（C）。Part 3&4常會出現詢問場所的題目，但是對話中會出現好幾次正確答案的相關線索，所以即使發現自己「錯過而沒聽到」某一句時，也不能放棄，要集中精神繼續聽內容。

字彙 □ kitchen appliance 廚房用品

42. What problem does the woman mention?
(A) An item is currently out of stock.
(B) A product is no longer available.
(C) A worker is temporarily occupied.
(D) A client is making unreasonable demands.

女性提到什麼問題？
（A）某項商品目前缺貨。
（B）已不再供應某項產品。
（C）工人暫時沒有空。
（D）客戶正在提出無理的要求。

答案 **(C)**

解析 題目是問女性提出的問題，所以正確答案的出處當然就在女性的發言內。女性一開始就提到Tom, our installation specialist, is working for another client until Thursday.（湯姆正在為另一位客戶工作，要到週四為止），而（C）簡單地將其換個說法，所以是正確答案。

字彙 □ make unreasonable demands 提出無理的要求

43. Why does the woman discourage self-installation?
(A) To protect the equipment
(B) To avoid injuries
(C) To secure employment
(D) To speed up the process

為什麼女性不鼓勵自行安裝？
（A）為保護設備
（B）為避免受傷
（C）為保障就業
（D）為加快過程

答案 **(A)**

解析 題目的主詞是女性，所以正確答案的出處當然就在女性的發言內。女性第二次發言時說It can seriously damage the product.（那有可能會嚴重損害產品），這句的It是指自行安裝設備一事，意為購買者自行安裝的話恐會損壞設備，所以建議由專業人員安裝以防損壞。由此可知正確答案是（A）。

字彙 □ self-installation 自行安裝

Questions 44 through 46 refer to the following conversation.

試題 44-46 請參考以下對話。

39

M: Q44 This is Greatscapes. How can I help you?

W: Hi, this is Bev Sunderman from GFK Tools. Q44 You guys take care of our lawn and yardwork. Anyway, the storm last night knocked down a huge tree, and we need it taken care of right away.

M: I'm sorry, but we've had so many calls that I don't think we can get there until Wednesday.

W: But Q45 it fell right at the company entrance to the road, so none of our employees or customers can get in or out of the parking lot.

M: Oh, well, in cases where it actually hinders business, Q46 we definitely give top priority.

W: Great, thank you. Is it possible to come soon?

M: Q46 It'll be done this morning.

M：這裡是大園藝（Greatscapes），能為您做什麼服務嗎？

W：嗨，我是GFK工具公司的貝福・桑德曼（Bev Sunderman）。我們公司的草坪和庭院工事都是委託你們維護的。總之，昨晚的暴風雨擊倒了一棵大樹，我們需要立刻處理。

M：很抱歉，但是我們接到了很多電話，我認為我們在週三以前無法過去。

W：但是它剛好倒在公司通往馬路的入口處，所以我們的員工或客人都無法進出停車場。

M：喔，好的，如果它確實妨礙了生意。我們當然優先處理。

W：太好了，謝謝。有可能很快過來嗎？

M：今天早上會處理好。

字彙 □ yardwork 庭院工事 □ knock down 擊倒～ □ hinder 妨礙～

44. Where does the man most likely work?

(A) At a city service department

(B) At a construction company

(C) At a landscaping company

(D) At a telephone company

男性最有可能在哪裡工作？

（A）城市服務部門

（B）建築公司

（C）景觀公司

（D）電話公司

答案 **(C)**

解析 男性一開始說This is Greatscapes.（這裡是大園藝）。對此，女性回答You guys take care of our lawn and yardwork.（我們公司的草坪和庭院工事都是委託你們維護的）。由此可判斷男性在維護草坪及庭院工事的公司上班，所以（C）是正確答案。

45. What is the problem? 發生了什麼問題？

(A) Employees have taken the day off. （A）員工休假了。

(B) A company's driveway is blocked. （B）公司的車道被堵住了。

(C) Fallen trees have ruined a company's lawn. （C）倒下來的樹損壞了公司的草坪。

(D) A tree was fallen onto a company building. （D）一棵樹倒在公司的大樓上。

答案 **(B)**

解析 女性第二次發言時說it fell right at the company entrance to the road（它剛好倒在公司通往馬路的入口處），這句的it是指前面提到的a huge tree（一棵大樹）。（C）和（D）雖然都提到了造成問題的那棵「樹」，也出現lawn（草坪）及company（公司）等「對話中提到的單字」，但是不符合對話的內容。

字彙 □ driveway 私有車道 □ ruin 損壞～

46. What will the man do for the woman? 男性將為女性做什麼？

(A) Find another company to assist her right away （A）找另一家公司來立即協助她

(B) Put her on the schedule for Wednesday （B）把她排進週三的行程

(C) Help her call workers to clean up the area （C）幫她打電話給工作人員清理該區

(D) Send someone to her company today （D）今天派人到她的公司

答案 **(D)**

解析 在女性說明狀況後，男性第三次發言時回答we definitely give top priority.（我們當然優先處理）。接著更針對女性提問「何時處理」，而具體地向對方表示It'll be done this morning.（今天早上會處理好）。（D）將這些狀況簡潔地表達，所以是正確答案。

Questions 47 through 49 refer to the following conversation.

試題 47-49 請參考以下對話。

40

W: Say, Miles, I heard you went for an interview last week. How did it go?

M: Not so well, I guess. Q47 There were dozens of other candidates, and I haven't heard anything from them since.

W: Well, you're qualified enough, so I wouldn't be so pessimistic if I were you. Why don't you give them a follow-up call? Q48 It will show them how much you would like to get the job and that's always a good thing.

M: I really don't think there's much point. But Q49 I sent my résumé to several other companies, so let's hope for the best.

W：嘿，邁爾斯（Miles），我聽說你上週去面試。結果如何？

M：不太好，我猜。還有數十多位其他的應徵者，我從那之後都沒有聽到他們傳來的何消息。

W：嗯，你的條件夠好，所以如果我是你，我不會這麼悲觀。你何不撥個後續追蹤電話給他們？這將展現你有多麼想要這份工作，那麼做總是好的。

M：我真的不覺得那會有多大意義。但是我已經把我的簡歷表寄給其他幾家公司，所以讓我們期待最好的結果。

字彙 □ dozens of～ 數十多的～、多數的～ □ qualified 有能力的、具備必要條件的 □ pessimistic 悲觀的 □ follow-up call 後續追蹤電話

47. Why is the man pessimistic?

(A) He doesn't have enough qualifications.

(B) He thinks he won't get the job.

(C) He failed an important exam.

(D) He received a bad evaluation.

男性為什麼悲觀？

（A）他沒有足夠的資格。

（B）他認為自己不會得到這份工作。

（C）他沒有通過重要的考試。

（D）他收到不好的評價。

答案 **(B)**

解析 這題是問男性的心情。像這種詢問情緒的試題並不常見，但有時還是會出現在正式測驗中。男性一開始就表示There were dozens of other candidates, and I haven't heard anything from them since.（還有數十多位其他的應徵者，我從那之後都沒有聽到他們傳來的何消息。），男性對於前往面試的公司全然沒有給予任何聯絡而感到悲觀。（B）將這種情況換另一種說法，所以是正確答案。dozen意為「12個、12的」，而dozens　of～則是「數十多的～、多數的～」。

48. What does the woman say about a follow-up call?
(A) It gives a good impression.
(B) It is better than sending an e-mail.
(C) It should be made as soon as possible.
(D) It demonstrates his responsibility.

女性對後續追蹤電話有什麼看法？
（A）給人留下好印象。
（B）比寄電子郵件好。
（C）最好盡快做。
（D）展現了他的責任感。

答案 **(A)**

解析 女性第二次發言時，向對方建議撥打後續追蹤電話之後，說了It will show them how much you would like to get the job and that's always a good thing.（這將展現你有多麼想要這份工作，而那樣做總是好的），正面地認為「這總是一件好事」。（A）將這些內容換一種說法It gives a good impression.（給人留下好印象），所以是正確答案。

49. What does the man say he has done?
(A) Phoned the employer
(B) Sent a recommendation letter
(C) Applied to other places
(D) Consulted a professional

男性說他已經做了什麼？
（A）打電話給雇主
（B）寄出推薦信
（C）應徵其他地方
（D）諮詢專業人士

答案 **(C)**

解析 男性第二次發言時說I sent my résumé to several other companies.（我已經把我的簡歷表寄給其他幾家公司）。表示他寄了簡歷表給其他幾家公司，所以（C）是正確答案。（B）和（D）看似有道理，但卻是對話中完全沒提到的內容。

Questions 50 through 52 refer to the following conversation.
試題 50-52 請參考以下對話。

41

W: I'm hoping to start classes next year to get my business degree, but Q50 that'll depend on whether I have enough savings by then.

M: Q51 Make sure to find out more about what your company offers. Q52 Many companies help employees pay for continuing education because they know it'll benefit the company.

W: Q52 That certainly would be fantastic. I'll see what the case is with my company.

M: A business degree is a great idea. It may even land you a promotion when you're done.

W：為了取得我的商學院學位，我希望明年開始上課，但得看我到時候是否有足夠的存款。

M：務必去了解更多有關你公司能提供的福利。很多公司幫助員工支付繼續教育的費用，因為他們知道這將有助於公司。

W：那樣的話就真的太棒了。我會去了解我公司的情況。

M：商學院學位是個好主意。當你完成後，它甚至有可能讓你升職。

字彙 ☐ business degree 商學院學位 ☐ saving 存款 ☐ make sure to *do* 務必要～ ☐ benefit 有助於～

50. What are the speakers mainly discussing?
說話者主要在討論什麼？

(A) Moving up in a company（A）公司內的晉升
(B) Financing extra schooling（B）籌措額外教育的資金
(C) Satisfying work requirements（C）滿足工作要求
(D) Teaching business classes（D）教商務課程

答案 **(B)**

解析 女性表達「想上學」後，接著說that'll depend on whether I have enough savings by then（得看我到時候是否有足夠的存款）。男性聽到後建議對方可利用公司的資金補助，所以話題是在談論如何籌措上學的資金。因此正確答案是（B）。

字彙 ☐ move up 晉升 ☐ finance 籌措～資金 ☐ extra schooling 額外的教育 ☐ business class 商務課程

51. What does the man suggest the woman do?
男性建議女性做什麼？

(A) Check her company's policy
(B) Get special training at work
(C) Apply for a federal scholarship
(D) Ask her boss for a raise

（A）查清楚她的公司政策
（B）在工作中獲得特別的培訓
（C）申請國家獎學金
（D）向她的老闆要求加薪

答案 **(A)**

解析 男性一開始就表示Make sure to find out more about what your company offers.（務必去了解更多有關你公司能提供的福利）。建議對方最好要查清楚公司是否可以提供什麼支援。（A）簡潔地將它換一種說法，所以是正確答案。

字彙 □ apply for～ 申請～ □ federal scholarship 國家獎學金 □ raise 加薪

52. What does the woman imply when she says, "I'll see what the case is with my company"?
當女性說「I'll see what the case is with my company」時，隱含什麼意思？

(A) She will pay for her school by herself.
(B) She doubts her company will help her.
(C) She hopes her company can support her.
(D) She will ask the company to educate employees.

（A）她將自己支付學費。
（B）她懷疑公司會幫助她。
（C）她希望公司可以支援她。
（D）她會要求公司教育員工。

答案 **(C)**

解析 這題是問說話者的意圖，想一想在什麼情形下才會說那句話。對於男性建議「公司或許會提供資金支援」一事，女性回答That certainly would be fantastic.（那樣的話就真的太棒了）。因為是在這樣的情形下對話，女性才會對公司提供資金支援有所期待。因此，正確答案是（C）。

字彙 □ doubt 懷疑～

Questions 53 through 55 refer to the following conversation.

試題 53-55 請參考以下對話。

42

M1: Q54 Hi. This is Mark Cooper. We have a BEX-2000 copy machine at our office. Q53 It had been working fine for years until yesterday when it stopped working properly. When we put paper into the feed, it comes out crumpled and then the whole machine shuts off.

M2: I see. Did you use any kind of special paper other than standard copier paper when this happened?

M1: We only buy our copier paper from BEX stores. Q54 We need to print out hundreds of course guidelines to hand out to our students tomorrow. Can you fix it as soon as possible?

M2: It sounds like a case of worn-out exit rollers. Q55 We'll send one of our technicians this afternoon and he can change them for you.

M1：嗨，我是馬克．庫柏（Mark Cooper）。我們辦公室裡有一台型號BEX-2000的印表機。它已經順利運作好幾年了，一直到昨天停止正常運作。當我們把紙放入紙匣後，它出來會變皺，然後整個機器自行關機。

M2：了解。這種情況發生時，您是否使用標準影印紙之外的特殊紙張呢？

M1：我們只從BEX商店購買影印紙。為了明天要發給我們的學生，我們需要印出數百份課程綱要。你們能盡快來修好嗎？

M2：這情況聽起來好像是老舊的出紙滾輪所致。今天下午我們會派一名技術人員過去，他可以為您更換。

字彙 ☐ feed 機器內的材料供應裝置 ☐ crumpled 皺皺的 ☐ hand out～ 發放～ ☐ worn-out 老舊的 ☐ exit roller 出紙滾輪

53. What is the problem?

(A) A delivery of office supplies was delayed.
(B) A wrong type of material has been used.
(C) A device is not working properly.
(D) An office supplies store has been closed.

發生了什麼問題？

（A）辦公用品配送延誤。
（B）使用了錯誤類型的材料。
（C）裝置無法正常運作。
（D）辦公用品店已經關門了。

答案 **(C)**

解析 詢問其中一位說話者所面臨的問題是什麼，這是典型的題型。第一個出現的男性說It had been working fine for years until yesterday when it stopped working properly.（它已經順利運作好幾年了，一直到昨天停止正常運作。）。運作一直很順利的影印機昨天不再正常運作，這就是這次發生的問題。因此正確答案是（C）。

54. Where does Mark most likely work?

馬克最有可能在哪裡工作？

(A) At an electronics store

(B) At a school office

(C) At a school cafeteria

(D) At a stationery company

（A）電器行

（B）學校辦公室

（C）學校的自助餐廳

（D）文具公司

答案 (B)

解析 第一位男性說This is Mark Cooper.（我是馬克．庫柏），由此可知他的名字就叫馬克。接著他又說We have a BEX-2000 copy machine at our office.（我們辦公室裡有一台型號BEX-2000的印表機），再加上他第二次發言時提到We need to print out hundreds of course guidelines to hand out to our students tomorrow.（為了明天要發給我們的學生，我們需要印出數百份課程綱要。），所以正確答案是（B）。

字彙 □ stationery company 文具公司

55. What will the technician most likely do?

技術人員將最有可能做什麼？

(A) Visit the office tomorrow

(B) Bring another kind of paper

(C) Replace old components

(D) Order a new unit

（A）明天拜訪辦公室

（B）帶另一種紙張

（C）更換舊的零組件

（D）訂購新的裝置

答案 (C)

解析 這題要仔細聽對話，注意有關技術人員要做什麼的資訊。因為第二位男性在第二次的發言時說了We'll send one of our technicians this afternoon and he can change them for you.（今天下午我們會派一名技術人員過去，他可以為您更換。），由此可知technician（技術人員）會更換them（＝exit rollers），所以正確答案是（C）。而（A）的tomorrow（明天）如果換成today（今天）就是正確答案了。

字彙 □ component 零組件

Questions 56 through 58 refer to the following conversation.

試題 56-58 請參考以下對話。

43

W: Sam, Q56 here's the form you need to fill out before you take your vacation leave next month.

M: Thanks, Lena. Hey, what's wrong? You look tired. Is the department still understaffed?

W: Yes. Q57 We have too much work and not enough workers. But I heard that next year we will hire an outside company to take care of all payroll associated tasks, so it should get better.

M: Oh, yes, Q58 I remember there was an announcement about that in the company newsletter. People say that it's common for companies to do that these days.

W：山姆（Sam），這是你下個月要休假之前需要填寫的表格。

M：謝謝妳，麗娜（Lena）。嘿，怎麼了？妳看起來很累。這個部門仍然人手不足嗎？

W：是的。我們有太多的工作，而且人手不足。但是我聽說明年我們將聘請一家外部公司來處理所有支薪相關的業務，所以情況應該會好轉。

M：喔，是的，我記得公司快訊內有這個公告。聽人說，最近企業做這樣的事是很常見的。

字彙 □ payroll associated task 支薪相關的業務

56. What will probably happen next month?

(A) An employee will be transferred.

(B) A staff member will go on holiday.

(C) Some duties will be outsourced.

(D) Some departments will be merged.

下個月可能會發生什麼事？

（A）一名員工將被調職。

（B）一名員工將去度假。

（C）一些職責將會外包。

（D）一些部門將被合併。

答案 **(B)**

解析 這題要仔細聽對話，注意有關next month（下個月）的資訊。女性一開始就說here's the form you need to fill out before you take your vacation leave next month.（這是你下個月要休假之前需要填寫的表格。）。而休假的人，就是接下來說話，且在同一公司上班的男性。（B）只是將take your vacation leave（休假）換個說法為go on holiday（去度假），所以是正確答案。（C）雖然符合對話後段的內容，不過時間不是下個月而是明年。

字彙 □ outsource 將～外包

57. What does the woman say about her department?
(A) It is heavily cluttered.
(B) It lacks sufficient manpower.
(C) It will get some new recruits.
(D) It will move to another location.

關於她的部門，女性說了什麼？
（A）非常雜亂。
（B）缺乏足夠的人手。
（C）將有一些新員工。
（D）將搬到另一個地方。

答案 (B)

解析 從題目中可知，正確答案的出處應該就在女性的發言內，因此要仔細聽她說了什麼。女性在第二次的發言時，針對她的部門說了We have to much work and not enough workers.（我們有太多的工作，而且人手不足。）。由此可知工作太多，以致人力不足。（B）簡潔地將其換個說法，所以是正確答案。而（A）的cluttered也是會出現在測驗中的重要單字，請牢記它。

字彙 □ cluttered 雜亂的 □ manpower 人手 □ recruit 新成員、新員工

58. How did the man know payroll associated tasks would be outsourced?
(A) He heard rumors about it.
(B) He saw a notice on the bulletin board.
(C) He read about it in a publication.
(D) He received a memo from his boss.

男性如何得知支薪相關的業務將會被外包？
（A）他聽到傳聞。
（B）他在公告欄上看到一則通知。
（C）他在一份出版物中讀到的。
（D）他收到老闆給的備忘錄。

答案 (C)

解析 男性第二次的發言提到I remember there was an announcement about that in the company newsletter.（我記得公司快訊內有這個公告）。這句的that就是指前一句女性所說的next year we will hire an outside company to take care of all payroll associated tasks（明年我們將聘請一家外部公司來處理所有支薪相關的業務）。（C）只是將company newsletter（公司快訊）換個說法為publication（出版物），所以是正確答案。

Questions 59 through 61 refer to the following conversation.

試題 59-61 請參考以下對話。

44

W: Q60 Sorry we can't do this meeting in person. Q59 I'm just lucky I could get my car to a garage that could work on it right away.

M: It happens to all of us at some point.

W: Anyway, I'm glad I brought my work laptop home with me last night. So, shall we start this conference call?

M: Yeah. Q61 Did you get a chance to make the changes to the contract last night as planned?

W: Yes. Take a quick look at it and tell me what you think—I just e-mailed it to you.

M: I like what you've done so far. Thanks for addressing the warranty issue. But let's clarify the last line a bit. Here's my idea...

W：很抱歉我們不能親自見面進行這次的會議。實在很幸運，我還能把車開到能立即進行修理的修車廠。

M：這樣的事隨時都有可能發生在任何人身上。

W：不論如何，很高興昨晚我有把工作用的筆記型電腦帶回家。所以，我們要開始電話會議了嗎？

M：是的。昨晚你有沒有機會依照計畫修正合約呢？

W：有的。請看一下並告訴我你的想法——我剛剛傳電子郵件給你了。

M：我喜歡你目前為止所做的。謝謝你處理擔保的問題。但是讓我們把最後一行字弄清楚。這是我的想法……

字彙 □ in person（本人）親自、面對面 □ at some point 在某個時間點 □ conference call 電話會議 □ e-mail 用電子郵件傳送～ □ so far 到目前為止 □ address 處理～ □ warranty issue 擔保的問題 □ clarify 把～弄清楚

59. Why can't the woman do the meeting in person? 女性為什麼無法親自見面參加會議？

(A) She did not get any work done last night. （A）她昨晚沒有完成任何工作。

(B) She is getting her laptop repaired. （B）她正在修她的筆記型電腦。

(C) She had trouble with her vehicle. （C）她的車發生故障。

(D) She double-booked for half of the meeting. （D）她預約的會議有一半時間重疊了。

答案 **(C)**

解析 女性一開始就說I'm just lucky I could get my car to a garage that could work on it right away.（實在很幸運，我還能把車開到能立即進行修理的修車廠。）。這就是在表達無法親自見面參加會議的原因，所以正確答案是（C）。

字彙 □ double-book 預約時間重疊

60. What does the man mean when he says, "It happens to all of us at some point"?
(A) The woman has entered a new stage in life.
(B) The woman had to make a difficult decision.
(C) The woman should be much more careful.
(D) The woman should not worry about it.

當男性說「It happens to all of us at some point」時，代表什麼意思？
（A）女性進入了人生的新階段。
（B）女性必須做很難的抉擇。
（C）女性應該要更加小心。
（D）女性不應該擔心。

答案 **(D)**

解析 理解這句話的前後「狀況」，選出符合該狀況的選項內容。在男性說這句話之前，女性懷著歉意地說Sorry we can't do this meeting in person.（很抱歉我們不能親自見面進行這次的會議）。而男性是針對這個來做回應，由此可知他要表達的是「不需要在意無法親自見面進行會議」。所以（D）是正確答案。

61. What was the woman supposed to do last night?
(A) Write down her ideas about an e-mail
(B) Work on a document
(C) Speak to someone about a warranty
(D) Negotiate a contract with a company

女性昨晚應該做什麼？
（A）寫下對於一封電子郵件的想法
（B）處理文件
（C）與某人討論一項擔保
（D）和公司交涉一份合約

答案 **(B)**

解析 因為男性第二次的發言向女性詢問Did you get a chance to make the changes to the contract last night as planned?（昨晚你有沒有機會依照計畫修正合約？），因此正確答案是（B）。work on～是「處理～」，所以是「處理文件」，也就是「修正文件」的意思。

字彙 ☐ write down 寫下～ ☐ work on～ 處理～ ☐ warranty 擔保 ☐ negotiate *A* with *B* 與B交涉A

Questions 62 through 64 refer to the following conversation with three speakers and map.

試題 62-64 請參考以下 3 人對話及地圖。 45

M: Jean, I'm going to try to find the post office so I can get this to the Sandberg Corporation ASAP. Is it that beautiful building next to Rhiner's Bank?

W1: That's the old opera house. But in the same area, Q63 you'll find it between an Italian restaurant and a library.

W2: The library is in an old book shop, so it doesn't look like a typical library.

M: Oh, okay. Q63 Across from a men's clothes shop. Q62 I'll figure this town out soon.

W2: By the way, when will you be back? I need to talk to you about our new project.

M: It'll be a while. Q64 I've got a 12 o'clock lunch consultation with a client at Everett Café. But I'll visit your desk when I'm back.

W2: Sounds good.

W1: If you get lost, just give one of us a call.

M：珍（Jean），為了儘快把這個寄到山德柏格（Sandberg）公司，我將試著去找郵局在哪。它是那個緊鄰萊茵爾（Rhiner's）銀行的漂亮建築物嗎？

W1：那是老歌劇院。但是郵局在同一區域，你可以在義大利餐廳和圖書館之間找到它。

W2：圖書館在一間舊書店內，所以它看起來不像典型的圖書館。

M：喔，好的。在男士服裝店對面。我很快就能弄清楚這個市鎮了。

W2：順便提一下，你什麼時候回來？我需要跟你談談有關我們的新計畫。

M：它會花一段時間。我已和一位客戶約好12點在艾佛里特咖啡（Everett Café）的午餐會議了。但是當我回來時，我會去你的座位找妳。

W2：聽起來不錯。

W1：如果你迷路了，只要打個電話給我們其中一位就好。

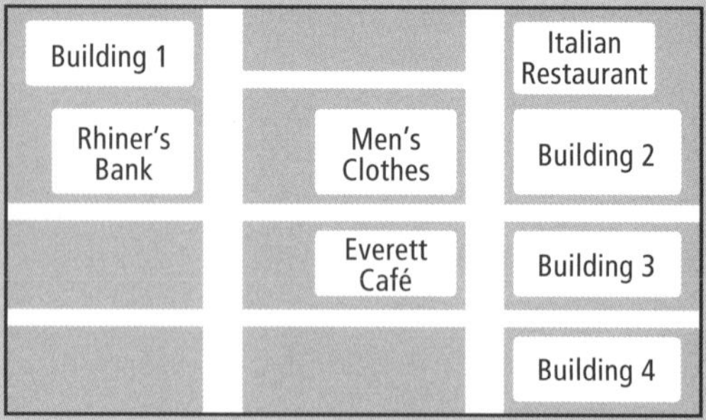

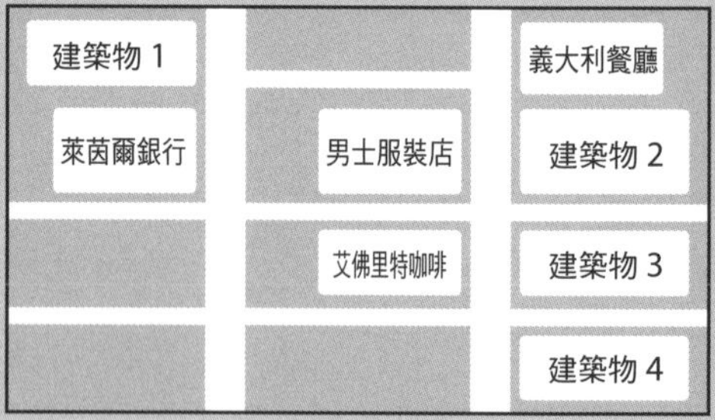

字彙 □ ASAP（as soon as possible的縮寫）儘快 □ typical 典型的 □ across from～ 在～對面
□ figure out～ 將～弄清楚 □ by the way 順便提一下 □ a while 一會兒 □ Sounds good. 聽起來不錯。

62. What is indicated about the man?
(A) He has an account at Rhiner's Bank.
(B) He is new to the area.
(C) He needs to buy a new suit.
(D) He is not very observant.

關於男性的敘述何者正確？
（A）他在萊茵爾銀行有一個帳戶。
（B）他對這個地區是陌生的。
（C）他需要買一套新的西裝。
（D）他不是很善於觀察。

答案 (B)

解析 男性第二次發言時說I'll figure this town out soon.（我很快就能弄清楚這個市鎮了）。也就是說，目前他對這條街的事物尚未完全了解。由此可知，正確答案是（B）。

字彙 □ account 帳戶 □ observant 善於觀察的

63. Look at the graphic. Which building is the post office?
(A) Building 1
(B) Building 2
(C) Building 3
(D) Building 4

請看圖。郵局是哪一棟建築物？
（A）建築物1
（B）建築物2
（C）建築物3
（D）建築物4

答案 (B)

解析 遇到圖表問題時，記得一邊看圖表上「與選項相異之處（＝組合資訊）」，一邊聽對話內容。如此一來，在尋找題目中的目標建築物時就更有利作答。第一位女性一開始提到you'll find it between an Italian restaurant and a library.（你可以在義大利餐廳和圖書館之間找到它。），而男性在第二次發言時說Across from a men's clothes shop（在男士服裝店對面）。由此可知，郵局是建築物2，圖書館是建築物3。

64. Why will the man be gone for a while?
(A) He will probably get lost.
(B) He wants to get to know the town.
(C) He wants to try the Italian restaurant.
(D) He has plans to meet someone.

男性為什麼會不在辦公室一段時間？
（A）他可能會迷路。
（B）他想要了解這個市鎮。
（C）他想嘗試義大利餐廳。
（D）他計畫與某人見面。

答案 (D)

解析 男性第三次發言中，已表達了暫時不在的原因是I've got a 12 o'clock lunch consultation with a client at Everett Café.（我已和一位客戶約好12點在艾佛里特咖啡的午餐會議了）。（D）只是將該情況換個簡潔的說法，所以是正確答案。

字彙 □ for a while 一會兒

Questions 65 through 67 refer to the following conversation and schedule.

試題 65-67 請參考以下對話及時間表。 46

W: Donald, I'm going to sign up for the 6-week Employee Training Program today, but Q65 I wanted to check with you on times first.

M: Q65 Q66 Good idea since one of us always has to be around to answer questions over the phone.

W: Exactly. Do you have a preference for when you'd like me available?

M: You know, Q67 I think we really need you at the desk in the mornings because I like to get certain daily tasks done early. And we're always bombarded by calls right after lunch, so I feel we both need to be here then.

W: All right, I'll take that into account when I make my selection.

M: Great, thanks.

W：唐納德（Donald），我今天要報名為期六週的員工培訓課程，但是我想先與你確認一下時間。

M：好主意，因為我們當中總是得有一人留守，負責接電話回答問題。

W：沒錯，那你有特別希望我什麼時候在嗎？

M：你知道嗎，我認為我們真的需要妳早上要在辦公桌前，因為我喜歡儘早完成某些特定的日常工作。而且我們總是在午餐後就馬上被電話轟炸，所以我覺得我們倆那段時間都需要在這裡。

W：好的，在我做出選擇時，我會考慮到這一點。

M：太好了，謝謝妳。

Employee Training Program Times
8:00 A.M.-10:00 A.M.
10:00 A.M.-12:00 P.M.
1:00 P.M.-3:00 P.M.
Q67 3:00 P.M.-5:00 P.M.

員工培訓課程時間表
8:00 A.M. – 10:00 A.M.
10:00 A.M. – 12:00 P.M.
1:00 P.M. – 3:00 P.M.
3:00 P.M. – 5:00 P.M.

字彙 ☐ sign up for～ 報名～ ☐ check with～ 與～確認 ☐ *be* bombarded by calls 被電話轟炸
☐ take that into account 考慮到這一點

65. What is the woman trying to do?
(A) Establish a more effective daily routine
(B) Find someone to teach a program
(C) Decide on a temporary work schedule
(D) Choose days to be away from the office

女性試圖做什麼？
（A）建立更有效的日常工作流程
（B）尋找教課的人
（C）決定短期內的工作時間表
（D）選擇不在辦公室的日子

答案 **(C)**

解析 女性一開始就提到想參加培訓課程，所以向對方表示I wanted to check with you on times first.（我想先與你確認一下時間）。男性對此回答Good idea since one of us always has to be around to answer questions over the phone.（好主意，因為我們當中總是得有一人留守，負責接電話回答問題），可知雙方是在商量臨時的上班時間。對話到這個階段時，給人感覺（D）也可能是正確答案。但是從接下來的男性發言可判斷，女性可離開辦公室的期間僅「數小時」，因此正確答案是（C）。

字彙 □ establish 建立～ □ daily routine 日常事務、程序 □ *be* away from the office 不在辦公室

66. Why is the woman consulting the man?
(A) They often have lunch together.
(B) They share some responsibilities.
(C) He generally gives good advice.
(D) He is the department manager.

為什麼女性找男性商量？
（A）他們經常共進午餐。
（B）他們共同分擔一些責任。
（C）他通常會給予好的建議。
（D）他是部門經理。

答案 **(B)**

解析 男性一開始說one of us always has to be around to answer questions over the phone（好主意，因為我們當中總是得有一人留守，負責接電話回答問題）。由此可知，這兩位說話者是做一樣的工作內容（接聽來電）。所以正確答案是（B）。

67. Look at the graphic. When will the woman most likely take the training program?
(A) 8:00 A.M.-10:00 A.M.
(B) 10:00 A.M.-12:00 P.M.
(C) 1:00 P.M.-3:00 P.M.
(D) 3:00 P.M.-5:00 P.M.

請看圖。女性最有可能什麼時候參加培訓課程？
（A）8:00 A.M.－10:00 A.M.
（B）10:00 A.M.－12:00 P.M.
（C）1:00 P.M.－3:00 P.M.
（D）3:00 P.M.－5:00 P.M.

答案 **(D)**

解析 男性第二次發言時說I think we really need you at the desk in the morning because I like to get certain daily tasks done early. And we're always bombarded by calls right after lunch, so I feel we both need to be here then.（我認為我們真的需要妳早上要在辦公桌前，因為我喜歡儘早完成某些特定的日常工作。而且我們總是在午餐後就馬上被電話轟炸，所以我覺得我們倆那段時間都需要在這裡。）。男性向女性表達了希望上午～午餐後她都能接聽來電。因此，女性參加培訓課程最適合的時間是下午3點～下午5點，所以正確答案是（D）。

Questions 68 through 70 refer to the following conversation and business card.

試題 68-70 請參考以下對話及名片。

47

W: I wanted to follow up on our conversation on Friday. Here's my friend's business card. I think your invention would be of great use to Amherst Aerospace and their affiliates.

M: Thanks. I think so, too. Q68 Q69 And since your friend's company is so big and successful, their endorsement of my invention could help me finally quit my regular job and launch my own business. Q70 I'll call him and see what he thinks.

W: Q70 I don't think that'll work.

M: Oh, I see why. I'll contact them when I get to my computer later.

W：我想繼續我們週五的對話內容。這是我朋友的名片。我認為你的發明對阿默斯特航太公司（Amherst Aerospace）及其附屬公司會非常有幫助。

M：謝謝。我也這麼認為。而且因為你朋友的公司規模如此龐大及成功，我的發明如果有他們的支持，就可以幫助我，終於能辭去固定工作並開創自己的事業。我會打電話給他並聽看看他的想法。

W：我認為那行不通。

M：喔，我知道原因了。那麼等我晚點用電腦時再聯繫他們。

AMHERST AEROSPACE
125 Lowry Ln, Amherst, RI (865) 555-1000

Theodore Dubrovka
President

* Q70 meetings must be in person, by appointment, 1-4 P.M.; contact secretary at: sec@amherstaerospace.com

阿默斯特航太公司
125號 洛瑞巷，
阿默斯特，羅德島州（RI）（865）555-1000

西奧多・杜布羅夫卡
董事長

* 必須親自會面，採預約制，1-4 P.M.；
請與秘書聯繫：
sec@amherstaerospace.com

字彙 ☐ follow up on～ 進行～的後續 ☐ affiliate 附屬公司 ☐ endorsement 支持 ☐ quit 辭去～
☐ work 行得通

68. What are the speakers mainly discussing?　說話者主要在討論什麼？

(A) A friend's new idea　（A）朋友的新想法

(B) Recent job offers　（B）最近的工作機會

(C) Investing in a company　（C）投資一間公司

(D) A business referral　（D）企業轉介

答案 (D)

解析 一開始，女性發言到一半時，即把名片遞給男性。收下名片的男性說And since your friend's company is so big and successful, their endorsement of my invention could help me finally quit my regular job and launch my own business.（而且因為你朋友的公司規模如此龐大及成功，我的發明如果有他們的支持，就可以幫助我，終於能辭去固定工作並開創自己的事業。）。由此可知，女性在向男性介紹工作相關的資訊，（D）只是簡單地換個說法而已，所以是正確答案。

字彙 □ referral 轉介

69. What does the man want to do?　男性想做什麼？

(A) Become self-employed　（A）自己做老闆

(B) Invest in the friend's company　（B）投資朋友的公司

(C) Invent something for Amherst Aerospace　（C）為阿默斯特航太公司發明一些東西

(D) Collaborate with the woman　（D）與女性合作

答案 (A)

解析 從上一題（第68題）解析中，男性說的同一句話可知，他想要自己創業。（A）self-employed只是將它換個說法而已，所以是正確答案。

字彙 □ self-employed 自僱的　□ collaborate with～ 與～合作

70. Look at the graphic. Why can't the man consult with the woman's friend over the phone?　請看圖。為什麼男性不能透過電話與女性的朋友商談？

(A) This company only accepts calls in the afternoon.　（A）該公司僅接受下午來電。

(B) The company secretary meets with everyone first.　（B）公司秘書要先與每個來訪的人見面。

(C) Discussions are conducted face-to-face.　（C）討論需要面對面進行。

(D) The woman's friend is often out of the office.　（D）女性的朋友經常不在辦公室。

答案 (C)

解析 男性第一次的發言時提到I'll call him and see what he thinks.（我會打電話給他並聽看看他的想法。）。但是名片下方有載明meeting must be in person（必須親自會面）。女性回答他I don't think that'll work.（我認為那行不通），所以正確答案是（C）。

字彙 □ face-to-face 面對面

Questions 71 through 73 refer to the following telephone message.
試題 71-73 請參考以下電話留言。

49

Hi. This is Denise Erasmo from Human Resources with a message for Erik Cole. Erik, Q71 we haven't received your self-evaluation form yet, and it was due on Wednesday. I know Q72 you have your hands full preparing for the conference in Singapore, but can you send it to us before you leave for the conference next week? The formal performance review is coming up next month and Q73 headquarters has requested that all forms be sent to them before then. Thanks.

你好，我是人力資源部門的丹尼斯・艾拉斯莫（Denise Erasmo），要留言給艾瑞克・柯爾（Erik Cole）。艾瑞克，我們尚未收到你的自我評估表，它在週三就過繳交期限了。我知道你目前忙著全力為新加坡的會議做準備，但是可否請你在下週出發去會議之前將它傳給我們？正式的績效考核將在下個月進行，總公司已經要求所有的表格都要在那之前傳送給他們。謝謝。

字彙 □ self-evaluation form 自我評估表 □ formal 正式的 □ performance review 績效考核

71. Why is the speaker calling the man?
(A) He failed to meet a deadline.
(B) He missed a meeting.
(C) He performed poorly on a test.
(D) He has not returned a message.

為什麼說話者打電話給男性？
（A）他未在截止日前完成規定。
（B）他錯過一場會議。
（C）他在測驗中表現不佳。
（D）他沒有回覆訊息。

答案 **(A)**

解析 題目問的the man，是指聽電話留言的男性。留言者在講完招呼語後接著說we haven't received your self-evaluation form yet, and it was due on Wednesday.（我們尚未收到你的自我評估表，它在週三就過繳交期限了）。由此可知，聽留言的男性似乎還未提出已於週三截止的自我評量表。（A）將該狀況換個委婉的說法，所以是正確答案。對於電話留言，請大家要特別注意開頭的部分，不要漏聽了。

72. What will the man most likely do next week?
(A) Take a business trip
(B) Present a report
(C) Have an interview
(D) Go on vacation

男性下週最有可能做什麼？
（A）出差
（B）提交報告
（C）參加面試
（D）去度假

答案 **(A)**

解析 預覽題目看到next week（下週），在聽留言時就要意識到這是重要的關鍵詞。電話留言的中間部分提到you have your hands full preparing for the conference in Singapore, but can you send it to us before you leave for the conference next week?（我知道你目前忙著全力為新加坡的會議做準備，但是可否請你在下週出發去會議之前將它傳給我們？）。由此可知，聽留言的男性為了出席新加坡的會議，下週會出差到新加坡。所以正確答案是（A）。

73. According to the woman, what will happen to the forms?
(A) They will be reviewed by the board of directors.
(B) They will be sent to headquarters.
(C) They will be used at a performance.
(D) They will be handed to Erik Cole.

根據女性所述，這些表格將會發生什麼事？
（A）它們將由董事會考核。
（B）它們會被送到總公司。
（C）它們會被用於表演。
（D）它們會被交給艾瑞克・柯爾。

答案 **(B)**

解析 聽留言內容時，要密切注意與forms（表格）有關的資訊。留言的最後提到headquarters has requested that all forms be sent to them（總公司已經要求所有的表格都要傳送給他們），由此可知總公司要求傳送所有的表格。（B）直接敘述要傳送到headquarters（總部），所以是正確答案。

Questions 74 through 76 refer to the following advertisement.
試題 74-76 請參考以下廣告。

50

For more than 25 years, Q74 Whitecare Laundry Service has provided Ottawa's hospitality industries with top quality services. To make life easier for our clients, Q75 we provide flexible collection and delivery hours. After the linens are collected they go through Q74 a variety of cleaning processes which ensure the highest level of disinfection without damaging the textiles. Q76 We use energy-efficient machinery with low water usage and near zero emissions to protect the environment around us. You can depend on Q74 Whitecare Laundry Service for all your linen needs. Call 555-1892 to request our professional services or to learn more about us.

長達25年以上的時間，潔白洗衣服務（Whitecare Laundry Service）一直為渥太華（Ottawa）的飯店服務業提供最優質的服務。為了讓我們客戶的日子更便利，我們提供彈性的收送時間。收集床單後，它們會經歷各種清潔過程，確保最高標準的消毒而不會損壞紡織品。我們使用低耗水量及接近零排放廢氣的節能機器來保護我們周圍的環境。您所有的床單需求都可以仰賴潔白洗衣服務。請致電555-1892預約我們專業的服務，或了解更多有關我們的資訊。

字彙 ☐ hospitality industry 飯店服務業 ☐ collection and delivery hours 收送時間 ☐ linen 亞麻布製品、床單 ☐ disinfection 消毒 ☐ textile 紡織品 ☐ energy-efficient 高效節能的 ☐ emission 排廢氣

74. What type of business is being advertised?
(A) A hotel chain
(B) A textile corporation
(C) A food delivery service
(D) A laundry company

這是在廣告什麼類型的行業？
（A）連鎖飯店
（B）紡織公司
（C）食品配送服務
（D）洗衣公司

答案 **(D)**

解析 開頭就提到Whitecare Laundry Service。雖然單憑這句就可以選出正確答案，不過萬一漏聽了，中間和最後階段也都分別提到了a variety of cleaning processes（各種清潔過程）和Whitecare Laundry Service，有利於彌補前面錯過的部分。所以正確答案是（D）。

字彙 ☐ textile corporation 紡織公司

75. According to the speaker, what is flexible?

(A) Payment method

(B) Delivery time

(C) Service costs

(D) Pick-up location

根據說話者所述，什麼是有彈性的？

（A）付款方式

（B）配送時間

（C）服務費用

（D）取貨地點

答案 (B)

解析 這題應該要意識到的關鍵字是flexible（有彈性的）。廣告前半段說we provide flexible collection and delivery hours.（我們提供彈性的收送時間）。因為是指建立靈活的收送時間，所以正確答案是（B）的Delivery time。collection and delivery hours字面之意即是「收件和遞送時間」。

76. What does the speaker suggest about the cleaning process?

(A) It only takes a short time.

(B) It is fully automated.

(C) It involves using cutting-edge computers.

(D) It is environmentally friendly.

針對清潔過程，說話者表示什麼？

（A）只需要很短的時間。

（B）完全自動化。

（C）包括使用最尖端的電腦。

（D）它是環保的。

答案 (D)

解析 廣告末段提到We use energy-efficient machinery with low water usage and near zero emissions to protect the environment around us.（我們使用低耗水量及接近零排放廢氣的節能機器來保護我們周圍的環境）。可知其作業過程是以保護周圍環境為優先，（D）簡潔地將它換個說法，所以是正確答案。雖說有使用energy-efficient machinery，但是並沒有提到（C）的cutting-edge computers。

字彙 ☐ cutting-edge 最尖端的 ☐ environmentally friendly 環保的

Questions 77 through 79 refer to the following talk.
試題 77-79 請參考以下談話。

51

In this training session, Q77 I'm going to share with you skills to improve communication in the workplace. Q78 This may not seem important, but you'd be surprised to know this. Research shows that better communication reduces employee stress, increases productivity, enhances the company's image as a whole, and brings greater customer satisfaction. After a week, I'll be e-mailing you all a link for a questionnaire. It won't take long but Q79 your responses will help me understand whether things have improved in your workplace due to this session. So let's get started. Please take one of these handouts and pass the rest on.

這次的訓練講習，我將與你們分享改善職場溝通的技巧。這或許看似不重要，但你們聽到這項資訊一定會很驚訝。研究報告顯示，更好的溝通可以降低員工壓力，增加生產力，將公司整體形象提升，並帶來更高的客戶滿意度。一週之後，我會將問卷調查的連結用電子郵件寄給你們所有人。這不會花很長時間，但你的回答將有助於我了解，是否藉由這堂講習讓您在職場的情況有所改善。那麼，我們開始吧！請自行取一份講義再將其餘的傳遞下去。

字彙 □ session 講習 □ as a whole 整體上 □ questionnaire 問卷調查 □ due to～ 由於～
□ pass on～ 將～傳遞下去

77. What is the talk mainly about?
(A) Reducing employee turnover
(B) Improving compliance to rules
(C) Communicating effectively
(D) Meeting deadlines

這段談話主要是在說什麼？
（A）減少人員流動率
（B）提高遵守規則的情況
（C）有效地溝通
（D）趕上繳交期限

答案 **(C)**

解析 演講者一開頭就說I'm going to share with you skills to improve communication in the workplace（我將與你們分享改善職場溝通的技巧）。（C）只是將improve communication換個說法為Communication effectively，所以是正確答案。而其他的選項都與整段談話無關。

字彙 □ turnover 人員流動率 □ compliance to rules 守規、遵守規則

78. What does the speaker mean when he says, “you'd be surprised to know this”?

(A) He will talk about what he thinks few people know.

(B) It is not difficult to communicate well.

(C) He decided to hold the training session suddenly.

(D) Changes in the workplace may suddenly occur.

當演講者說「you'd be surprised to know this」時，代表什麼意思？

（A）他將談到他認為很少人會知道的內容。

（B）溝通良好並非難事。

（C）他突然決定舉行訓練講習。

（D）職場上的變化可能突然發生。

答案 **(A)**

解析 上一題（第77題）的正確答案出處後有提到「這或許看似不重要」，隨後接的就是這一題問的you'd be surprised to know this（你們聽到這項資訊一定會很驚訝）。而（A）最能夠表達演講者說這句話時背後的想法。

79. Why will the speaker e-mail the listeners after a week?

(A) To send all the handouts

(B) To get their feedback

(C) To respond to their questions

(D) To remind them about the next session

說話者為什麼一週後要寄電子郵件給聽者？

（A）寄送所有講義

（B）為了得到他們的反饋

（C）回答他們的問題

（D）提醒他們下一次的講習

答案 **(B)**

解析 後半段的談話提到I'll be e-mailing you all a link for a questionnaire.（我會將問卷調查的連結用電子郵件寄給你們所有人），後面接著說「你的回答將有助於我了解，是否藉由這堂講習讓您在職場的情況有所改善」。由此可知，寄問卷調查是為了「得到他們的反饋」，所以正確答案是（B）。

Questions 80 through 82 refer to the following telephone message. 52

試題 80-82 請參考以下電話留言。

Good afternoon, Mr. Long. This is Peter Hummel from Nick's Truck Rentals. Q80 We received your online reservation, and we're happy to confirm that a cargo van has been reserved for you for September 15 from 10 A.M. The vehicle can be picked up at your nearest Nick's Truck Rental Center, which is on Jardine Avenue. Since you have chosen the same drop-off location option, please return the vehicle to the same Rental Center. Please be warned that if you cancel within 24 hours of pick-up time, Q81 a 40-dollar penalty fee will be assessed. We'd also like to tell you that Q82 we provide printable worksheets which you can use to list articles belonging to your household to make your moving easier, at www.nickstruckrentals.com.

午安，龍（Long）先生。我是尼克卡車租賃（Nick's Truck Rentals）的彼得．胡梅爾（Peter Hummel）。我們收到您的線上預約，很高興向您確認，一輛自9月15日10 A.M.起租的箱行車已為您預留。這輛車可以在離您最近的尼克卡車租賃中心領取，就在渣甸（Jardine）大道上。由於您選擇了相同的歸還地點，因此請將車輛返回同一處租賃中心。請注意，如果您在起租時間的24小時內取消，將會被處以40美元的罰款。在此我們也想告知您，在www.nickstruckrentals.com的網頁內，我們提供了可列印使用的工作表，您可列出屬於您家的所有物品，使您的搬家過程更輕鬆。

字彙 □ cargo van 箱型車 □ drop-off location 歸還地點、交付地點 □ pick-up time 起租時間 □ assess 處以～罰款 □ printable 可列印的 □ list 將～編列成表 □ article 項目、商品 □ household 家庭、戶

80. What is the purpose of the telephone message? 電話留言的目的是什麼？

(A) To make a reservation （A）做預約

(B) To give details about a booking （B）提供預約詳情

(C) To change an order （C）更改訂單

(D) To provide a cost estimate （D）提供成本估算

答案 (B)

解析 像這類詢問電話中處理的事項，也就是詢問全文目的的題目，是Part 4經常出現的題型之一。一開始留言者就說 We received your online reservation, and we're happy to confirm that a cargo van has been reserved for you for September 15 from 10 A.M.（我們收到您的線上預約，很高興向您確認，一輛自9月15日10 A.M.起租的箱行車已為您預留。），由此可知，這是為了通知已接受預約事宜而撥打的電話。後面則是針對租賃方法及取消等細節做說明，所以正確答案是（B）。而（A）是指預約本身，注意不要混淆了。

81. How much is the penalty charge?

(A) 10 dollars
(B) 15 dollars
(C) 24 dollars
(D) 40 dollars

罰款是多少？

（A）10美元
（B）15美元
（C）24美元
（D）40美元

答案 **(D)**

解析 集中精神注意聽有關penalty charge的話題。留言的最後階段提到a 40-dollar penalty fee will be assessed.（會被處以40美元的罰款），所以正確答案是（D）。請記住assess除了有「對～評價、估價」的意思，還有「處以～（稅金、罰款）」之意。

字彙 □ penalty charge 罰款

82. What can the listener obtain from the Web site?

(A) A form for making an inventory
(B) A worksheet to calculate the total cost
(C) A timetable to facilitate moving
(D) A copy of the rental agreement

聽留言者可以從網站得到什麼？

（A）可編製清單的表格
（B）可計算總成本的工作表
（C）有助於搬遷的時間表
（D）租賃合約的副本

答案 **(A)**

解析 先掌握這題是有關Web site（網站）的部分，就能準確聽懂重點。留言者最後總結we provide printable worksheets which you can use to list articles belong to your household to make your moving easier, at www.nickstruckrentals.com.（在www.nickstruckrentals.com的網頁內，我們提供了可列印使用的工作表，您可列出屬於您家的所有物品，使您的搬家過程更輕鬆。）。不但提供了能列印出來的工作表，而且可以用來將家中物品逐項列成清單，（A）只是將它換個說法為inventory，所以是正確答案。

字彙 □ inventory 清單、存貨 □ facilitate 使～容易、促進

Questions 83 through 85 refer to the following news broadcast.

試題 83-85 請參考以下新聞廣播。

53

And now for business news. More and more Q83 companies are using global mobility programs to effectively utilize their workforce on an international scale. Glomore is a company which helps employers run these programs by offering relocation solutions that fit the companies' policies and budgets. Glomore spokesperson Andrew Chang says Q84 they did see a slowdown in business last year due to the economic crisis, but demands for their services are rising rapidly and it is expected to continue. And he points out that although the primary business centers like Hong Kong, Singapore, New York and London are still popular destinations, Q85 they have been dealing increasingly with relocations to African and Eastern European countries.

現在播報商業新聞。越來越多的企業都採用全球流動性計畫，以有效地利用他們具國際規模的勞動力。葛羅莫爾（Glomore）是一家協助雇主執行這些計畫的公司，藉由提供符合企業政策和預算的外派方案，葛羅莫爾發言人張安卓（Andrew Chang）表示，由於經濟危機，他們去年的確遇到業務衰退，但是對該公司服務的需求正在快速成長，且預計會持續下去。他指出，儘管香港、新加坡、紐約和倫敦等主要商業中心仍是受歡迎的目的地，他們已經開始在處理越來越多往非洲和東歐各國的外派調度了。

字彙 □ global mobility 全球流動性 □ utilize 利用、活用～ □ workforce 勞動力、總員工數 □ slowdown 衰退 □ primary 首要的、主要的

83. What is the news broadcast about?

(A) Increased international shipping costs

(B) Global environmental protection programs

(C) New promotional strategies for companies

(D) Relocation of employees to foreign countries

新聞廣播的內容與什麼有關？

（A）國際運輸成本增加

（B）全球環境保護計畫

（C）各企業的新促銷戰略

（D）將員工調派到國外

答案 **(D)**

解析 Part 4最常出現和全文目的、內容相關的題型。本文開頭就提到companies are using global mobility programs to effectively utilize their workforce on an international scale.（企業採用全球流動性計畫，以有效地利用他們具國際規模的勞動力。），所以正確答案是（D）。雖然聽到global mobility programs（全球流動性計畫）很難具體地想像它是什麼，但是後面接著說明to effectively utilize their workforce on an international scale，應該就能想像該計畫的大致內容了。

84. What does Mr. Chang say about last year?
(A) Demand for Glomore's products increased.
(B) Business was slow for Glomore.
(C) Glomore had to lay off some employees.
(D) Glomore had to close down its overseas office.

張先生說了什麼有關去年的事？
（A）對葛羅莫爾的產品需求增加。
（B）葛羅莫爾的業務進展緩慢。
（C）葛羅莫爾不得不解雇部分員工。
（D）葛羅莫爾不得不關閉海外辦事處。

答案 **(B)**

解析 將last year視為關鍵字，專心聽正確解答的出處。中間部分提到了they did see a slowdown in business last year（他們去年的確遇到業務衰退），由此可知去年公司的業務低迷。而（B）將該狀況簡而言之，所以是正確答案。

字彙 □ lay off～ 解雇～

85. Which area is Glomore increasingly involved with?
(A) Asia
(B) The United States
(C) Western Europe
(D) Africa

葛羅莫爾與哪一地區有關的業務日益增加？
（A）亞洲
（B）美國
（C）西歐
（D）非洲

答案 **(D)**

解析 專心聽有關地區的內容。新聞的最後有提到they have been dealing increasingly with relocations to Africa and Eastern European countries（他們已經開始在處理越來越多往非洲和東歐各國的外派調度了。）。這句話明白地表達，該公司已經在處理往非洲和東歐各國的調派業務，所以正確答案是（D）。（C）的Western Europe（西歐）是錯誤的。這題如能確實聽懂細節部分，就可百分之百迎刃而解。

字彙 □ *be* involved with～ 與～有關

Questions 86-88 refer to the following telephone message.
試題 86-88 請參考以下電話留言。

54

Hello, Mr. Schindler. This is Emily from Frosted Sweets. Q87 Thank you for inquiring about our desserts for the party your company is hosting! To answer your question, um, yes, Q86 we do make gluten-free cakes, but Q88 since people's tastes for gluten-free may be different, before you go ahead with an order, it's always best to try these things first. Every two weeks, Frosted Sweets holds what we call a Taste Test Night where customers can try a variety of our desserts. We always have a few gluten-free items there, so please consider joining us at our next event this Thursday at 6.

哈囉，辛德勒（Schindler）先生。我是糖霜甜點店（Frosted Sweets）的艾蜜莉（Emily）。感謝您為 貴公司主辦的派對來詢問我們的甜點！先來回答您的問題，嗯，是的，我們有做無麩質蛋糕，但因為人們對無麩質食品可能會有不同喜好，在決定訂購之前，最好都要先試嚐。每隔兩週，糖霜甜點店會舉辦一場我們稱為「試吃之夜」的活動，讓客人可以試嚐各種甜點。在活動現場，我們總是有一些無麩質食品，所以請考慮參加我們下次的活動，將在這週四6點舉辦。

字彙 □ gluten-free 無麩質的（不使用小麥等類穀物中所含的蛋白質，也就是麩質製成的食品）
□ go ahead with an order 決定訂購

86. Where does the caller most likely work?
(A) At a tent rental company
(B) At a bakery
(C) At an ice cream shop
(D) At a party supply store

留言者最有可能在哪裡工作？
（A）在帳篷出租公司
（B）在烘焙店
（C）在冰淇淋店
（D）在派對用品店

答案 **(B)**

解析 留言前半段提到we do make gluten-free cakes（我們有做無麩質蛋糕）。可知留言者是在做蛋糕的地方工作，所以正確答案是（B）。bakery除了可指麵包店之外，還有製作糕點類（包括蛋糕）的店。

87. What does the listener need desserts for?
聽留言者為何需要甜點？

(A) A work event
(B) A birthday party
(C) A graduation party
(D) A family reunion

（A）職場活動
（B）生日派對
（C）畢業派對
（D）家庭團聚

答案 **(A)**

解析 留言者一開始就提到Thank you for inquiring about our desserts for the party your company is hosting!（感謝您為貴公司主辦的派對來詢問我們的甜點）。（A）只是將the party your company is hosting抽象地換個說法，所以是正確答案。

88. What does the caller mean when she says, “it's always best to try these things first”?
打電話者說「it's always best to try these things first」時，她的意思是什麼？

(A) The listener should try baking a gluten-free cake.
(B) The listener should buy some desserts to test out.
(C) The listener should bring a good recipe.
(D) The listener may not like the gluten-free items.

（A）聽留言者應該嘗試烘焙無麩質蛋糕。
（B）聽留言者應該購買一些甜點試吃。
（C）聽留言者應該帶來一個好食譜。
（D）聽留言者可能不喜歡無麩質的商品。

答案 **(D)**

解析 在題目所指的這句話之前，留言者說了since people's tastes for gluten-free may be different（因為人們對無麩質食品可能會有不同喜好）。意指「對無麩質的喜好」因人而異，所以表達了希望對方在訂購之前最好先試嚐一下。因此，最適合表達說話者意圖的是（D）。

字彙 ☐ test out 測試～

Questions 89 through 91 refer to the following news broadcast.
試題 89-91 請參考以下新聞廣播。

55

Q89 The Boston area is bracing to get slammed by Hurricane Richard this weekend. It is traveling up the coast quickly and causing delays everywhere it goes. The Boston airport has already canceled thousands of flights for the next three days, and area hotels are reaping the benefits. The latest report is that Q90 all hotel rooms in a 20-mile radius have been reserved. To the contrary, rental car agencies aren't faring so well. Q91 While a small number of people have decided to drive rental cars home instead of waiting out the storm, most are canceling their reservations, making agencies concerned about the lost business.

波士頓（Boston）地區正在為本週末即將受到理查（Richard）颶風猛擊而做好準備。它正迅速地沿著海岸線北上，並在各地引起交通延誤。波士頓機場已經取消接下來三天的數千個航程，該區的飯店因而受惠。最新的報告顯示，半徑20英哩範圍的所有飯店房間皆已預定一空。相反地，租車公司的生意就沒有進行得那麼好了。雖然少數人決定租車開回家而不是等待暴風雨過去，但大多數人還是取消預約，讓租車公司很擔心業務的流失。

字彙 □ brace 做好準備 □ get slammed by～ 受到～的猛擊 □ travel up～ 往～北上 □ coast 海岸 □ reap the benefits 受惠 □ radius 半徑 □ to the contrary 相反地 □ fare 進展

89. What is the broadcast mainly about?
這則廣播主要是關於什麼內容？

(A) Technical difficulties at an airport
(B) Bad weather approaching an area
(C) The decline of a city's tourism
(D) Major delays during construction season

（A）機場的技術難點
（B）惡劣的天氣接近地區
（C）城市的旅遊業下滑
（D）施工期間的主要延誤

答案 **(B)**

解析 廣播一開始就說The Boston area is bracing to get slammed by Hurricane Richard this weekend.（波士頓地區正在為本週末即將受到理查颶風猛擊而做好準備）。可知這是因颶風接近而帶來影響的相關內容，所以正確答案是（B）。

90. How are hotels in the area affected?

(A) Stranded travelers are sleeping in the ballrooms.

(B) Reservations are rapidly being canceled.

(C) Rooms are being shared by strangers.

(D) All of them are completely booked.

該地區的飯店如何受到影響？

（A）被困住的旅客夜宿在宴會廳。

（B）預約被快速地取消。

（C）客房被陌生人共用。

（D）所有飯店全被預定一空。

答案 **(D)**

解析 廣播到一半時提到all hotels rooms in a 20-mile radius have been reserved（半徑20英哩範圍的所有飯店房間皆已預定一空）。（D）簡潔地將其換個說法，所以是正確答案。

字彙 □ stranded 被困住的 □ ballroom 宴會廳 □ stranger 陌生人

91. What does the speaker mean when he says, “rental car agencies aren't faring so well”?

(A) They cannot fulfill all of their reservations.

(B) They are losing a lot of customers.

(C) Their cars are being ruined.

(D) There are complaints about their customer service.

當說話者說「rental car agencies aren't faring so well」，他的意思是什麼？

（A）他們無法滿足所有預約需求。

（B）他們正失去很多客戶。

（C）他們的車被毀了。

（D）有接到抱怨他們的客戶服務的投訴。

答案 **(B)**

解析 題目這句話後面接的是，While a small number of people have decided to drive rental cars home instead of waiting out the storm, most are canceling their reservations, making agencies concerned about the lost business.（雖然少數人決定租車開回家而不是等待暴風雨過去，但大多數人還是取消預約，讓租車公司很擔心業務的流失。）。可知租車公司因颶風的緣故而處於客戶流失的情況，所以正確答案是（B）。faring是動詞fare的現在分詞。

字彙 □ ruin 毀壞～

Questions 92 through 94 refer to the following talk.
試題 92-94 請參考以下談話。

56

Good morning, all. Following last month's security assessment, Q92 OMAR Technologies has decided to upgrade its perimeter control systems. Some of you may have noticed Q92 Q93 intercoms and surveillance cameras being set up in buildings A and B last week. In addition, we will be enforcing stricter rules. Currently, the access control badges issued to employees and authorized contractors are updated annually. But under the new policy, they will be updated every 6 months. On top of that, we'd like to ask all our employees to keep important papers locked up in secure cabinets and Q94 keep their work stations neat and orderly to make identifying strange objects or unauthorized persons easier. Thank you.

早安，各位。繼上個月的安全評估之後，歐瑪（OMAR）科技公司決定升級其周邊控制系統。你們當中有些人可能已經注意到上週在A棟和B棟設置了對講機和監控攝影機。此外，我們將執行更嚴格的規定。目前，發給員工和被授權的承包商的進出控制識別證每年更新一次。但是根據新政策，它們將每六個月更新一次。除此之外，我們想請所有的員工將重要的文件妥善鎖在帶鎖置物櫃中並保持他們的工作區井然有序，以便更容易識別奇怪的物品或未經授權的人員。謝謝。

字彙 □ perimeter control system 周邊控制系統 □ intercom 對講機 □ surveillance camera 監控攝影機 □ enforce（強制）執行～ □ on top of～ 除～之外 □ lock up～ 將～妥善鎖好 □ neat and orderly 井然有序

92. What is the talk about?
(A) Customer relations
(B) Security measures
(C) Emergency procedures
(D) Wellness guidelines

這段談話在說什麼？
（A）客戶關係
（B）安全措施
（C）緊急程序
（D）健康指南

答案 **(B)**

解析 說話者一開始就提到OMAR Technologies has decided to upgrade its perimeter control system.（歐瑪科技公司決定升級其周邊控制系統）。即使不懂perimeter control system是什麼意思，但是因為後面接的句子是intercoms and surveillance camera being set up in building A and B last week（上週在A棟和B棟設置了對講機和監控攝影機），應該可了解這是在說有關安全方面的設備升級內容，（B）只是簡單地換個說法，所以是正確答案。

字彙 □ security measures 安全措施 □ wellness 健康

93. What happened last week?
(A) An updated version of a product was released.
(B) Construction of some buildings began.
(C) Electronic devices were installed.
(D) A professional assessment was conducted.

上週發生了什麼事？
（A）發表了產品的更新版本。
（B）開始蓋一些建築物了。
（C）安裝了電子裝置。
（D）進行了專業的評估。

答案 (C)

解析 有關last week（上週）的內容，是出現在談話的前半段，也就是上一題（92題）正確答案的出處。從intercoms and surveillance camera being set up in building A and B last week可知上週裝了對講機和監控攝影機。（C）只是將這些裝置換個說法為electronic devices，所以是正確答案 。

94. What are employees asked to do?
(A) Attend a photo session
(B) Back up important files
(C) Lock the break room doors
(D) Keep the office tidy

員工被要求做什麼？
（A）參加攝影講習
（B）備份重要文件
（C）將休息室上鎖
（D）保持辦公室整潔

答案 (D)

解析 談話到最後階段時，說話者對聽者說keep their work stations neat and orderly（保持他們的工作區井然有序）。意即表達了希望大家將工作區保持井然有序的狀態，（D）將neat and orderly換個說法為tidy，所以是正確答案。

字彙 □ tidy 整潔的、井然的

Questions 95 through 97 refer to the following advertisement and list.
試題 95-97 請參考以下廣告及列表。

56

Do you find it difficult to go to a hair salon? Well, I've got a solution. Hi. I'm hair stylist José Martinez, and Q95 I make home visits for people like you. I bring all the necessary equipment, and of course I clean up afterward. I can do a range of things including haircuts, perms, colorings, and formal styling. Q96 And I speak Spanish, too! Q97 If you are interested and haven't tried my services, you can receive a special deal. I'm sure you'll be referring your friends to me in no time.

José Martinez	
Q97 First user	$15 off
Frequent user	$5 off
Family user	$7 off
Premium member	$20 off

去美髮院對您來說有困難嗎？我有一個解決方法。嗨，我是髮型師荷西・馬汀茲（José Martinez），可以為像您這樣的客人做到府服務。我會帶所有必要的設備，當然事後我會清理乾淨。我會做一系列包括剪髮、燙髮、染髮和正式場合造型的服務。而且我也會說西班牙語！如果您有興趣並且還沒有試過我的服務，您可以獲得特別優惠。我相信您很快就會把您的朋友介紹給我。

荷西・馬汀茲	
首次用戶	折扣15美元
經常用戶	折扣5美元
家庭用戶	折扣7美元
高級會員	折扣20美元

字彙 □ afterward 後來 □ a range of～ 一系列的～ □ refer *A* to *B* 將A介紹給B □ in no time 很快

95. Why is the speaker's service special?
(A) He does not use any equipment.
(B) He takes people to and from salons.
(C) He specializes in styles for the elderly.
(D) He goes to clients' houses.

為什麼說話者的服務是特別的？
（A）他不使用任何設備。
（B）他帶人往返美髮院。
（C）他專為老年人設計造型。
（D）他到客人家裡。

答案 **(D)**

解析 說話者在前半段提到I make home visits for people like you.（可以為像您這樣的客人做到府服務）。意即他可以針對到美髮院有困難的人做到府服務，所以（D）是正確答案。

字彙 □ to and from 往返 □ specialize in～ 專攻～

96. What do we learn about the speaker? 我們從文中得知有關說話者的什麼資訊？

(A) He is bilingual. （A）他是雙語人士。

(B) He sees more people in a day than usual. （B）他在一天之中看到的人比往常多。

(C) He has an assistant to help clean up. （C）他有一名助理幫忙清理。

(D) He works very quickly. （D）他工作迅速。

答案 **(A)**

解析 廣告文到一半時，說話者提到And I speak Spanish, too.（而且我也會說西班牙語）。表示除了當下說的英文之外，他也會說西班牙文，所以正確答案是（A）。

字彙 □ bilingual 雙語的（會說兩種語言的）

97. Look at the graphic. Which amount of discount is the speaker talking about? 請看圖表。說話者談到哪一項折扣金額？

(A) $5 off （A）折扣5美元

(B) $7 off （B）折扣7美元

(C) $15 off （C）折扣15美元

(D) $20 off （D）折扣20美元

答案 **(C)**

解析 一邊專心看圖表左欄，一邊聽語音內容。說話者在最後階段說If you are interested and haven't tried my services, you can receive a special deal.（如果您有興趣並且還沒有試過我的服務，您可以獲得特別優惠。）。可知這句話的「折扣對象」就是First user（首次用戶），所以正確答案是（C）。圖表問題要將「談話內容與圖表上所記載的事項」做結合才能作答。而正確的選項內容通常不會出現在談話中，因此，如果沒有聽全文內容並搭配圖表，這兩者的資訊缺一就無法作答了。

Questions 98 through 100 refer to the following talk and list.

試題 98-100 請參考以下談話及列表。

58

Good afternoon, everybody. Q98 I know several of you haven't been with us for long, so... well...I know you'll get used to things soon, but I want to stress the importance of placing orders from our warehouse timely. When our project managers give you any orders for materials, they generally expect to receive them within 24 hours. Unfortunately, last week we didn't handle one order on time. Q99 One of our project managers, Michael, needed to finish a job by Friday at noon, but the materials didn't come in until later that day. He said his customer was very unhappy about this delay. Q100 So please make it a rule to put in orders as soon as you get them rather than waiting for several to do at once.

午安，各位。我知道你們當中有幾位和我們沒有共事很久，所以……好吧……我知道你們很快就會習慣這些事情，但我想強調及時從倉庫下訂單的重要性。當我們的產品經理給你任何材料的訂單時，他們通常希望在24小時內收到材料。遺憾的是，上週我們沒有準時處理一筆訂單。我們的一位產品經理麥克（Michael），他需要在週五中午之前完成一項工作，但是這些材料一直到當天晚些時候才到。他說他的客戶對這此延誤非常不悅。因此請養成一收到訂單就立刻下單的習慣，而不是等累積數筆後才一起處理。

Delivery Schedule

Orders placed by noon
→ Next morning delivery (9 A.M.)
Q99 Orders placed after noon
→ Next afternoon delivery (1 P.M.)

交貨時間表

中午之前的訂單
→隔天早上交貨（9 A.M.）
中午過後的訂單
→隔天下午交貨（1 P.M.）

字彙 □ get used to～ 習慣於～ □ timely 及時地 □ make it a rule to *do* 養成～習慣
□ put in～ 提出～、放入～ □ at once 一起、同時

98. What do we learn about some of the listeners? 我們從文中得知有關一些聽者的什麼資訊？

(A) They often work with customers. （A）他們的工作經常與客戶接觸。

(B) They arrived late to the office. （B）他們晚到辦公室。

(C) They used to be contractors. （C）他們曾經是承包商。

(D) They are new to the company. （D）他們是公司的新手。

答案 (D)

解析 說話者一開始就對聽者說I know several of you haven't been with us for long（我知道你們當中有幾位和我們沒有共事很久）。因此正確答案是（D）。

字彙 □ used to *do* 曾經做～

99. Look at the graphic. When was Michael's order most likely processed? 請看圖表。麥克的訂單最有可能是什麼時候被處理的？

(A) Thursday before noon （A）週四上午

(B) Thursday after noon （B）週四中午過後

(C) Friday before noon （C）週五上午

(D) Friday after noon （D）週五中午過後

答案 (B)

解析 談話到一半時提到One of our project managers, Michael, needed to finish a job by Friday at noon, but the materials didn't come in until later that day.（我們的一位產品經理麥克，他需要在週五中午之前完成一項工作，但是這些材料一直到當天晚些時候才到。），意即麥克要用的材料在週五下午才送到，再參照圖表可知，「下午送達的訂單」是在「前一日中午過後下單」的，因此正確答案是（B）。

100. What does the speaker ask the listeners to do? 說話者要求聽者做什麼？

(A) Order extra items to have on hand （A）訂購額外的品項放在手邊

(B) Take care of orders right away （B）立即處理訂單

(C) Expedite all special orders （C）加速所有特殊訂單

(D) Learn project managers' order patterns （D）了解產品經理的訂單模式

答案 (B)

解析 說話者最後表示，So please make it a rule to put in orders as soon as you get them（因此請養成一收到訂單就立刻下單的習慣）。意即要求聽者「收到訂單後要馬上處理」，所以正確答案是（B）。

字彙 □ on hand 手邊 □ expedite 加快～

PART 5

101.

A restructuring of the major divisions will end up taking place after SO & T ------- Supersoft next month.

(A) foresees (B) acquires
(C) rests (D) merges

索恩提（SO & T）下個月收購超級軟體（Supersoft）後，最終將會發生主要部門的改組。

答案 (B)

解析 若單從前後語意來看，（B）acquire（收購～）和（D）merge（合併）這兩個選項都可能是正確答案。但空格後面因為有受詞Supersoft，必須要選及物動詞才對。所以正確答案是（B）。（D）merge with～是指「和～合併」。（A）foresee意為「預知」。（C）rest意為「讓～擱置、休息」。

字彙 □ restructuring 重建、改組 □ end up *doing* 最終～ □ take place 發生

102.

The annual shareholders' meeting will be held in the Hamptons in ------- with company tradition.

(A) connecting (B) keeping
(C) realizing (D) concluding

年度股東大會將依照公司的傳統在漢普敦斯（Hamptons）舉行。

答案 (B)

解析 選項字彙都是動詞的ing型態。注意空格前後是in ------- with，填入（B）就是「依照～」的意思。（A）connect意為「連接」。（C）realize意為「領悟、了解～」。（D）conclude意為「推斷出結論」。

103.

For being a senior partner at Berizon and Rukoil Law Firm, frequent travel to other countries is one of the -------.

(A) recoupment (B) requirements
(C) reflections (D) refurbishment

對於成為貝莉森和路克伊爾（Berizon and Rukoil）律師事務所的資深合夥人來說，經常前往其他國家出差是必要條件之一。

答案 (B)

解析 選項都是字首re的名詞。空格前面是one of the（～之一），所以作答選項可縮小為複數的名詞（B）和（C）。從前後語意可判斷「經常海外出差」是「條件」之一，所以正確答案是（B）requirements意為「必要條件、要求」。（A）recoupment意為「補償」。（C）reflection意為「反射」。（D）refurbishment意為「整修」。

104.

Mr. Moskovitz reviewed the latest proposal and ------- it to the manager for approval.

(A) continued (B) extinguished

(C) forwarded (D) converted

莫斯科維茲（Moskovitz）先生審核了最新的提案並將它轉交給經理批准。

答案 (C)

解析 選項字彙都是動詞的過去式。空格後面是A to B的句型，以這種形式當受詞，且能傳達語意的（C）forward為正確答案。forward *A* to *B*是指「將A轉交給B」。（D）convert雖然也可接*A* to *B*，但是convert *A* to *B*的意思是「將A轉換、改變為B」，不符合整個語意。（A）continue意為「繼續～」。（B）extinguish意為「使～破滅」。

105.

Von Vai Industry's new fall line of siding for houses is guaranteed to ------- the look of your house.

(A) quicken (B) depict

(C) exemplify (D) enhance

逢瓦工業（Von Vai Industry）新的房屋外牆板秋季系列，保證可以提升您房屋的外觀。

答案 (D)

解析 想一下new fall line（新的秋季系列）保證能為the look of your house（您房屋的外觀）達到什麼效果呢？以（D）enhance（提升）傳達的語意最正確。（A）quicken意為「加快～」。（B）depict意為「描寫～」。（C）exemplify意為「作為～的例子、舉例說明」。

字彙 □ siding 外牆板 □ guarantee 保證～

106.

Please write your name on the label in the space provided and ------- it to the top of the bottle.

(A) abide (B) affix

(C) detach (D) confine

請在提供的標籤空白處寫下你的名字，並將它貼在瓶子的頂端。

答案 (B)

解析 整句的內容是「請在標籤上寫名字，並將它 ------- 在瓶子的頂端」。從前後語意可知（B）是正確答案，affix *A* to *B*是指「將A貼在B」。其他選項分別是（A）abide意為「忍受～」，（C）detach是affix的相反詞，意為「拆下～」。（D）confine意為「限制～」，所以從語意來思考才能解出正確答案。

107.

Donations to the Takashi Tanaka & Family Home will be greatly appreciated, yet are only -------.

(A) optional (B) usable
(C) individual (D) candid

對田中隆暨家庭之家（Takashi Tanaka & Family Home）的捐款都將被受感謝，然而捐款只是隨意的。

答案 **(A)**

解析 空格是當補語的形容詞。因為有連接詞yet表達轉折語氣，所以整句內容是「雖然捐款受到感謝，然而-------」。將（A）optional（隨意的、可選擇的）填入空格內，語意最通順。（B）usable意為「可使用的」。（C）individual意為「個人的」。（D）candid意為「坦率的」。

字彙 □ donation 捐款 □ appreciate 感謝～

108.

The new attorneys must be under the supervision of a senior manager for several months before they are ------- any clients.

(A) garnered (B) assumed
(C) incurred (D) assigned

在被分配到任何客戶之前，新進的律師必須由資深經理監督幾個月。

答案 **(D)**

解析 選項都是動詞-ed的型態，因為空格前面有be動詞，所以可判斷是被動語態。空格後面的any clients（任何客戶）也是該動詞的受詞，因此要選帶有兩個受詞的授予動詞才是對的。正確答案是（D）assign，而assign *A B*是「將B分配給A」的意思。（A）garner意為「獲得～」。（B）assume意為「承擔、假定為～」。（C）incur意為「擔負、遭受、招致～」。

字彙 □ attorney 律師 □ supervision 監督、監管

109.

Due to the ------- of a self-development training program at Ballmer Company, staff absenteeism has been reduced to 10 percent.

(A) implementation (B) temptation
(C) independency (D) indemnity

由於包默爾公司（Ballmer Company）自我發展訓練計畫的實施，員工的缺勤已降至百分之十。

答案 **(A)**

解析 題目的意思是「由於計畫的 -------，使員工的缺勤降低」。假設是計畫的「實施」，則前後語意通順，所以正確答案是（A）implementation意為「實施」。請大家也要熟記該字的動詞implement，意為「實施（計畫或政策等）」。（B）temptation意為「誘惑」。（C）independency意為「獨立」。（D）indemnity意為「損害賠償、賠償金」。

字彙 □ self-development 自我發展 □ absenteeism 缺勤 □ reduce 減少～

110.

Follow the ------- of steps to unlock the emergency exit door, or you will not be able to open it again.

(A) orbit (B) sequence

(C) instruction (D) expertness

按照一連串步驟打開緊急出口的門鎖，否則你將無法再次打開它。

答案 (B)

解析 為了打開緊急出口的門鎖，必須要按照什麼呢？正確答案是（B），the sequence of steps是「一連串的步驟」的意思。而形容詞sequent（連續發生的）、相關字consequent（因某結果而引起的）以及consequently（結果、因此），也是常出現在多益正式測驗的字彙，請大家要一起記住。（A）orbit意為「運行軌道」。（C）instruction意為「指示」。（D）expertness意為「熟練、專業」。

字彙 □ unlock 打開～鎖 □ emergency exit 緊急出口

111.

Bale Energy is seeking an alternative lubricant that is ------- in quality to the brand that they have been using over the past decade.

(A) quantity (B) comparable

(C) pilot (D) substantial

貝爾能源（Bale Energy）正在尋找一種替代的潤滑油，其品質要可比得上過去十年他們使用的品牌。

答案 (B)

解析 關鍵在空格後面出現的to。如果選（B），句型結構就是*be* comparable to～（比得上～），且前後語意通順，因此是正確答案。雖然空格後面馬上接in quality（品質方面），或許很難意識到to，不過請記住這種含副詞片語的題型，還是偶爾會出現喔！（A）quantity意為「數量」。（C）pilot意為「引導員、試驗性的」。（D）substantial意為「可觀的」。

字彙 □ alternative 替代的 □ lubricant 潤滑油

112.

Tokyo has an ------- public transit system with many subway, train and bus lines.

(A) attachable (B) ensuing

(C) assertive (D) extensive

東京擁有廣大的公共交通系統，包括許多地鐵、火車和巴士線路。

答案 (D)

解析 選擇適當的形容詞來修飾public transit system（公共交通系統）。選項中符合語意的是（D）extensive意為「廣大的」。而（B）ensuing也是形容詞，意思是「接著發生的、隨後的」。記住不要與ensure（保證～）混淆。（A）attachable意為「可附上的」。（C）assertive意為「堅定自信的」。

113.

Fortunately, the readings for the chemical analysis were well ------- the acceptable range for safety.

(A) within (B) slight

(C) amid (D) mutually

幸運的是，化學分析的讀數完全在可接受的安全標準範圍內。

答案 (A)

解析 題目內容是「幸運的是，讀數是在安全標準範圍 -------」。將（A）within「在～之內」填入空格內的語意最通順，所以是正確答案。（C）amid「在～之中、在～之間」是介系詞，不能用well修飾，所以不正確。（B）slight意為「微小的」。（C）mutually意為「互相」。

字彙 □ reading（儀器等的）讀數、顯示值

114.

The manager spoke most ------- about focusing on customer satisfaction, although he failed to address several topics during the last meeting.

(A) independently (B) previously

(C) eloquently (D) evasively

上次開會時，經理對於專注客戶滿意度一事口才流利地發表了談話，不過有好幾個主題卻沒提到。

答案 (C)

解析 連接詞although是正確答案的關鍵。題目內容是「儘管經理未能提到幾個主題，但在客戶滿意度方面做了最 ------- 的談話」。如果選（C）eloquently（口才流利地、雄辯地）的話，前、後兩個子句的內容可形成對比，並適當地連結前後關係，因此是正確答案。（A）independently意為「獨立地」。（B）previously意為「事先」。（D）evasively意為「逃避地」。

115.

The area has the largest ------- of coffee plants in the country due to the favorable climate in the southern hills.

(A) concentration (B) conversion

(C) compost (D) correspondence

由於南部山區氣候宜人，該地區擁有國內最大的咖啡種植密集度。

答案 (A)

解析 試題內容是「由於氣候宜人，咖啡種植 ------- 最大」。可以用the largest（最大）來修飾，且語意通順的名詞是（A）concentration（密集）。the largest concentration of～是「最大密集程度的～」的意思。（C）compost（堆肥）或許是很陌生的單字，不過還是得要牢記。（B）conversion意為「轉換」。（D）correspondence意為「通訊」。

116.

------- of consumers who bought Berizon's new laptop were not entirely satisfied with the quality.

(A) Some (B) Any

(C) A large number (D) A few

許多購買倍利森（Berizon）新筆記型電腦的消費者對品質並不完全滿意。

答案 (C)

解析 some of～（一些～）、any of～（任何～）以及a few of～（幾個～）的後面如果要接consumers（消費者），都需要加限定詞the、its和their等。a large number of～（許多～）後面是不需要限定詞的。因此正確答案是（C）。

字彙 □ entirely 全然、完全地

117.

On November 20, the sales department is going to ------- a new policy that will take effect as soon as the current one expires.

(A) chaperon (B) introduce

(C) derive (D) command

11月20日，銷售部門將推行一項新政策，並將於目前政策到期後立即生效。

答案 (B)

解析 以new policy（新政策）作受詞，且語意通順的是（B）introduce意為「推行～」。（A）chaperon意為「陪伴～」。（C）derive意為「取得、源自～」。（D）command意為「命令～」。

字彙 □ take effect 生效

118.

Unless oak doors are treated with a chemical stabilizer, they have a tendency to ------- in a humid climate.

(A) append (B) intensify

(C) expand (D) inflate

除非橡木門有經過化學安定劑處理，否則它們在潮濕的氣候中容易膨脹。

答案 (C)

解析 從試題內容「橡木門在潮濕的氣候中容易 -------」可推測，空格應該要填入意為「（吸濕而）膨脹」的單字。雖然（C）和（D）似乎都是候選答案，不過因為（D）inflate是「（因空氣或氣體等的）膨脹」的意思，所以正確答案是（C）expand意為「擴張、膨脹」。（A）append意為「附加、添加～」。（B）intensify意為「增強、變劇烈」。

字彙 □ oak 橡木 □ chemical stabilizer 化學安定劑 □ tendency 傾向

119.

All the recipes in this book are ------- enough to be adjusted to individual preferences.

(A) miscellaneous (B) versatile

(C) prototypical (D) unabridged

這本書內的所有的食譜是多方面適用的，能夠依個人喜好調整。

答案 (B)

解析 從「能夠依個人喜好調整」的敘述來判斷，空格如果填入形容詞（B）versatile（多方面適用的）來表達該內容，則語意通順。（A）miscellaneous意為「五花八門的」。（C）prototypical意為「典型的」。（D）unabridged意為「未刪除的、完整的」。

120.

The amber grapes are used to make ice wine, the most ------- and expensive wine in the world.

(A) renowned (B) utter

(C) seasoned (D) devoted

琥珀色的熟葡萄被用來釀造冰酒，也就是世界上最有名且最昂貴的葡萄酒。

答案 (A)

解析 這題是要選一個形容詞和expensive（昂貴的）一起修飾wine（葡萄酒）。除了（A）renowned（有名的）之外，用其他選項來修飾wine都不適合，所以正確答案是（A）。（B）utter（完全的）雖然是形容詞，要記住它當動詞時也有「說出～」的意思。（C）seasoned意為「調過味的、經驗豐富的」。（D）devoted意為「專心致志的、獻身的」，是多益正式測驗常出現的單字。

字彙 □ amber grapes（熟成的）琥珀色葡萄

121.

Actually, ------- all the applications reviewed, Mr. Persson's is by far the most impressive one.

(A) out (B) toward

(C) of (D) onto

事實上，在所有複審過的申請書中，佩爾森（Persson）先生的是到目前為止最令人印象深刻的。

答案 (C)

解析 這是表達形容詞最高級的句子，不過句型一開始先用of～來表示「哪個範圍中」的最佳物件。因此正確答案是（C）。題目句的by far（目前為止）有助於強調最高級。

122.

In preparation for the arrival of the DM25, the older version, the DM20 will be ------- phased out over the next three months.

(A) sufficiently (B) excessively
(C) gradually (D) inadvertently

為了DM25的到來做好準備，未來三個月內將逐漸地讓舊版本DM20逐步淘汰。

答案 (C)

解析 這題主要的意思是「未來三個月內將 ------- 讓DM20逐步淘汰」。選項中的副詞，可修飾經過某段期間的情形者，以（C）gradually（逐漸地）最正確。（A）sufficiently意為「充分地」。（B）excessively意為「過度地、過份地」。（D）inadvertently意為「不經意地」。

字彙 □ in preparation for～ 為～做好準備 □ phase out～ 使～逐步淘汰

123.

Most of the workers may find the daily tasks ------- due to the intrinsic nature of the work.

(A) disposed (B) repetitive
(C) unfortunate (D) preceding

由於該工作的本質，大多數的工人可能會覺得日常任務是重複的。

答案 (B)

解析 即使不知道空格後面的intrinsic nature（本質）是什麼意思，如果能從「什麼單字適合用來形容the daily task（日常任務）」的角度去思考，應該就可以選出正確答案。每天都要進行的事，就是（B）repetitive意為「重複的」。（D）preceding意為「先前的」，常以the preceding year（去年）的型態出題，請大家要注意。（A）disposed意為「有～的傾向」。（C）unfortunate意為「不幸的、遺憾的」。

字彙 □ intrinsic 本身的、固有的

124.

Students who have yet to submit their plans for their next research project must submit those documents ------- after the completion of them this evening.

(A) exceptionally (B) particularly
(C) promptly (D) inwardly

尚未對下一個研究主題提出計畫的學生們，必須在今天晚上完成後立即提出那些文件。

答案 (C)

解析 這題要選出使語意通順的副詞，來修飾空格後after所接的內容。promptly after～意為「在～之後立即」，所以正確答案是（C）。immediately after～幾乎是同樣的意思，請一起背起來。（A）exceptionally意為「例外地」。（B）particularly意為「特別地」。（D）inwardly意為「在內部、暗自地」。

125.

The Italian food festival downtown has become so popular that almost all local residents avoid going into the city -------.

(A) never　(B) slightly
(C) scarcely　(D) altogether

市中心的義大利美食節已經變得如此受歡迎，以致幾乎所有當地的居民完全避免進入城市。

答案 (D)

解析 這題大意是「美食節變得很受歡迎，所以當地居民 ------- 避免去城市」。選項中可以修飾avoid（避免～），且符合前後意思的是（D）altogether意為「完全」。（B）slightly意為「稍微地」不適合修飾avoid。（A）never意為「從不～」。（C）scarcely意為「幾乎不～」。

字彙 □ resident 居民

126.

Before we make a decision on purchasing the property, we are currently having an ------- undertaken to determine the true value of it.

(A) advantage　(B) appraisal
(C) aggregate　(D) absorption

在決定購買房地產之前，為了查明其真正的價值，我們目前正在進行一項評估。

答案 (B)

解析 包括空格在內的這段話意思是「為了查明真正的價值，我們目前正在進行 -------」。假定是房地產的價值被「評估」的話，那麼整句語意通順，因此正確答案是（B）appraisal（評估）。（D）absorption意為「吸收」，請將它的動詞absorb（吸收～）也一起記起來吧！（A）advantage意為「優點」。（C）aggregate意為「聚集」。

字彙 □ property 房地產　□ determine 查明～

127.

The extra 30-minute break time added to the workday may explain the facility's high ------- over the last year.

(A) entry　(B) induction
(C) mandate　(D) output

在一天的工作作息中額外加入的30分鐘休息時間，是過去一年機構高產量的可能原因。

答案 (D)

解析 把工作中的休息時間再加長30分鐘，因此使工作的生產力提高。所以正確答案是（D）output意為「生產性」。（C）mandate意為「委任、命令」，請大家也把當動詞時的意思「委任～的統治、命令～」一併記住。（A）entry意為「入場、登錄」。（B）induction意為「誘導」。

128.

City officials ------- to widen the road in order to ease traffic congestion in this area.

(A) proposed (B) braced
(C) advocated (D) asserted

為了緩解這個地區的交通壅堵，市府官員們提議放寬道路。

答案 (A)

解析 空格後面是to widen，所以要選後面可接不定詞to且符合語意的動詞。選項中只有propose（提議～）符合該條件，所以正確答案是（A）。（B）brace意為「做好準備～」，後面雖然可接不定詞to，但是意思不通順。（C）advocate意為「主張～、倡導」。（D）assert意為「斷言～、強力主張」。

字彙 □ city officials 市府官員們 □ widen 放寬～

129.

Several industry analysts predict the market is heading into the worst recession ------- the last decade.

(A) for (B) in
(C) during (D) to

一些產業分析師預測市場正走向過去十年中最嚴重的衰退。

答案 (B)

解析 這題的主要內容是「分析師預測市場正走向最嚴重的衰退」。能夠放在the last decade前面且語意通順的是（B）in，意思是「過去十年中」。

字彙 □ industry analyst 產業分析師 □ predict 預測～ □ head into～ 走向～ □ recession 經濟衰退、不景氣

130.

Berkshire Group will try to offer consumers more accurate information on a wide range of goods so that they can make an ------- decision.

(A) informal (B) informed
(C) informative (D) informing

柏克希爾集團（Berkshire Group）將嘗試為消費者提供更多有關各種不同商品的準確資訊，以便他們能夠做出明智的決定。

答案 (B)

解析 題目內容是「為了能夠做出 ------- 決定，柏克希爾集團將嘗試提供有關商品的準確資訊」。informed decision意思是「（取得資訊後所做出）明智的決定」，最適合當作so that（以便～）之後的內容，所以正確答案是（B）。（A）informal意為「不拘形式的、非正式的」。（C）informative意為「有益的（資訊等）」。（D）inform意為「通知～」。

字彙 □ accurate 準確的 □ a wide range of～ 各種不同的～、範圍廣泛的～

PART 6

Questions 131-134 refer to the following advertisement.
試題 131-134 請參考以下的廣告。

-------(131.). We specialize in helping business professionals enhance core skills and keep up on evolving trends through our business seminars, which we have -------(132.) over the years to meet today's challenges. We offer more than 120 training seminars in dozens of subject areas of business management and staff development, -------(133.) interpersonal skills, time management, and supervisory skills. Our seminars are conducted in person at 40 executive conference centers around the country. Register today and join the tens of thousands of managers, leaders, and professionals -------(134.) careers and organizations have been strengthened by their participation in LPL's seminars.

自一九四九年以來，LPL公司已是經營管理和員工培訓方面的領導者。透過本公司多年來不斷精進以面對當今挑戰的商務研討會，我們專門協助商務專業人士提高核心能力並跟上不斷發展的趨勢。我們在企業管理和員工發展等幾十個主題領域提供了超過120個培訓研討會，例如人際關係的技巧、時間管理和監督能力。我們的研討會都是親授，於全國40個行政會議中心舉辦。今天就登錄並加入成千上萬的經理、領導者和專業人士群吧！他們的職業生涯和組織都已因為參與LPL研討會而得到加強。

131. (A) Read the following testimonials from LPL's satisfied professional participants.
(B) Thank you for participating in LPL's recent employee training seminar.
(C) LPL has been a leader in management and employee training since 1949.
(D) An online consulting company called LPL has just opened.

132. (A) refined
(B) authorized
(C) surpassed
(D) approved

133. (A) on the whole
(B) regardless of
(C) by the way
(D) for instance

134. (A) who
(B) whose
(C) whom
(D) who's

字彙 □ specialize in～ 專門～ □ enhance 提高～ □ evolve 發展
□ in dozens of subject areas 在幾十個主題領域 □ interpersonal 人際關係的 □ supervisory 監督的
□ executive conference center 行政會議中心 □ strengthen 加強～

131.

答案 (C)

解析 空格後面接We specialize in helping business professionals enhance core skills and keep up on evolving trends through our business seminars（透過本公司的商務研討會，我們專門協助商務專業人士提高核心能力並跟上不斷發展的趨勢），由此可知這是一篇主辦研討會的機構廣告文，所以正確答案是（C）。（A）引述testimonial（推薦文），但空格後面並非延續該內容，所以不正確。（B）是對參加研討會的人們表達感謝。（D）與文中前半段提到的over the years（這些年來）相牴觸，所以這個選項讓前後文完全不符。

字彙 □ testimonial 推薦文

132.

答案 (A)

解析 空格要填入的過去分詞，其動作對象是該形容詞子句的先行詞our business seminars（我們的商務研討會）。如果這段文字的意思是「多年來不斷精進的研討會」，則前後語意通順，所以正確答案是（A）refined（改善、精進）。（B）authorize意為「授權～」。（C）surpass意為「優於～」。（D）approve意為「核准～」。

133.

答案 (D)

解析 空格前面提到「超過120個培訓研討會」，後面更具體表達「那些研討會中有什麼樣的內容」。因此，正確答案是意為「例如」的（D）for instance，而for instance後面就是接「具體例子」。（A）on the whole意為「一般說來」。（B）regardless of意為「不管～」。（C）by the way意為「順便一提」。

134.

答案 (B)

解析 選項中有關係代名詞和who's（＝who is / has）。空格前面是先行詞professionals（專業人士），後面接careers（職業生涯）。如果這是代表「前面擁有後面」的關係，則語意通順，正確答案就是當所有格用的關係代名詞（B）whose。

Questions 135-138 refer to the following letter.
試題 135-138 請參考以下的信件。

Mr. Edward Walton
207 Elkhorn Drive
Wheaton, IL 60189

Dear Mr. Walton,

This is it, your last chance to sign up for another year of *Industry Robots* magazine at the low price of $34.99, the best rate offered to date. Plus, respond now and get your -------(135.) copy of *Robotic Trends Guidebook*! Don't risk missing a single issue. Go online to renew now, or send us the -------(136.) Renewal Request!

Last year, *Industry Robots* featured the Biennial International Robot Classic. We promise that this year will be -------(137.) fascinating in the robotics world! We won't offer this low rate again, so hurry! Renew today! And don't pass up this opportunity to get our special guidebook for robotic trends at no cost to you!

Sincerely,

Betty Lundin

P.S. -------(138.). Make sure the mailing address above is correct so that all 12 issues arrive on time.

愛德・沃爾頓先生
艾克宏大道207號
惠頓，伊利諾州60189

親愛的沃爾頓先生，

就是現在，您能以34.99美元的低價訂購《工業機器人》（*Industry Robots*）雜誌的最後機會，是至今提供最好的價格。另外，現在回覆就可獲得一本免費贈送的《機器人趨勢指南》（*Robotic Trends Guidebook*）！不要冒險錯失任何一期。立即上網續訂，或是將隨信附寄的續訂需求表寄給我們！去年，我們（工業機器人）做了國際機器人經典雙年展（the Biennial International Robot Classic）特刊。我們承諾今年的機器人世界也將同樣令人著迷！我們將不再提供這麼低的價格，所以快行動吧！今天就續訂！不要放棄這個機會，免費獲取我們為機器人趨勢所做的特別指南喔！

誠摯祝福
貝蒂・路丁

附註：請協助我們讓您的雜誌準確寄到您家大門。請確認上述郵寄地址是否無誤，以便所有12期刊物準時送達。

135. (A) digital
(B) award-winning
(C) complimentary
(D) instant

136. (A) dispatched
(B) enclosed
(C) outlined
(D) combined

137. (A) exactly
(B) properly
(C) uniformly
(D) equally

138. (A) Help us deliver your magazines to your door without fail.
(B) We have a 100% money-back guarantee if you're not satisfied.
(C) Have us give a free subscription of our magazine to a colleague.
(D) Your first issue of the year is scheduled to arrive in a few days.

字彙 □ risk 冒著～的危險 □ feature 做～特刊 □ fascinating 令人著迷的
□ pass up～ 放棄～ □ mailing address 配送地址

135.

答案 (C)

解析 這題是要選一個形容詞來修飾空格後面的copy of *Robotic Trends Guidebook*（一本《機器人趨勢指南》）。空格前面有Plus（另外），且該字前一句提到了有關「用便宜的價格訂購雜誌」的「優待」。因此Plus後面如果也是「相當於優待的內容」，則前後語意通順，所以正確答案是（C）complimentary（贈送的）。（A）digital意為「數位的」。（B）award-winning意為「獲獎的」。（D）instant意為「立即的」。

136.

答案 (B)

解析 空格前後都是「雜誌續訂」事宜。建議讀者不管上網續訂或是使用Renewal Request（續訂需求表）都可以。本篇是「信件」，如果填入（B）enclosed（附件的）就是指「隨信附寄的續訂需求表」，語意通順。（A）dispatched意為「被發送的」。（C）outlined意為「概述的～」。（D）combined意為「結合的」。

137.

答案 (D)

解析 空格前面提到*Industry Robots*《工業機器人》去年做了特刊，而今年也承諾要「提供令人著迷的期刊內容」。選項都是副詞，要修飾後面的fascinating，而（D）equally（一致的）正好表達了「今年也和去年一樣」的意思，所以是正確答案。（A）exactly意為「正確地」。（B）properly意為「適當地」。（C）uniformly意為「一致地」。

138.

答案 (A)

解析 空格後面說Make sure the mailing address above is correct so that all 12 issues arrive on time.（請確認上述郵寄地址是否無誤，以便所有12期刊物準時送達。）。這是在請對方確認「地址是否無誤」，而與這句相關的內容是選項（A）。（B）和（C）完全與配送無關。（D）是對已續約的對象表達配送的訊息，前後語意不符。

Questions 139-142 refer to the following notice.
試題 139-142 請參考以下的通知。

NOTICE

Employee parking permits will -------(139.) on August 3. All employees must reapply for a permit for the upcoming year, as a valid parking permit is required for every vehicle that parks on campus. This can be done online at www.fsu.edu/parking. Employees are entitled to a -------(140.) permit sticker only.* However, those with unpaid parking citations are not eligible to receive a new parking permit until outstanding citations -------(141.). Employees will be sent an e-mail to inform them of their outstanding fine amount.

A brochure containing information about university parking and traffic policies will be sent along with each renewed parking permit. The permit holder is responsible for understanding the policies for parking on campus. -------(142.). They are always happy to provide assistance.

*Since multiple permit stickers are not issued, employees who drive more than one vehicle to campus must contact the Parking Office to register the extra license plates.

通知

員工停車許可證將於8月3日到期。所有員工必須重新申請下一年度的許可證，因為每個停放在校園的車輛都需要有效的停車許可證。這可以在www.fsu.edu/parking線上完成。員工僅能有一張許可證貼紙。*但是，在未付的違規罰單已付完之前，那些未付違規停車罰單者是沒有資格獲得新停車許可的。這些員工們將會收到電子郵件，通知他們未付的罰款金額。

內含大學停車及交通政策資訊的小冊子將與每張更新的停車許可證一起寄送。許可證持有者有責任了解校園停車政策。如有任何問題請聯繫停車場辦公室。他們隨時很樂意提供協助。

*由於不核發多個許可證貼紙，駕駛多輛車進入校園的員工們必須聯繫停車場辦公室，以便登記額外牌照。

139. (A) expire
(B) renew
(C) arrive
(D) change

140. (A) discounted
(B) temporary
(C) single
(D) congenial

141. (A) paid
(B) be paid
(C) will be paid
(D) have been paid

142. (A) You must visit the Web site to print your own copy.
(B) Please contact the Parking Office with any questions.
(C) Thank you for responding to our notice so quickly.
(D) Employees may park in any available space on campus.

字彙 □ reapply for～ 重新申請～ □ *be* entitled to～ 有～的資格 □ parking citation 違規停車罰單
□ *be* eligible to *do* 有資格做～ □ outstanding citation 未付的違規罰單
□ outstanding fine amount 未付的罰款金額 □ along with～ 和～一起 □ multiple 多個
□ license plate 車輛牌照

139.

答案 (A)

解析 這題要從前後句的意思，來判斷對應主詞Employee parking permits（員工停車許可證）的動詞。因為空格後面提到All employees must reapply for a permit for the upcoming year（所有員工必須重新申請下一年度的許可證），由此可知員工已申請過一次許可證。如果把不得不重新申請的情況想成是「因許可證到期，所以有重新申請之必要」，則語意通順，因此正確答案是（A）。（B）renew意為「更新」。（C）arrive意為「到達」。（D）change意為「改變」。

140.

答案 (C)

解析 這是要從冠詞a和permit sticker（許可證貼紙）之間填入語意通順的單字。空格後面有only（僅、只有）加強語氣，所以意為「僅能有一張」的（C）single（單一的）是正確答案。請把〈a single＋名詞〉是「唯一的～」的意思記起來。通知文最後也明確提到「不核發多個許可證貼紙」，所以這也是解答這題時的依據。（A）discounted意為「已折扣的」。（B）temporary意為「臨時的」。（D）congenial意為「愉快的」。

141.

答案 (D)

解析 這題雖然是問「時態和語態」，但是從選項的各句就可以判斷答案。主詞是outstanding citation（未付的違規罰單），所以將空格的意思視為「已被付清」的被動語態最適當。而且空格前面提到those with unpaid parking citations are not eligible to receive a new parking permit（那些未付違規停車罰單者是沒有資格獲得新停車許可的），由此可知付清停車違規罰單者才有資格獲得新的許可證。也就是「完成支付（現在完成）」→「可以獲得許可證（現在式）」這樣的時間流程是正確的，所以正確答案是（D）。

142.

答案 (B)

解析 空格後面是They are always happy to provide assistance（他們隨時很樂意提供協助）。可知空格內有出現代名詞They（他們）所代表的人物，而且他們將「給予協助」。因此正確答案是（B）。They就是Parking Office（停車場辦公室）的工作人員，他們會回答有關停車規則的問題，所以前後連貫，語意通順。

Questions 143-146 refer to the following article.
試題 143-146 請參考以下的文章。

SEATTLE — -------(143.). Because of this, Amber Richards, vice president of client services at Barkley, Inc., will now have the opportunity to contribute articles to *Fremd Magazine* and share her decades of business insight with tens of millions of readers. The Council is an -------(144.) only community for successful professionals who have been recognized publicly by organizations or in publications. The Council searched dozens of qualified candidates and then hand-selected Richards before offering her a position. Richards looks forward to telling a wider -------(145.) about the special programs and technology developed by Barkley, Inc. Moreover, she feels she can gain a better understanding of -------(146.) other professionals are thinking through their comments on her articles on Fremd.com. *Fremd Magazine* can be read in print and on the Internet in over 10 languages. Find more information at www.fremdagencycouncil.com.

143. (A) The Fremd Agency Council is happy to announce the formation of a new group.
(B) The Fremd Agency Council is on the lookout for new members for their community.
(C) Amber Richards was selected as a member of the Fremd Agency Council.
(D) Amber Richards is a candidate vying for a position on the Fremd Agency Council.

144. (A) online
(B) English
(C) administrator
(D) invitation

145. (A) turnout
(B) market
(C) gathering
(D) audience

146. (A) whom
(B) what
(C) where
(D) when

西雅圖（SEATTLE）——安博．理查茲（Amber Richards）被選為佛雷德機構委員會（Fremd Agency Council）的成員。正因為如此，巴克利（Barkley）公司客服部副總，安博．理查茲現在將有此機會為《佛雷德雜誌》（Fremd Magazine）撰寫文章，並與數千萬讀者分享她數十年的商業見解。該委員會為一邀請制社團，會員為已被組織或出版物公開認可的成功專業人士。委員會先是尋找了數十名符合資格的候選人，才精心挑選出理查茲，並在那之後，向她提出加入會員的邀請。理查茲期待告訴更廣泛的讀者有關巴克利公司開發而成的特殊程式和技術。此外，透過Fremd.com網頁上對於她的文章的評論，她認為自己將可以更深入了解其他專業人士在想什麼事。《佛雷德雜誌》不但有印刷本，還可以在網路上用10種以上的語言閱讀。請至www.fremdagencycouncil.com網頁，查找更多訊息。

字彙 □ insight 洞察力、見解 □ tens of millions of～ 數千萬的～ □ hand-select 精心挑選～

143.

答案 (C)

解析 報導的中間部分提到The Council searched dozens of qualified candidates and then hand-selected Richards before offering her a position.（委員會先是尋找了數十名符合資格的候選人，才精心挑選出理查茲，並在那之後，向她提出加入會員的邀請。），因此可知理查茲被委員會選為成員。而空格後面也描述了理查茲成為委員會會員後將做什麼，所以符合前後句意思的是（C）。

字彙 □ formation 組成 □ *be* on the lookout for～ 費心尋找～ □ vie for～ 為～爭奪

144.

答案 (D)

解析 空格後面接的下一句是The Council searched dozens of qualified candidates and then hand-selected Richards before offering her a position.（委員會先是尋找了數十名符合資格的候選人，才精心挑選出理查茲，並在那之後，向她提出加入會員的邀請）。由此可知是委員會從眾多有資格的候選人中精心挑選後，給予理查茲會員身份。這個身份並不是誰都可以獲得，必須要受到委員會賞識才行。所以正確答案是（D）invitation（邀請）。

145.

答案 (D)

解析 空格前面的telling是tell somebody about～「告訴某人有關～」的意思。而選項中代表人的只有（D）audience（觀眾、閱聽人）。a wide audience意思是「廣泛的讀者、聽眾」。

146.

答案 (B)

解析 選項中有關係代名詞和關係副詞。空格的前面是介系詞of，所以後面要接名詞或名詞子句。如果把what引導的名詞子句填入空格的話，就完成what other professionals are thinking（其他專業人士在想什麼事）的名詞子句，前後語意通順。所以正確答案是（B）。

PART 7

Questions 147-148 refer to the following text-message chain.
試題 147-148 請參考以下一連串的文字通訊。

Manning, Alex (8:33 A.M.)
Q147 How's it going with sponsorship for the charity walk?

Frey, Theresa (8:35 A.M.)
I have to figure everything out myself. I wish Mr. Elliot had written up a manual before he left the company.

Manning, Alex (8:36 A.M.)
I understand. But at the same time, are you learning a lot in the process?

Frey, Theresa (8:38 A.M.)
Absolutely. And while I think our booklet with information about our organization, charity, and sponsors is great, I think we need to do more.

Manning, Alex (8:38 A.M.)
Like what?

Frey, Theresa (8:40 A.M.)
Q148 We could easily have an area at the charity walk where our sponsors could set up tables.

Manning, Alex (8:41 A.M.)
What are you saying?

Frey, Theresa (8:42 A.M.)
Q148 It would give them an in-person presence. They could hang their company banners, give out information, and maybe even have a quick activity to engage kids.

Manning, Alex (8:43 A.M.)
I like it. Q147 It could help us get more sponsors and therefore more money for the charity.

艾力克斯．曼寧 (8:33 A.M.)
慈善競走活動的贊助進行得怎麼樣了？

德瑞莎．佛雷 (8:35 A.M.)
我必須自己搞懂每件事。真希望當時艾略特（Elliot）先生在離職之前有寫好（交接）手冊。

艾力克斯．曼寧 (8:36 A.M.)
我了解。但是同時，你在過程中有學到很多嗎？

德瑞莎．佛雷 (8:38 A.M.)
肯定有的。雖然我認為小冊子上寫著有關我們的組織、慈善機構和贊助商的資訊很棒，但我認為我們需要做更多。

艾力克斯．曼寧 (8:38 A.M.)
例如什麼？

德瑞莎．佛雷 (8:40 A.M.)
我們其實很容易可以在慈善競走場地安排一個區域讓贊助商擺設桌子。

艾力克斯．曼寧 (8:41 A.M.)
你的意思是？

德瑞莎．佛雷 (8:42 A.M.)
這樣就可讓他們親自到場。他們可以懸掛公司的橫布條、分送資訊，或許甚至能辦個簡易活動來吸引小朋友參加。

艾力克斯．曼寧 (8:43 A.M.)
我喜歡這主意。它可以幫我們獲得更多贊助商，並因此為慈善機構提供更多資金。

字彙 ☐ sponsorship 贊助 ☐ figure out～ 理解～ ☐ in-person 親自 ☐ engage 吸引～

147. What is the discussion mainly about?
這篇討論主要是有關什麼內容？

(A) Hiring a new organization leader
(B) Raising funds for an event
(C) Advertising for a nonprofit organization
(D) Ms. Frey's recent training

（A）聘用新的組織領導者
（B）籌集活動的資金
（C）為非營利組織廣告
（D）佛雷女士最近的研修

答案 **(B)**

解析 對話一開始8:33 A.M.，曼寧先生就說How's it going with sponsorship for the charity walk?（慈善競走活動的贊助進行得怎麼樣了？）。由此可知這段內容是在聊有關贊助方面的對話，加上曼寧先生最後提到It could help us get more sponsors and therefore more money for the charity.（它可以幫我們獲得更多贊助商，並因此為慈善機構提供更多資金），所以他們之間聊的是有關取得贊助商的「集資」事宜。選項（B）簡潔地表達該狀況，因此是正確答案。

148. At 8:41 A.M., what does Mr. Manning most likely mean when he writes, "What are you saying"?
8:41 A.M.，曼寧先生寫下「What are you saying?」這句最有可能是什麼意思？

(A) He does not like the idea.
(B) He is feeling insulted.
(C) He wants Ms. Frey to give another example.
(D) He wants an explanation.

（A）他不喜歡這個主意。
（B）他覺得被侮辱。
（C）他希望佛雷女士再舉其他例子。
（D）他想聽解釋。

答案 **(D)**

解析 在這句話之前，佛雷女士說了We could easily have an area at the charity walk where our sponsors could set up tables.（我們其實很容易可以在慈善競走場地安排一個區域讓贊助商擺設桌子。）。而曼寧先生即是針對那句話回應「What are you saying?」（你的意思是？），所以佛雷女士馬上接著聊天話題，將上述內容具體詳細的重新說明。從這些可看出是曼寧先生不理解佛雷女士的意思，所以正確答案是（D）。

Questions 149-150 refer to the following article.
試題 149-150 請參考以下的文章。

Density-2000 Wins Again	丹西堤-2000（Density-2000）再次獲勝
Q149 Globe-biz.net has released its list of top-selling mobile phones for this month. According to the list, Q150 Density-2000 by Bensen is in first place for the third consecutive month. In second place is Hyuwa-90 by Hyuwa Electronics.	全球商業網（Globe-biz.net）已發布本月最暢銷的手機名單。根據這份名單，班森（Bensen）公司的丹西堤-2000連續第3個月位居首位。其次是鈺樺電子（Hyuwa Electronics）的鈺樺-90（Hyuwa-90）。
It has been quite a year for Bensen, with its Density-2000 selling 35 million units worldwide. Bensen also overtook Hyuwa, becoming the biggest mobile phone manufacturer in January this year.	隨著該公司的丹西堤-2000在全球銷售達3500萬支，今年對班森公司而言是大有斬獲的一年。班森也超越了鈺樺，在今年一月成為最大的手機製造商。
More details on Density-2000 are available on page 27 — Q149 find out if the features that attract thousands are suitable for you.	更多有關丹西堤-2000的詳細資料請見第27頁——來看看吸引成千上萬人的特色是否也適合您。

字彙 □ top-selling 最暢銷的 □ in first place 位居首位
□ for the third consecutive month 連續第三個月 □ overtake 超越～

149. Where would the article most likely appear?
(A) In a technology magazine
(B) In a historical novel
(C) In a scholarly journal
(D) In a business report

這篇文章最有可能出現在哪裡？
（A）科技雜誌
（B）歷史小說
（C）學術期刊
（D）營業報告

答案 **(A)**

解析 文章一開頭就寫Globe-biz.net has released its list of top-selling mobile phones for this month.（全球商業網已發布本月最暢銷的手機名單），由此可知本篇文章的主題是「手機的銷售」。最後一句find out if the features that attract thousands are suitable for you.（來看看吸引成千上萬人的特色是否也適合您。），意思是希望讀者參考選購該款手機，所以正確答案是（A）。

150. What is indicated in the article?
(A) Hyuwa-90 has sold more than Density-2000.
(B) Hyuwa is the largest mobile phone manufacturer.
(C) Density-2000 has been a best-selling product for 3 months.
(D) Bensen sold less than 35 million mobile phones last year.

有關文章中的內容，何者敘述正確？
（A）鈺樺-90的銷售量已超過丹西堤-2000。
（B）鈺樺-90是最大的手機製造商。
（C）丹西堤-2000已經連續3個月都是最暢銷的產品。
（D）班森公司一年賣不到3500萬支手機。

答案 **(C)**

解析 What is indicated～?這樣的題型，作答關鍵在於要精讀文章，直到可以分辨選項間的差異，不過這題的正確解答出處，其實就出現在文章一開始沒多久。Density-2000 by Bensen is in the first place for the third consecutive month.（班森公司的丹西堤-2000連續第三個月位居首位），由此可知丹西堤-2000是連續三個月賣最好的商品，所以正確答案是（C）。

Questions 151-152 refer to the following advertisement.
試題 151-152 請參考以下的廣告。

Get the Professional Look with MP Solutions!	透過MP有解公司（MP Solutions）獲得專業的外觀！
How can MP Solutions improve your business? The way in which you present your material says a lot about your company. Create sophisticated, professional-looking documents by using our thermal binding system. We offer only the highest performance machines in the market.	MP有解公司如何改善您的生意？ 您呈現自家東西的方式決定大眾對貴公司的觀感。來使用我們的熱黏合裝訂系統創作一份精緻、專業外觀的文件吧！我們只提供市場上找得到性能最高的機器。
We provide: Fast delivery The machines are normally delivered and are ready for use within 2-3 days from the time of your call.	我們提供以下服務： 快速配送 通常機器會在接到來電後2～3天之內送達，並可以直接使用。
Q152 User support Customers will be provided with an exclusive phone number where an expert will answer any questions you may have.	用戶支援 提供客戶專用的電話號碼，讓專家回答您可能遇到的任何問題。
Flexible lease terms Q151 Our machines are available for short or long-term lease. At this time, items are not available for retail purchases.	彈性的租賃條款 我們的機器可用於短期或長期租賃。現階段，本品項不開放零售購買。

字彙 □ sophisticated 精緻、複雜的 □ thermal binding system 熱黏合裝訂系統 □ exclusive 專用的

151. What type of service does MP Solutions offer?
(A) Document shipping service
(B) Equipment rental service
(C) Printer maintenance service
(D) Fashion consultation service

MP有解公司提供哪些類型的服務？
（A）文件配送服務
（B）設備租賃服務
（C）印表機維修服務
（D）時尚諮詢服務

答案 (B)

解析 廣告內列舉服務的最後一項提到Our machines are available for short or long-term lease.（我們的機器可用於短期或長期租賃。）。由此可知這是一家有提供短期及長期租賃機器的公司，所以正確答案是（B）。雖然從廣告中間位置的Fast delivery（快速配送）項下的The machines are normally delivered（通常機器～送達）可知它是一家提供機器的公司，但是決定性的正確依據是最後一項說明的lease（租賃）。

152. What is suggested in the advertisement?
(A) Orders are delivered to destinations overnight.
(B) A support service is available to customers.
(C) Payment can be made in installments.
(D) Support is offered to users 24 hours a day.

廣告中提到了什麼？
（A）訂貨於翌日送達目的地。
（B）客戶可以獲得支援服務。
（C）付款可以分期支付。
（D）每天24小時為客戶提供支援。

答案 (B)

解析 用戶支援這項底下寫著Customers will be provided with an exclusive phone number where an expert will answer any questions you may have.（供客戶專用的電話號碼，讓專家回答您可能遇到的任何問題。）。由此可知公司有用戶支援制度，所以正確答案是（B）。（A）並非overnight（翌日）而是2–3天之內。（D）廣告文中沒有提到24 hours a day（每天24小時），敘述完全不符。

字彙 ☐ in installments 分期付款

Questions 153-155 refer to the following Web page.
試題 153-155 請參考以下網頁。

Pinecone Entertainment
Home
About us
Rates
DJs

Q153 Our entertainment division offers tailor-made packages to suit functions of up to 300 people. Our four DJs devote an enormous amount of time to music research and Q154(D) meet with clients beforehand to discuss requests. Our goal is your satisfaction! Q154(A)(C) With our lighting and audio-visual effects, we can create just the mood you are looking for!

松果娛樂
首頁
關於我們
費用
唱片騎師

我們的娛樂部門提供客製化的整套節目，適合多達300人的活動。我們的四位唱片騎師投入大量時間於音樂研究，並事先與客戶見面討論需求。我們的目標就是讓您的滿意！藉由我們的燈光和視聽效果，可以精準創造您追求的氣氛！

Mr. Enzo Rankin of Dacota Financial Institute says, "Thank you for your performance at our gala dinner. Judging from the fact that you were able to extend your services for a few hours and from the compliments we received from guests, I must say hiring you was a great idea. Q155 Our guests came from all walks of life and all of them were happy."

達柯塔（Dacota）金融機構的恩佐·藍金（Enzo Rankin）先生說：「感謝你們在我們的慶祝晚宴上的表演。從您們能夠延長幾個小時的服務時間，以及我們從客人那兒得到的讚美來判斷，我必須說委託 貴公司真的是一個很棒的主意。我們的客人來自各行各業，他們都很開心。」

字彙
- ☐ tailor-made 客製化的
- ☐ function 集會、活動
- ☐ devote *A* to *B* 投注A於B
- ☐ an enormous amount of～ 大量的～
- ☐ beforehand 事先、提前地
- ☐ gala dinner 慶祝晚宴
- ☐ judging from～ 從～來判斷、可看出
- ☐ from all walks of life 來自各行各業的

153. What is indicated about Pinecone Entertainment's service?
(A) It is customized for each client.
(B) It guarantees 100 percent satisfaction.
(C) It is suitable for events of all sizes.
(D) It must be reserved one week in advance.

關於松果娛樂的服務，何者推論正確？
（A）依每個客戶需求來訂做。
（B）保證百分之百的滿意。
（C）適用於所有規模的活動。
（D）必須提前一週預約。

答案 **(A)**

解析 文章首句就說Our entertainment division offers tailor-made packages（我們的娛樂部門提供客製化的整套節目），由此可知這家公司提供客製化服務。（A）將它換個說法為customized（訂做），所以是正確答案。

154. What is NOT provided by Pinecone Entertainment?
(A) Lighting adjustment
(B) Market research
(C) Audio-visual effects
(D) Pre-event meeting

松果娛樂不提供什麼？
（A）照明調整
（B）市場調查
（C）視聽效果
（D）事前會議

答案 **(B)**

解析 選項（A）、（C）、（D）分別在本文前半段出現。如果這三點都和文中內容相符，就可判斷剩下的選項即是正確答案，並在答案卡標記作答。注意不要把music research（音樂研究）和（B）Market research混淆了。

155. What is mentioned in Mr. Rankin's comment?
(A) The event ended earlier than expected.
(B) The attendants were happy with the food quality.
(C) The guests came from a variety of backgrounds.
(D) The company had been recommended by a guest.

藍金先生的評論中提到什麼？
（A）活動比預期提早結束。
（B）出席者對食物的品質很滿意。
（C）客人來自各種不同的背景。
（D）該公司當初是被一位客人推薦的。

答案 **(C)**

解析 文章後半段藍金先生的評論中提到Our guests came from all walks of life（我們的客人來自各行各業）。from all walks of life的意思是「來自各行各業的」，因此正確答案是（C），但是如果不知道它的意思時，就採用刪去法也可行喔！從you were able to extend your services for a few hours（您們能夠延長幾個小時的服務時間）這句可知活動比預定時間晚結束，所以（A）是錯的。

Questions 156-159 refer to the following e-mail.
試題 156-159 請參考以下的電子郵件。

From: Margaret Klimov [Mklimov@lonetech.com]
To: Jim Barros [Jbarros@lonetech.com]
Subject: Ice Hockey Event
Date: Wednesday, March 7

Hi Jim,

I wonder if you got the message I left on your desk on Monday. Q156 Q159(A) Have you already reserved the bus to Yolanda Ice Hockey Stadium? If so, please notify me of the pick-up time and meeting point as I am making Q159(B) the final copy of the itinerary of the event to distribute to staff members at tomorrow's meeting.

Incidentally, Q157 there are a few dozen sheets of name tag stickers in the storage room if you need them for the event. I thought there were some paper cups and napkins left over from last year's picnic but didn't find any. The storage room is usually open on weekdays, but if it's locked, you can get the key from Elena in the accounting department.

Q158 Q159(D) I read in the newspaper that the weather will be nice on Friday. I hope you will all enjoy yourselves, and Q159(C) I look forward to hearing all about it when you return!

Margaret

發信者：瑪格麗特・克里莫夫
[Mklimov@lonetech.com]
收信者：吉姆・巴洛斯
[Jbarros@lonetech.com]
主旨：冰上曲棍球活動
日期：3月7日星期三

嗨，吉姆，

我想知道你是否收到我星期一留在你桌上的訊息。你預約好前往尤蘭達（Yolanda）冰上曲棍球體育場的巴士了嗎？如果已預約，請通知我接送的時間和集合點，因為我正在製作明天會議上要發給同仁們的活動行程最後版本。

順便提一下，如果活動上你需要姓名標籤貼紙，儲藏室有幾十張。還有我以為去年野餐有留下一些紙杯和餐巾紙，但我沒找到。儲藏室通常在平日開放，但是如果有上鎖，你可以從會計部的艾琳娜（Elena）那兒拿到鑰匙。

我在報上看到星期五的天氣不錯。希望你們大家都能盡情享受，期待你們回來時，我可以聽到所有關於活動的一切。

瑪格麗特

字彙 ☐ incidentally 順便提一下

156. What is the purpose of the e-mail?
寫這封電子郵件的目的是什麼？

(A) To inform a colleague of an office clean-up
(B) To reserve a bus for a sports team
(C) To obtain missing information
(D) To ask about existing stocks

（A）通知同事辦公室清掃事宜
（B）為一支體育隊伍預約巴士
（C）獲取不足的資訊
（D）詢問目前庫存

答案 (C)

解析 詢問書信的目的，是多益測驗常見的題型。第一段說Have you already reserved the bus to Yolanda Ice Hockey Stadium? If so, please notify me of the pick-up time and meeting point（你已預約了前往尤蘭達冰上曲棍球體育場的巴士嗎？如果已預約，請通知我接送的時間和集合點），由此可知電子郵件發信者想知道接送的時間和集合點。（C）只是將它抽象地換個說法表達，所以是正確答案。

157. What can be found in the storage room?
(A) Adhesive labels
(B) Disposable cups
(C) Picnic baskets
(D) Paper towels

儲藏室可以找到什麼？
（A）黏性標籤
（B）一次性使用的杯子
（C）野餐籃
（D）紙巾

答案 (A)

解析 這題要把storage room（儲藏室）當作關鍵字來閱讀文章內容。第二段提到there are a few dozen sheets of name tag stickers in the storage room（儲藏室有幾十張姓名標籤貼紙），所以在倉庫的是名牌標籤貼紙。（A）將它換個說法表達，所以是正確答案。而下一句I thought there were some paper cups and napkins... but didn't find any.（我以為……有一些紙杯和餐巾紙，但我沒找到），表示（B）的cup（杯子）還無法確定它的有無。（C）的籃子和（D）的紙巾在信中都沒被提到。因此（B）、（C）、（D）都是錯的。

字彙 □ adhesive label 黏性標籤 □ disposable 一次性使用的

158. When will the outing take place?
(A) Monday
(B) Wednesday
(C) Friday
(D) Sunday

出遊活動何時舉行？
（A）星期一
（B）星期三
（C）星期五
（D）星期日

答案 (C)

解析 電子郵件末段時，發信者寫著I read in the newspaper that the weather will be nice on Friday.（我在報上看到星期五的天氣不錯。）因為主題是尤蘭達（Yolanda）冰上曲棍球活動，可由此判斷活動是星期五舉行，所以正確答案是（C）。（A）的星期一是發信者將訊息留在桌上的那天。（B）的星期三是電子郵件的發送日。

159. What is probably NOT true about the event?
(A) Transportation will be arranged.
(B) Schedules will be handed out beforehand.
(C) All employees will participate.
(D) The weather is expected to be sunny.

有關這次活動，下列何者為非？
（A）會安排交通方式。
（B）會事先發行程表。
（C）所有員工都將參加。
（D）預期天氣晴朗。

答案 (C)

解析 （A）信中有提到要安排巴士。（B）待行程表完成後，預計隔天要發出去。（D）報紙上的預測寫著the weather will be nice on Friday（星期五的天氣將會不錯），所以剩下的（C）就是正確答案。電子郵件上雖沒寫到所有員工都要參加，但是從最後一句即可知，郵件的發信者不會參加。

Questions 160-162 refer to the following e-mail.
試題 160-162 請參考以下的電子郵件。

From: Jimmy Chang [Jchang@ssf.com]
To: Colin Peters [Cpeters@osc.org]
Subject: GMT Technologies
Date: April 29

Dear Mr. Peters,
Following the near miss incident at the Abo factory last week, I was assigned to conduct an assessment of worker safety in twelve GMT factories. Upon careful inspection, I found all safety equipment at the factories in good working condition. — [1] —. However, twenty-five accidents and ten near misses were reported within GMT facilities last year. This year, there have so far been a total of five accident reports. Q162 The analysis of incidents shows that 40 percent of the injuries were caused by falling. — [2] —. Q160 Regrettably, many of the reported incidents could have been avoided if workers followed basic safety rules, such as using ladders to reach higher shelves, wiping any spills on the floor and not leaving unnecessary tools lying around.
My conclusion is that the number of accidents can be significantly lowered by reinforcing workplace safety through Q161(D) rewarding workers who demonstrate safe behavior, Q161(B) encouraging workers to participate in developing safety programs, and Q161(A) placing signs and guidelines in appropriate locations. — [3] —. My full report is attached to this e-mail for the review of the Oakland Safety Commission. — [4] —.
Jimmy Chang
SSF, Inc.

發信者：吉米・張 [Jchang@ssf.com]
收信者：柯林・彼得斯 [Cpeters@osc.org]
主旨：GMT科技公司
日期：4月29日

親愛的彼得斯先生，
上週在阿保（Abo）工廠發生了有驚無險的事件之後，我被指派對十二家GMT工廠進行工安評估。經過仔細的檢查後，我發現工廠的所有安全設備都處於良好的運作狀態。然而，去年在GMT廠內獲報有二十五起事故及十件有驚無險的事件。今年，到目前為止共有五起事故報告。這份事故分析顯示，40%的傷害是由跌落引起的。這包括從台階、椅子、凳子上跌下來，以及在潮濕或不平表面的地板上滑倒。遺憾的是，如果工人遵守基本的安全規定，很多獲報的事件就可以被避免，例如使用梯子以搆到更高的貨架、擦拭地板上任何的溢出物，以及不任由非所需工具散落各處。
我的結論是，藉由加強工作場所的安全，可以大大地降低事故的次數，如透過獎勵行為安全的工人、鼓勵工人參與制定安全方案，並在適當的地點放置標誌和指南等方法。我的完整報告附加在這封電子郵件內，以供奧克蘭安全委員會（Oakland Safety Commission）審查。

吉米・張
SSF公司

字彙 □ near miss incident 有驚無險的事件、倖免事故的人為疏失 □ *be* assigned to *do* 被指派做～
□ regrettably 遺憾的是 □ significantly 在相當大的程度上、大大地 □ reinforce 加強、強化～

160. What is indicated as the main reason for the incidents?
(A) A malfunction in the machinery
(B) Failure to follow regulations
(C) Lack of human resources
(D) Too much overtime work

有關這些事件的主要原因，何者推論正確？
（A）機器故障
（B）未遵守規定
（C）缺乏人力資源
（D）過多的加班工作

答案 (B)

解析 郵件內文中間提到Regrettably, many of the reported incidents could have been avoided if workers followed basic safety rules（遺憾的是，如果工人遵守基本的安全規定，很多獲報的事件就可以被避免）。調查結果是，目前為止發生的很多事故，如果工人有遵守基本的安全規則就可以預防。（B）Failure to follow regulations簡單直接地總結該狀況，所以是正確答案。

161. What is NOT a suggestion made by Mr. Chang?
(A) Putting up signs on site
(B) Getting workers involved in some programs
(C) Making stricter rules to protect confidentiality
(D) Rewarding employees who act safely

哪一項不是張先生的建議？
（A）在現場放置標誌
（B）讓工人參與一些方案
（C）制定更嚴格的規定以保護機密性
（D）獎勵行為安全的員工

答案 (C)

解析 張先生的建議，在郵件最後一段有歸納總結。（C）Making stricter rules to protect confidentiality是跟保護機密有關，與以安全性為主題的郵件內容無關。

字彙 □ put up～ 放置～ □ confidentiality 機密性

162. In which of the positions marked [1], [2], [3] and [4] does the following sentence best belong?
"This included falling from steps, chairs, stools and slipping on wet or uneven surfaces on the floor."
(A) [1]
(B) [2]
(C) [3]
(D) [4]

下面這一句應該插入標記 [1]、[2]、[3]、[4] 的哪一個位置？
「這包括從台階、椅子、凳子上跌下來，以及在潮濕或不平表面的地板上滑倒。」
（A）[1]
（B）[2]
（C）[3]
（D）[4]

答案 (B)

解析 插入句是在舉例「各種不同的跌落狀況」。因為這句的主詞This是代指前述的某項主題，所以在插入句的位置前面應該要有以「跌落」為總結的語句。而符合該條件的位置就是 [2]。如果This指的就是 [2] 前面的falling（跌落），則語意通順，所以正確答案是（B）。

Questions 163-164 refer to the following book review.
試題 163-164 請參考以下的書評。

Book of the Month
Reviewed by Michael Gottenberg

本月一書
由麥克・格騰堡評論

Meals and Magic
By Lorenzo Carreras
Illustrated. 258 pages
Don Juan Publishing. £19.99

書名：《餐食與魔法》
作者：洛倫佐・卡雷拉斯
含插圖　全書共258頁
東傳出版售價19,99英鎊

Bookstores today are filled with stacks of books dedicated to helping you with creating great healthy dishes in no time. But have you ever wondered how those images of steaming home-cooked pasta or lamb curry that make your mouth water are taken?

現今書店裡擺滿的許多書籍，皆旨在助你快速地創作美味又健康的料理。但是你有沒有好奇過，熱騰騰的自製義大利麵或羊肉咖哩，那些讓你垂涎三尺的圖像是怎麼拍出來的呢？

Wonder no more — Lorenzo Carreras takes you behind the scenes in his new book *Meals and Magic*. Q163 A self-confessed food enthusiast, Carreras interviews chefs, photographers and editors to discover the secret behind creating magnificent food photographs.

不用再猜想了——洛倫佐・卡雷拉斯的新書《餐食與魔法》將帶你到幕後。自認是個食物熱愛者的卡雷拉斯採訪了各大主廚、攝影師及編輯們，發現到製作華麗食物照片背後的秘密。

The book is filled with tricks experienced photographers use to make the dishes look fresh, such as brushing oil over finished food to add shine, and hiding hot towels behind the plate to create steam. Even if you are not a professional cook, Q164 it will be simple to apply the tips in the book to take amazing snapshots of your own culinary handiwork.

這本書詳載許多技巧，為經驗豐富的攝影師所愛用，以使菜餚看起來新鮮，例如在已完成的食物上刷油以增加光澤，並在盤子後面藏著熱毛巾來製造蒸氣。即使你不是專業廚師，也能輕鬆應用本書中的訣竅，為自己的烹飪佳作拍攝出色快照。

字彙
☐ stacks of～ 大量的～　☐ dedicated to～ 致力於～　☐ in no time 快速的、立刻
☐ home-cooked 自家做的　☐ make *one*'s mouth water 讓人垂涎三尺　☐ wonder no more 不用再猜想了
☐ self-confessed 自認的　☐ enthusiast 對～熱愛的人　☐ magnificent 華麗的、宏大的
☐ brush 用刷子塗上～、輕輕掠過　☐ tip 訣竅、提示　☐ culinary 烹飪的　☐ handiwork 手工製品、自製品

163. What is indicated about Mr. Carreras?
(A) He is a skilled photographer.
(B) He works with Michael Gottenberg.
(C) He is passionate about food.
(D) He cooks delicious meals.

關於卡雷拉斯先生，何者推論正確？
（A）他是一位技巧熟練的攝影師。
（B）他和麥克·格騰堡一起工作。
（C）他對食物充滿熱情。
（D）他做美味的料理。

答案 **(C)**

解析 雖然這篇是針對卡雷拉斯先生的著作所做的書評，不過對於他是怎麼樣的人在第二段有做說明。由A self-confessed food enthusiast這句可知卡雷拉斯先生自認為是個食物熱愛者。（C）將它換個說法為passionate about food，所以是正確答案。

字彙 □ passionate 熱情的、熱烈的

164. What is suggested about the photographic techniques described in the book?
(A) They were developed over many years.
(B) They determine the sales of a product.
(C) They require professional equipment.
(D) They can easily be adopted by amateurs.

有關書中描述的攝影技巧，何者推論正確？
（A）它們是經多年開發而成的。
（B）它們決定了產品的銷售。
（C）它們需要專業設備。
（D）它們能輕易地被業餘愛好者應用。

答案 **(D)**

解析 書評最後提到it will be simple to apply the tips in the book to take amazing snapshots of your own culinary handiwork.（能輕鬆應用本書中的訣竅，為自己的烹飪佳作拍攝出色快照）。而應用書上所寫的訣竅，即使非專業人士也能輕易上手，（D）將它換個說法為can easily be adopted by amateurs，所以是正確答案。

字彙 □ determine 決定～　□ adopt 吸收、採納～

Questions 165-168 refer to the following online chat.
試題 165-168 請參考以下線上對話。

FRANCIS BOHR (3:42 P.M.) Have you noticed that some of Q165 our cooks' and waiters' uniforms seem to have food on them even when they start their shift?	法蘭西絲・波爾 （3:42 P.M.） 你是否注意到我們的一些廚師和服務人員的制服上，即使在他們才剛開始輪班時也似乎沾有食物？
ED KAEHLER (3:44 P.M.) Yeah. Sometimes I see them leaving their uniforms here when they go home, so I guess they're not laundering them regularly.	艾迪・凱勒 （3:44 P.M.） 是啊，有時候我看到他們要回家時，把他們的制服留在這裡，所以我猜他們並沒有經常洗。
FRANCIS BOHR (3:45 P.M.) Hmm, I'm thinking it might be worth it to invest in a uniform service.	法蘭西絲・波爾 （3:45 P.M.） 嗯，我在想可能值得花點錢雇用制服業者。
ED KAEHLER (3:45 P.M.) What would that entail?	艾迪・凱勒 （3:45 P.M.） 那將意味著什麼呢？
FRANCIS BOHR (3:46 P.M.) Q166 We would no longer buy uniforms for workers. The service would own them, so they'd pick them up, launder them, and deliver clean ones. I know it would be more expensive, but it would help with cleanliness and our image in general.	法蘭西絲・波爾 （3:46 P.M.） 我們不再為員工買制服。業者將擁有這些制服，所以他們會回收，洗完制服再送來乾淨的。我知道這樣會花更多的費用，不過它將有助於潔淨和我們整體的形象。
ED KAEHLER (3:48 P.M.) Oh, that's an idea. Q167 So workers would change their clothes before and after their shifts. They'd have to come to work a bit early then, but I'm sure they'd get used to that.	艾迪・凱勒 （3:48 P.M.） 喔，那是個主意。所以員工們會在輪班前、後換衣服。屆時他們必須要早一點上班，但是我相信他們會習慣於那樣的。
FRANCIS BOHR (3:49 P.M.) Right. But Q168 I think most workers would be happy with the change, especially the high schoolers who probably don't like doing laundry at all!	法蘭西絲・波爾 （3:49 P.M.） 對。但是我認為大多數員工會對這個改變感到高興，特別是那些可能一點也不喜歡洗衣服的高中生！

字彙 □ launder 洗滌～ □ *be* worth it to *do* 做～是值得的 □ invest in～ 投資～ □ entail 使需要、意味～ □ help with～ 有助於～ □ in general 整體、一般的 □ get used to～ 習慣於～ □ high schooler 高中生 □ not... at all 一點也不～

165. For what type of business does Ms. Bohr most likely work?

(A) Food service

(B) A laundry service

(C) A delivery company

(D) A retail clothing company

波爾女士最有可能從事哪一類型的行業？

（A）餐飲服務業

（B）洗衣服務業

（C）送貨公司

（D）零售服裝公司

答案 **(A)**

解析 波爾女士下午3點42分的發言提到our cooks' and waiters' uniforms（我們的廚師和服務人員的制服）。從這句可知，波爾女士的工作場所有廚師和給薪的員工。所以正確答案是（A）。

166. What is Ms. Bohr considering?

(A) Checking workers' uniforms daily

(B) Requiring workers to buy their own uniforms

(C) Cleaning uniforms at the workplace

(D) Renting uniforms for the staff

波爾女士正在考慮什麼？

（A）每天檢查員工的制服

（B）要求員工購買自己的制服

（C）在工作場所清洗制服

（D）為工作人員租用制服

答案 **(D)**

解析 波爾女士下午3點46分的發言提到We would no longer buy uniforms for workers. The service would own them, so they'd pick them up, launder them, and deliver clean ones.（我們不再為員工買制服。業者將擁有這些制服，所以他們會回收，洗完制服再送來乾淨的。）。這句是提議「向業者租制服」的內容，因此正確答案是（D）。

167. At 3:48 P.M., what does Mr. Kaehler mean when he writes, "Oh, that's an idea"?

(A) He feels the plan will help them keep workers longer.

(B) He is unsure about the cost.

(C) He is thinking favorably about the idea.

(D) He believes the change will not help.

3:48 P.M.，凱勒先生寫到「Oh, that's an idea」，這代表什麼意思？

（A）他覺得這個計畫會幫助他們讓員工待更久。

（B）他對成本有疑慮。

（C）他對這個想法表示贊同。

（D）他相信改變將無濟於事。

答案 **(C)**

解析 這是針對波爾女士下午3點46分的發言而回應「Oh, that's an idea」（喔，那是個主意）。後面接著就是凱勒先生回答同意波爾女士提議的內容，所以正確答案是（C）。

168. What is indicated about the company?

(A) It has expanded outside the city.

(B) It employs young workers.

(C) It is dealing with financial problems.

(D) It needs to reduce its employee numbers.

有關該公司的推論，何者正確？

（A）已擴展到城市外。

（B）雇用年輕員工。

（C）正在處理財務問題。

（D）需要減少員工人數。

答案 **(B)**

解析 波爾女士最後的發言說I think most workers would be happy with the change, especially the high schoolers who probably don't like doing laundry at all（我認為大多數員工會對這個改變感到高興，特別是那些可能一點也不喜歡洗衣服的高中生）。（B）將這句話的 high schoolers換成young workers來表達，所以是正確答案。

Questions 169-171 refer to the following article.
試題 169-171 請參考以下文章。

Drought Hurts Milk Production

乾旱損害牛奶的生產

The drought over much of the south-eastern region is putting pressure on dairy farmers. Over the last seven months, the region has experienced a 35 percent decrease in the production of crops such as corn and soybeans. This has resulted in the doubling of crop prices, which in turn has impacted the price of animal feed.

遍及東南地區的乾旱正帶給酪農壓力。過去七個月，該地區的玉米和大豆等農作物產量已減少了35%。結果造成農作物價格翻倍，並進一步影響了動物飼料的價格。

Compared to last year, Q169 the cost of animal feed has increased by 20 percent and many farmers are being forced to use cheaper, less nutritious cattle feed. Not only has this led to a drop in the total production of milk, but Q170 it is affecting the density and creaminess of the product.

與去年相比，動物飼料的成本增加了20%，而且許多農民被迫使用更便宜、營養更少的牛飼料。不僅導致牛奶總產量下降，而且影響了產品的濃度和乳脂感。

Those who refuse to compromise on quality are driven to take on more debt, or to simply leave the field. Q171 Analysts say many of the small dairy farmers will be forced out of business while larger farms and corporate milking operations may have to go through major restructuring.

那些拒絕在品質上妥協的人會被迫承擔更多債務，或者完全離開這個領域。分析師表示，許多小型酪農將被迫停業，而較大型的農場和企業化經營的牛乳業者可能不得不進行重大重整。

字彙 ☐ drought 乾旱 ☐ dairy farmer 酪農 ☐ soybean 大豆 ☐ *be* forced to *do* 被迫做～
☐ cattle feed 牛飼料 ☐ compromise 妥協 ☐ milking operation 牛乳業者

169. What is indicated about animal feed?
(A) It is mainly manufactured in the south-eastern region.
(B) It is in low supply across the world.
(C) It generally does not contain a lot of vitamins.
(D) It has gotten more expensive than before.

有關動物飼料的推論，何者正確？
（A）主要在東南地區生產。
（B）世界各地供給量低。
（C）一般不含大量維生素。
（D）它比以前更貴了。

答案 (D)

解析 文章第二段提到the cost of animal feed has increased by 20 percent and many farmers are being forced to use cheaper, less nutritious cattle feed.（動物飼料的成本增加了20%，而且許多農民被迫使用更便宜、營養更少的牛飼料）。說明了因動物飼料價格高，不得不用便宜又營養少的飼料代替的現狀。因此，（D）是正確答案。

170. The word “affecting” in paragraph 2, line 4, is closest in meaning to
(A) continuing
(B) surrendering
(C) influencing
(D) concerning

第二段第四行的單字「affecting」意思接近下列哪一個？
（A）繼續
（B）放棄
（C）影響
（D）關於

答案 (C)

解析 affecting在it is affecting the density and creaminess of the product（它影響了產品的濃度和乳脂感）這句的意思是「影響」。因此，正確答案是（C）influencing。這句的主詞it，指的是前面提到的to use cheaper, less nutritious cattle feed（更便宜、營養更少的牛飼料）。考同義字變換的題目，如果從「單字放在該句是什麼意思」來思考，就可以選出正確答案了。

171. What is suggested by analysts?
(A) Larger corporations should help small farmers.
(B) Both small and large farmers will have a hard time.
(C) Small farmers will need to make more products.
(D) Large farms will be hit the hardest by the drought.

分析師指出什麼？
（A）較大的企業應該幫助小農。
（B）小、大農都將渡過一個困難時期。
（C）小農需要生產更多產品。
（D）大農場將受旱災的打擊最大。

答案 (B)

解析 有關分析師的見解，文章的最後一段有提到。Analysts say many of the small dairy farmers will be forced out business while larger farms and corporate milking operations may have to go through major restructuring（許多小型酪農將被迫停業，而較大型的農場和企業化經營的牛乳業者可能不得不進行重大重整），見解中指出不僅是小農要停業，大農也可能必須改革。（B）將該狀況簡潔地表達，所以是正確答案。

Questions 172-175 refer to the following letter.
試題 172-175 請參考以下的信件。

March 28 Mr. Jonathan Lee 767 Kensington Drive Springfield, VT 05465	3月28日 強納森・李先生 肯辛頓大道767號 春田，佛蒙特州05465
Dear Mr. Lee,	親愛的李先生，
Q172 After house hunting for several months, I was delighted to discover your beautiful home located at 767 Kensington Drive. Since I enjoy hiking as a hobby, Q173(B) Q175 the wooded surroundings near the house is perfect for me. — [1] —. Moreover, Q173(A) I was impressed by the consideration given to the floor layout. Q173(C) The location of the two bedrooms on the upper floor gives a lot of privacy and shuts out noise from the living room on the first floor. — [2] —.	經過幾個月的找房後，我很高興能找到您位於肯辛頓大道767號的美麗家園。因為我樂於把健行當作一種嗜好，這棟房子附近樹木繁茂的環境對我來說是完美的。離春田市中心這麼近就能找到如此自然和安靜的地方是很罕見的，剛巧我的辦公室也就在附近。此外，我對樓層配置的貼心留下深刻的印象。上層兩間臥室的位置提供很多隱私，阻斷從一樓客廳傳來的噪音。
Q172 I have carefully considered my offering price and have decided to offer $139,000. — [3] —. Q174 My reason for not offering the asking price of $143,000 is because I noticed that the floorboards in several rooms need to be fixed, and the living room wall needs a new paint job. I think it is a fair offer compared to local housing prices. — [4] —. Q174 For example, a similar two-bedroom house just one block away on Dexter Avenue sold for $128,000.	我仔細考慮並決定出價139,000美元。我之所以沒有提出您要價的143,000美元是因為我注意到幾個房間的地板需要修補，且客廳牆壁需要重新油漆。我認為與當地房價相比，這是一個合理的出價。例如，只離一個街區遠的德克斯特大道（Dexter Avenue）有間類似的兩房住宅成交在128,000美元。
Thank you for considering my offer. I look forward to hearing from you.	謝謝您考慮我的出價。期待您的回音。
Sincerely, Russ Taylor Russ Taylor	誠摯祝福 羅斯・泰勒（簽名） 羅斯・泰勒

字彙 □ house hunting 找房子 □ wooded 樹木繁茂的 □ upper floor 上層
□ offering price 出價 □ asking price（賣方的）要價

172. Who most likely wrote the letter?
(A) A property owner
(B) A real estate agent
(C) A home buyer
(D) A next-door neighbor

誰最有可能寫這封信？
（A）房屋所有人
（B）房地產經紀人
（C）房屋買主
（D）隔壁鄰居

答案 **(C)**

解析 寫信者羅斯．泰勒一開始寫著After house hunting for several months（經過幾個月的找房後），但是光憑這句還不足以作為正確答案的關鍵依據。一直到第二段I have carefully considered my offering price and have decided to offer $139,000.（我仔細考慮並決定出價139,000美元。）這句為止才能解答這一題。這兩個訊息加起來，就可判斷是寫信者要買房。因此正確答案是（C）。

173. What is NOT indicated about the house?
(A) It has a well thought-out layout.
(B) It is surrounded by woods.
(C) It has more than one floor.
(D) It has been soundproofed.

有關這棟房子的描述，下列何者為非？
（A）它有個精心規劃的格局。
（B）周圍是樹林。
（C）它超過一層樓。
（D）它已有隔音裝置了。

答案 **(D)**

解析 關於房子的資訊，總結寫在第一段。信中完全沒有談到隔音裝置相關的內容，所以正確答案是（D）。（C）more than one 是要表達「有兩個以上」的意思。

字彙 □ well thought-out 經過深思熟慮的 □ soundproofed 有隔音裝置的

174. What is suggested about the asking price of the house?
(A) It has been reduced.
(B) It is comparatively high.
(C) It is similar to others on the market.
(D) It is not negotiable.

有關房子的要價，何者推論正確？
（A）它已經降價了。
（B）相較之下，它較為價高。
（C）它與市場上的其他產品相似。
（D）不可協商。

答案 **(B)**

解析 關於房子的要價資訊，寫在信件最後的部分。泰勒不但說「沒有出價143,000美元」，還表示「只離一個街區遠的德克斯特大道有間類似的兩房住宅成交在128,000美元」。這就是在說明賣方要價「高」的理由，而（B）將該狀況抽象表達為It is comparatively high.，所以是正確答案。

175. In which of the positions marked [1], [2], [3] and [4] does the following sentence best belong?
"It is rare to find such nature and calm so close from downtown Springfield, where incidentally my office is located."
(A) [1]
(B) [2]
(C) [3]
(D) [4]

下面這一句應該插入標記 [1]、[2]、[3]、[4] 的哪一個位置？
「離春田市中心這麼近就能找到如此自然和安靜的地方是很罕見的，剛巧我的辦公室也就在附近。」
（A）[1]
（B）[2]
（C）[3]
（D）[4]

答案 **(A)**

解析 如果可以找到插入句所說的such nature and calm（如此自然和安靜的地方）是指什麼，就會知道這句應該放在什麼位置。文中提到有關住宅地點的敘述是the wooded surroundings near the house，意為住宅就在森林旁邊很理想。由此可知插入句的such nature and calm就是指the wooded surroundings，所以正確答案是（A）。

字彙 □ *be* rare to *do* 是很罕見的

Questions 176-180 refer to the following e-mails.
試題 176-180 請參考以下兩封電子郵件。

To: Joanna Flore [jflore@lgar.com]
From: Erika Smith [SmithE@joosta.com]
Date: November 1, 10:25 A.M.
Subject: Introducing Joosta, Inc.

Dear Ms. Flore,

Hello! I am writing to introduce you to our company, Joosta, Inc. We are a German company which designs and produces top quality wooden toys. Our products have been widely enjoyed in Germany for over fifteen years. All our toys are made from safe, premium quality material and Q179(B) each one is crafted by hand by an expert toymaker in Germany. Within the country, our products are sold in such reputable department stores as Axi and Rian Guus.

Q176 Currently, we are working to develop our clientele in the North American region. Q177 This is why we have prepared a sample package which you, as a retailer in North America, Q178 can receive for free by filling out the attached form and sending it back to us. It is important that you fill out all the entries on the form to ensure a swift delivery.

Q179(A)(B) Included in the package are a few of our most popular toys and some items from our brand-new children's apparel line. After you experience our products first-hand, you can then decide whether to place further orders with us.

We look forward to working with you.

Sincerely,

Q180 Erika Smith, Manager
Joosta, Inc.

收信者：喬安娜・佛羅爾 [jflore@lgar.com]
發信者：艾立卡・史密斯 [SmithE@joosta.com]
日期：11月1日，10:25 A.M.
主旨：介紹喬斯達公司

親愛的佛羅爾女士，

您好！我寫這封信是要向您介紹我們公司，喬斯達公司。我們是一家設計和生產高品質木製玩具的德國公司。我們的產品在德國廣受喜愛已超過十五年。所有的玩具都是用安全、優質的材料製成的，每一件都是由一位德國專業玩具製造師手工製作。在國內，阿克西（Axi）和里安古斯（Rian Guus）等信譽良好的知名百貨商店都有銷售我們的產品。

目前，我們正努力拓展北美地區的顧客。這就是我們準備樣品包的原因，而您身為一名北美的零售商，只要填寫隨信附上的表格並將它傳回給我們，就可以免費獲得該樣品包。重要的是，您要填寫表格上所有的項目以確保樣品迅速送達。整套樣品包括一些我們最受歡迎的玩具和我們全新兒童服裝系列中的一些品項。在您親自體驗我們的產品後，再決定是否更近一步向我們下訂單。

我們期待與您合作。

誠摯祝福
艾立卡・史密斯，經理
喬斯達公司

To: Joanna Flore [jflore@lgar.com]
From: Adrian Appel [AppelA@joosta.com]
Date: November 7, 9:00 A.M.
Subject: Sample Pack

Dear Ms. Flore,

We are delighted to hear of your interest in our products. A sample package is on its way! Should

收信者：喬安娜・佛羅爾 [jflore@lgar.com]
發信者：安德里安・阿沛爾 [AppelA@joosta.com]
日期：11月7日，9:00 A.M.
主旨：樣品包

親愛的佛羅爾女士，

我們很高興您對我們的產品有興趣。樣品包正在

you decide to place an order, simply fill out and Q179(D) return the order sheet enclosed in the package.

In an effort to reduce our carbon footprint, Q179(C) we no longer provide printed literature with our sample packs. However, detailed product information and technical documentation can be downloaded from our Web site.

Q180 Regarding your question concerning high-volume order discount, the manager will get back to you with details in a separate e-mail which will be sent shortly.

Thank you.

Adrian Appel, Customer Representative

Joosta, Inc.

寄送途中！如果您決定下訂單，只需填妥並寄回附在樣品包內的訂單表即可。

為了減少碳排放量，樣品包內我們不再提供印刷品。但是，可以在我們的網站下載詳細的產品訊息和技術文件。

關於您提出大量訂單折扣的問題，經理將很快在另一封電子郵件中回覆您細節。

謝謝！

安德里安．阿沛爾，客服代表

喬斯達公司

字彙 □ premium 優質的、高價的 □ clientele 顧客 □ swift 迅速的 □ carbon footprint 碳排放量 □ printed literature 印刷品 □ technical documentation 技術文件 □ high-volume 大量的

176. What can be inferred about Joosta, Inc.?

(A) It is a family-owned company.

(B) It is expanding its business.

(C) Its products are manufactured abroad.

(D) Its main customer base is in North America.

關於喬斯達公司，何者推論正確？

（A）它是一家家族企業。

（B）它正在擴展事業。

（C）其產品在國外製造。

（D）主要客戶群在北美。

答案 (B)

解析 喬斯達公司是第一封電子郵件的發信者史密斯（Smith）任職的公司。第二段他提到Currently, we are working to develop our clientele in the North American region.（目前，我們正努力拓展北美地區的顧客。），可知這家公司現在要開拓北美地區的顧客。因此，正確答案是（B）。雖然正在開發北美的客戶群，但並不意味著已成了主要客源，所以（D）是錯誤的。

177. Who most likely is Ms. Flore?

(A) A representative of a manufacturing company

(B) A customer of a department store

(C) A store owner in North America

(D) A wood supplier based in Germany

誰最有可能是佛羅爾女士？

（A）製造公司的代表

（B）百貨公司的客戶

（C）北美的店家

（D）德國的木材供應商

答案 (C)

解析 第一封電子郵件第二段提到，This is why we have prepared a sample package which you, as a retailer in North America（這就是我們準備樣品包的原因，而您身為一名北美的零售商），可知佛羅爾女士是北美的零售商。因此，正確答案是（C）。

178. What is Ms. Flore encouraged to do?
(A) Let customers try out Joosta, Inc. products
(B) Return a document to receive complimentary samples
(C) Complete and send a form to enter a contest
(D) Read customer reviews on Joosta, Inc.'s Web site

佛羅爾女士被鼓勵做什麼事？
（A）讓客人試用喬斯達公司的產品。
（B）傳回文件以獲得免費樣品。
（C）填寫並傳送表格以參加比賽。
（D）閱讀喬斯達公司網站上的客戶評論。

答案 (B)

解析 177題正確答案出處的後半段提到，「只要填寫隨信附上的表格並將它傳回，就可以免費獲得該樣品」。而（B）將該情況總結為Return a document to receive complimentary samples，因此是正確答案。

179. What is NOT included in the package?
(A) Some garments
(B) Handmade toys
(C) A product catalogue
(D) An order form

樣品包內不含下列何者？
（A）一些服裝
（B）手工玩具
（C）商品目錄
（D）訂單表格

答案 (C)

解析 第一封電子郵件最後寫著Included in the package are a few of our most popular toys and some items from our brand-new children's apparel line.（整套樣品包括一些我們最受歡迎的玩具和我們全新兒童服裝系列中的一些品項。），可知（A）和（B）都包括在內。另外，第二封電子郵件的第一段最後提到return the order sheet enclosed in the package，可見（D）也包含在內。因此，正確答案是（C）。從「不提供印刷品」和「可以在我們的網站下載詳細的產品訊息」等內容，也可以判斷商品目錄並沒有放入其中。

字彙 □ garment 服裝

180. What is indicated about high-volume orders?
(A) A separate price list will be sent.
(B) The toy designs do not allow for mass production.
(C) Joanna Flore will need to meet with the manager.
(D) Erika Smith will provide more information.

關於大量訂購，何者敘述正確？
（A）將另外傳送價目表。
（B）玩具設計不允許大量生產。
（C）喬安娜．佛羅爾將需要與經理見面。
（D）艾立卡．史密斯將提供更多資訊。

答案 (D)

解析 這是要同時參考兩封信件的題型。第二封電子郵件最後一段提到Regarding your question concerning high-volume order discount, the manager will get back to you with details in a separate e-mail（關於您提出大量訂單折扣的問題，經理將很快在另一封電子郵件中回覆您細節），可知有關大量訂單的電子郵件將由喬斯達公司的經理來回覆。而且，從第一封電子郵件的最後署名可知，艾立卡．史密斯就是這家公司的經理，所以正確答案是（D）。

字彙 □ mass production 大量生產

Questions 181-185 refer to the following article and letter.
試題 181-185 請參考以下報導與信件。

NEWPORT — Potential visitors to the Newport Flower Show are not the only ones hoping for better summer weather. As the unusually rainy summer forces many flower shows to be canceled, organizers hope the same won't happen to Q183 their show which brings in approximately 40,000 visitors to the town each year. The show, which is hosted by the Newport Horticultural Society and costs £300,000 to stage, is a big boost to Newport's economy.
Q181 "I don't think the event will be canceled totally, but I'm afraid it will be severely curtailed like the flower shows at Stony Shade or Templeton," said Rolf Kelly, a Newport business owner.
This year at the Newport Flower Show, Q182 on top of the usual display of various flowers and over 100 fantastic English-style gardens, a demonstration by the rescue dog team will take place. Also, a glass pavilion has once again been set up to house the many species of roses.
Bob Martin, President of the Newport Horticultural Society says, "We have prepared a stunning range of events with the help of the local community. For example, this is our first attempt to incorporate animals into our show, which we hope will be appreciated by people of all ages but especially by our younger guests."

紐波特（NEWPORT）——期待夏季天氣更好的並非只有紐波特花卉展的潛在遊客們。由於異常多雨的夏季迫使很多花卉展取消，主辦單位希望同樣的事不會發生在這場每年為該市鎮帶來約40,000名遊客的展覽。該展是由紐波特園藝協會主辦，共耗資300,000英鎊籌劃，對紐波特的經濟有很大的推動力。「我不認為這個活動會被取消，但我擔心它會像石之蔭（Stony Shade）或坦伯頓（Templeton）的花卉展一樣受到嚴重縮短，」紐波特的一名老闆羅爾夫・凱利（Rolf Kelly）這麼說。

今年在紐波特花卉展上，除了既有的各種花卉展示和超過100個夢幻般的英式花園，將加上救援犬隊的示範表演。此外，用來容納多樣品種玫瑰花的玻璃展示館也會再次設置。

紐波特園藝協會主席鮑伯・馬丁（Bob Martin）說，「我們在當地社區的協助下準備了一系列極精采的活動。例如，這是我們首次嘗試將動物納入我們的展覽，我們希望這些活動能受到所有年齡層的人青睞，尤其是我們的年輕客群。」

August 31
Mr. Bob Martin
Newport Horticultural Society
287 Bane Street
Newport, South Wales
NP18 6G5
Dear Mr. Martin,
I would like to congratulate you on the success of last week's flower show. I'm happy to hear that Q183 you had a turnout of around 40,000 visitors despite adverse weather conditions. I visited the

8月31日
鮑伯・馬丁先生
紐波特園藝協會
班恩街287號
紐波特，南威爾斯
紐波特（NP）18 6G5

親愛的馬丁先生，
我謹恭喜您上週花卉展的成功。儘管惡劣的天氣狀況，很高興聽到大約有40,000名遊客出席來看展。我自己在展覽開放期間參觀了

show twice during its opening days myself. Q182 I loved the glass pavilion section last year and the roses were magnificent this year as well.

Q184 Q185 I deeply appreciate the kind suggestion by the Newport Horticultural Society of donating flowers and plants for the Newport Hospital playground. Unfortunately, however, at this time we do not have enough funds or manpower to plant and maintain them. Nevertheless, we thank you for thinking of us.

Sincerely,

Jing Wong

Jing Wong, Director

兩次。我喜歡去年的玻璃展示館區，而今年的玫瑰花也非常壯觀。

我深切地感謝紐波特園藝協會提議為紐波特醫院的兒童遊戲區捐贈鮮花和植物。然而遺憾的是，目前我們沒有足夠的資金或人力來種植和維護它們。不過，我們感謝您想到我們。

誠摯祝福

靜・翁（簽名）

靜・翁，董事

字彙 □ boost to～ 對～的推動力 □ curtail 縮短～ □ on top of～ 除了、加在～上
□ stunning 極漂亮的、令人驚嘆的 □ incorporate *A* into *B* 將A納入B □ turnout 出席人數
□ adverse weather conditions 惡劣的天氣狀況

181. Why is Mr. Kelly concerned?

(A) A major town event has been canceled.

(B) The water shortage has damaged plants.

(C) Business has been slow in Newport.

(D) Some other flower shows were cut short.

為什麼凱利先生在擔心？

（A）一個大型城市活動已被取消。

（B）缺水造成植物受損。

（C）紐波特的商業一直很不景氣。

（D）一些其他的花卉展被縮短展期。

答案 **(D)**

解析 文章的第二段提到"I don't think the event will be canceled totally, but I'm afraid it will be severely curtailed like the flower shows at Stony Shade or Templeton," said Rolf Kelly（「我不認為這個活動會被取消，但我擔心它會像石之蔭或坦伯頓的花卉展一樣受到嚴重縮短，」羅爾夫・凱利這麼說）。凱利先生擔心的就是，活動會像其他的花卉展一樣被縮短展期。而（D）將be severely curtailed換個說法為were cut short，所以是正確答案。

字彙 □ *be* cut short 被縮短

182. What feature is new to this year's show?

(A) Glass pavilion

(B) English gardens

(C) Rescue dog demonstration

(D) Children's playground

今年的展覽有什麼新的特色？

（A）玻璃展示館

（B）英式花園

（C）救援犬的示範

（D）兒童遊樂場

答案 **(C)**

解析 有關今年展覽的其他資訊，在文章第三段有提到。on top of the usual display of various flowers and over 100 fantastic English-style gardens, a demonstration by the rescue dog team will take place.（除了既有的各種花卉展示和超過一百個夢幻般的英式花園，將加上救援犬隊的示範表演。），由此可知會有救援犬隊的示範表演。所以，正確答案是（C）。（A）的glass pavilion在文章中有說是has once again been set up（再次設置），而且信

件中也提到了I love the glass pavilion section last year（我喜歡去年的玻璃展示館區），表示該館去年就有，所以這個選項不正確。

183. What can be inferred about the turnout?
(A) It was poorer than expected.
(B) It was more than usual.
(C) It was less than last year.
(D) It was about the same as usual.

關於出席人數，何者推測正確？
（A）比預期差。
（B）比平常多。
（C）比去年少。
（D）大約和往年一樣。

答案 (D)

解析 文章的第一段提到their show which brings in approximately 40,000 visitors to the town each year.（這場每年為該市鎮帶來約40,000名遊客的展覽），可知展覽每年會吸引約40,000名的人群。另外，信中第一段也提到you had a turnout of around 40,000 visitors，可知今年也和往年一樣約有40,000人的參展人數。所以，（D）是正確答案。

184. What is the purpose of the letter?
(A) To congratulate an award winner
(B) To report on the outcome of an event
(C) To give thanks for a monetary donation
(D) To decline a proposed offer

寫這封信的目的是什麼？
（A）祝賀獲獎者
（B）報告活動的結果
（C）感謝捐款
（D）婉拒提出的奉獻

答案 (D)

解析 寫這封信的原因可在信件的第二段找到。寫著「我深切地感謝紐波特園藝協會提議為紐波特醫院的兒童遊戲區捐贈鮮花和植物。然而遺憾的是，目前我們沒有足夠的資金或人力來種植和維護它們」等這樣的內容來婉拒協會的奉獻。（D）簡潔地換個說法為To decline a proposed offer，所以是正確答案。

185. What type of organization does Mr. Wong most likely work for?
(A) A regional committee
(B) A local school
(C) A health service
(D) A charity organization

翁先生最有可能在什麼類型的機構工作？
（A）地區委員會
（B）當地學校
（C）醫療服務
（D）慈善組織

答案 (C)

解析 寫信者就是翁先生。這題的正確解答出處和184題一樣。翁先生在第二段婉謝了對紐波特醫院的奉獻提議，且最後一句we thank you for thinking of us.（我們感謝您想到我們。）用了we當主詞來婉謝。從以上可推測，寫這樣內容的人應該是紐波特醫院的相關人員，所以正確答案是（C）。

Questions 186-190 refer to the following itinerary, information, and comment.
試題 186-190 請參考以下的行程表、資訊與評論。

ITINERARY

Day 1: Jandara - Arrival
Arrival and welcome meeting at 7 P.M. Feel free to explore the city or join the optional tour of the Galli Temple ($15).

Day 2: Jandara
Enjoy an orientation walk of Jandara. Visit your leader's favorite spots around the city, including the spice market, Leroni Palace, Souvenir Alley, and a rooftop lunch which offers a great view of the city. Then take an afternoon cruise down the Anderly River and have an ethnic dinner with the group.

Q189 Day 3: Nalan
Transfer to Nalan in the morning. Spend a slow day with a host family and experience the way of life in this quaint village. Enjoy home-cooked meals and stay the night as a guest in your family's dwelling.

Day 4: Nalan / Rudapi / Achad
Bid farewell to your host family after breakfast and head to the city of Rudapi. Rudapi was an important stop on the Turley Trail thousands of years ago and is home to some of the most unique architecture in the country. During your free time today, join an optional tour around this streetless city ($10) or wander around by yourself. Sleep in nearby Achad.

Day 5: Achad / Marnitka / Nidapolis
Take a morning stroll through this charming seaside town and enjoy the cobbled streets and outdoor cafés. Meet at 10 A.M. for a tour of the Achad Museum. Then, head to Marnitka for an up-close view of the famous white cliffs. Stay the night in the ancient village of Nidapolis.

行程表

第1天：珍達拉（Jandara）－抵達
抵達後，7 P.M.歡迎會。輕鬆探索城市或參加迦利寺（Galli Temple）（15美元）自費行程。

第2天：珍達拉
享受一趟介紹珍達拉周圍環境的徒步遊覽。拜訪您的領隊在這個城市中最喜歡的地點，包括香料市場、雷隆尼皇宮（Leroni Palace）、紀念品小徑和在提供絕佳市景的屋頂上午餐。然後下午搭船遊安德里河（Anderly River）順流而下，與團體共進風味晚餐。

第3天：納蘭（Nalan）
早上往納蘭移動。與寄宿家庭度過慢活的一天，並體驗在古色古香的村莊的生活方式。在寄宿家庭住處享受家常飯菜和以訪客身分住宿一晚。

第4天：納蘭／路達比（Rudapi）／阿嘉德（Achad）
早餐後向寄宿家庭道別並前往路達比市。在數千年前，路達比是特立小道上（Turley Trail）的一個重要停留站，也是該國一些最獨特建築的所在地。在您今天的自由活動時間，可自費參加遊覽行程逛逛這個沒有街道的城市（10美元）或自己四處閒逛。今晚入宿附近的阿嘉德。

第5天：阿嘉德／馬尼特卡（Marnitka）／尼達波里斯（Nidapolis）
您可以在這個迷人的海濱小鎮清晨漫步，享受鵝卵石街道和戶外咖啡館。10 A.M.集合參觀阿嘉德博物館。然後前往馬尼特卡，近距離觀看知名的白色懸崖。今晚入宿尼達波里斯的古村。

Day 6: Nidapolis / Bendalay
Start the morning with a local cooking class and visit Nidapolis' ancient ruins before transferring to Bendalay. View the city's modern architecture during a walk along the waterfront, and stop at a café for a chat with one of the city's many university students. Q186 Stay overnight in a converted palace built in 1838.

第6天：尼達波里斯／班達拉利（Bendalary）
參加當地的料理教室做為晨間的序幕，並在前往班達拉利之前參觀尼達波里斯的古遺跡。沿著海邊散步並觀看城市的現代建築，然後找間咖啡館休息一下，從該城市許多的大學生中找個人聊天。晚間入宿建於1838年的宮殿改建成的旅館。

Day 7: Bendalay / Jandara
Take an optional morning tour of the famous Bendalay battlefield ($10) before heading back to Jandara for some free time. Consider visiting the Jandara Handicraft Co-op for souvenirs. A group goodbye dinner will be held at the hotel.

第7天：班達拉利／珍達拉
上午自由參加導覽，參觀著名的班達拉利戰場（10美元），之後返回珍達拉自由活動。可考慮參觀珍達拉手工藝合作社買紀念品。晚間於飯店舉行團體再會晚餐。

Day 8: Jandara - Departure
Depart any time today.

第8天：珍達拉 – 離開
今日隨時離開。

字彙 □ explore 探索～ □ rooftop lunch 屋頂上的午餐 □ transfer to～ 往～移動 □ quaint 古雅的、奇特有趣的 □ dwelling 住處 □ bid farewell to～ 向～道別 □ streetless 沒有街道的 □ wander around 四處閒逛 □ take a stroll 漫步 □ cobbled 鵝卵石的 □ up-close 近距離的 □ cliff 懸崖 □ ruin 遺跡 □ converted 改建的 □ battlefield 戰場 □ handicraft 手工藝 □ Co-op 合作事業

Style of travel: Classic
Q187(C) See the highlights of the region and experience the culture, all at a great price.

旅遊風格：經典的
參觀該地區的亮點及體驗文化，一切價格實惠。

Physical rating: 2
Q187(A) Q188 Generally, the walking on this tour is light and not too challenging for most fitness levels. However, the optional tour on Day 1 includes many steps.

體力等級：2
整體來說，這次的旅遊行走路線輕鬆，對大部分人的體能程度來說不算太難。但是第一天的自費行程包括許多步行。

Age requirement: None
All travelers under 18 years of age must be accompanied by an adult.

年齡要求：無
所有18歲以下的旅客必須由成人陪同。

Service level: Standard
Accommodations are tourist-class and comfortable. Q187(D) Travelers will experience a mix of public and private transport.

服務等級：標準
住宿為旅遊經濟型且舒適環境。旅客們將體驗到大眾和私人兩種交通工具。

Trip type: Small group
This tour provides a small group experience with a maximum of 16 travelers but an average of 12.

旅行類型：小團體
此行程為小團體活動，最多16位旅客，但平均12位。

字彙 □ highlight 亮點 □ physical rating 體力等級 □ generally 一般地 □ a mix of～ ～的混合
□ with a maximum of～ 最多～

EXPLORE TOURS	探索旅遊
Comment	評論
Name: Raj Singh	姓名：拉吉．辛格
I love getting a feel for what a country is really like, in both the big city and the countryside. This tour did not disappoint. Q189 I think the highlight of my trip was the time I spent in Nalan. I also enjoyed the other travelers, and I often look affectionately at the wonderful picture taken with everyone. Q190 The only thing I wish we had more time for was getting gifts to bring home.	不論是在大城市或是鄉間，我愛感受一個國家真正的樣子。這次旅行沒有讓我失望。我認為我的旅行亮點是我在納蘭度過的時光。我也很喜歡其他的旅客，我經常鍾愛地看著與大家合影的精彩照片。我唯一希望的是，我們有更多的時間來買帶回家的禮物。

字彙 □ affectionately 鍾愛地、深情地

186. What kind of accommodation will travelers sleep in on Day 6?
(A) A historical building
(B) A hotel on the waterfront
(C) A university dormitory
(D) A dwelling in ancient ruins

旅客們第六天會入宿什麼樣的住處？
（A）歷史建築
（B）海邊的酒店
（C）大學宿舍
（D）古老遺跡中的住家

答案 **(A)**

解析 第一篇行程表的第六天最後寫著Stay overnight in a converted palace built in 1838.（晚間入宿建於1838年的宮殿改建成的旅館）。（A）將其簡潔地換個說法，因此是正確答案。

187. What is NOT indicated about the tour?
(A) People in any physical shape can join.
(B) The entire itinerary is included in the price.
(C) Travelers can see the country's main sights.
(D) Local transportation will be utilized.

有關該旅遊的敘述，何者為非？
（A）任何體能程度的人都可以參加。
（B）價格包含全部行程。
（C）旅客們可以看到該國的主要景點。
（D）將利用當地的交通。

答案 **(B)**

解析 第二篇文章前半段提到Generally, the walking on his tour is light and not too challenging for most fitness levels.（整體來說，這次的旅遊行走路線輕鬆，對大部分人的體能程度來說不算太難。），這句和（A）的內容一致。另外，前面一段提到的See the highlights of the region and experience the culture（參觀該地區的亮點及體驗文化），和（C）的內容一致。而同樣在這篇文章後段提到Travelers will experience a mix of public and private transport.（旅客們將體驗到大眾和私人兩種交通工具），這句則和（D）的內容一致，所以剩下與內容不符的（B）是正確答案。

188. In the information, the word "light" in paragraph 2, line 1, is closest in meaning to

(A) bright
(B) easy
(C) small
(D) pleasant

在資訊文中，第二段第一行的單字「light」意思接近下列哪一個？

（A）明亮的
（B）容易的
（C）小的
（D）令人愉悅的

答案 **(B)**

解析 light在Generally, the walking on his tour is light and not too challenging for most fitness levels.（整體來說，這次的旅遊行走路線輕鬆，對大部分人的體能程度來說不算太難。）這句之中，用來當作是challenging（有挑戰性的）的反義詞，也就是「不難」的意思，和（B）的easy（容易的）意思最相近。

189. What does Mr. Singh indicate he liked best about the tour?

(A) The size of the group
(B) The homestay
(C) Walking the Turley Trail
(D) Seeing unique architecture

辛格先生表示這次旅遊他最喜歡什麼？

（A）團體的規模
（B）寄宿家庭
（C）走在特立小道上
（D）看到獨特的建築

答案 **(B)**

解析 辛格先生在第三篇文的前半段說I think the highlight of my trip was the time I spent in Nalan.（我認為我的旅行亮點是我在納蘭度過的時光）。而第一篇文的第3天行程是在納蘭，由此可知辛格先生指的是「與寄宿家庭度過慢活的一天」。所以，正確答案是（B）。

190. What did Mr. Singh feel was missing from the tour?

(A) Ample shopping opportunities
(B) Cultural experiences
(C) A group photograph
(D) A visit to the countryside

辛格先生覺得這次旅行少了什麼？

（A）充裕的購物機會
（B）文化體驗
（C）團體照
（D）參觀鄉村

答案 **(A)**

解析 第三篇文的最後，辛格先生說The only thing I wish we had more time for was getting gifts to bring home.（我唯一希望的是，我們有更多的時間來買帶回家的禮物。）。意指唯一可惜的是「買禮物的時間不夠」，而（A）將它簡潔地換個說法，所以是正確答案。

Questions 191-195 refer to the following e-mail, Web page, and memo.
試題 191-195 請參考以下的電子郵件、網頁與內部通知。

To: Ignacio Ortiz
<ortiz-i@hemingwayfinancial.com>
From: Fiona Hoople
<hoople-f@hemingwayfinancial.com>
Subject: A thought
Date: July 18

Ignacio,
Q191 Take a look at this Web site I came across: www.jobmatch.com. It's funny how a solution to the problem you and I were just talking about appeared. I think with this new tool, you're going to find that you have a lot more time and a lot fewer headaches in the winter! Anyway, hope this helps.
Fiona

收信者：伊格納西・歐帝斯
[ortiz-i@hemingwayfinancial.com]
發信者：費歐娜・胡普爾
[hoople-f@hemingwayfinancial.com]
主旨：一個想法
日期：7月18日

伊格納西：
看一下我偶然發現的網站：www.jobmatch.com。真有趣，你和我剛才正討論的問題，就出現了解決辦法。我想有了這個新工具，冬天時，你會發現自己有更多的時間和更少的麻煩事！無論如何，希望這對你有幫助。
費歐娜

www.jobmatch.com
JOB MATCH
Log in Create a FREE account
Home Post a Job Search Résumés Employer FAQs

Recruiting has never been as easy as 1-2-3…until now. Create a FREE account with Job Match, post a job, and have résumés at your fingertips in no time. Q191 When you send us information about a job using our site, we save you time by automatically posting it to hundreds of job boards for you. And customize a questionnaire for applicants to answer to help the screening process go quickly and smoothly. Q192 No more sifting through résumé after résumé to find appropriate applicants for your specific job! We will analyze your requests and send you the best candidates. Finally, with one click, give those applicants a thumbs up or a thumbs down, and we will send replies on behalf of your company updating the applicants on their status.

www.jobmatch.com
工作配對網
登入 新設免費帳戶
首頁 刊登職缺 搜尋履歷 雇主常見問題

徵人從來不是像1、2、3……數數般那麼容易，但現在不一樣了。透過工作配對網新設免費帳戶、刊登職缺並即時滑動您的指尖來掌握履歷。當您使用我們的網站送來一份職缺的相關資訊時，我們會為您節省時間，自動將它發佈到上百個徵人網站上。並客製化一份問卷讓求職者回答，以使篩選過程進行得快速且順利。不用再為了幫您的特定職缺找合適求職者，而無盡地篩選著履歷。我們將分析您的要求，並傳送最佳求職者給您。最後，您只需要點擊一下，對這些求職者按下合格或不合格，我們將代表 貴公司傳送回覆並更新求職者的狀態。

Want more? Q193 Make use of our premium tools for a minimal monthly fee. You can't go wrong with Job Match. So go on, click the button below and try ALL of our tools for free during a 7-day trial!
FREE TRIAL

還想要更多嗎？那就以最低月租費來使用我們的升級版工具。選擇工作配對網準沒錯。來吧！點擊底下的按鈕圖案，在7天試用期間內免費使用我們的所有工具！
免費試用

字彙 ☐ fingertip 指尖 ☐ sift through～ 篩選～ ☐ a thumbs up or a thumbs down 合格或不合格、贊成或反對 ☐ can't go wrong with～ 選～一定不會出錯

MEMO
Dear Staff:
Interview season is approaching! I know I'm giving this memo to you early this year— Q194(C) a new tool has helped streamline the process of choosing candidates. A big thank you to Fiona Hoople for introducing me to it. Anyway, Q194(B)(D) interviews will still take place next month, and we'll have 15 candidates and two interviewers for each session like usual. Q195 The whole process usually takes about a week. If you are interested in volunteering to help me, please e-mail me at ortiz-i@hemingwayfinancial.com. I appreciate your consideration.
Ignacio Ortiz
Human Resources

內部通知
親愛的各位同仁：
面試季即將到來！我知道今年我提早給這份通知——有新的工具已幫助簡化篩選求職者的過程。非常感謝費歐娜．胡普爾把它介紹給我。無論如何，下個月仍將舉行面試，我們將如往常一樣，每個時段有15位求職者和兩位面試官。整個過程通常需要一週左右。如果有興趣自願協助我的人，請傳電子郵件至ortiz-i@hemingwayfinancial.com。感謝您的考慮。
伊格納西．歐帝斯
人力資源部門

字彙 ☐ streamline 將～簡化

191. What is implied about Mr. Ortiz?
(A) He has started a recruiting business.
(B) He is looking for new employment.
(C) He has more work than he can handle.
(D) He has the job of hiring new employees.

有關歐帝斯先生，何者暗示正確？
（A）他已經開創了一個人力招募事業。
（B）他正在尋找新的工作。
（C）他的工作量超出了他的能力範圍。
（D）他的職責是雇用新員工。

答案 **(D)**

解析 第一篇文是胡普爾女士向歐帝斯本人傳達「www.jobmatch.com這個網站，對你的工作應該很有幫助」。第二篇文是www.jobmatch.com的網頁，說明利用該網頁「可以順利地篩選合適的求職者」。由此可知，歐帝斯先生的職務是「負責招募人員的工作」。所以，正確答案是（D）。

192. In the Web page, the word “appropriate” in paragraph 1, line 7, is closest in meaning to
(A) significant
(B) definite
(C) suitable
(D) accurate

在網頁中，第一段第七行的單字「appropriate」意思接近下列哪一個？
（A）重要的
（B）明確的
（C）適合的
（D）準確的

答案 **(C)**

解析 appropriate在No more sifting through résumé after résumé to find appropriate applicants for your specific job!（不用再為了幫您的特定職缺找合適求職者，而無盡地篩選著履歷）這句之中是「適合的」的意思。因此，（C）suitable是正確答案。

193. What type of Job Match users pay a fee?
(A) Those creating applicant questionnaires
(B) Those who have found good job candidates
(C) Those using high-quality features
(D) Those posting to many job sites

什麼樣的工作配對網用戶需要付費？
（A）製作求職者問卷的人
（B）已找到好求職者的人
（C）使用高品質功能的人
（D）將職缺刊登到許多求職網站的人

答案 **(C)**

解析 第二篇文快結尾時提到Make use of our premium tools for a minimal monthly fee.（以最低月租費來使用我們的升級版工具。）。意指唯有使用升級版工具才會發生費用，所以正確答案是（C）。

194. What is NOT suggested about interviews this year?
(A) They are taking place now.
(B) The number of applicants per session are the same as before.
(C) A tool is making the process faster.
(D) Two people will be involved in giving each interview.

有關今年的面試，何者推論為非？
（A）現在正在進行。
（B）每個時段的應徵人數與以往相同。
（C）工具使過程更快。
（D）將有兩個人會參與主持每次的面試。

答案 **(A)**

解析 第三篇前半段提到... a new tool has helped streamline the process of choosing candidates.（有新的工具已幫助簡化篩選求職者的過程。）這句符合（C），而interviews will still take place next month, and we'll have 15 candidates and two interviews for each session like usual（下個月仍將舉行面試，我們將如往常一樣，每個時段有15位求職者和兩位面試官）這句內容分別與（B）和（D）一致。至於（A）在全文中完全沒有被提到。

195. What does Mr. Ortiz mention about the process of selecting applicants?
(A) He must recruit volunteers this week.
(B) Ms. Hoople will take charge of it this year.
(C) It will last about seven days.
(D) It will not utilize Job Match.

有關篩選求職者過程，歐帝斯先生提到什麼？
（A）他這週一定要招募志工。
（B）胡普爾女士今年將負責它。
（C）它將持續七天左右。
（D）它不會利用工作配對網。

答案 **(C)**

解析 第三篇文中間，歐帝斯先生說The whole process usually takes about a week.（整個過程通常需要一週左右。）。因此，正確答案是（C）。

Questions 196-200 refer to the following article, information, and review.
試題 196-200 請參考以下的文章、資訊與評論。

Ways to Move Through Airports Faster

更快通過機場的方式

Airports are busy, and there are often long lines due to staff reductions. Since wait times are unpredictable, it helps to save a few minutes here and there. Try these five tips to speed your way through the airport the next time you travel:

機場很繁忙，且由於人員的減少而經常大排長龍。因為等待的時間無法預測，所以到處都省個幾分鐘就很有幫助。下次您旅行時，不妨嘗試以下五個訣竅來加快通過機場的速度：

- Q199 Check in online and print your boarding pass before you leave for the airport. This can save a lot of time if there are lines at the check-in kiosks.

‧在前往機場之前先辦理網路報到並印出登機證。如果自助報到機有人排隊，這可以節省很多的時間。

- Before you leave for the airport, weigh your bags and make sure they are not above the maximum limit. It takes a lot of time to rearrange bags or to pay extra fees.

‧在前往機場之前先秤您的行李重量並確保它們沒有超過上限。重新整理行李或支付額外費用需要花很多的時間。

- Have your ID and boarding pass in an easily accessible location like a pocket or a special place in your wallet or purse. This way, you can get them quickly when you need them.

‧將您的身分證件和登機證放在易於取得的位置，如口袋或錢包裡特定的地方。這麼一來，當您需要它們時就能夠快速拿取。

- Apply for the Airport Pre-Check program. Q196 If approved, you will be considered a "safe traveler" and will be awarded access to a special line at security checkpoints whenever you use any airport nationwide. In this line, the procedures are less strict than the procedures in regular lines.

‧申請機場預檢程序。如果獲准，您將被視為「安全旅客」，不論在國內任何機場，您在安檢站都能獲准使用專用路線。這條路線的安檢程序不像一般路線那麼嚴格。

- If you go through regular security lines, wear slip-on shoes, have liquids in clear bags, and buy an airport-friendly laptop bag.

‧如果您是走一般的安檢路線，要穿方便穿脫的鞋、液體類裝進透明袋內，並且購買便於機場安檢的筆記型電腦專用包。

字彙 ☐ check-in kiosk 自助報到機 ☐ slip-on shoes 方便穿脫的鞋

AIRPORT PRE-CHECK

Frequently Asked Questions

Q: What are the allowed methods of payment for the $100 Airport Pre-Check application fee?

A: We accept credit cards or money orders from a bank.

Q: I usually book flights through third-party Web sites or travel agencies. How can I make sure my tickets reflect my authorized Airport Pre-Check status?

A: Q197 When you are approved for the Airport Pre-Check program, you will receive an Authorized Traveler Number (ATN). Input this number when booking tickets online or give it to your travel agent so that it is indicated on your ticket.

Q: I am traveling with family. Are they allowed to use the special line with me?

A: Q200 People who are not authorized under the Airport Pre-Check program are not allowed to pass through the special security line unless they are 12 years of age or below and accompanying an authorized family member.

機場預檢

常見問題

Q：100美元的機場預檢申請費允許什麼支付方式？

A：我們接受銀行核發的信用卡或匯票。

Q：我通常透過第三方網站或旅行社預定航班。我要如何確保我的機票顯示已通過機場預檢的身分？

A：當您通過機場預檢程序後，您將會收到一組經授權旅客編號（ATN）。當您在網路預訂機票時請輸入此編號，或是將編號給旅行社以便在機票上註明。

Q：我和家人同行。他們可以和我一起使用專用路線嗎？

A：未經機場預檢程序授權的人不得通過專用路線，除非是12歲或以下者，且必須由經過授權的家庭成員陪同。

字彙 □ third-party 第三方 □ Airport Pre-Check status 機場預檢的身分

https://www.airportexperience.com/top-five-ways-to-move-through-airports-faster /reviews

June 25

Q199 I have found that these top five tips save time in varying degrees. When I don't check bags, the first one saves me a lot of time since I can go straight to security. When I do check bags, I still have to wait in a line, and often the airport worker prints out a new boarding pass anyway. What I find really speeds me through the airport is the tip about security. While it requires a lot of effort to get approved, including an in-person interview, background check, finger-printing, and $100, it is worth it. Not only is there a special line for approved travelers, which is definitely

https://www.airportexperience.com/top-five-ways-to-move-through-airports-faster/reviews

6月25日

我發現上面的五個訣竅節省時間的程度不同。當我不託運行李時，第一個訣竅幫我省下很多時間，因為我可以直接進入安檢。當我行李要託運時，我仍然需要排隊等候，且機場工作人員通常不管如何還是會印出新的登機證。我發現真正讓我迅速通過機場的是有關安檢的訣竅。雖然需要花很多工夫才能取得核准，包括親自面談、身分背景調查、指紋採集和100美元，但它是值得的。

shorter than the regular lines, but Q198 we also don't have to take off our shoes, belts, or coats, and we don't have to take our laptops out of our bags. The one complaint I have with the system is that when the regular lines are very busy, airport workers often allow non-approved travelers to go through the special line. At many times, these are the elderly, who move slowly and must have the procedures for the special line explained to them, which holds up the line. It also doesn't speed things up when traveling with family if they haven't all gone through the same approval process. Q200 I was traveling with my 14-year-old daughter recently and was very annoyed because, while I got through security quickly, I had to wait a long time for her to get through.

經核准的旅客不僅享有絕對比一般路線還短的專用路線，我們也不必脫鞋、解皮帶或脫外套，甚至不必從包包裡拿出筆記型電腦。我對該程序有一點要抱怨的是，當一般路線非常繁忙時，機場工作人員通常允許未經核准的旅客通過專用路線。很多時候，這些都是行動緩慢的老人，而且必須向他們解釋專用路線的程序，這樣就會拖延這條路線的速度。和家人同行時，如果他們沒有經過同樣的核准程序，那也不會加快通關速度。我最近和14歲的女兒一起旅行就讓我非常不悅，因為雖然我快速通過安檢，但為了等她通過，我必須要等很久。

字彙 □ background check 身分背景調查 □ finger-printing 指紋採集 □ annoy ～讓人不悅

196. In the article, the word "awarded" in paragraph 5, line 2, is closest in meaning to

(A) transferred
(B) donated
(C) decorated
(D) granted

在文章中，第五段第二行的單字「awarded」意思接近下列哪一個？

（A）轉讓
（B）捐贈
（C）裝飾
（D）准予

答案 **(D)**

解析 awarded在and will be awarded access to a special line（將能獲准使用專用路線）這個短句中，是「給予」的意思。因此，（D）granted是正確答案。

197. What is indicated about travelers who are Airport Pre-Check approved?

(A) They carry a special pre-check card.
(B) They are assigned a special number.
(C) They must be 12 years old or older.
(D) They must buy tickets through special agents.

有關通過機場預檢的旅客們，何者敘述正確？

（A）他們帶一張預檢專用卡。
（B）他們會收到一組專用編號。
（C）他們必須年滿十二歲。
（D）他們必須透過專門代理人員買票。

答案 **(B)**

解析 第二篇文的第二段內容提到When you are approved for the Airport Pre-Check program, you will receive an Authorized Travel Number（ATN）（當您通過機場預檢程序後，您將會收到一組經授權旅客編號）。意指一旦通過機場的預檢程序，旅客就會收到經授權的旅客編號，（B）換個說法用special number來表達，所以是正確答案。

198. How is the special line different from the regular line?
(A) There are more employees working there.
(B) It exists specifically for elderly travelers.
(C) Travelers do not have to remove clothing.
(D) No one has to go through metal detectors.

專用路線和一般路線有何不同？
（A）有更多員工在那裡工作。
（B）它是特別為年長旅客而存在的。
（C）旅客不需要脫衣服。
（D）沒有人必須通過金屬探測。

答案 **(C)**

解析 第三篇文中間提到we also don't have to take off our shoes, belts, or coats, and we don't have to take our laptops out of bags（我們也不必脫鞋、解皮帶或脫外套，甚至不必從包包裡拿出筆記型電腦）。因為是排在「專用路線」，可以獲得上述的特權，所以正確答案是（C）。

199. Which tip does the reviewer feel saves time when traveling with carry-ons only?
(A) Online check-in
(B) Weighing bags at home
(C) Placing certain items in a pocket
(D) Wearing specific clothing

只有帶隨身行李旅行時，評論者認為哪些訣竅可以節省時間？
（A）網路辦理登機
（B）在家秤行李的重量
（C）將某些物品放入口袋
（D）穿著特定的衣物

答案 **(A)**

解析 第三篇文一開始，評論者就說When I don't check bags, the first one saves me a lot of time since I can go straight to security.（當我不託運行李時，第一個訣竅幫我省下很多時間，因為我可以直接進入安檢），意指沒有託運行李時，「第一個訣竅」即有助於節省時間。這正符合第一篇文說的「辦理網路報到」，所以正確答案是（A）。

200. What is implied about the daughter of the person writing the review?
(A) She traveled at a different time than her parent.
(B) She preferred to use the regular line.
(C) She did not apply for the pre-check program.
(D) She had too many bags for the pre-check line.

有關評論者的女兒，何者暗示正確？
（A）她與父母在不同時間旅行。
（B）她比較喜歡一般路線。
（C）她沒有申請預檢程序。
（D）她在過預檢路線時帶了太多行李。

答案 **(C)**

解析 第三篇文最後提到I was traveling with my 14-year-old daughter recently and was very annoyed because, while I got through security quickly, I had to wait a long time for her to get through.（我最近和14歲的女兒一起旅行就讓我非常不悅，因為雖然我快速通過安檢，但為了等她通過，我必須要等很久）。由此可知評論者的女兒14歲，而且無法通過專用路線。原因就是第二篇文第三段提到的，未經授權的人不得通過專用路線，可見她沒有申請預檢，所以正確答案是（C）。

✂ 請沿線剪下

Training 基礎練習 答案卡

Part 3

No.	ANSWER A	B	C	D	No.	ANSWER A	B	C	D
1	Ⓐ	Ⓑ	Ⓒ	Ⓓ	11	Ⓐ	Ⓑ	Ⓒ	Ⓓ
2	Ⓐ	Ⓑ	Ⓒ	Ⓓ	12	Ⓐ	Ⓑ	Ⓒ	Ⓓ
3	Ⓐ	Ⓑ	Ⓒ	Ⓓ					
4	Ⓐ	Ⓑ	Ⓒ	Ⓓ					
5	Ⓐ	Ⓑ	Ⓒ	Ⓓ					
6	Ⓐ	Ⓑ	Ⓒ	Ⓓ					
7	Ⓐ	Ⓑ	Ⓒ	Ⓓ					
8	Ⓐ	Ⓑ	Ⓒ	Ⓓ					
9	Ⓐ	Ⓑ	Ⓒ	Ⓓ					
10	Ⓐ	Ⓑ	Ⓒ	Ⓓ					

Part 4

No.	ANSWER A	B	C	D	No.	ANSWER A	B	C	D
1	Ⓐ	Ⓑ	Ⓒ	Ⓓ	11	Ⓐ	Ⓑ	Ⓒ	Ⓓ
2	Ⓐ	Ⓑ	Ⓒ	Ⓓ	12	Ⓐ	Ⓑ	Ⓒ	Ⓓ
3	Ⓐ	Ⓑ	Ⓒ	Ⓓ					
4	Ⓐ	Ⓑ	Ⓒ	Ⓓ					
5	Ⓐ	Ⓑ	Ⓒ	Ⓓ					
6	Ⓐ	Ⓑ	Ⓒ	Ⓓ					
7	Ⓐ	Ⓑ	Ⓒ	Ⓓ					
8	Ⓐ	Ⓑ	Ⓒ	Ⓓ					
9	Ⓐ	Ⓑ	Ⓒ	Ⓓ					
10	Ⓐ	Ⓑ	Ⓒ	Ⓓ					

Part 5

No.	ANSWER A	B	C	D	No.	ANSWER A	B	C	D	No.	ANSWER A	B	C	D
1	Ⓐ	Ⓑ	Ⓒ	Ⓓ	11	Ⓐ	Ⓑ	Ⓒ	Ⓓ	21	Ⓐ	Ⓑ	Ⓒ	Ⓓ
2	Ⓐ	Ⓑ	Ⓒ	Ⓓ	12	Ⓐ	Ⓑ	Ⓒ	Ⓓ	22	Ⓐ	Ⓑ	Ⓒ	Ⓓ
3	Ⓐ	Ⓑ	Ⓒ	Ⓓ	13	Ⓐ	Ⓑ	Ⓒ	Ⓓ	23	Ⓐ	Ⓑ	Ⓒ	Ⓓ
4	Ⓐ	Ⓑ	Ⓒ	Ⓓ	14	Ⓐ	Ⓑ	Ⓒ	Ⓓ	24	Ⓐ	Ⓑ	Ⓒ	Ⓓ
5	Ⓐ	Ⓑ	Ⓒ	Ⓓ	15	Ⓐ	Ⓑ	Ⓒ	Ⓓ	25	Ⓐ	Ⓑ	Ⓒ	Ⓓ
6	Ⓐ	Ⓑ	Ⓒ	Ⓓ	16	Ⓐ	Ⓑ	Ⓒ	Ⓓ	26	Ⓐ	Ⓑ	Ⓒ	Ⓓ
7	Ⓐ	Ⓑ	Ⓒ	Ⓓ	17	Ⓐ	Ⓑ	Ⓒ	Ⓓ	27	Ⓐ	Ⓑ	Ⓒ	Ⓓ
8	Ⓐ	Ⓑ	Ⓒ	Ⓓ	18	Ⓐ	Ⓑ	Ⓒ	Ⓓ	28	Ⓐ	Ⓑ	Ⓒ	Ⓓ
9	Ⓐ	Ⓑ	Ⓒ	Ⓓ	19	Ⓐ	Ⓑ	Ⓒ	Ⓓ	29	Ⓐ	Ⓑ	Ⓒ	Ⓓ
10	Ⓐ	Ⓑ	Ⓒ	Ⓓ	20	Ⓐ	Ⓑ	Ⓒ	Ⓓ	30	Ⓐ	Ⓑ	Ⓒ	Ⓓ

Part 5 Review of Training

No.	ANSWER A	B	C	D	No.	ANSWER A	B	C	D	No.	ANSWER A	B	C	D
1	Ⓐ	Ⓑ	Ⓒ	Ⓓ	11	Ⓐ	Ⓑ	Ⓒ	Ⓓ	21	Ⓐ	Ⓑ	Ⓒ	Ⓓ
2	Ⓐ	Ⓑ	Ⓒ	Ⓓ	12	Ⓐ	Ⓑ	Ⓒ	Ⓓ	22	Ⓐ	Ⓑ	Ⓒ	Ⓓ
3	Ⓐ	Ⓑ	Ⓒ	Ⓓ	13	Ⓐ	Ⓑ	Ⓒ	Ⓓ	23	Ⓐ	Ⓑ	Ⓒ	Ⓓ
4	Ⓐ	Ⓑ	Ⓒ	Ⓓ	14	Ⓐ	Ⓑ	Ⓒ	Ⓓ	24	Ⓐ	Ⓑ	Ⓒ	Ⓓ
5	Ⓐ	Ⓑ	Ⓒ	Ⓓ	15	Ⓐ	Ⓑ	Ⓒ	Ⓓ	25	Ⓐ	Ⓑ	Ⓒ	Ⓓ
6	Ⓐ	Ⓑ	Ⓒ	Ⓓ	16	Ⓐ	Ⓑ	Ⓒ	Ⓓ	26	Ⓐ	Ⓑ	Ⓒ	Ⓓ
7	Ⓐ	Ⓑ	Ⓒ	Ⓓ	17	Ⓐ	Ⓑ	Ⓒ	Ⓓ	27	Ⓐ	Ⓑ	Ⓒ	Ⓓ
8	Ⓐ	Ⓑ	Ⓒ	Ⓓ	18	Ⓐ	Ⓑ	Ⓒ	Ⓓ	28	Ⓐ	Ⓑ	Ⓒ	Ⓓ
9	Ⓐ	Ⓑ	Ⓒ	Ⓓ	19	Ⓐ	Ⓑ	Ⓒ	Ⓓ	29	Ⓐ	Ⓑ	Ⓒ	Ⓓ
10	Ⓐ	Ⓑ	Ⓒ	Ⓓ	20	Ⓐ	Ⓑ	Ⓒ	Ⓓ	30	Ⓐ	Ⓑ	Ⓒ	Ⓓ

Part 7

No.	ANSWER A	B	C	D	No.	ANSWER A	B	C	D	No.	ANSWER A	B	C	D
1	Ⓐ	Ⓑ	Ⓒ	Ⓓ	11	Ⓐ	Ⓑ	Ⓒ	Ⓓ	21	Ⓐ	Ⓑ	Ⓒ	Ⓓ
2	Ⓐ	Ⓑ	Ⓒ	Ⓓ	12	Ⓐ	Ⓑ	Ⓒ	Ⓓ	22	Ⓐ	Ⓑ	Ⓒ	Ⓓ
3	Ⓐ	Ⓑ	Ⓒ	Ⓓ	13	Ⓐ	Ⓑ	Ⓒ	Ⓓ	23	Ⓐ	Ⓑ	Ⓒ	Ⓓ
4	Ⓐ	Ⓑ	Ⓒ	Ⓓ	14	Ⓐ	Ⓑ	Ⓒ	Ⓓ	24	Ⓐ	Ⓑ	Ⓒ	Ⓓ
5	Ⓐ	Ⓑ	Ⓒ	Ⓓ	15	Ⓐ	Ⓑ	Ⓒ	Ⓓ					
6	Ⓐ	Ⓑ	Ⓒ	Ⓓ	16	Ⓐ	Ⓑ	Ⓒ	Ⓓ					
7	Ⓐ	Ⓑ	Ⓒ	Ⓓ	17	Ⓐ	Ⓑ	Ⓒ	Ⓓ					
8	Ⓐ	Ⓑ	Ⓒ	Ⓓ	18	Ⓐ	Ⓑ	Ⓒ	Ⓓ					
9	Ⓐ	Ⓑ	Ⓒ	Ⓓ	19	Ⓐ	Ⓑ	Ⓒ	Ⓓ					
10	Ⓐ	Ⓑ	Ⓒ	Ⓓ	20	Ⓐ	Ⓑ	Ⓒ	Ⓓ					

✂ 請沿線剪下

Practice Test 實戰試題 答案卡

LISTENING SECTION

Part 1

No.	ANSWER A B C D
1	Ⓐ Ⓑ Ⓒ Ⓓ
2	Ⓐ Ⓑ Ⓒ Ⓓ
3	Ⓐ Ⓑ Ⓒ Ⓓ
4	Ⓐ Ⓑ Ⓒ Ⓓ
5	Ⓐ Ⓑ Ⓒ Ⓓ
6	Ⓐ Ⓑ Ⓒ Ⓓ

Part 2

No.	ANSWER A B C	No.	ANSWER A B C	No.	ANSWER A B C
1	Ⓐ Ⓑ Ⓒ	11	Ⓐ Ⓑ Ⓒ	21	Ⓐ Ⓑ Ⓒ
2	Ⓐ Ⓑ Ⓒ	12	Ⓐ Ⓑ Ⓒ	22	Ⓐ Ⓑ Ⓒ
3	Ⓐ Ⓑ Ⓒ	13	Ⓐ Ⓑ Ⓒ	23	Ⓐ Ⓑ Ⓒ
4	Ⓐ Ⓑ Ⓒ	14	Ⓐ Ⓑ Ⓒ	24	Ⓐ Ⓑ Ⓒ
5	Ⓐ Ⓑ Ⓒ	15	Ⓐ Ⓑ Ⓒ	25	Ⓐ Ⓑ Ⓒ
6	Ⓐ Ⓑ Ⓒ	16	Ⓐ Ⓑ Ⓒ		
7	Ⓐ Ⓑ Ⓒ	17	Ⓐ Ⓑ Ⓒ		
8	Ⓐ Ⓑ Ⓒ	18	Ⓐ Ⓑ Ⓒ		
9	Ⓐ Ⓑ Ⓒ	19	Ⓐ Ⓑ Ⓒ		
10	Ⓐ Ⓑ Ⓒ	20	Ⓐ Ⓑ Ⓒ		

Part 3

No.	ANSWER A B C D	No.	ANSWER A B C D
1	Ⓐ Ⓑ Ⓒ Ⓓ	11	Ⓐ Ⓑ Ⓒ Ⓓ
2	Ⓐ Ⓑ Ⓒ Ⓓ	12	Ⓐ Ⓑ Ⓒ Ⓓ
3	Ⓐ Ⓑ Ⓒ Ⓓ	13	Ⓐ Ⓑ Ⓒ Ⓓ
4	Ⓐ Ⓑ Ⓒ Ⓓ	14	Ⓐ Ⓑ Ⓒ Ⓓ
5	Ⓐ Ⓑ Ⓒ Ⓓ	15	Ⓐ Ⓑ Ⓒ Ⓓ
6	Ⓐ Ⓑ Ⓒ Ⓓ		
7	Ⓐ Ⓑ Ⓒ Ⓓ		
8	Ⓐ Ⓑ Ⓒ Ⓓ		
9	Ⓐ Ⓑ Ⓒ Ⓓ		
10	Ⓐ Ⓑ Ⓒ Ⓓ		

Part 4

No.	ANSWER A B C D	No.	ANSWER A B C D
1	Ⓐ Ⓑ Ⓒ Ⓓ	11	Ⓐ Ⓑ Ⓒ Ⓓ
2	Ⓐ Ⓑ Ⓒ Ⓓ	12	Ⓐ Ⓑ Ⓒ Ⓓ
3	Ⓐ Ⓑ Ⓒ Ⓓ	13	Ⓐ Ⓑ Ⓒ Ⓓ
4	Ⓐ Ⓑ Ⓒ Ⓓ	14	Ⓐ Ⓑ Ⓒ Ⓓ
5	Ⓐ Ⓑ Ⓒ Ⓓ	15	Ⓐ Ⓑ Ⓒ Ⓓ
6	Ⓐ Ⓑ Ⓒ Ⓓ		
7	Ⓐ Ⓑ Ⓒ Ⓓ		
8	Ⓐ Ⓑ Ⓒ Ⓓ		
9	Ⓐ Ⓑ Ⓒ Ⓓ		
10	Ⓐ Ⓑ Ⓒ Ⓓ		

READING SECTION

Part 5

No.	ANSWER A B C D	No.	ANSWER A B C D	No.	ANSWER A B C D
1	Ⓐ Ⓑ Ⓒ Ⓓ	11	Ⓐ Ⓑ Ⓒ Ⓓ	21	Ⓐ Ⓑ Ⓒ Ⓓ
2	Ⓐ Ⓑ Ⓒ Ⓓ	12	Ⓐ Ⓑ Ⓒ Ⓓ	22	Ⓐ Ⓑ Ⓒ Ⓓ
3	Ⓐ Ⓑ Ⓒ Ⓓ	13	Ⓐ Ⓑ Ⓒ Ⓓ	23	Ⓐ Ⓑ Ⓒ Ⓓ
4	Ⓐ Ⓑ Ⓒ Ⓓ	14	Ⓐ Ⓑ Ⓒ Ⓓ	24	Ⓐ Ⓑ Ⓒ Ⓓ
5	Ⓐ Ⓑ Ⓒ Ⓓ	15	Ⓐ Ⓑ Ⓒ Ⓓ	25	Ⓐ Ⓑ Ⓒ Ⓓ
6	Ⓐ Ⓑ Ⓒ Ⓓ	16	Ⓐ Ⓑ Ⓒ Ⓓ	26	Ⓐ Ⓑ Ⓒ Ⓓ
7	Ⓐ Ⓑ Ⓒ Ⓓ	17	Ⓐ Ⓑ Ⓒ Ⓓ	27	Ⓐ Ⓑ Ⓒ Ⓓ
8	Ⓐ Ⓑ Ⓒ Ⓓ	18	Ⓐ Ⓑ Ⓒ Ⓓ	28	Ⓐ Ⓑ Ⓒ Ⓓ
9	Ⓐ Ⓑ Ⓒ Ⓓ	19	Ⓐ Ⓑ Ⓒ Ⓓ	29	Ⓐ Ⓑ Ⓒ Ⓓ
10	Ⓐ Ⓑ Ⓒ Ⓓ	20	Ⓐ Ⓑ Ⓒ Ⓓ	30	Ⓐ Ⓑ Ⓒ Ⓓ

Part 6

No.	ANSWER A B C D	No.	ANSWER A B C D
1	Ⓐ Ⓑ Ⓒ Ⓓ	11	Ⓐ Ⓑ Ⓒ Ⓓ
2	Ⓐ Ⓑ Ⓒ Ⓓ	12	Ⓐ Ⓑ Ⓒ Ⓓ
3	Ⓐ Ⓑ Ⓒ Ⓓ	13	Ⓐ Ⓑ Ⓒ Ⓓ
4	Ⓐ Ⓑ Ⓒ Ⓓ	14	Ⓐ Ⓑ Ⓒ Ⓓ
5	Ⓐ Ⓑ Ⓒ Ⓓ	15	Ⓐ Ⓑ Ⓒ Ⓓ
6	Ⓐ Ⓑ Ⓒ Ⓓ	16	Ⓐ Ⓑ Ⓒ Ⓓ
7	Ⓐ Ⓑ Ⓒ Ⓓ		
8	Ⓐ Ⓑ Ⓒ Ⓓ		
9	Ⓐ Ⓑ Ⓒ Ⓓ		
10	Ⓐ Ⓑ Ⓒ Ⓓ		

Part 7

No.	ANSWER A B C D	No.	ANSWER A B C D	No.	ANSWER A B C D
1	Ⓐ Ⓑ Ⓒ Ⓓ	11	Ⓐ Ⓑ Ⓒ Ⓓ	21	Ⓐ Ⓑ Ⓒ Ⓓ
2	Ⓐ Ⓑ Ⓒ Ⓓ	12	Ⓐ Ⓑ Ⓒ Ⓓ		
3	Ⓐ Ⓑ Ⓒ Ⓓ	13	Ⓐ Ⓑ Ⓒ Ⓓ		
4	Ⓐ Ⓑ Ⓒ Ⓓ	14	Ⓐ Ⓑ Ⓒ Ⓓ		
5	Ⓐ Ⓑ Ⓒ Ⓓ	15	Ⓐ Ⓑ Ⓒ Ⓓ		
6	Ⓐ Ⓑ Ⓒ Ⓓ	16	Ⓐ Ⓑ Ⓒ Ⓓ		
7	Ⓐ Ⓑ Ⓒ Ⓓ	17	Ⓐ Ⓑ Ⓒ Ⓓ		
8	Ⓐ Ⓑ Ⓒ Ⓓ	18	Ⓐ Ⓑ Ⓒ Ⓓ		
9	Ⓐ Ⓑ Ⓒ Ⓓ	19	Ⓐ Ⓑ Ⓒ Ⓓ		
10	Ⓐ Ⓑ Ⓒ Ⓓ	20	Ⓐ Ⓑ Ⓒ Ⓓ		

✂ 請沿線剪下

Final Test 終極模擬測驗 答案卡

LISTENING SECTION

Part 1		Part 2						Part 3						Part 4					
No.	ANSWER A B C D	No.	ANSWER A B C	No.	ANSWER A B C	No.	ANSWER A B C D	No.	ANSWER A B C D	No.	ANSWER A B C D	No.	ANSWER A B C D	No.	ANSWER A B C D	No.	ANSWER A B C D	No.	ANSWER A B C D
1	Ⓐ Ⓑ Ⓒ Ⓓ	11	Ⓐ Ⓑ Ⓒ	21	Ⓐ Ⓑ Ⓒ	31	Ⓐ Ⓑ Ⓒ	41	Ⓐ Ⓑ Ⓒ Ⓓ	51	Ⓐ Ⓑ Ⓒ Ⓓ	61	Ⓐ Ⓑ Ⓒ Ⓓ	71	Ⓐ Ⓑ Ⓒ Ⓓ	81	Ⓐ Ⓑ Ⓒ Ⓓ	91	Ⓐ Ⓑ Ⓒ Ⓓ
2	Ⓐ Ⓑ Ⓒ Ⓓ	12	Ⓐ Ⓑ Ⓒ	22	Ⓐ Ⓑ Ⓒ	32	Ⓐ Ⓑ Ⓒ Ⓓ	42	Ⓐ Ⓑ Ⓒ Ⓓ	52	Ⓐ Ⓑ Ⓒ Ⓓ	62	Ⓐ Ⓑ Ⓒ Ⓓ	72	Ⓐ Ⓑ Ⓒ Ⓓ	82	Ⓐ Ⓑ Ⓒ Ⓓ	92	Ⓐ Ⓑ Ⓒ Ⓓ
3	Ⓐ Ⓑ Ⓒ Ⓓ	13	Ⓐ Ⓑ Ⓒ	23	Ⓐ Ⓑ Ⓒ	33	Ⓐ Ⓑ Ⓒ Ⓓ	43	Ⓐ Ⓑ Ⓒ Ⓓ	53	Ⓐ Ⓑ Ⓒ Ⓓ	63	Ⓐ Ⓑ Ⓒ Ⓓ	73	Ⓐ Ⓑ Ⓒ Ⓓ	83	Ⓐ Ⓑ Ⓒ Ⓓ	93	Ⓐ Ⓑ Ⓒ Ⓓ
4	Ⓐ Ⓑ Ⓒ Ⓓ	14	Ⓐ Ⓑ Ⓒ	24	Ⓐ Ⓑ Ⓒ	34	Ⓐ Ⓑ Ⓒ Ⓓ	44	Ⓐ Ⓑ Ⓒ Ⓓ	54	Ⓐ Ⓑ Ⓒ Ⓓ	64	Ⓐ Ⓑ Ⓒ Ⓓ	74	Ⓐ Ⓑ Ⓒ Ⓓ	84	Ⓐ Ⓑ Ⓒ Ⓓ	94	Ⓐ Ⓑ Ⓒ Ⓓ
5	Ⓐ Ⓑ Ⓒ Ⓓ	15	Ⓐ Ⓑ Ⓒ	25	Ⓐ Ⓑ Ⓒ	35	Ⓐ Ⓑ Ⓒ Ⓓ	45	Ⓐ Ⓑ Ⓒ Ⓓ	55	Ⓐ Ⓑ Ⓒ Ⓓ	65	Ⓐ Ⓑ Ⓒ Ⓓ	75	Ⓐ Ⓑ Ⓒ Ⓓ	85	Ⓐ Ⓑ Ⓒ Ⓓ	95	Ⓐ Ⓑ Ⓒ Ⓓ
6	Ⓐ Ⓑ Ⓒ Ⓓ	16	Ⓐ Ⓑ Ⓒ	26	Ⓐ Ⓑ Ⓒ	36	Ⓐ Ⓑ Ⓒ Ⓓ	46	Ⓐ Ⓑ Ⓒ Ⓓ	56	Ⓐ Ⓑ Ⓒ Ⓓ	66	Ⓐ Ⓑ Ⓒ Ⓓ	76	Ⓐ Ⓑ Ⓒ Ⓓ	86	Ⓐ Ⓑ Ⓒ Ⓓ	96	Ⓐ Ⓑ Ⓒ Ⓓ
7	Ⓐ Ⓑ Ⓒ	17	Ⓐ Ⓑ Ⓒ	27	Ⓐ Ⓑ Ⓒ	37	Ⓐ Ⓑ Ⓒ Ⓓ	47	Ⓐ Ⓑ Ⓒ Ⓓ	57	Ⓐ Ⓑ Ⓒ Ⓓ	67	Ⓐ Ⓑ Ⓒ Ⓓ	77	Ⓐ Ⓑ Ⓒ Ⓓ	87	Ⓐ Ⓑ Ⓒ Ⓓ	97	Ⓐ Ⓑ Ⓒ Ⓓ
8	Ⓐ Ⓑ Ⓒ	18	Ⓐ Ⓑ Ⓒ	28	Ⓐ Ⓑ Ⓒ	38	Ⓐ Ⓑ Ⓒ Ⓓ	48	Ⓐ Ⓑ Ⓒ Ⓓ	58	Ⓐ Ⓑ Ⓒ Ⓓ	68	Ⓐ Ⓑ Ⓒ Ⓓ	78	Ⓐ Ⓑ Ⓒ Ⓓ	88	Ⓐ Ⓑ Ⓒ Ⓓ	98	Ⓐ Ⓑ Ⓒ Ⓓ
9	Ⓐ Ⓑ Ⓒ	19	Ⓐ Ⓑ Ⓒ	29	Ⓐ Ⓑ Ⓒ	39	Ⓐ Ⓑ Ⓒ Ⓓ	49	Ⓐ Ⓑ Ⓒ Ⓓ	59	Ⓐ Ⓑ Ⓒ Ⓓ	69	Ⓐ Ⓑ Ⓒ Ⓓ	79	Ⓐ Ⓑ Ⓒ Ⓓ	89	Ⓐ Ⓑ Ⓒ Ⓓ	99	Ⓐ Ⓑ Ⓒ Ⓓ
10	Ⓐ Ⓑ Ⓒ	20	Ⓐ Ⓑ Ⓒ	30	Ⓐ Ⓑ Ⓒ	40	Ⓐ Ⓑ Ⓒ Ⓓ	50	Ⓐ Ⓑ Ⓒ Ⓓ	60	Ⓐ Ⓑ Ⓒ Ⓓ	70	Ⓐ Ⓑ Ⓒ Ⓓ	80	Ⓐ Ⓑ Ⓒ Ⓓ	90	Ⓐ Ⓑ Ⓒ Ⓓ	100	Ⓐ Ⓑ Ⓒ Ⓓ

READING SECTION

Part 5						Part 6				Part 7									
No.	ANSWER A B C D	No.	ANSWER A B C D	No.	ANSWER A B C D	No.	ANSWER A B C D	No.	ANSWER A B C D	No.	ANSWER A B C D	No.	ANSWER A B C D	No.	ANSWER A B C D	No.	ANSWER A B C D	No.	ANSWER A B C D
101	Ⓐ Ⓑ Ⓒ Ⓓ	111	Ⓐ Ⓑ Ⓒ Ⓓ	121	Ⓐ Ⓑ Ⓒ Ⓓ	131	Ⓐ Ⓑ Ⓒ Ⓓ	141	Ⓐ Ⓑ Ⓒ Ⓓ	151	Ⓐ Ⓑ Ⓒ Ⓓ	161	Ⓐ Ⓑ Ⓒ Ⓓ	171	Ⓐ Ⓑ Ⓒ Ⓓ	181	Ⓐ Ⓑ Ⓒ Ⓓ	191	Ⓐ Ⓑ Ⓒ Ⓓ
102	Ⓐ Ⓑ Ⓒ Ⓓ	112	Ⓐ Ⓑ Ⓒ Ⓓ	122	Ⓐ Ⓑ Ⓒ Ⓓ	132	Ⓐ Ⓑ Ⓒ Ⓓ	142	Ⓐ Ⓑ Ⓒ Ⓓ	152	Ⓐ Ⓑ Ⓒ Ⓓ	162	Ⓐ Ⓑ Ⓒ Ⓓ	172	Ⓐ Ⓑ Ⓒ Ⓓ	182	Ⓐ Ⓑ Ⓒ Ⓓ	192	Ⓐ Ⓑ Ⓒ Ⓓ
103	Ⓐ Ⓑ Ⓒ Ⓓ	113	Ⓐ Ⓑ Ⓒ Ⓓ	123	Ⓐ Ⓑ Ⓒ Ⓓ	133	Ⓐ Ⓑ Ⓒ Ⓓ	143	Ⓐ Ⓑ Ⓒ Ⓓ	153	Ⓐ Ⓑ Ⓒ Ⓓ	163	Ⓐ Ⓑ Ⓒ Ⓓ	173	Ⓐ Ⓑ Ⓒ Ⓓ	183	Ⓐ Ⓑ Ⓒ Ⓓ	193	Ⓐ Ⓑ Ⓒ Ⓓ
104	Ⓐ Ⓑ Ⓒ Ⓓ	114	Ⓐ Ⓑ Ⓒ Ⓓ	124	Ⓐ Ⓑ Ⓒ Ⓓ	134	Ⓐ Ⓑ Ⓒ Ⓓ	144	Ⓐ Ⓑ Ⓒ Ⓓ	154	Ⓐ Ⓑ Ⓒ Ⓓ	164	Ⓐ Ⓑ Ⓒ Ⓓ	174	Ⓐ Ⓑ Ⓒ Ⓓ	184	Ⓐ Ⓑ Ⓒ Ⓓ	194	Ⓐ Ⓑ Ⓒ Ⓓ
105	Ⓐ Ⓑ Ⓒ Ⓓ	115	Ⓐ Ⓑ Ⓒ Ⓓ	125	Ⓐ Ⓑ Ⓒ Ⓓ	135	Ⓐ Ⓑ Ⓒ Ⓓ	145	Ⓐ Ⓑ Ⓒ Ⓓ	155	Ⓐ Ⓑ Ⓒ Ⓓ	165	Ⓐ Ⓑ Ⓒ Ⓓ	175	Ⓐ Ⓑ Ⓒ Ⓓ	185	Ⓐ Ⓑ Ⓒ Ⓓ	195	Ⓐ Ⓑ Ⓒ Ⓓ
106	Ⓐ Ⓑ Ⓒ Ⓓ	116	Ⓐ Ⓑ Ⓒ Ⓓ	126	Ⓐ Ⓑ Ⓒ Ⓓ	136	Ⓐ Ⓑ Ⓒ Ⓓ	146	Ⓐ Ⓑ Ⓒ Ⓓ	156	Ⓐ Ⓑ Ⓒ Ⓓ	166	Ⓐ Ⓑ Ⓒ Ⓓ	176	Ⓐ Ⓑ Ⓒ Ⓓ	186	Ⓐ Ⓑ Ⓒ Ⓓ	196	Ⓐ Ⓑ Ⓒ Ⓓ
107	Ⓐ Ⓑ Ⓒ Ⓓ	117	Ⓐ Ⓑ Ⓒ Ⓓ	127	Ⓐ Ⓑ Ⓒ Ⓓ	137	Ⓐ Ⓑ Ⓒ Ⓓ	147	Ⓐ Ⓑ Ⓒ Ⓓ	157	Ⓐ Ⓑ Ⓒ Ⓓ	167	Ⓐ Ⓑ Ⓒ Ⓓ	177	Ⓐ Ⓑ Ⓒ Ⓓ	187	Ⓐ Ⓑ Ⓒ Ⓓ	197	Ⓐ Ⓑ Ⓒ Ⓓ
108	Ⓐ Ⓑ Ⓒ Ⓓ	118	Ⓐ Ⓑ Ⓒ Ⓓ	128	Ⓐ Ⓑ Ⓒ Ⓓ	138	Ⓐ Ⓑ Ⓒ Ⓓ	148	Ⓐ Ⓑ Ⓒ Ⓓ	158	Ⓐ Ⓑ Ⓒ Ⓓ	168	Ⓐ Ⓑ Ⓒ Ⓓ	178	Ⓐ Ⓑ Ⓒ Ⓓ	188	Ⓐ Ⓑ Ⓒ Ⓓ	198	Ⓐ Ⓑ Ⓒ Ⓓ
109	Ⓐ Ⓑ Ⓒ Ⓓ	119	Ⓐ Ⓑ Ⓒ Ⓓ	129	Ⓐ Ⓑ Ⓒ Ⓓ	139	Ⓐ Ⓑ Ⓒ Ⓓ	149	Ⓐ Ⓑ Ⓒ Ⓓ	159	Ⓐ Ⓑ Ⓒ Ⓓ	169	Ⓐ Ⓑ Ⓒ Ⓓ	179	Ⓐ Ⓑ Ⓒ Ⓓ	189	Ⓐ Ⓑ Ⓒ Ⓓ	199	Ⓐ Ⓑ Ⓒ Ⓓ
110	Ⓐ Ⓑ Ⓒ Ⓓ	120	Ⓐ Ⓑ Ⓒ Ⓓ	130	Ⓐ Ⓑ Ⓒ Ⓓ	140	Ⓐ Ⓑ Ⓒ Ⓓ	150	Ⓐ Ⓑ Ⓒ Ⓓ	160	Ⓐ Ⓑ Ⓒ Ⓓ	170	Ⓐ Ⓑ Ⓒ Ⓓ	180	Ⓐ Ⓑ Ⓒ Ⓓ	190	Ⓐ Ⓑ Ⓒ Ⓓ	200	Ⓐ Ⓑ Ⓒ Ⓓ

刊登照片來源一覽表

Training

p.16	3	©Tomoyuki Hosoda
	4	©Tomoyuki Hosoda
	10	©Tomoyuki Hosoda
	12	©Tomoyuki Hosoda
	13	©Tomoyuki Hosoda
	14	©Tomoyuki Hosoda
p.17	25	©Kyoko Hasegawa
	27	©Tomoyuki Hosoda
	31	©Tomoyuki Hosoda
p.18	38	©Tomoyuki Hosoda
	39	©Tomoyuki Hosoda
	40	©Tomoyuki Hosoda

Practice Test

p.23	1	©Kyoko Hasegawa

國家圖書館出版品預行編目資料

高效拆解！新制多益TOEIC® TEST 990滿分攻略 /
濱崎潤之輔著；葉紋芳譯
-- 初版 -- 臺北市：瑞蘭國際, 2019.11
400面；19×26公分 --（外語學習；63）
ISBN：978-957-9138-37-6（平裝）
1.多益測驗

805.1895 108015007

外語學習系列 63

高效拆解！新制多益TOEIC® TEST 990滿分攻略

作者｜濱崎潤之輔・譯者｜葉紋芳・責任編輯｜鄧元婷、王愿琦
校對｜鄧元婷、王愿琦

封面設計、內文排版｜余佳憓

瑞蘭國際出版

董事長｜張暖彗・社長兼總編輯｜王愿琦
編輯部
副總編輯｜葉仲芸・主編｜潘治婷・副主編｜鄧元婷
設計部主任｜陳如琪
業務部
經理｜楊米琪・主任｜林湲洵・組長｜張毓庭

出版社｜瑞蘭國際有限公司・地址｜台北市大安區安和路一段104號7樓之1
電話｜(02)2700-4625・傳真｜(02)2700-4622・訂購專線｜(02)2700-4625
劃撥帳號｜19914152 瑞蘭國際有限公司・瑞蘭國際網路書城｜www.genki-japan.com.tw

法律顧問｜海灣國際法律事務所　呂錦峯律師

總經銷｜聯合發行股份有限公司・電話｜(02)2917-8022、2917-8042
傳真｜(02)2915-6275、2915-7212・印刷｜科億印刷股份有限公司
出版日期｜2019年11月初版1刷・定價｜599元・ISBN｜978-957-9138-37-6
2022年05月二版1刷

PRINTED WITH SOY INK 本書採用環保大豆油墨印製

瑞蘭國際

瑞蘭國際